Cursed with a poor sense of direction and a propensity to read, **Annie Claydon** spent much of her childhood lost in books. A degree in English Literature followed by a career in computing didn't lead directly to her perfect job—writing romance for Mills & Boon— but she has no regrets in taking the scenic route. She lives in London: a city where getting lost can be a joy.

Ann McIntosh was born in the tropics, lived in the frozen north for a number of years, and now resides in sunny central Florida with her husband. She's a proud mama to three grown children, loves tea, crafting, animals—except reptiles!—bacon and the ocean. She believes in the power of romance to heal, inspire, and provide hope in our complex world.

STRANDED WITH THE ISLAND DOCTOR

ANNIE CLAYDON

ONE-NIGHT FLING IN POSITANO

ANN McINTOSH

MILLS & BOON

First published in Great Britain 2022
by Mills & Boon, an imprint of HarperCollins*Publishers* Ltd,
1 London Bridge Street, London, SE1 9GF

www.harpercollins.co.uk

HarperCollins*Publishers*
1st Floor, Watermarque Building,
Ringsend Road, Dublin 4, Ireland

Stranded with the Island Doctor © 2022 Annie Claydon

One-Night Fling in Positano © 2022 Ann McIntosh

ISBN: 978-0-263-30132-8

07/22

MIX
Paper from
responsible sources
FSC™ C007454

This book is produced from independently certified FSC™ paper
to ensure responsible forest management.
For more information visit www.harpercollins.co.uk/green.

Printed and Bound in Spain using 100% Renewable Electricity
at CPI Black Print, Barcelona

STRANDED WITH THE ISLAND DOCTOR

ANNIE CLAYDON

MILLS & BOON

With grateful appreciation for friends in a crisis

CHAPTER ONE

DR MEL MURPHY liked to keep busy. She wouldn't even have been on this holiday if it weren't for her daughter Amy and new son-in-law, who had gifted it to her as a thank-you for helping organise their wedding, and 'keeping us sane'. The thank-you was unnecessary, but the thought that her daughter had grown into the kind of person who would think to do such a thing was immeasurably precious.

She'd arrived on Nadulu Island, in the Maldives, on Saturday, and been shown to one of the small, luxurious cabins that were suspended over the clear blue water like a string of pearls. The view was magnificent, the movement of the sea beneath her calming. Mel had unpacked and decided to go for a walk.

White sand and tall palm trees encircled the island, and it had taken just over an hour to arrive back where she'd started. She'd gone to the hotel bar, ordered a many-coloured cocktail and made the acquaintance of a few of the other guests staying here.

Everything was calm and tranquil, from the lapping of the waves to the smiles and unhurried pace of the island. Maybe Amy had been right and everyone needed a break, even from the most carefully balanced and rewarding of lives. Mel could almost feel herself winding down and although she had the nagging feeling that she must have missed *something* that needed to be done, she was reconciling herself to letting everything beyond the sapphire-blue of the sea get along without her for three weeks.

This island of calm had seemed like an impossible goal for much of her life. Mel had battled the crippling anxiety that had followed in the wake of her relationship with Amy's father, like the wash of one of the speedboats on the horizon. When Michael had left, a week before Amy's first birthday, it had seemed that there was no future at all beyond the next ten minutes. But her family had picked her back up again, and slowly Mel's horizons had begun to widen. Her parents had looked after Amy while Mel went back to university to finish her medical degree. Over the years the dreams that she'd thought were gone for ever, standing on her own two feet and making a career and a good home for her daughter, had gradually materialised.

She'd done it all for Amy, in the belief that one of the best things she could pass down to her was a good example, and now everything was changing again. Her precious girl was grown, with a husband, a career and a home of her own. Mel had planned for this, just as she planned for everything. Those carefully laid building blocks, the four days a week spent travelling into the heart of London to work as a consultant neurologist, then three days involved with the village community where she lived and her favourite local medical charity, would sustain her. They'd help protect Mel from the anxiety that had plagued her for so many years after Michael had left, his last unwanted gift to her.

She took the wooden walkway out across the water and back to her cabin, to read until her drooping eyelids told her it was time for an early night. The hotel's brochure promised a busy activities programme, and maybe she'd try one of the water sports on offer tomorrow…

* * *

The morning dawned bright and clear, she supposed much like most other mornings here. Breakfast was ordered, delivered and eaten, and Mel made sure that the bag slung across her body contained enough sunscreen. A pair of Bermuda shorts and a cotton top would be suitable for any adventure that presented itself this morning.

As she closed the sliding doors of her cabin, one of the hotel staff came hurrying along the walkway, knocking at each of the sliding glass doors and waiting to deliver a message. As a nod to the unhurried pace of the island, Mel didn't walk towards her to see what was going on, but waited, taking in the scent of the warm sea.

'The manager, Mr Manike, has asked that all guests come to the reception area, for a meeting which is to be held in the main restaurant. Thank you.'

Since there seemed to be no alternative on offer Mel smiled. She supposed that it didn't really matter what the meeting was about, she had all day and nowhere in particular to be.

'Okay. Thanks, I'm on my way.'

The hotel entrance was surprisingly busy, people standing in groups and talking to each other, the hotel staff moving amongst them. The young man behind the reception desk seemed inundated with enquiries and had a queue to deal with. The laissez-faire atmosphere of the place seemed to be slipping and Mel caught the attention of a young woman, clad in the hotel's uniform.

'What's going on?'

The woman smiled. 'Everything's all right.'

Not what she'd asked, although it was nice to know. But something prickled at the back of Mel's neck. As a doctor, she was well aware of the fact that *everything's all right* generally meant that there was a suspicion that something might not be.

'So…' How to phrase this? 'What's everyone doing here?'

Another smile. 'We've had news that there is some heavy rain in the area. It's not a problem, ma'am, the hotel is fully equipped to deal with such things. It may miss us altogether.'

Heavy rain didn't sound like anything to panic about, even if the pictures in the hotel brochure did imply that the skies would be unremittingly cloudless for the duration of one's visit. She'd heard that rainstorms here weren't uncommon, and the hotel must be able to deal with them as a matter of course. Mel wondered exactly what level of rain was needed to provoke the kind of bustle that she was seeing around her.

'You mean a hurricane?'

The woman laughed nervously. 'Oh, no, ma'am, we don't get hurricanes in this area. Just rain.'

Maybe Mel should go halves with her and assume a tropical storm. But the woman's attention had been caught by one of her colleagues, who had called to her and beckoned her over, and there was no chance to ask. The hotel guests were being shepherded into the large dining area, open to the sea on one side, where seats had been laid out in neat rows rather than informally grouped. Mel wondered if this might be an opportunity to gather a little more information, gravitating towards two women who were sitting alone together.

'Is this seat taken?'

'No.' The woman who answered her looked to be in her mid-thirties, and her tan showed that she'd been here for longer than just a day. 'It's terrible, isn't it?'

Out of habit, her most reassuring smile sprang to Mel's

lips. 'I don't really know what's happening. One of the concierges says rain.'

'I'm sure that's underplaying things. There's going to be a big storm, we heard about it this morning.' The two women nodded conspiratorially, obviously privy to a little local knowledge. 'It's going to spoil our holiday.'

'And we're in one of the cabins, out on the water.' Her companion looked as if she was about to burst into tears. 'Even here in the main building…those palm trees don't look at all safe, do they?'

Mel considered the palm trees, waving gently in the breeze outside. They were huge, probably here long before the hotel had been built. She'd have to consult the internet, but common sense told her that if they'd survived any length of time on the island then they had a natural advantage in the face of storms.

'They seem quite flexible. Isn't it the more rigid type of tree that generally comes down during a storm?'

Her answer didn't quell the anxiety that Mel was trying very hard not to think about. Nor did it appear to console the woman, who looked as if she was about to burst into tears. Mel shot her a reassuring smile as Mr Manike stepped out in front of them, and every head turned towards him.

'Ladies and gentlemen.' His soft-spoken tones were amplified by a microphone. 'I will update you on exactly what is happening. We have received a warning of rain and winds of up to gale force eight which are approaching us. If the storm maintains its current course then it will be with us at some time during the afternoon.'

A murmur ran around the assembled guests. Mel tried to recall the late-night weather report on the radio, back in England, and whether gale force eight was anything to worry about.

'There is nothing to worry about.' Mr Manike appeared to have anticipated the question before anyone got the chance to ask. 'We will move all of the guests who are staying in the water cabins, to spend the night in the hotel building, purely as a precautionary measure. I can assure you that we will be quite safe, the hotel has been built to withstand any kind of weather and we are currently putting the storm shutters in place. We will have a safe and pleasant evening.'

There was a barrage of shouted questions and Mr Manike appealed for quiet, saying that he would answer everyone's concerns. Hands shot up, and one by one he addressed the questions. No, there was no possibility of evacuating onto the mainland, it was a lot safer to stay here. Yes, everyone from the cabins would be given first class rooms in the hotel building and no one would be asked to share. Yes, the storm was expected to pass and everyone could resume their holidays. No, he couldn't say exactly when.

This was just the kind of thing that was prone to make her feel anxious, vague risks coupled with equally vague reassurances. Maybe this was payback time for having thought that all the world's problems would just drift past her, carried away by the tide…

Mel straightened herself, trying to concentrate on coping mechanisms. This wasn't her fault, and no amount of thinking about it was going to change the weather. There were people here on the island who could deal with this much better than she could, and she should let them get on with it. She still couldn't help wishing that someone would give her a clear and concise explanation of the situation and something to do…

Or… Something to take her mind off the thousand different scenarios that were beginning to jostle in her head.

Suddenly, as if in answer to an unspoken prayer, one of the double doors into the restaurant flipped open and someone walked in.

At last! This man had an unmistakable air of action and purpose about him. A magnetism that would have made Mel shiver in any situation, but right now it had the added bonus of driving every other thought from her head. Tanned and a little lined, his dark curly hair showing a few streaks of white, he had the look of someone whose experience was something that any woman would be glad to be on the receiving end of. He wore a canvas jacket and heavy boots, as if he were about to cut his way through a jungle.

You Tarzan, me Jane.

Maybe not the kind of guy you'd want to indulge in a long conversation with, the way he walked was a little too swaggering. Very nice to look at though, even if touching was probably not a good idea, and he was ideal for taking her mind off things for the next ten minutes.

The manager caught sight of him and beckoned him over, temporarily ignoring the next shouted question. There was a click as the microphone was muted and the two spoke briefly, nodding in agreement about something.

'Is there anyone here with medical training? I understand that a Dr Murphy is a guest at the hotel…' Tarzan had a cut-glass English accent and was smiling now. Before Mel had properly admitted to herself that it was a nice smile, she was on her feet.

'I'm Dr Murphy.' She bit her lip before she could admit that her name *wasn't* Jane.

'Great. This way…' Tarzan turned, making for the exit without looking back at her. A man of the jungle who was clearly used to having his every word obeyed by the creatures around him. Mel threaded her way past the line of seated guests and found that he was holding the door open for her.

'Has someone been hurt?' The manager had gone back to answering questions and Mel stopped in the doorway, blocking his path. If someone *had* been hurt then it would be a little more appropriate to just tell her what was going on and allow her to lead the way.

Tarzan gave a quick shake of his head, gesturing her through the door and closing it behind them. 'No, I'm here to see the wife of a member of staff. She's in perfect health, but she *is* pregnant and her due date is today. I'm going to have to decide how best to provide her with medical care over the next twenty-four hours.'

Was there really such a thing as a come-to-bed voice, or was a sudden appreciation of his scent and the look in his dark eyes messing with her head? It was a bit more to the point to ask why he assumed that *he* was qualified to make medical decisions.

'I'm a neurologist, but I have ten years' experience of working with a childbirth trust and I've delivered many babies during that time.' Mel folded her arms, waiting for him to acknowledge that leaving any decisions to her might be a good idea.

His brow creased slightly, as if that came as a surprise. 'Your internet profile didn't mention anything about a childbirth trust...'

'That's because I generally keep my work separate from my personal interests.' Mel rattled off the web address for the Trust. 'It's good to know that you took the time to look me up. Are you going to return the favour and tell me who *you* are?'

That grin of his was straight off a cinema screen. Mel reminded herself that cinema screens weren't real life.

'Rafe Davenport. I'm temporarily the doctor for this area. I'm not sure what the web says about me…'

He might have mentioned that he too was a doctor but he'd clearly been too busy taking charge. Mel resisted the temptation to take her phone from her bag and do an internet search, right then and there.

'I'm sure I can manage to find you. You're based here on the island?'

'No, I flew in this morning. I know you're supposed to be on holiday, but any help you feel able to give would be appreciated.'

Another thing that Dr Davenport needed reminding of. 'You think that sorry, I'm *on holiday* is an option for any doctor?'

The quick shake of his head told her that it wasn't an option for him, and Mel wished he'd thought to extend her the same courtesy. But even if there had been any choice in the matter, being annoyed by Dr Davenport's extraordinary magnetism seemed a better alternative than sitting around and worrying about things she couldn't do anything to change.

'We have a walk ahead of us. Have you got more suitable shoes? Maybe jeans…?'

Nowhere was all that far to go in this place, and Mel assumed he was referring to some kind of short cut, through the densely wooded centre of the island. Although, of course, he wasn't going to say *where* they were going, that would be far too much information. Dr Davenport had decided he was in charge and it seemed that he intended to stay that way.

'I have jeans in my cabin.' Mel couldn't resist taking a dig at him. 'Suitable shoes tends to vary, according to where I'm planning to go.'

He grinned again and she raised an eyebrow. Mel hadn't been aware that she was joking.

'We need to get to the other side of the island, and the quickest way is through those trees.' He gestured towards the thickly wooded area that occupied the centre of the island 'I'll go and fetch my things from the plane and see you by the walkway to the cabins.'

He turned, walking purposefully out of the reception area and onto the beach. A small sea plane was moored against the jetty and Mel made for the wooden walkway that led to her cabin. Flipping the lock on the sliding glass doors that led to the living area, she banged them shut again, just in case Dr Davenport thought it was a good idea to join her and pick out the most suitable thing for her to wear for a trek across the island.

Rafe would admit he probably *had* been a little economical with the details, and that Dr Murphy had been quite right in quizzing him. He put the omissions down to his curious preoccupation with whether her smile would have the same effect on him in person as the electronic version had done. He was still waiting. Dr Murphy clearly hadn't found a great deal to smile about yet.

Before he'd left Male', the capital of the long string of islands that made up the Maldives, he'd spoken with the manager here and learned that a doctor was a guest at the hotel. Keeping Mr Manike on the line, he'd searched the internet and found a Dr Amelia Murphy, a consultant neurologist, practising at a select private hospital in London. He'd described the woman in the photograph in front of him, failing to mention his own reaction to her smile, which was no one's business but his own, and Mr Manike had confirmed that this was the right person.

Rafe had decided to take this good news with a pinch

of caution. A doctor was a doctor, everyone had the same basic training. Ideally he would have preferred someone who had some recent experience of childbirth or emergency medicine and, although Dr Murphy was most probably excellent in her own environment, the island didn't have the battalions of support staff and cutting-edge equipment to support her that she'd likely be used to in the private sector. But beggars couldn't be choosers and Rafe was accustomed to making good use of every resource at his disposal.

The smile was the real problem. Or…actually not a problem at all… It was his reaction to it that disturbed Rafe. The way she looked at the camera, quiet assurance in the curve of her perfect lips. He'd always been attracted to women who would present him with challenges, and when he added Dr Murphy's undeniable beauty to the equation he couldn't deny the answering thump of his heart. It was enough to distract any man from the most pressing of missions, and he needed to stay focused. But he also needed her help, and had decided that staying one step ahead of her would avoid any unwelcome interferences.

And… Dr Murphy had put him straight without any trouble at all, which had left him grinning at her like a starry-eyed fool. As he walked to the sea plane, he found himself pulling his phone from his back pocket and typing the web address she'd given him into the browser.

Bad move. The picture of her on the childbirth trust's website was a little more informal, her smile warmer and yet somehow more purposeful. Rafe flipped past it quickly, reading that she was a trustee of the charity and clearly something of a campaigner, advocating for culturally appropriate and individual care for women during their pregnancy. The group pictures that followed left him in no doubt that she based her advice on hands-on involvement.

He resisted the temptation to sit in the cockpit of the plane and take a closer look at the pictures. Dr Murphy might have proved her worth in many different situations but not in the one that faced them right now. Until she did that, he would keep his eye on the goal of keeping everyone safe during the oncoming storm, and Dr Murphy would stay firmly in his rear-view mirrors.

He put his phone back into his pocket and hauled the medical kit from the plane, shouldering it and walking back towards the cabin that he'd seen her disappear into when he'd furtively looked over his shoulder to catch another glimpse of her. The sea was a little higher than usual maybe, lapping a little less gently against the massive posts that supported the cabins, and the warm breeze was a little stiffer than normal. But they had time. He'd contacted the Meteorological Office when he'd got here and although Mr Manike had sensibly told everyone to be ready for the storm this afternoon, it wasn't expected to reach the island until this evening.

As he leant over the rail outside her cabin, looking down at the sea, the sliding doors snapped open behind him and Rafe jumped, swinging round. Dr Murphy was clad in a pair of slim-fitting jeans and a no-nonsense pair of walking boots. The strap of a zipped nylon bag was looped across her body, and if he wasn't very much mistaken it was a travelling medical kit. The sight of his own, larger, backpack didn't seem to deter her and she closed and locked the doors.

'Ready?' When she looked up at him he noticed that her eyes were a more compelling blue than in the photographs, more like the water swirling beneath them. Suddenly Rafe felt unsteady, as if they too had the power to sweep him off his feet.

Not a good idea when there was a storm coming. Not a good idea, full stop.

'Yep. This way.' He started to walk back to the beach, hearing her footsteps behind him.

You could turn your back on a fire, and yet still feel its heat. And, despite her quiet, well measured façade, Dr Murphy did have a touch of fire about her. Her hair was strawberry blonde and he imagined that in her youth it had been as red as the hottest of embers. And her attitude made it very obvious that she stood no nonsense from anyone.

Even the thought of her made his heart thump, the way it had when he had first met his wife. The way that Rafe had thought it never would again when Annu had died. He could tell himself until he was blue in the face that keeping Dr Murphy at arm's length was a simple matter of keeping focused and dealing with a potentially disastrous situation, but that wasn't the whole story. Feeling the intoxicating sensation of attraction for someone he hardly knew carried with it a sense of the overwhelming grief he'd felt when he'd lost Annu.

It was unsettling because he couldn't control it. And because, despite all of the reasons why he shouldn't, he was still looking forward to crossing swords with the beautiful Dr Murphy.

CHAPTER TWO

RAFE'S STRIDE SEEMED to lengthen as he walked up the beach. Mel matched his pace, trying to avoid the indignity of having him turn and wait for her at the line of trees that ran behind the hotel building. He stopped anyway, looking back at the calm sea and the blue sky.

'When is the storm expected to hit us?' It would be nice to have some kind of a timeframe on all of this.

'This evening some time. It could last for a couple of days.'

'The manager said it would be here this afternoon. He didn't say how long it would last but the implication was that it wouldn't be as long as a couple of days.'

He looked down at her as if she were interrupting a serious line of thought with frivolous questions, and Mel felt a tingle of outrage. Michael had done something of the sort, refusing to answer perfectly reasonable questions about where he'd been until the early hours of the morning, until Mel had finally stopped asking. Her judgement had begun to seem flawed and unreasonable, and she'd been reduced to anxious waiting, going through every possible scenario in her head.

She'd had to work hard to leave that behind. And Rafe was going to have to get used to the idea that even though her expertise didn't run to tropical storms she wasn't entirely useless.

'Mr Manike's a sensible man. Get everyone ready ahead of time, and don't panic people with estimates.'

Right. So it was okay to panic *her,* was it? Anyone in her shoes would be a little afraid of the unknown, and Mel's fears were no different to anyone else's. She knew the difference between irrational anxiety and a perfectly normal reaction to the situation you found yourself in.

'And…it's going to be bigger than normal? I heard that heavy rain isn't unusual here, and the hotel seems to be taking a bit of notice of this one.'

Rafe nodded. 'Yeah, this one is probably going to be heavier than usual.'

'But you can't evacuate anyone?' Mel shrugged. 'Some of the people here have been asking about that…'

He raised an eyebrow, giving her a crooked half-smile. Mel wondered whether that was the way he got everyone to just comply with his instructions—pure smouldering magnetism.

'Where do you want to go?'

'I'm not going anywhere. I just wondered if there *was* anywhere to go.'

'Not really. The storm's moving in a westerly direction so even if we had the resources to take people to Sri Lanka, which we don't, we'd be heading straight towards it. This is one of the safer islands to be on, there's a very wide shelf between the open sea and the beach, which acts to deaden any high waves. And it's pretty much circular.'

He turned, taking the path that led towards the mass of trees in the centre of the island. Mel decided not to ask why circular was better than any other shape. She could look that up on the internet later.

The internet was a wonderful resource, particularly

when you were trying to stay one step ahead of someone. While she'd been getting into her jeans and boots, Mel had managed to do a little multi-tasking, propping her phone on the bed and searching for Dr Rafe Davenport.

'So you work out of a hospital in Sri Lanka?'

He shot a delicious glance over his shoulder and kept walking. 'Yeah, Colombo, but I'm not there all that much. I'm part of a team that provides medical support for people in situations like this. When we're not needed in disaster situations we visit rural areas that are hard to get to. Anywhere that medical treatment is needed and there's some obstacle to that.'

Mel would overlook the term *disaster situations.* There was no point in worrying about every possible permutation of that. As far as she could see there were no disasters happening right now. 'You seem to know the island pretty well.'

'I've been here before, on a number of occasions.'

'And you've flown all the way from Colombo this morning?'

Rafe grinned, shaking his head. 'If I'd tried that in a sea plane I'd be swimming by now. They don't have that kind of range. I was in Male' with a group of doctors who are working on a unified disaster plan for the area, and I commandeered a plane and got myself here.'

Of course. The everyday process of just *asking* for a plane probably didn't occur to him. Commandeering sounded far more his style. As the path ahead began to curve gently to the left, Rafe kept walking straight ahead, plunging into the lush undergrowth. Mel pushed through the vegetation behind him, glad of her jeans and boots. In her experience the straightest route wasn't always the best, but Rafe clearly disagreed.

'I looked at the web address you gave me...' His words

floated back towards her and Mel ignored the impulse to wonder whether he'd liked what he saw. He didn't have to like her to accept that she knew what she was talking about.

'And...?'

'I'd been wondering whether my patient might prefer a woman doctor.'

So she'd got the job on the basis of her gender. And talking to Rafe's back was beginning to irritate her as well.

'That's for her to say, isn't it? And, in my experience, quite a lot of people prefer a doctor who knows what they're doing.'

He turned suddenly, flashing a smile over his shoulder that made her legs go to jelly. 'Touché, Dr Murphy.'

'Since you know all about me now, probably best to call me Mel.' Maybe his lips wouldn't curve quite so seductively if they had fewer syllables to work with.

'Rafe.' Apparently he didn't mind too much when people answered him back. That was just as well, because Mel answered back.

At the moment she didn't have much breath for answering back. She stopped for a moment, resting her hand on the trunk of an enormous palm, and Rafe gave her a querying look.

'These trees...' Mel had a sudden and irresistible desire to save face. 'They look as if they've been here for a while.'

'You're wondering about whether the ones around the hotel might come down in the storm?'

'It had crossed my mind.'

'Well, you're right, these have been here for a while and weathered quite a few storms. It's interesting...'

He started walking again, launching into a description of how a palm trunk was made of spongy material and not wood, which made it liable to bend instead of break.

Threw in a note about taking care not to be caught by the whipping motion of the trunk, just in case she was feeling too reassured by the knowledge, and broke off to slither down an incline, turning and holding his hand out to her. Mel ignored it. If he could make it with the heavy pack he was carrying, then she was sure she could too.

'You know palms are more closely related to grass, corn and rice than to other trees. And they're pretty old. The first palm trees were around when dinosaurs roamed the earth.'

'Good. I like a survivor.'

Rafe nodded. 'Me too.'

This might just be the first thing that they agreed on.

Reaching the sandy beach on the other side of the island was a relief. They walked out of the shaded claustrophobia of the woodlands into a slightly stiffer breeze than had been blowing when they'd entered and it was finally possible to put a little more distance between herself and Rafe. He was heading purposefully towards a group of brick-built bungalows and, as Mel was beginning to expect, there were no explanations.

Rafe stopped to help a woman lift a heavy shutter into place and then continued towards a bungalow on the far edge of the compound. A man was sitting upright in one of the cane chairs on the veranda and sprang to his feet, obviously awaiting their arrival.

'Dr Davenport. I'm glad you could come.'

Those were obviously the words that Rafe lived for. He was the kind of guy who liked to be needed. To be followed and adored… Wait. Mel could see herself following and adoring that broad-shouldered frame as well, if she wasn't careful. And after the night when Michael had substituted coming home late with not coming home at all, she didn't follow *or* adore. She'd devoted herself to her daughter, her work and the small village community where she lived, in that order. She understood the kind of life that fed her, and what could break her.

Almost break her. Michael had broken her, reducing her to a mess of fear and uncertainty, but she was a lot tougher than she'd been back then. Anxiety wasn't something that ever quite left you, but she could deal with it now. Mel hadn't had a panic attack in years.

But Rafe was making her heart beat faster. His steady gaze made her feel flustered and hot, and it was an effort to gather her thoughts. What she needed was a good old-fashioned crisis to give her one overwhelming problem to focus on, rather than a myriad of inconsequential ones.

Careful what you wish for. Mel surveyed the bungalows around her, storm shutters fixed to the doors and windows. The sound of loud complaint, which had been overwhelming at the hotel, might be noticeably absent here, but these people could do without a crisis that might deprive them of their homes. One which might even threaten the life of a mother and her unborn child. Mel silently apologised to the world in general for forgetting that, and joined Rafe on the steps of the covered veranda that ran around the house.

'This is Dr Mel Murphy…' He gestured towards the man who had come to meet them. 'This is Haroon Khaleel. His wife Zeena is going to be having a baby boy any day now and we're here to see that all goes well.'

'Dr Murphy.' Haroon smiled, holding out his hand. 'It's good of you to come. I heard you're here on holiday.'

'It's my pleasure…' Mel shook Haroon's hand and Rafe interrupted.

'Dr Murphy works with a childbirth trust in England, and we're lucky to have her here.' Clearly it was all right to say that *about* her, even if he seemed to have some objection to saying it to her.

'Ah. Indeed.' Haroon beamed at her, ushering her towards the front door, which was the only method of entry into the house that wasn't boarded up.

'Do you need me?' Rafe called after her, and Mel felt her lip curl as she turned towards him.

'I'll be fine. I'd prefer to make my own examination.' Zeena was about to have her very full attention, and Mel would leave nothing to chance. If that was going to annoy Rafe, then it was an added bonus of doing her job well.

'Great… I'll be over there…' Rafe pointed to a group of women who were struggling to fix a large shutter over a pair of patio doors, and Mel resisted the temptation to roll her eyes. Tarzan never missed an opportunity to be helpful, and neither did Rafe Davenport.

A thorough examination showed that Zeena was in the best of health and that the estimate of her due date was accurate. The baby would be coming very soon, probably at much the same time that the storm was expected to hit. Something needed to be done now, to ensure the safety of both mother and baby.

Despite that, the atmosphere around her was calm and unhurried, which gave Mel time to consider all of the things that could go wrong in greater depth. She sat on the veranda, tapping her finger anxiously against the full glass of lemonade on the table beside her, waiting for Rafe to stop what he was doing and come and discuss what they were going to do next.

His jacket was slung over the railings that bounded one of the verandas and the action of a stiff breeze on the thin collarless shirt he wore underneath didn't leave much to the imagination. In the absence of anything else to distract her, it was tempting to allow her imagination to take all it could get, and picture him wet through…

Enough. Mel concentrated on her finger, willing it to stay still. She needed to be a little more assertive and take control of a situation that threatened the lives of both Zeena and her baby. Taking control of Rafe wouldn't be such a bad thing either, even if that did seem a more baffling process.

'Will you be all right here while I go and talk to Dr Davenport?'

'Of course. You will need to make the arrangements.' Zeena smiled lazily towards where Rafe and her husband were working together, helping with the storm shutters on a neighbouring bungalow. She trusted her husband and the community around her to do what was best for her, and Mel felt a sharp pang of envy. Trust was the one thing that had been noticeably missing, along with Amy's father, when Mel had given birth.

Picking up her glass of lemonade, she walked over to Rafe, waiting while he and Haroon manoeuvred a shutter into place. Rafe turned to her, smiling, and walked over to where she stood.

'Ah, thanks.' He took the glass from her hand and drained it. Then he had the audacity to put the empty glass back into her hand. A sudden flash of uncertainty in his eyes, quickly masked, showed Mel that he knew exactly what he'd just done.

And he'd just love it if she made a thing of it, wouldn't he? Mel smiled up at him.

'You're welcome. You want to know the results of my examination?'

'Um… Yes. Please.' For one moment he was at a disadvantage and Mel felt an inappropriate lurch of triumph in her stomach. She handed Rafe the piece of paper that she'd written the results of her examination on.

'This looks good…' He scanned the paper. 'It's consistent with the notes Zeena's usual doctor gave me.'

'And you didn't think to tell me that you'd been briefed on her medical history?' Lemonade was one thing, but the welfare of a patient was quite another.

He gave a shrug. 'You said you didn't need me.'

He'd thought to test her, more likely. That was the kind of thing that happened with experienced doctors and medical students. Mel felt the back of her neck bristle with outrage.

'You didn't say you had Zeena's notes. There's a reason for making notes, and it's called *working together.* You've heard of pooling experience?' She raised one eyebrow.

'Yes, of course.' He didn't seem much chastened by her rebuke and walked over to his backpack, fetching a battered folder full of notes and handing it to Mel. 'Maybe you'd like to review them and add yours.'

That melting smile. The one that was brighter than the morning sunshine and more lulling than the gentle roll of the waves. *That* was the thing that Mel was going to have to be most careful of. The rest she could deal with without too much difficulty.

'Thank you.' She took the folder, tucking it under her arm in a gesture that implied she'd be keeping hold of it. 'As you've seen from my notes, Zeena's baby will be coming at any time now. I'm assuming you've brought medical supplies with you and I'll need you to make them available to me here, as I'll be staying with her from now on.'

Rafe nodded thoughtfully. 'I think it would be best to transfer her over to the hotel.'

Mel looked around her. 'Does Zeena need to make that

journey? Everyone here seems pretty organised and ready for the storm.'

'They are, they're used to this kind of thing and the houses are built to withstand storms. But in this situation I think it's better to concentrate our resources in one place. Many of the men are already working over at the hotel, and if Zeena's here then we'll have two locations to cover. That'll probably be impossible once the storm hits.'

In the plethora of shouted questions, no one back at the hotel had thought to ask how the families of the men working there might be faring.

'So you're thinking of moving Zeena so that we can provide medical services to everyone at the hotel as well.' Mel frowned. Annoyingly, that sounded like a good alternative to her own proposal. 'It sounds logical, even if it is a little unfair.'

Rafe nodded. 'The hotel has an unusually well equipped medical suite which… I probably should have shown it to you before we left.'

'Yes, you probably should.' Mel couldn't resist agreeing with him.

'There are patient beds available in private rooms, and Zeena will be better off there. And we'll be able to cover the hotel as well. It's a win-win situation.'

Mel thought for a moment. Rafe didn't seem to care too much about her feelings, but he was basing his decisions on what was best for everyone. She couldn't fault him in that and it occurred to her that there was a little more to Rafe than met the eye.

'Okay, I agree. Although if anyone at the hotel runs away with the idea that the islanders are seeking refuge there and forgets to thank them for their help, I may have something to say about it.'

He chuckled, the glint in his eyes telling Mel that she'd

said pretty much what he'd hoped she might. Maybe he was thinking that there was a little more to *her* than met the eye as well, and the idea brought a sizzling tingle to her spine.

'That's a very good idea. I may join you.'

CHAPTER THREE

RAFE WATCHED AS Mel walked back to Zeena, sitting down with her on the veranda. He couldn't shake his fascination with Mel. It wasn't like or dislike but an unthinking tug that transcended any opinion he might have of her, and made him crave her presence.

It had made him wary. She was an unknown quantity, not used to working in this environment, and he had to get the measure of her. That measure should be based on cold, hard logic, not something that fell into the same category as a teenage crush.

But he couldn't fault Mel's judgement. She asked questions and came to the right conclusions. She clearly thought that he was testing her, and she wasn't far wrong, but she'd come through those tests with flying colours.

Maybe he should back off for a moment and examine his own motives a little more carefully. Making sure that an unknown doctor was up to the job was one thing, and he didn't regret withholding information until he'd seen what conclusions Mel came to on her own. But using his natural caution to distance himself from his own feelings was quite another thing, however necessary it seemed at the moment.

He'd come to Sri Lanka soon after he'd fully qualified as a doctor, the years of study and practical experience having made him feel a little stuck in one place. And then he'd met Annu. Straight out of medical school in Colombo, she was several years behind him in her training, but if Rafe had felt that he could take his seniority for granted, Annu had shown him differently. She was fiery and confrontational and had made him earn every single piece of the respect that she'd ultimately handed him.

There had been no way he couldn't fall in love with her. Two doctors working together, who stretched each other to their limits. A woman who was as beguiling as she was beautiful. What else was Rafe to do but beg her to marry him?

The thought of the ceremony still brought longing to his heart. Annu had seemed like a queen, in white and gold, and Rafe had been admitted into a family that was as welcoming as it was large. Ten months later, their son Ashok Chandra Davenport had been born.

At first he'd thought that Annu's fatigue was just the sleepless nights, nursing a new baby. Then he'd convinced her to go for some tests, and the cancer had been discovered. All that Rafe had been able to do was to watch, hoping that each new treatment option might be more effective than the last, while his young wife's fire flickered, and finally died.

He had thought he might die of grief too, but he had a son and he needed to survive. Not just survive, but make a good life. Going back to England now was out of the question. Rafe's family consisted of a couple of aunts, who'd taken very little interest in keeping in touch with a busy medical school student when his parents had died in a road accident. Ash's cousins, uncles, aunts and grandparents were involved and for the most part loving relatives and the boy needed his mother's family as much as he did his father. Rafe had stayed, for the love of his son, and then for the love of a country and its people, who had made him their own and given him purpose.

But he'd never found a woman who could replace Annu. In truth, he hadn't really looked, preferring to expend his energies on bringing his son up and a busy medical career, but then Dr Mel Murphy had found him. Mel was very different from his wife in many ways, but the feeling that his heart was going to jump out of his chest was just the same as when he had first met Annu.

He could ignore it. The same way he'd ignored every other woman who'd thought that a young and then not-so-young widower would be looking to replace the wife that he'd lost. He'd had the one true love of his life, and Annu had left him with a son. Once was enough to last a lifetime.

Wasn't it?

Rafe had never questioned the thought, and he wouldn't do so now.

A two-seater beach buggy wasn't the most usual mode of transport for a pregnant woman, but Rafe was used to using whatever was available and Zeena got into the vehicle with a smile. Rafe drove while Zeena's husband walked alongside her, chatting to her. Mel was part of the trail of women and children, who had opted to take the route around the island instead of the shorter path through the centre, because everyone here stuck with the most vulnerable member of the community.

When they arrived at the hotel a few of the men who were working there stopped to wave. Children ran to their fathers, and were hugged and sent back to their mothers again, so that they could be settled into the accommodation that Mr Manike had waiting for them. It may not be as comfortable as their own homes, but it was spacious and afforded shelter from the storm. Rafe led the way to the hotel's medical suite, and Mel followed with Zeena and Haroon.

'Wow! This is…' Mel looked around her as she walked through the small lobby and into a bright, modern consulting room which boasted equipment and supplies to meet almost any medical emergency.

'A bit over the top?' It was obvious what Mel was thinking.

'Yes, actually. Very useful in the circumstances, but definitely over the top.'

Her face was a picture of surprise, and Rafe couldn't help smiling. 'This was one of the conditions that the developers had to meet when they applied to build here: a medical suite that could handle cases from here and neighbouring islands. We're a relatively long way from Male' and the main hospital.'

Mel frowned. 'A medical suite's not much use without a doctor.'

'There's a visiting doctor for the area, but she's in Colombo at the moment, as part of the working party that brought me to Male'. This is her base when she visits this group of islands.'

'And I suppose it's a reassuring picture to put in the brochure?'

She missed nothing. 'I expect so. But the manager's made full use of what he's been given and made sure that the suite is fit for purpose. It's not just a showpiece.' Rafe turned to Zeena, ushering her through the consulting room and into the private corridor beyond, which led to the patients' accommodation, opening the first door he came to.

'Is this okay for you, Zeena? This room's the biggest, but there are three other rooms and since you're our only in-patient you can take your pick.'

'This is very good. Thank you.' Zeena walked into the

room and sat down on the bed, beckoning to her husband, who stepped forward and joined her.

'Right then. We'll leave you to get settled, and then you can have some visitors.' Rafe was under no illusions that there would be plenty of visitors. In fact, elbowing his way through the crowd was likely to be his first consideration if Zeena suddenly went into labour.

'I'll see you later.' Mel gave the couple a warm smile and turned, making her way back up the corridor to the consulting room. Rafe followed her, trying very hard not to notice the relaxed grace with which she moved.

A knock sounded and one of the concierges popped his head around the entrance door to the consulting room. 'Dr Murphy. Dr Davenport...' There was some kind of commotion going on behind him, at the entrance to the medical suite, and the man looked back before slipping through the door and closing it firmly.

'The guests have seen your return. There are many questions, and I assume these must be of a medical nature...'

Rafe turned the corners of his mouth down. He wasn't so sure about that. There was something about being a doctor that allowed people to assume that he was also an authority on keeping safe in any emergency. As it happened he knew quite a bit, but Mr Manike was doing that job extremely well.

But, before he could sound a note of caution, Mel had followed the concierge, out of the medical suite. He heard her gasp of surprise as she was surrounded by the knot of talking people who were waiting at the entrance door to the lobby.

The concierge was doing his best to calm everyone down and restore some order, but suddenly Mel was the centre of everyone's attention. Unwittingly, she'd put herself right in the firing line and everyone was raising their voice so they could be heard over everyone else.

She was partly obscured by the mass of people around her, but he saw her raise her hand shakily to her forehead, as if to shield herself from the wall of noise and people. The concierge looked at her questioningly and her impassive silence seemed only to encourage everyone to press closer and speak more loudly.

And she didn't turn. In a situation where she was clearly out of her depth and needed someone to help her, she didn't look back at him. Rafe grudgingly admitted that he wished she had, telling himself that he'd done nothing to deserve the role of Mel's protector, even though all of his instincts were telling him that he wanted it.

A mind trained to observe and diagnose was automatically running through all of the possibilities. Agoraphobia? Panic attack? Or had the tension in the air got to her and played on those fears that anyone thrust into this kind of situation would feel? Now wasn't the time to stand back and try to assess the situation.

'Quiet!' Rafe raised his voice above the hubbub. He saw Mel jump and resisted the impulse to wade into the melee and pull her out.

Everyone stopped talking suddenly and looked at him. Now that he had control, Rafe knew exactly what to do. Panic was the one thing that Mr Manike had been trying to avoid, because that was the way people got hurt, and a firm hand was needed.

'Form a line, please. Right here, behind this gentleman…' He guided the nearest person to him to one side of the corridor. The man was grinning smugly at being first in the queue and everyone else got behind him, jockeying for position.

Mel had turned towards him, regarding him silently.

Her cheeks were a little red and her eyes seemed just a little moist. He couldn't think about that now, and he couldn't show weakness. Right now, not showing weakness was all about asserting his authority and getting everyone to do what he said without stopping to discuss the matter.

'Who is here with a question?' No one seemed obviously ill or injured and the first thing he needed to do was to restore order, so he could find out who *did* need medical assistance.

Almost every hand shot up. There was something to be said for a queue. It seemed to reawaken everyone's memory of the order of a schoolroom. Just one woman, clearly frustrated by her place halfway down the queue, spoke.

'What about the facilities here in the hotel? Shouldn't guests have first priority?'

He saw Mel stiffen suddenly, squaring her drooping shoulders. 'There are more than enough medical resources here if everyone shares. The islanders have relocated so that medical personnel assigned to them are available if needed by hotel guests.'

Great answer. And Mel's indignant fire seemed to have burned off whatever it was that had put her at a loss in this situation. She was still shaking, but she was visibly pulling herself together.

A few people were nodding, and a woman standing next to the one who'd asked the question voiced her opinion that the arrangement was more than fair. That was good to hear, but Rafe didn't want to encourage any discussion about medical priorities because they weren't going to change. He held his hand up for silence.

'I understand that you all have questions, and they'll be dealt with in due course. Is there anyone here with a medical issue that requires attention?' Rafe glanced at the end of the queue. It was the people who couldn't fend for themselves and push to the front that he was most interested in right now.

A woman's hand went up. 'My little boy...' She had a young child with her, who she was holding protectively against her legs. He strode down the line towards them, ushering the woman to one side.

Suddenly Mel was there, at his elbow. 'I'll take them.'

Rafe nodded, jerking his thumb towards the entrance of the medical suite. She got his meaning immediately, guiding the woman and her child into the lobby of the consulting room.

'Any other concerns about current medical issues or medication?' Rafe looked up and down the line.

'I have a question about my medication...' A man gestured to catch his attention.

'So do I.' A woman spoke up and Rafe beckoned towards the concierge.

'Right, I want you both to stand over there, please.' The concierge ushered them both to the other side of the corridor, standing with them, as they each gestured to the other to go first in the line of two.

'Anyone else?' Apparently not. 'Okay, I'll be coming down the line with paper, so you can write your questions down. I'll be holding a meeting this afternoon and they'll all be addressed there.'

A couple of women opened their handbags, withdrawing paper and pens, handing spares out to the people next to them in the queue. Everyone was calm now and starting to look at the person next to them instead of just themselves, which was exactly what Rafe needed.

He ducked into the consulting room, apologising to Mel's patient for the intrusion, and fetched a pad, grabbing up a handful of pens from the holder on the desk. Then he started to work quickly down the line, giving out paper and asking again if anyone had any medical concerns that he needed to know about.

This was exactly why he needed to keep his distance from Mel. In a crowd of people where one little boy needed to see a doctor, and two others had medical queries, he'd been able to see only her. Allowing his own attraction for her to run riot and take over his thoughts would only get in the way of what he was here to do.

And feeling again what he'd felt when he'd first met Annu allowed the possibility of feeling what he'd felt when she'd died. It might not be entirely logical to put himself into the role of Mel's protector, but Rafe's instincts seemed to have come to a different decision. That alone was more terrifying than the most ferocious of storms.

'Okay?' Half an hour later Rafe returned to the consulting room, finding Mel sitting alone behind the desk.

'Yes, the boy had been sick a couple of times this morning. I think it's a stomach upset from unfamiliar food rather than a bug, but I've called Mr Manike and asked him to arrange for the family to be isolated for the time being just in case. There's no fever and I'll check back later on how he's doing.'

Rafe nodded. That wasn't really what he'd wanted to know. He'd been hoping that Mel might tell him how *she* was. Clearly she preferred to keep that to herself.

'I've spoken to a couple of people who were concerned about their medication. No problems there, but it's good to know who we need to keep an eye on.'

Mel nodded. It seemed that she had a better idea of their current priorities than he did at the moment. 'A board would be useful, so we can have all that information in one place. I wonder if Mr Manike has something we could use?'

'I expect so, I'll go and ask him. I've already spoken to him briefly about holding a meeting this afternoon to address some of the questions that people have, and he thinks that's a good idea. He's going to send a couple of pairs of scrubs down for you as well.'

Mel looked at him steadily. No surprise, no questions. Her face was devoid of emotion, and Rafe suspected this was a strategy on her part. Something was going on behind the façade that she didn't want him to know about.

'The doctor who usually visits the island uses them, and he has some that he ordered for her. Looking the part can help in these situations. It gives people confidence.'

She nodded. Mel hadn't had any reservations in telling him exactly what was going on in her head when they'd first met, and he felt shut out now.

'Gives me confidence too.'

That was as far as Rafe felt he could go in encouraging her to talk, but Mel didn't bite.

'You seem to be doing just fine.' She gestured towards the paper in his hand. 'If you give me the questions I'll organise them into a list, while you go and see if you can rustle up an information board and some marker pens.'

That was a polite invitation to leave. He should take it.

'Okay. I'll be with Mr Manike if you want me…' Rafe was sure she wouldn't, and he should take this opportunity of severing himself from the rapidly growing feelings that threatened to turn his world upside down.

CHAPTER FOUR

RAFE DAVENPORT.

Mel had accompanied her young patient and his mother back to their room, and made sure he was settled and comfortable. Then she'd returned, taking refuge behind the authority of the large desk in the consulting room. Since her own defences were so low at the moment she needed something to fend him off.

Concentrating on a whiteboard and scrubs, neither of which were strictly necessary at the moment, had done the trick and Rafe had left her alone. Mel considered the idea. She shouldn't need to fend Rafe off at all. He was a doctor and that meant they were working towards the same thing. She should be pleased that he was here, and that she didn't have to face what was coming on her own.

Maybe it was yet another lesson in what she could, and couldn't, deal with. She was afraid of the oncoming storm and what havoc that might wreak, but that was a normal and reasonable reaction to real threats and she could deal with that. A pregnant woman was a concern, but she was confident that she could meet Zeena's needs. The challenge brought only a heightened sense of concentration, not the thoughtless mess of panic that had threatened to render her helpless and useless when she'd found herself caught up in the crowd of shouting people.

Rafe Davenport…?

Mel swallowed hard as her hands began to shake suddenly. Rafe was the trigger, the thing she couldn't deal with. She closed her eyes, trying to breathe slowly through the panic.

It couldn't be a coincidence that the last time she'd felt so anxious was when she'd been with Michael. She'd had relationships since then, but she'd made sure that they were all polite and convenient, with unchallenging men who in truth weren't any more than just friends. But polite and convenient simply wasn't possible with a gorgeous adventurer like Rafe. Her emotions were getting the better of her and she had no idea where that might lead.

Rafe was the kind of man who could push a well-ordered life into chaos. His challenging unpredictability didn't just make her feel suddenly alive, it provoked the kind of anxiety reaction that could stop her dead in her tracks.

Enough. She had a handle on this now, and she needed to do something to work off the fight or flight feeling that was still pounding in her veins. Her anxiety stemmed from situations where she felt out of control, and Mel needed to do something, *anything,* to convince herself that she had some traction over her life.

The list of questions could wait. She wanted to be on her feet and doing something. The row of cupboards on the wall, some of which could only be reached with the help of a small stepladder stowed neatly in the corner, was much more inviting. It would be useful to know what was available, and where it was kept.

She started at one end, opening each door in turn and making a mental note of what was where. There was a cupboard full of dressings, that could be called into use for anything from a cut finger to a broken limb. An ordered mind had thought everything through, and provided all kinds of diagnostic and examination equipment. And...

It made sense. This was an island, and there was no possibility of popping around the corner to the nearest chemist. People were on holiday, so romance probably vied with stomach bugs as the most common ailment a doctor had to deal with. And it was nice to offer a bit of variety. But was a full height cupboard's worth of condoms really necessary?

Mel didn't get the chance to investigate any further. A knock sounded on the door and she banged the cupboard door shut before calling to whoever was waiting outside. The manager, Mr Manike, entered, carrying a bundle wrapped in paper.

'Pink or blue, Dr Murphy?' He smiled, putting the package down on the desk and opening it.

'What...?' Mel's mind was still on the range of condoms. Mr Manike brought her back down to earth with a bump by withdrawing two pairs of scrubs, still in their plastic wrappers.

Pink had the kind of friendly feel about it that would be great for delivering a baby. Blue was a colour that indicated seniority in her own hospital, and that might apply a splash of confidence in her dealings with Rafe.

'May I take one of each, please, Mr Manike?'

'Of course.' Mr Manike deposited an extra pair of each colour onto the desk for good measure. 'I hope they will fit. I order a medium woman's size for our usual doctor.'

'That's fine, thank you.' Mostly scrubs came in whatever size you could manage to get into, but Mr Manike's quiet attention to detail was very calming.

'I have also taken the liberty of bringing one of our usual doctor's white jackets. I am sure she would offer it if she were here. Freshly laundered, with not too much starch.'

'Perfect.' Mel grinned at the thought that the amount of starch was going to matter when caught in the terrifying centre of a storm. 'Not too much starch is just right, thank you. Do you know where Dr Davenport is, by any chance?'

'I spoke to him briefly on my way here about a white-board and pens, and I believe he is now with one of our work teams discussing how best to secure the sea plane. He tells me that you are dealing with a list of questions in preparation for the proposed meeting this afternoon.' Mr Manike withdrew a sheet of paper from his pocket. 'Here is the user name and password for the laptop our regular doctor uses, in case you need it.'

Mel hadn't even thought of the laptop that she'd pushed to one side on the desk. 'Thank you, that's useful.'

'We are asking all of the guests in the water cabins to pack their things, and are arranging for suitable accommodation in the main building. I have arranged for a room to be put at your disposal.'

Breath of fresh air. Fresh air that Mel could actually make some use of without her chest beginning to heave with the beginnings of panic. Mr Manike's painstaking efficiency was a fine antidote to Rafe.

'Thank you again. I may stay here in the medical suite, so I'm available for anyone who needs me. Is there a camp bed that I could use?'

'The medical suite does have accommodation for visiting doctors, but you are a guest, Dr Murphy.'

'Right now I'm a doctor, and I'd like to be here.'

Mr Manike nodded, suddenly brisk now that he'd said all he'd come to say. 'As you wish. Please let me know if there is anything I can do to make you more comfortable.'

As the door closed quietly behind him, Mel sucked in a breath. She could decide not to dwell on the light in Rafe's eyes, the way he made her feel so alive when he smiled.

Nor did she need to take any notice of his body, or his scent, and definitely not how the touch of his fingers might feel. She could deal with the situation she'd found herself in, and she could deal with Rafe as well.

'Three o'clock.'

Mel had turned her attention to the list of questions and then gone to collect her things from her water cabin. As she wheeled her suitcase back to the hotel, she made a point of ignoring the fact that Rafe was helping board up the windows of the medical suite. She wasn't having any truck with *distractingly gorgeous* and Rafe was one of those men who seemed at his best whenever physical exertion was involved.

'What's happening at three?' She shaded her eyes as she looked up at him.

'The meeting.' Rafe swung down the ladder, wiping his forearm across his brow as he walked over to where she stood. *Very* annoyingly sexy, but he didn't seem to be able to help it.

'Ah. I've typed the list of questions if you want to look over it beforehand.'

Rafe shook his head. 'Thanks. I'll wing it and work down the list when I get there.'

She should have expected that. 'Line everyone up in a queue if they start to get rowdy...?'

That sounded less like a joke than she'd meant it to be, and more like a criticism. That really wasn't fair. Rafe had dealt with the situation a lot better than she had. The look of silent amusement on his face told her that he knew it as well, but he had the decency not to say so.

'You did what needed to be done. I guess instinct takes over in these kinds of situations, and everyone tends to act out of character.' It was as close as Mel was going to get to an apology, because apologies required explanation. Rafe had obviously noticed her own loss of control but perhaps he wouldn't mention it.

He shrugged, changing the subject. 'Has Mr Manike sorted you out with a room for the night?'

'I'd like to stay close to Zeena. There's accommodation for doctors in the medical suite, isn't there?'

'There is.'

Rafe turned, signalling to the men he was working with that he would be a minute, and then opening the door that led into the building. He led her through the consulting room and down the corridor, past the patient rooms, to a door at the end.

There were three comfortable-looking beds, each with curtains that could be drawn around them for privacy. On one side an open door led to a small kitchen, and Rafe gestured towards another closed door on the other side of the room.

'There's a shower room through there, although it's important not to use taps or showers during an electrical storm, so the staff will be around later on to put tape across the basin and shower cubicle in the bathroom.'

'Is that going to be enough in the guest rooms?'

'No, there's always someone who decides that a shower is worth risking a jolt if lightning hits the water system, so they're locking and taping bathroom doors in the guest rooms. But here we'll need to be able to wash in case of any medical emergencies, so they'll be delivering a couple of plastic barrels of water and a bowl, that we can use. Is your phone charged?'

'Um…yes, I think so. Can we use our phones?'

'Yeah, if the phone mast stays in one piece. I've got some batteries and a portable charger, but we need to go easy on any phone use because we don't know how long this is going to last. The staff are covering and taping electrical sockets as well.'

'Right. No running water, no electrical devices. What about light?'

'There's emergency lighting here and in most areas of the hotel, and that's powered by the main generator, so we should be okay there.' Rafe stepped forward, picking up a small holdall that lay beside one of the beds. 'I'll let you settle in…'

'Wait. Where are you going to sleep?' Rafe had clearly staked his claim to one of the beds, in the expectation that Mel would be occupying one of the guest rooms.

A flash of embarrassment showed in his eyes. 'I'll…um…find somewhere.'

This was ridiculous. And an opportunity to show herself, or maybe Rafe, she wasn't sure which, that she could spend the night a few feet away from him without dissolving into sleepless panic.

'That's not necessary. I went to medical school, the same as you did.'

He chuckled. 'So tired that you could sleep anywhere?'

'And with anyone.' Mel bit her lip. That hadn't come out quite the way she'd meant it to, but at least Rafe's expression didn't give any indication that he'd registered the faux pas.

'If you're sure.'

'Positive.' Mel walked over to the bed that was furthest from the one his holdall had been next to and parked her case next to it. 'This will be fine, and it's probably just as well if we're in the same place if we're needed.'

He nodded and put his own bag back down again. 'Right then. I'll finish up with the windows and then I should probably clean up a bit before the meeting.'

It wouldn't do to have Rafe looking this good in front

of a whole hotel full of guests. They might miss any number of important pieces of safety and medical information.

'I'll leave you to it then, and check in on Zeena again, to see how she's doing.'

Rafe nodded. It seemed they *could* work out a basic split in responsibilities if they put their minds to it, and that was all good. Smiling at him didn't seem so very challenging now, and Mel even allowed her eyes to linger on his back for a few extra moments as he walked away.

Mel had spent an hour with Zeena and her husband. Speaking to the couple together gave her the opportunity to ask a few more questions about their expectations for the birth, and to make sure that she'd missed nothing in terms of providing a nurturing environment for them that took account of both their personal wishes and their Muslim faith.

Then Haroon looked at his watch. 'Time to go. Would you like to come, Zeena?'

Zeena shifted uncomfortably. 'Yes, I'd like to take a walk.'

Instead of walking up and down the corridor for a while, it seemed that Haroon and Zeena had a particular destination in mind. Mel followed them to the restaurant, where they joined the rest of the islanders in one corner, for Rafe's health and safety talk.

'Surely you know everything he's going to say already?' Mel leaned across, murmuring to Zeena.

'Yes. But we have come to support him.' Zeena smiled. 'Dr Davenport will tell everyone that everything will be all right, and we will agree.'

That sounded like a plan. And when Rafe joined Mr Manike, who was waiting to start the meeting, the room fell silent. He looked the part. A clean, crisp shirt and a pair of chinos. Hair still slightly wet from the shower, which

tamed his curls a little. A broad, reassuring smile and…
Rafe just had a presence. It was difficult not to feel that
he knew exactly what he was doing, and that next to him
was the safest place you could possibly be.

He ran through everything, taking in all of the questions that had been asked and giving clear and concise
instructions about what to do in response to a number
of different scenarios. Watching out for any wildlife that
might seek shelter in the hotel building. Staying inside,
even after the storm seemed to be passing, and waiting
until the hotel team had pronounced it was safe to leave
the building. Calling for help immediately if they were ill
or injured in any way, and waiting for the medical team
to come to them. He made it all seem easy.

'In short…' he gave a smile that would bolster anyone's
spirits '…sit tight, do as the hotel staff ask you, and you'll
be able to resume your holidays as soon as the storm sub-
sides. And you'll have a story to take back home with you.'

A ripple of laughter ran around the restaurant. Rafe
invited further questions but everyone seemed content
with what they'd heard. Zeena was nodding, her hand protectively across her stomach, and Mel had to admit that
if she was smiling then there couldn't be a great deal to
worry about.

'Oh, and by the way. We're fortunate that Dr Mel Murphy is here on holiday, and we'll both be on call tonight,
although we're confident we won't be seeing any of you in
our official capacity. But if you need her, Mel's here too.'

It was probably a good idea to point her out, so that people knew who she was. The clapping that rippled around
the restaurant in response to Rafe's gesture of applause
wasn't strictly necessary though, and Mel shifted uncomfortably in her seat. But Zeena patted her on the back,

beaming, and the islanders' smiles seemed to be setting the tone for the behaviour of the hotel guests.

'When *is* the storm expected to be over?' Mel asked as they strolled back to the medical suite together, and Rafe shrugged.

'I said I can't give an exact time. Mother Nature goes at her own pace.'

'Now that it's moving closer, I imagine that it would be easier to predict, though.'

Rafe opened the door of the consulting room for her, waiting until Mel had walked inside and he'd closed the door behind them. 'There is some indication. The Meteorological Office says that there's a front moving in the other direction, and when it meets the storm it may stop it in its tracks.'

Cold fingers closed around her heart. 'Where will that be?'

'It's impossible to say right now. Maybe here, maybe thirty or forty miles east of the island. But if it's here, then the storm will last longer than just one night. Maybe two to three days. We'll have to wait and see. I've spoken with Mr Manike and we don't see any point in alarming people until we actually know the situation.'

Mel nodded. Everyone was calm at the moment and an atmosphere of camaraderie seemed to be developing. Maybe it *was* better to say nothing until they were sure. 'Okay. Thanks for telling me. Do the islanders know?'

'The islanders know that you can never really predict exactly how a storm's going to behave, or how long it'll last. They'll tell you to wait and see, and that it'll be over when it's over.'

'And that everything's going to be okay?' Suddenly Mel really needed to hear him say that. If Rafe said it, then perhaps she'd believe him.

'You're a doctor, you know it's never a good idea to make blanket predictions.' He fell silent, looking at her thoughtfully. Maybe he saw the terror that Mel was trying so hard to hide. 'But yeah. Everything's going to be okay.'

Mel was an enigma. She seemed so certain of herself, so capable, and yet Rafe couldn't forget that sudden glimpse of her vulnerable side. He'd been unable to shake the feeling that there was something wrong, something beyond the fact that no one with any sense was completely unafraid in the face of an emergency of a kind they'd never experienced before.

When a short queue of people had formed outside the consulting room door, mostly wanting reassurance, he'd wondered if he should deal with them, but she'd arranged for a line of chairs to be put out and chased him away. Activity seemed to quell her fears, and Rafe needed to get the sea plane under cover before the storm hit.

He changed out of his clean shirt, dragging a T-shirt over his head, and then rounded up the men he'd been working with to fix the storm shutters. It took a couple of hours to unload the medical supplies and move the light aircraft out of the water and up the beach, to a large outbuilding that was used to store the hotel's water sports equipment. Space had been found to accommodate the plane, and he secured it alongside the boats and kayaks that were being tied down to minimise any damage.

The wind was beginning to pick up now, kicking up small plumes of fine white sand on the beach. The sky was dark with clouds, coming in from the east, and Rafe made his way back to the hotel, ordering a crate of soft drinks from the bar for the men who'd been working all day, to wash some of the dust from their throats. Everything was ready, they'd done as much as they could, and now they just had to wait.

When he popped in to Zeena's room he half expected to find Mel there, but she wasn't. Zeena assured him that she was quite all right and that the baby would come whenever it came, telling him that Mel had been here but that she'd gone to see if she could get a couple of hours' sleep before the storm hit.

Something made him turn and walk to the end of the corridor. Maybe the thought that even the steeliest of hearts found it difficult to sleep before a storm, however sensible the suggestion seemed. Maybe some instinct telling him that he needed to know where Mel was and that she was all right.

The door was slightly ajar and the doctors' ready room seemed dark and quiet. Maybe Mel really was sleeping. Rafe hesitated in the doorway and then he caught the sound of a ragged breath.

She was crying. Alone in the dark, where no one could see her.

CHAPTER FIVE

THE QUIET BEFORE the storm. Mel had supposed that it was just a figure of speech, but it really *was* quiet. The air was heavy and humid, seeming to press down on her like a smothering blanket.

She'd eaten dinner with Zeena and her husband and, after checking her blood pressure and reassuring her that she was in great shape, left the couple alone together for the evening. Even if she didn't sleep, Mel reckoned that a couple of hours' rest might stand her in good stead for whatever was to come that night, but had found that it was too hot to slip under a blanket, and not comforting enough to lie on the bed without something to cover her.

The dark silence was corrosive, eating into her shell of measured confidence. She lay on her left side, then her right, and then on her back, and when she'd run out of positions that might potentially be comfortable Mel went to fetch a bottle of water from the kitchen, finding that even though the refrigerator was unplugged the bottles inside were still cool. As she closed the door a low rumble of distant thunder sounded. A mile away? Two? Twenty? The uncertainty of all this was killing her.

Backing out of the kitchen, she stumbled back towards her bed, pulling the curtains around it. Maybe she should call Amy…

Mel had decided not to call her daughter, on the basis that the storm would be over before Amy could possibly worry about not being able to contact her for their promised weekly catch-up. But if the storm lasted for days then communications might be affected for goodness only knew how long. Amy might call and then decide to look at the weather reports for this region.

She could call Amy and tell her that she was having a wonderful time, but that reception on her phone wasn't great and so not to worry if she didn't hear from her. Mel took her phone from her bag, calling Amy's number. Nothing. The phone was charged and even though she had only one reception bar that should be enough. She dialled again. Then again. She so badly wanted to hear Amy's voice.

She had to pull herself together. If she was crying when she called then Amy would know that something was up, and she'd worry. Mel took a couple of deep breaths and then tried again. The call didn't connect yet again, and Mel sank down onto the floor, the wall at her back giving her at least some measure of security.

She didn't know how long she'd stayed there for, her knees pulled up in front of her and her head in her hands, trying to stop herself from crying. When a soft footstep and the instinct that someone else was in the room made her open her eyes she was blinded for a moment by light streaming in from the doorway.

Why hadn't she thought to draw the privacy curtains around her bed? As her eyes adjusted to the light, she saw Rafe's solid shadow and froze, panic driving every excuse that she could think of for sitting on the floor in the darkness from her head.

Maybe he'd come to fetch something and he wouldn't notice her. Mel held her breath.

'I could do with someone to talk to. The waiting's getting to me.'

His voice was soft, almost tender. No…it was definitely tender. And even if this was very clearly his way of making her feel better, she didn't care because even his silhouette was reassuring. Mel took a sip of water from the bottle beside her to clear her throat.

'There's a spare seat here. Help yourself.'

'Thanks. I appreciate it.' He sat down on the floor next to her.

The foreboding shadows *were* suddenly less intimidating. And half-light might make her tears a little less obvious. Although Rafe was clearly aware of them, since he'd handed her a clean tissue. Mel wiped her eyes and blew her nose.

'Thanks. Did you get your sea plane sorted?'

'Yep. She's tied down in one of the outhouses, with the boats.' He nodded towards the phone, still clutched in her hand. 'Been trying to call someone?'

'My daughter. Amy.'

He leaned over, taking the phone from her grasp and putting it down on the floor between them. 'And what were you thinking of saying to her?'

Mel shrugged. 'Probably best to tell her all about it when I get home. I couldn't get through, anyway.'

'Yeah, everyone's either on the internet or trying to phone home at the moment, and getting stressed out about it. Why don't you message her? Your phone will connect as soon as there's a signal and you don't have to keep dialling.'

'Yeah. Later maybe, when I've worked out what to say.'

'That's a good idea too. Zeena's okay?'

Mel doubted that he didn't already know how Zeena was. He was probably just trying to take her mind off everything else for a moment, but the ploy seemed to be working.

'Yes, her vitals are stable, and the baby will be along any time now. I thought that she and her husband could do with some quiet time together.' Mel pressed her lips together, feeling the embarrassment of the situation seep into her. 'I'm not usually this edgy about waiting for things to happen.'

'No? I am, every time. It's the downside of being ready, I reckon. I wouldn't have it any other way, but my instinct tells me I'd rather be doing something.'

'Me too. Nothing's ever as bad as you think it's going to be in your head.'

Rafe nodded. He was so solid, and he exuded safety. Mel could feel her heart begin to steady, just at the sound of his voice, and his scent. A trace of machine oil and hard work, mingling with the stronger smell of soap. She would allow herself this, if it meant that she could meet the night ahead.

'So how's London these days? It's been a while since I was there.'

'It's much the same as it ever was, I guess. Always changing.'

Rafe smiled. 'Yeah. That was what I liked about it. Always the same, and yet always something new.'

'How long since you've been there?' There was a trace of reminiscence in his voice that said it had probably been a while.

'Eight…no, ten years. I took my son when he was fifteen, just to show him where his dad came from.'

'You have a son?'

Rafe shifted, taking his phone from his back pocket. Flipping through photographs, he found the one he was looking for and passed the phone over to Mel. A golden-skinned, dark-haired young man, who clearly shared his father's temperament. He was standing on the floats of a sea plane, much like the one that Rafe had arrived in, grinning at the camera, a deep blue cloudless sky in the background.

'Ash has just qualified as a doctor. He's working in Colombo at the moment.'

'He's like you.'

Rafe leaned over to look at the phone, his shoulder touching hers. 'You think so? I always reckoned he'd got the best of the bargain and took after my wife.'

His wife. Mel wondered whether she should feel that there was one lucky lady, or someone with a challenge on her hands. Whatever the case, Mel really shouldn't be feeling any of the warmth that his mere presence seemed to engender. She excused herself by remembering she'd been doing her best not to feel anything for Rafe ever since she'd met him.

'He looks as if he's just finished doing one thing and about to do another.'

That made him laugh. 'Yeah. If I remember rightly, he had just completed a few repairs and was about to take the plane up when I took that photograph.'

'Your wife's Sri Lankan?'

'Yes, she was. Annu died when Ash was ten months old. Cancer.'

And he still felt it. Of course he did. Time healed but it never dismissed that kind of pain entirely. There was a matter-of-factness about the way that Rafe said it, but it couldn't hide the quiver in his voice.

'I'm so sorry. That must have been terrible for you.'

'Yeah. The first few years were the worst, but having Ash to look after did a lot in encouraging me to pull myself together.'

'You've brought him up alone?'

Rafe's lips quirked in a slight smile. 'I suppose if by *alone* you mean with the help of Annu's extended family, some of whom weren't strictly speaking related to her, then yeah. I brought him up alone. They're the reason I stayed in Sri Lanka. I don't have much family back in England and Ash needed them as much as he did me.'

'No plans to go back now, though?' Rafe seemed so at home here.

'No. You can get to love Sri Lanka very easily. And there's enough to keep me occupied.'

'Flying around, dropping in on people who might need you?' He shrugged, and Mel let the question drop, reaching for her own phone. 'I've pictures of my own.'

'Oh. Let me see…'

Mel flipped to the picture of Amy that she particularly liked, taken in the porch at the church, smiling up at her new husband. 'That's my daughter, Amy.'

Rafe took the phone, a broad grin spreading across his face. 'I can tell. She's a lot like you. Beautiful.'

A little sizzle of heat chased the last of the chills of the night away. People often commented on how much Amy and Mel were alike, and if Rafe thought Amy beautiful…

She dismissed the thought. What else was anyone supposed to say when presented with a photograph of a bride?

'You must have been very young when you had her.'

That could be taken as a compliment as well, if you really tried. Mel decided not to try. 'I had Amy after I'd completed first year at university. I was able to defer my studies for a year, but my relationship with Amy's father broke up. My family came to the rescue too. They took us in and looked after Amy so that I could go back to university.'

'It makes all the difference in the world, doesn't it.' Rafe was scrolling through the photographs on his phone and when he found the one he wanted he handed it to Mel. 'That's Ash at five years old, with his grandparents.'

'He looks as if he's having a lot of fun with that paddling pool. Can I swipe?'

He chuckled. 'As much as you like. Ash always gives me a hard time over loading all of the photos of him when he was little, each time I get a new phone.'

'They don't understand, do they? When Amy starts her own family, she'll get it.' Mel found the folder that contained all of Amy's childhood photographs and handed her phone to Rafe.

'She's very cute. Can *I* swipe?'

'Knock yourself out. We'll see who gets to the end first…'

Something was growing, here in the darkness. Something tender, that was reflected in the faces in the photographs. She and Rafe had found common ground, and it was in the thing that meant the most to them both. Sitting close, feeling the brush of his arm against hers, seemed natural and reassuring.

His phone rang and Mel jumped. He leaned across, taking it from her hand, and she felt his scent wash through her senses, like an intoxicating wave. Maybe it was just as well that these moments were coming to an end. He listened for a moment, and then nodded.

'Okay. We'll be straight there.' He ended the call, turning to Mel. 'Looks as if we're done waiting.'

He was suddenly all movement, and there was no time to ask why his phone should be working when hers wasn't. At least the intermittent nature of the connection had saved Mel from doing anything that she'd regret later. Rafe got to his feet and when he held out his hand to her she took it, her legs and back a little stiff from sitting so long, hunched on the floor.

As he led the way swiftly out of the doctors' ready room the sound of thunder crashed around them, almost above their heads.

CHAPTER SIX

As HE PASSED Zeena's door, Rafe knocked and briefly looked in on her. She and her husband were sitting together playing draughts and clearly the baby wasn't going to be coming in the next fifteen minutes. Hopefully by then the current number one on his to-do list would be resolved.

And hopefully the impulse that time spent with Mel was the most important thing in the world would have sunk back into perspective as well. There had been a closeness between them that he hadn't allowed himself to feel in twenty-five years, and which he'd had no intention of allowing himself to feel again. His marriage had been a good one, a once in a lifetime experience. If he ever wavered in that belief, he only had to remember the pain that Annu's death had caused.

He led the way to Mr Manike's office, knocking on the door and opening it before he heard the call to come inside. Mr Manike was sitting in the small anteroom, in front of a whole bank of screens which showed the feeds from the various CCTV cameras.

'What's happening?' Mel stepped forward, addressing her question to Mr Manike, and Rafe couldn't help but smile. The side of her that took life by the scruff of the neck and hung on tight was back.

'Look. Here.' Mr Manike indicated one of the screens,

which showed a view of the lagoon and the water cabins. Mel leant forward to study the exact area that he was pointing to, and Rafe looked over her shoulder. He was crowding her a little so that he could see properly, but she didn't move away. He fancied she even moved a little closer.

'What's that? A light, in one of the cabins?' Mel asked.

'Looks like it.' Rafe stared at the glimmering point of white light on the black and white image. 'Someone's left a light on in one of the water cabins?'

'Maybe… Keep looking.' Mr Manike was still staring at the screen.

Then they saw it. A brief shadow passed in front of the light and Mel gasped, putting her hand to her mouth. 'There's someone out there!'

Someone who was clearly not very mindful of their own safety. 'Who's staying in that cabin?'

Mr Manike pulled a sheet of paper towards him. 'Mr and Mrs Cartwright. Young honeymooners. Mr Cartwright has been very keen in his participation in our more extreme water sports.'

Young honeymooners out for kicks. Rafe could imagine the kind of tragedy that might lead to all too well.

'Okay. I'll go and get them.' He turned, walking out into the main office, where a bundle of sou'westers was hanging on the peg that was usually reserved for Mr Manike's jacket. Rafe selected the largest and pulled it on.

'Wait… Rafe!' Mel caught his arm and instinctively he shook himself free. This was something he needed to do alone.

'Stay here. Zeena needs you…' She understood the unspoken as well as he did. If anything happened to him, then there would still be a doctor here to look after Zeena. He was largely surplus to requirements, the man who had lived when his talented wife, who had so much more to give to the world than he did, had died.

And he wouldn't let Mel risk herself. He was beginning to need that, more than he could admit to. Rafe heard her call his name, exasperation sounding in her voice, and he ignored her. Mel could be as exasperated as she liked, but he needed to have her safe.

He strode out of Mr Manike's office to the private door that led out onto the beach, nodding at the two men who were keeping an eye on it to make sure that no one used the only way out of here that wasn't boarded shut. As he pushed out into the oncoming storm, the wind pushed back. But he was stronger.

He *had* to be stronger, because there were two young people out there who might just be making the biggest mistake of their lives.

Typical! *Typical!* Just when Mel was thinking that Rafe was someone that she could trust, he snapped that connection like a dry twig under his foot. It was all the more hurtful because Michael had done that again and again, until finally Mel had questioned her every thought and deed.

'Can't you stop him?' She turned on Mr Manike in frustration.

'I think that any man might do the same.' Mr Manike was staring at the CCTV images, tracking Rafe's movements from one camera to another.

Not quite any man. She suspected that Rafe was a little more disposed to stepping in and playing the part of a lone hero than most, and it was irritating when they both had a job to do. The years had taught Mel to distinguish between her own shortcomings and those of others, and this one she could lay squarely at Rafe's feet.

And what Rafe didn't seem to grasp was that if there

was no stopping him, then there was no stopping Mel either. 'Have you got two volunteers, to go outside with me? Strong…'

Mr Manike considered the matter and then nodded. 'Of course.'

Clearly this had been his original plan, because in response to his call two burly men appeared, clad in waterproofs. Mel grabbed one of the sou'westers from the peg and slipped it on, finding that it wasn't so big that she couldn't find her hands somewhere in the sleeves.

'Right then.' She turned to the volunteers, one of whom she recognised from behind the bar last night. 'You're happy to go out there with me? I may need your help.'

'Don't worry, miss.' Adil, the bartender, smiled at her. 'Mushan and I will get you out there and back inside again, no problem.'

'Thank you. I want you to be careful and not to take any unnecessary risks. We can't help anyone else if we're not in one piece ourselves.' Mel wasn't quite sure how that applied to helping Rafe, because right now she was so furious with him she could march out there alone and pluck him from the eye of the storm. But Adil and Mushan weren't to be involved in that part of the operation.

Mr Manike produced a pair of safety glasses and Mel put them on, tucking the holding strap around the back of her head. It seemed she was about the only person who didn't quite know what to expect from the conditions outside, because Adil and Mushan both withdrew similar protection from their pockets.

As soon as she stepped through the door and onto the beach the wind almost knocked her off her feet, and Adil reached out to steady her. There was sand too, stinging her skin as it was whipped up by the wind, and Mel pulled the high collar of her sou'wester across her mouth. Together the three figures made their way down the beach and onto the wooden walkway that led to the water cabins. It creaked alarmingly under their weight and water was slopping against their feet, but the structure seemed sound enough and Adil nodded, clearly deeming it safe.

They were making better progress than Rafe, able to support each other as the wind buffeted them. Mel kept her eyes on him, catching her breath as he staggered in response to a particularly strong gust of wind. But he regained his footing and as he did so he looked behind him.

His gesture was crystal-clear in its meaning. Go back. Adil and Mushan hesitated, but when Mel pressed on ahead they followed her. When they reached Rafe he leaned towards her, shouting to make himself heard.

'Thought I told you not to come out here…'

'I thought *I* told you not to go alone…' Mel yelled back at him, wondering if this was going to turn into an argument.

But Rafe shrugged suddenly, taking her arm and guiding her along the walkway. Mel had to admit that it was very welcome, as the waves that were sloshing against her ankles were getting stronger now, threatening to whip her feet out from under her.

They could see the light in the furthest cabin more clearly now, and it seemed to be coming from the back of the structure, where the bedroom was situated. Maybe the young bride and groom had left something behind and decided to return for it. She couldn't imagine what could be so important that they would risk their safety for it, but people did thoughtless things at times.

Rafe reached the sliding doors of the cabin, feeling inside his jacket for a pocket multi-tool, and made short work of the lock. He opened the door, bundling Mel inside, and then followed Adil and Mushan, sliding the door closed behind them. The sudden absence of wind and noise almost took her breath away, and it was a moment before she could compose herself enough to look around.

'Mate… Trust me, sex in a storm sounds a great deal better than it actually is. Do us all a favour and get your wife out of here.' Rafe's voice was suddenly relaxed, almost jocular.

Mel looked up and saw the object of his comments standing by the sliding doors that led to the bedroom. A young man, with sun-blond hair and an impressive tan, wearing only a cocky smile. When he realised that Mel was regarding him, his grin became broader and he slowly covered his manhood with his hand.

'I wouldn't bother. Dr Murphy's undoubtedly seen anything you have to offer. Put your clothes on and let's be going.'

It seemed that Rafe's tone was working, and the young man started to turn. But then a young, equally blonde woman appeared in the bedroom doorway, clad only in a very skimpy towel. She yelped at the sight of the three burly men and ducked behind her husband. Adil and Mushan immediately turned their gazes to the floor, and even Rafe seemed to be making some effort to look somewhere else while still keeping control of the situation.

'Oh, please…'

Mel hadn't come out here to play games with the couple, and neither had the men, despite their obvious attempts at gentlemanly behaviour. She stepped forward, taking the woman by the shoulders and propelling her into the bedroom. A pair of woman's jeans lay tangled on the floor with a sweater, and Mel picked them up.

'Get these on. Now.'

'Hey. Don't sweat it…' The man had followed and was thankfully stepping into his own jeans.

'Enough with the attitude!' Rafe's brisk words floated through the open doorway, unmistakably an order now. 'Do as the lady says.'

'I think we should go, Ty...' The woman had pulled her sweater over her head and was wriggling into her jeans. 'This cabin isn't quite as stable as we thought...'

Just how stable had they thought a wooden cabin would be, suspended over the water in a gale? Mel never got the chance to ask, because a loud crash sounded against the floor-to-ceiling window, showering the bed with broken glass. Rafe was there suddenly, his arm around Mel's shoulders as he shepherded everyone out of the bedroom.

Mr and Mrs Cartwright suddenly got the message, in the most graphic way possible. Ty pulled on his sweater and Rafe ducked back into the bedroom, fetching the two pairs of trainers that were lying on the floor. Mel inspected both pairs for any broken glass before handing them to Ty and his wife to hurriedly put on.

'We stay together, right?' Rafe had obviously decided that the couple needed no more cajoling and was taking off his own sou'wester and wrapping it around the young woman's shoulders. 'You do exactly as Adil and Mushan tell you. Without question.'

'Yes, okay.' Ty was clearly doing his best not to lose too much face. 'Do as they say, Em.'

Mel rolled her eyes. For a moment Rafe's gaze caught hers, and his mouth twitched in a crooked smile. Then he opened the door of the cabin. Adil and Mushan went first and then Rafe beckoned to Ty and Em to follow them. When it was Mel's turn she felt Rafe's reassuring hand on her arm.

They were halfway along the walkway, back to the safety of the beach, when suddenly the wind seemed to drop a little. A moment of silence, and then the rain started, so heavy that it felt as if someone had just tipped a bucket of water over Mel's head. Ty let go of his wife, raising his arm to shield his face against the onslaught. Em staggered a little and lost her footing, falling onto the walkway. Before Rafe could reach her, a wave sloshed across the boards and she slid into the sea.

In normal circumstances that wasn't going to hurt anyone. Last evening, Mel had seen people stepping off the walkways and wading in the warm sea to their cabins. But now the waves were higher and could very easily knock someone off their feet, and who knew what kind of sharp objects were in the turbulent water?

But Rafe was there. She felt Adil take hold of her arm as Rafe swung his legs over the handrails and let himself down into the sea, where Em was struggling helplessly. When he grabbed her, lifting her out of the water, Mel saw blood mixed with the water that was running down his arms, but it was impossible to say whether it was his or Em's.

Mushan lifted Em over the handrail, setting her back down on her feet. Mel ran her hands over the sou'wester, looking for any tears that might signify a wound.

'Are you all right? Can you keep walking?'

'Yes… I'm okay, I can walk.' Em nodded.

'Right then. We'll take a look at you as soon as we get inside.' Mel was watching as Rafe climbed back over the railings, breathing her own sigh of relief when he was safely back on the walkway. Together the small party made their way back to the beach and as they approached the door into the hotel it opened, willing hands pulling them inside.

Mel seemed in her element. She'd despatched him to the doctors' ready room, to wash off the grime, and had taken

Em into one of the patient rooms, presumably for the same treatment. He drew a bowl full of water from the barrel that stood next to the hand basin and walked through to the shower room at the far end, putting the bowl on the tiled floor outside the cubicle. Rafe soaped his shoulders and arms, then picked up his flannel to wipe them, trying to avoid the areas that were already stinging from contact with soap and water.

The scrape on his forearm wasn't too bad but Rafe was pretty sure that the other wound would need stitches. Which was a shame because it was above his elbow on the back of his arm, which meant he couldn't reach it himself and he was going to have to ask Mel to stitch it for him. And the look she'd given him when she'd ordered him to go and clean himself up had left him in no doubt that she was still unhappy about his having gone out to fetch Ty and Em Cartwright on his own.

Hindsight was always twenty-twenty. He probably could have managed alone, and he stood by the guiding principle of his actions. If one of them was going to take their chances out there, then it was going to be him.

He heard a knock at the outer door and it opened a crack. 'Hey. How are you doing in there?' Mel was standing outside the bathroom, calling in.

'Fine, thanks.'

'You're not absolutely fine, are you? You're bleeding.'

'And how would you know that?'

He heard a loud, rather theatrical sigh. 'Because I saw blood when you lifted Em out of the water. And I've just given her a thorough once-over and she doesn't have a mark on her.'

'Did she swallow any water?' Maybe he could keep the subject on Em's possible injuries until he was at least dry and felt a bit more able to face the world.

'She says not, but I'll keep an eye on her. And meanwhile…'

The bathroom door swung open. Rafe reached for the door to the shower room and banged it shut, hearing her footsteps outside.

'Hey…!'

'I thought it was nothing I hadn't seen before.' There was a trace of amusement in her voice. Rafe rubbed his hand across his face, trying to wipe away his own smile.

'I don't want to bore you,' he called back to her.

'I'm sure you're underestimating yourself.' Mel was clearly intent on making the most of the fact that she was standing in between him and his clothes, which were in his bag at his bedside.

'It's generous of you to say so. I'll see you in the consulting room in ten minutes. If you wouldn't mind, I think I need a couple of stitches.'

'My pleasure. If you start feeling dizzy, call me.'

He was feeling dizzy already. Light-headed, and weak-kneed. None of that was anything to do with blood loss. It was more to do with the fact that Mel was just a few paces away from him.

'I'm sure you have something better to do than harangue me, Dr Murphy.'

'I'm sure I do, Dr Davenport.' He heard Mel's footsteps again, and the door closed behind her.

Rafe finished washing himself and walked through to inspect the wound on his arm in the mirror above the hand basin. It was still bleeding and he reached for a couple of paper handtowels to press against it, before wrapping a towel awkwardly around his hips with one hand. The towel probably wasn't strictly necessary. If Mel was going to torment him any more then he couldn't imagine that she'd lie in wait for him outside. Meeting him head-on seemed far more her style.

He smiled to himself grimly. Much as he liked crossing swords with Mel, this was one thing he wasn't going to compromise on.

She was very thorough, and very gentle. Rafe sat on the examination couch, rather more embarrassed than usual over the fact that Mel had stripped his T-shirt off to examine his shoulders and torso for any other signs of injury. She was currently sitting behind him, carefully pulling splinters of wood from the cut on his upper arm with the aid of a magnifying glass and a pair of tweezers.

'I think that's everything. You want to see for yourself?'

'I trust you.' Rafe was staring at the wall, wondering when Mel would decide that she'd been more than kind and he now deserved a telling-off.

'Really? You've picked *this* moment to trust me?' She murmured the words quietly, which made them seem all the more cutting, and Rafe sighed.

'Okay. You're angry, aren't you?'

'Yes, I'm angry. Hold still while I irrigate the wound and stitch it.'

In anyone else, the thought of angry stitches might have made him pause. But it seemed that Rafe *did* trust Mel enough to back off if emotion got the better of her. She'd already numbed the skin around his wound with a local anaesthetic and he felt only the cold dribble of antiseptic as it ran down towards his elbow, quickly mopped by a piece of cotton wool.

A slight push against his skin as the stitches went in. 'Five?' Rafe bit his tongue. Maybe he shouldn't question her judgement right now, or he was liable to find his lips stitched together.

'Six. If you decide to try any other stunts like the one you pulled tonight, I don't want you pulling them apart.'

'It wasn't a stunt, Mel. Someone needed to go out there, and it didn't make sense for the only two doctors in the place to go.'

'Hmm. Maybe we should both stay in separate rooms at all times, just in case something comes crashing through the ceiling.' The sixth stitch went in as smoothly as the other five and Mel reached round, handing him a mirror.

'That's great, thank you.' Rafe squinted at the six neat stitches. 'And you're taking it to ridiculous lengths. We need to work together and nothing's going to be crashing through the ceiling tonight. I just don't see that it's all that useful to deliberately put both of us at risk. I know my own capabilities.'

He pressed his lips together. Rafe hadn't wanted to bring up the moment when the clamour of a crowd of people around her had left Mel suddenly paralysed, because she clearly didn't want to talk about it. But it had happened and he couldn't ignore it.

'I get that. But you can't just decide you have a monopoly on mindless daring.' He felt the gentle sweep of her fingers as she dressed the wound and when Mel had finished Rafe went to pull his T-shirt back on.

'Wait…' He felt her hand on his shoulder. 'I'll dress that other scrape. It doesn't look as if it's going to stop bleeding unless it's covered.'

Now he could see her, carefully irrigating the deep graze on his forearm and securing a dressing over it. Somehow, she managed to be just as immaculate as she'd been before going out into a force eight gale and her hair still smelled faintly of roses.

'It's not mindless daring. What do you take me for?'

Her gaze flipped up towards his, giving him the inexplicable feeling that he was completely naked.

'I'm not sure what I take you for yet. What I *do* know is that we're supposed to be working together and you didn't see any need to discuss our next move with me.'

'You mean we could have talked about it, and *then* decided that I'd go and you'd stay here. By which time that window could have shattered all over Ty and Em and we'd be doing more than just dressing a couple of scrapes on my arm.'

'No. Discussion is a two-way process, Rafe. It doesn't mean trading a few words before we do what you intended in the first place. It's supposed to improve our response, not delay it.'

Fair enough. She had a point. And Rafe couldn't deny that he'd acted out of instinct, a wish to protect her, rather than strictly logically. He pulled his T-shirt back over his head.

'I'll admit I should have waited for Adil and Mushan. But if *you* were thinking logically and reasonably, what prompted you to come out with them?'

Mel's cheeks reddened slightly. 'Irritation.'

Now they were getting somewhere. Somewhere that felt as if it might allow for some acknowledgement of concern for each other, although Rafe would hold out as long as he could before he gave in to that.

'All right, then.' Maybe now was a good time to leave and let Mel think about that. He turned and she caught his arm.

'No, it's not all right. I didn't act very sensibly, and neither did you. If we're going to work together, then I think we'd better come to a more rational arrangement, don't you? Because I'm not just going to follow your lead in everything.'

He could see why that grated with Mel. Practically speaking, he understood the weather conditions better than she did, and what to look out for. But she wasn't the kind of woman who just waited for a man to tell her what to do. Just as he wasn't the kind of man who'd put a woman in danger. Rafe felt his anger subside as rational thought took hold.

'Nor should you. You were right to challenge me.'

Her gaze searched his face. In this moment, he wanted her approval more than he wanted anything.

'Maybe I didn't do it in quite the right way.'

'So let's start again, shall we? We're partners in this, and we make a joint response to everything.'

'You mean…discuss things first?' Mel wasn't going to let him wriggle out of this with a set of vague promises. She saw his hesitation and leaned forward towards him. The scent of roses alone was enough to break him.

'Yeah. Fair enough, we'll discuss.' Just as long as the discussion didn't include how he was beginning to feel about her. He hadn't allowed himself to feel this way since Annu died, and he wasn't allowing it now. But whatever it was that made Mel so fascinating to him paid no heed to what he did and didn't allow.

'Deal?' She held out her hand, and he took it. Small and soft, and yet with a determined grip.

'Yeah. Deal.'

CHAPTER SEVEN

THEY WERE GETTING SOMEWHERE. At least Rafe didn't seem to be about to rush off and try any more feats of daring, although it was difficult to see what feats might present themselves since everything seemed to be very much under control. When a call came through for a non-urgent visit to one of the guest rooms, he clearly felt that going together was an acceptable level of risk.

No one was getting very much sleep, and there was a small group in the bar who seemed intent on drinking the night away. Rafe grinned when Mel frowned up at him.

'The cocktails don't have any alcohol in them. Mr Manike announced that drinks were on the house tonight, but if you look you'll see the optics behind the bar are all empty. He knows it's not a good idea to have anyone getting drunk.'

'They look as if they're well on their way...' Another raucous round of laughter echoed across the otherwise empty bar.

'Power of suggestion. They're sitting in a bar, drinking something. If something happens they'll sober up pretty quickly.'

'Fair enough. When this is over I'll be ordering a single malt Scotch and savouring every sip of it.'

Rafe nodded. 'I might just join you. They have a good choice of single malts here.'

That would be something to look forward to. Mel had assumed that as soon as the danger from the storm had passed she wouldn't see Rafe for dust, but perhaps he'd stay for one leisurely drink in the sunshine. Before wheeling his sea plane out of its shelter and taking off to fly somewhere else.

They made their way upstairs, to Mr and Mrs Denby's room. The retired couple were on the holiday of a lifetime, and Mr Manike had reported that Mrs Denby was becoming very distressed by the noise and clatter of the storm.

'She won't stop crying.' Mr Denby was looking a little overwhelmed himself when he opened the door to their room. 'Have you got something you can give her to make her sleep?'

'Let's go and have a chat with her.' Rafe smiled breezily and Mel followed him into the room.

Mrs Denby was sitting in one of the armchairs, her arms hugged around her. Every time a gust of wind hit the shutters outside the windows she jumped, tears issuing from her eyes. Mel knelt down beside her, taking her hand.

'Hello there. I'm Mel.'

'Terri. You're the doctor?'

'Yes, that's right. We came to see how you were doing.'

'Oh, dear…' Terri dissolved into tears, and Mel felt Rafe press a paper handkerchief into her hand. 'This is so awful…'

'Yes, it's pretty loud, isn't it? But we're quite safe here.'

Terri gave Mel a disbelieving look. 'Are you sure?'

'Absolutely. This hotel's fully prepared for weather like this.'

One of the perks of being a doctor was that people tended to take your word for things. Mel had about as much experience of structural engineering as the next person, but Terri brightened a little at her assurance.

'There's a lizard in the room.' Terri pointed to a shadowy corner, where a small gecko clung to the wall. Sand-coloured, with dark markings along its back, the creature wasn't much longer than Mel's middle finger.

Rafe took a couple of steps towards the creature, careful not to frighten it. 'We can get rid of that for you.'

'Yes. It could bite or…anything.' Terri waved her hand in the direction of the gecko, which ignored her suggestions completely, staying motionless on the wall.

'You agree that a gecko-catching mission's in order, Dr Murphy?' Rafe's eyes flashed with humour.

'Absolutely. I'm looking forward to watching you try, Dr Davenport.' All of the geckos that Mel had seen during her short stay on the island had been shy creatures which darted out of sight as soon as she took a step towards them.

'I'll just be a moment.' Rafe grinned, leaving the room.

Mel took the precaution of taking Terri's pulse and checking her blood pressure while he was gone. Both very slightly elevated, but what was really wrong with her was that she was scared. In Mel's experience, a few well chosen words and something to do would be a lot more effective than sedatives, and Terri would be much better able to deal with her experience afterwards.

'I'm interested in seeing how he does with the gecko.' Mel smiled at Terri and got a smile back. When Rafe returned, holding a net with a long handle, Terri turned towards him to watch and Mel shot him a smile.

He knew that this had turned into a bit of light relief for Terri and maybe his first lunge with the net wasn't entirely in earnest. The gecko skittered across the wall, coming to a halt and regarding Rafe warily through its large bulging eyes, seemingly ready to race for cover again. But this time Rafe was too quick for it, dropping the net over it and carefully detaching it from the wall.

Terri smiled, clapping her hands together. 'Well done... Be careful though, it might be poisonous.'

'It's harmless. Probably come inside to get out of the storm.' Rafe grinned at Terri. 'I'll find somewhere for it where it won't bother you any more.'

'Thank you. I'd really rather it wasn't anywhere near me.' Terri was beginning to look a great deal better, and hardly jumped when a loud crash sounded from outside.

'I'll take it away right now.'

Half an hour later, she found Rafe in the doctors' ready room, staring at a glass tank which he'd clearly done a bit of work to convert into a comfortable home, with a large bowl of water, some fruit slices and a couple of small, leafy branches. The gecko was motionless on one of the twigs, staring back at him.

'How's Terri?' He didn't look up.

'She's fine. I took her and her husband down to the lounge, where Mr Manike's organised a quiz and some card games. There are plenty of the staff around to lift the mood if needed, and they'll keep an eye on her.'

'Great. Better than sedatives.' He turned, looking at her speculatively.

'Yes, much. Working through things takes a bit longer but it's a lot more effective.' Mel sat down next to him on the bed, looking into the glass tank.

She took a deep breath. 'I've got something to say... About working together.' If she committed herself then she couldn't back out when it came to the point of actually saying the words.

'Yeah?'

Mel swallowed hard. What if telling Rafe that she suffered from an anxiety disorder made him see her differently? He never hesitated and how could his adventurous spirit ever really understand? He might make allowances for her to get them both through the storm, but suddenly she wanted a lot more than that.

The silence was killing her. Suddenly, Rafe smiled. 'We could just close our eyes and jump...'

'You'd like that, wouldn't you.' She smiled back at him. 'Wouldn't you?'

So she was an adventurer too. Suddenly the words seemed easier.

'This morning, outside the medical suite, when I was surrounded by all those people... I had an anxiety reaction and I froze.'

He nodded thoughtfully. 'What happened to you didn't strike me as a reaction to what was going on around you.'

He'd hit the nail right on the head. Anxiety wasn't a response to the real world, it was a response to her own internal world. One where she was stripped of the resources that she'd built up around her to safeguard her life.

'Yes... It's an anxiety disorder. It doesn't mean that I can't deal with what's going on here, Rafe. But I thought you needed to know because...if we're going to work together then we need to know each other's weaknesses.'

'In my experience people with anxiety disorders are very far from weak. They struggle with very real obstacles and symptoms.' He pursed his lips. 'But you're a doctor, Mel. You know this, don't you?'

She knew it. Sometimes she got a little tired of saying it. 'People can think differently.'

His lip curled. 'They'd be the people who would laugh in your face if you suggested that it was possible to snap out of a broken leg.'

'I imagine so.'

'And you think I'm one of them? That I'd consider this a weakness and it would affect the way I work with you?'

Maybe she had. Rafe was a complex, compelling man and she couldn't help caring what he thought of her. She'd listened too well to her fears and misjudged him.

'That would be very wrong of me, wouldn't it.'

'I'm glad you think so.' He shot her an intoxicating smile, laying his hand on his heart. 'I would have been mortally wounded if you'd got the wrong idea about me.'

'Stop it, Rafe. I'm sorry, okay? You're the one who's been testing me all day.' She couldn't help returning his smile.

'That's how I know for sure that you're a tough cookie and a good doctor. Someone who'll be great in a crisis.'

'So you're not going to apologise for that? I could have tested you out, but I didn't.'

He made out that the words were hard to say, but his eyes were bright with humour. 'I'm sorry. Okay?'

Yes. Suddenly everything was okay. Even the crash of thunder seemed to have receded into the distance, and they were safe and protected here. Mel leaned back on her elbows on the bed, stretching her legs out in front of her to ease the slight ache of fatigue in her back.

'You want to talk about it?' Rafe was obviously tired too and had flopped backwards onto the bed, staring at the ceiling. But yes… Mel did want to talk about it.

'Nothing much to say. You know how it is, bringing a child up on your own.' Maybe she should let him sleep. Let them both sleep, while they could.

'I was never on my own. I had a great deal of support from Annu's family. And I was already qualified, so I didn't have to study as well.' He was still alert and seemed to want to listen.

'I couldn't have done it without my family. And, to be

honest, Amy's father leaving was the beginning of everything getting better, although it didn't seem much like it at the time.'

'Not the one for you then.'

Mel shook her head. 'I'd known Michael since I was sixteen. Teenage crush. We decided to go to the same university, and the first year was great. We had a good time. Then I got pregnant. Amy was the best mistake I ever made. The best I ever will make.'

Rafe chuckled. 'Yeah, I get you there. Ash was one of the best things that Annu and I ever did.'

He'd had a good marriage. Mel envied him that, even though he'd lost his wife. 'Michael and I didn't do much else that was good. He seemed okay about it when I told him I was pregnant, and said we'd get married when the baby was born.'

'He wanted to wait?'

In retrospect, that had been the first warning sign. 'He said that I'd want to look my best at the wedding.'

Rafe shot her an incredulous look. 'I've always rather liked that pregnancy glow... But that's not really the point, is it?'

'No, it's not the point at all. He was making excuses. Michael always liked to be at the centre of things, and he didn't see why my being pregnant should deprive him of anything that he enjoyed. I'd decided to stay at university until the end of the academic year and it was tiring. He started going out on his own and... I never really knew when he'd be coming back.'

'So you had to shoulder all of the responsibility in the relationship.'

She liked that Rafe seemed to always see the realities of a situation. She could now. 'He reckoned that just being there was enough and I was lucky that he was standing by me. I was young and I bought that line. The first time I really questioned it was when I had Amy. Michael was off somewhere doing something, I don't know what, and I couldn't contact him.'

'That's unforgivable.' Rafe's tone was suddenly ice-cold.

'Well, I managed it somehow. Largely because by that time I didn't feel that I was worth a great deal more. I thought that things would get better, but they didn't. I wasn't losing the baby weight fast enough and I was no fun any more.'

'Ah. So everything was your fault then?'

'That was his line, and I bought it. I'd taken a year off from my studies and money was very tight. He spent most of what we had, staying out nights and coming home with lame excuses. I thought that if I could just read the situation a little better, and be what he wanted, then things would be okay. I was trying to make it work for Amy's sake.'

She'd been so wrong. Mel could see that now. And she could see how the anxiety had grown, watching Michael and trying to anticipate his fickle moods.

Rafe had sat up straight, his frame tense and rigid in the silence.

'Say something, Rafe...'

He turned to face her. 'Something you don't already know for yourself? Not sure I can come up with anything.'

'Say it anyway.' Mel wanted to hear it. On his lips, the words seemed more powerful.

'What he did was cruel and irresponsible. The unforgivable part of it is that he made you believe that it was your fault and not his.' Rafe paused, his gaze searching her face. 'Did you forgive him?'

He understood what had really hurt her. And Rafe had

allowed for her muddled emotions, in a way that Mel hadn't always been able to.

'A week before Amy's first birthday, Michael just didn't come back. There was no word from him, but a couple of days later I collected Amy from the nursery on my way back from lectures and found that he'd taken most of his clothes. When Mum and Dad came for Amy's birthday party they saw what had happened and packed all of our things up, squashed them into the car and took us home. I still remember going to bed that night, feeling that I had someone to look after me...'

That simple feeling had been so strong that it got to her, even now. Mel felt herself choking on the emotion of it all. And Rafe didn't flinch away from it, he just hung on in there and waited.

'Mum and Dad really stepped up for me. I'm the eldest of five, and they took care of Amy along with my youngest brother and sister. I could continue with my studies and I was able to come home and spend some time with her, instead of doing housework and cooking. I was getting panic attacks by that time. I had been ever since Amy was born and I worried about her constantly, but things seemed to be getting better. Then Michael called. Apparently the grass wasn't greener on the other side, and he wanted us back together again.'

Rafe was having a hard time keeping silent. She could see it on his face. But still he said nothing.

'I said that I could forgive him but that we had to discuss how things might change. He told me I'd always had unrealistic expectations of him, and put the phone down.'

'So you un-forgave him?' Rafe finally gave in, and added something of his own expectations to the story.

'Not right then. He wouldn't come to Mum and Dad's house to see Amy because he said it was a hostile environment for him, and every now and then he'd call me and ask me to meet up so that he could see her. Sometimes he'd turn up, and sometimes not. He'd talk about getting back together, but there was always something I'd done which gave him a reason not to. Then one day, when Amy was four, we were waiting in the coffee shop for him and Amy started to cry. He was terribly late, and she was bored and wanted to go home. Michael turned up, took one look at her and asked me how on earth he could be expected to care for a kid who cried all the time.'

It had been another moment of clarity. Another turning point. Mel let it hang in the air for a moment, because it had cut through all of Michael's excuses.

'I'd been seeing someone for the panic attacks, and I went to see my therapist the following week and told her that I was never going to let him treat Amy the way he'd treated me.' Mel smiled at the memory. 'That was when I un-forgave him for good.'

'And your daughter?' Rafe seemed to know instinctively what the next big challenge had been.

'Amy has a right to know Michael if she wants to, but it's my job to protect her. I went to see a family lawyer and told him that I wanted him to help me work out a set of ground rules that were centred around Amy's well-being. Meeting up in safe places for her rather than what Michael said were safe places for him, for instance.'

Rafe nodded, his brow creasing. 'It's a difficult thing to balance.'

'As it turned out there wasn't much balancing to do.' Mel shrugged. 'Michael didn't like the implication that he was the second most important person in the room, and simply disappeared from our lives. About the only thing that Amy remembers about him is that she couldn't rely on him, and when she was old enough to make her own decisions she made it quite clear that she had no interest in pursuing any relationship with him. When she got married she asked my dad to give her away. It was one of the best parts of the day, seeing how proud he was when he walked her down the aisle.'

'And what about you? You have all you want?'

No one ever questioned that now. Maybe here, without the trappings of her life around her, it was possible to see a little more clearly.

'The anxiety hasn't ever quite left me, as you saw today, but I have coping mechanisms and it's under control. I have peace, and the life that I want.'

Rafe nodded. 'One of the best things about getting older. You work your way around to accepting the way you are, without trying to be perfect. Saves a lot of time, doesn't it.'

'Yes, it seems to.' Mel wondered what it was that Rafe had to accept about himself. Maybe she could ask…

'No Mr Right?'

Mel thought about her answer for a moment. She wanted to tell Rafe a little bit more than she probably should. Perhaps that was one more thing she could accept about herself.

'No. Mum and Dad always encouraged me to go out with my friends and to meet people, but once bitten, twice shy, I guess.' That made her sound unreachable and some part of her wanted Rafe to reach her. 'I was persuaded that I might try dating again when Amy was in her teens, but nothing ever came of it. It was all very polite and discreet.' So discreet sometimes that Mel had hardly known herself that she was in a relationship.

The difference between that and the way Rafe challenged her made her catch her breath. The glint in his eye was never particularly polite or discreet, and it reminded her that it was the risk, the meeting of two minds that didn't necessarily agree and two people who could work that out that made any relationship exciting enough to hold on to. Even if holding on was more than she'd ever been able to handle.

'So you're unforgiven too?' He interrupted her reverie with an awkward question.

'What makes you say that? My therapist oversaw a rather long process of forgiving myself.'

'Once bitten, twice shy implies that you think all men are like your ex-partner.'

'No! I don't think that at all. It's obviously not the case.'

'Then logically…maybe it's you?'

No one could challenge her the way that Rafe did. And engaging with that challenge made her feel stronger and not weaker. Mel wasn't at all sure how that worked.

'I don't know. There are always two sides to a relationship, and I accepted Michael's behaviour far too easily…' Mel shook her head. 'I think that accepting happiness is a thing too, whatever shape it comes in.'

It was Rafe's turn to think about an idea now. Maybe his wife's death had made it difficult for him to see happiness in terms of anything other than what he'd lost.

'Maybe… You might be right.' He rubbed his hand over his face, as if trying to knock his thoughts back into place.

He was tired, and so was she. It had been a good talk, and Mel was grateful to him for listening. Even more grateful that he'd accepted and understood, even if her therapist had drilled it into her that she never needed to be grateful just to be accepted.

'I suppose we should try to get some rest.'

'Yeah.' Rafe stretched his arms, catching his breath at just the point when Mel reckoned the stitches on his left arm would start to pull. 'The hotel staff will wake us if we're needed.'

'How long have you been up?' It occurred to Mel that he'd probably already made the flight from Male' this morning, before she'd even finished breakfast.

'Since…early.' He suppressed a yawn. 'A couple of hours and I'll be fine.'

He did seem suddenly very tired. Maybe the efforts of the day, or maybe just that their conversation had gone as far as it could. Or perhaps just force of habit from their years spent training. A junior doctor took whatever sleep they could get, whenever they could get it.

'I'll go and look in on Zeena. Get some sleep.'

She left him alone in the doctors' ready room, returning to find that Rafe seemed to have just flopped over onto the bed and fallen asleep as soon as his head hit the pillow, his legs still hanging over the side of the bed. Mel unlaced his boots, pulling them off, and he stirred a little as she lifted his legs up onto the bed. By the time she'd covered him with a sheet though, he was fast asleep again.

She took off her own boots and lay down on the bed on the other side of the room. Probably best not to get undressed, as she might be hitting the ground running.

It seemed strange to close her eyes, knowing that there was someone else in the room. But the soft, regular sound of Rafe's breathing, almost drowned out by the storm and punctuated by the gecko's soft chirping, was a powerful tranquilliser. Her own breaths seemed to mirror his as she started to doze.

CHAPTER EIGHT

THE QUIET BUT insistent knocking penetrated his dreams. Rafe sat upright, fighting with the sheet that covered him. He didn't remember lying down on the bed, or taking off his boots, but he must have done so. He definitely didn't remember the sheet...

He stumbled in the direction of the door, stubbing his toe on the way. By the time he pulled it open, he was awake.

'Is the baby coming?'

Haroon gave him a broad, excited smile. 'We think so.'

'Go back to your wife then. We'll be right there.'

Rafe switched the light on and saw Mel sleeping soundly, despite the crash of thunder and the sound of rain outside. For a moment he hesitated. She was lying on top of the bedcovers, still wearing the jeans and T-shirt she'd had on during the evening. She looked peaceful, and so very beautiful.

He reached out, his fingers brushing against her shoulder, and she didn't stir. So he tried shaking her and the result was much the same as his own awakening. Only when Mel sat up straight in her bed, her hair sticking out at several different angles, her cheek still flushed from the pillow, she looked utterly lovely.

'Uh... Baby...?'

'Yep.'

'Don't just stand there then. Get moving, Rafe…'

The mad scramble slowed to a brisk walk as they made their way towards Zeena's room, Mel tying her hair back as she went and looking irresistible in pink scrubs. Zeena's contractions seemed to be coming regularly now and two of her neighbours, obviously chosen to be her birth partners, were already with her. Haroon was hovering nervously by the door.

Mel stepped forward, the smile on her face giving no clue that she'd been fast asleep two minutes ago.

'Would you like Haroon to stay a little longer?'

Zeena shook her head, pressing her lips together in pain. 'No… No, tell him to go…'

'Rafe?' Mel looked up at him and he ushered Haroon from the room. A little cluster of men were waiting for him by the door of the medical suite, and Rafe promised to come and fetch him as soon as there was any news.

When he returned, Mel had washed her hands and was tying a surgical apron around her waist. Zeena had her hand clamped across her mouth to stop herself from crying out when the contractions came.

'Hey, Zeena. It's okay to let it out.'

'I don't want Haroon to…worry…'

'He'll be fine, he's out of earshot. And this is your time, Zeena. I want you to breathe the way your midwife taught you and give me a yell whenever you want to. It'll help, won't it?' Mel smiled at the women with Zeena, who both nodded in agreement.

Mel did everything that was needed, leaving Rafe to monitor the baby's heartbeat and Zeena's vital signs. It was more than just medicine, though. The atmosphere in the room was loving and encouraging, three women helping another to bring a new life into the world. Three hours later, at four in the morning, Zeena's baby son was born.

Rafe had been present at many births since that of his son. But the only thing that could compare with this was the feeling of holding his own child for the first time. It was obvious that Mel's approach centred around each mother's individual needs, and she had made this birth into an affirmation of life, a positive and moving experience.

As Zeena's baby was delivered there were no more words. Mel signalled to Rafe to fetch Haroon and before the cord was cut the lights were dimmed and the new father took his son in his arms. The first human sound that the child would hear was his father, whispering the call to prayer into his right ear. Mel had remembered that too, and respected Zeena and Haroon's religious traditions.

Watching Haroon with his son in his arms brought tears to Rafe's eyes. Not for the wife he'd lost, or the son that he loved so much. These were thankful tears. He hadn't thought that he would experience this feeling again, but somehow Mel had created an atmosphere in the room that had touched everyone there.

She attended to Zeena, suggesting that Rafe might take some photographs of the baby for the proud parents. Then Mel took a few photos of her own, and they left the young couple alone with their baby.

'Nicely done.' Rafe grinned at her as they walked together back up the corridor. 'No one noticed that you had any concerns.'

'I'm rather hoping that I don't. What do you think?' Mel handed him the phone, opening the door of the doctors' ready room.

She'd zoomed in on the tiny baby's face, and Rafe studied the photograph carefully. Then swiped to the next photograph. Mel had got a better angle and it was immediately clear what was bothering her.

'Looks like a cataract. In his left eye…' Rafe enlarged the image on the small screen. 'I can't see if there's one in the right.'

That would make a difference. Most often, both eyes were affected if a baby was born with cataracts due to illness or hereditary factors. Just one eye meant that the cause was more likely to be some kind of injury in the womb. Mel nodded.

'I looked carefully but I didn't see one. That doesn't mean there isn't one there, and the left eye is just more noticeable. We'll have to investigate.'

And that meant alerting the new parents to the idea that their baby might have a problem. Always a difficult conversation, but Rafe reckoned that if anyone was equal to it then Mel was.

'I have a good friend in London who's an eye specialist, and maybe she can give us some pointers.' She'd taken her phone from her pocket and was staring at it. 'I've only got one bar, though…'

'Try her.' Rafe glanced at his own phone. 'I've only got one bar too, so that's no better. The phone mast is probably still up and working. It's just that the storm's making reception difficult.'

She nodded, flipping open a messaging app and typing furiously. She pressed *send* and then sent another couple of messages, enclosing the photographs she'd taken. 'It looks as if they've been sent. It'll be past ten in the evening in London so I might have to wait until the morning, and hope we have some reception then.'

Mel sat on the bed, putting her phone down. It seemed so easy, natural even, to sit down next to her.

'We'll give them half an hour together. Then we can

go in and do some more checks on the baby.' He stared straight ahead, clasping his hands together. What he really wanted to do was give Mel a hug.

'Yeah. I've done all of the initial checks, but they don't know that. We can say it's routine...' He felt the mattress move as her phone buzzed and Mel jumped. She snatched up her phone, stabbing at the *answer call* button.

'Maddie...?'

The image on the screen was breaking up a little, but it was good enough. Rafe could see a blonde woman in a red sleeveless dress.

'Mel... You caught me at a dinner party. I thought you were meant to be on holiday?'

'I am. Well, I was. We have a tropical storm making things a bit more interesting.' Mel smiled. 'This is Dr Rafe Davenport, and we've just delivered a baby.'

Generous. Mel had delivered the baby and he'd largely just watched. But now wasn't the time for any extraneous information, when the connection to a woman who could give them the expertise they needed was so slender. Rafe returned Maddie's wave and smiled.

'So...what medical resources do you have?' Maddie too was ready to get straight down to business, despite her attire.

'We've got good clinic facilities, and we can do just about anything in terms of examination... Maddie...?'

The image on her phone froze and after a few worrying seconds unfroze. 'Okay, I got that. What about hospitals?'

Mel looked at Rafe.

'There are hospitals in Male', which is on the main island, but we can't get there right now because of the storm.'

'They'll have the facilities to deal with infant eye surgery?' Maddie's face froze again in a frown.

'Not necessarily. Leave that with me. I'll get whatever's needed.'

'Good. Okay, Mel, this is what you need to look for. I'm going to message you with a checklist, but I'll tell you now in case it doesn't get through.'

'Wait…' Mel was looking around for a piece of paper, and Rafe got to his feet, fetching a notebook and pen from his own bedside. She nodded an acknowledgement and turned her attention back to the phone. 'Fire away, Maddie.'

Rafe had a few messages to send too. He got to his feet, gesturing to his own phone when Mel looked up momentarily, and retreated to the corridor. No one was around, but he closed the door behind him, standing next to it in the corridor so that Mel wouldn't be interrupted. This might be their only chance of getting some specialist advice for the next few days, and it was precious.

CHAPTER NINE

MADDIE HAD COME through for her. Despite being at a dinner party, she'd managed to find somewhere quiet and called her back. Mel looked at the page of notes in front of her, reading them through.

'Thanks so much, Maddie. I owe you one. Don't forget to call Amy for me, will you?'

'I won't. I'll tell her that you may not be in touch for a while but you're safe and not to worry. I won't mention that you appear to be trapped on a very small tropical island with *the* most gorgeous guy.' Maddie's intent expression was switching back to party mode now that she'd said all she needed to.

'Trapped in a medical centre with no sleep, you mean…'

'Mel! I'm sure you could make the most of it if you tried.' The poor connection couldn't disguise Maddie's smirk. Maybe Mel should take a leaf out of her book and indulge in a few of the simple pleasures in life, instead of worrying about where they might lead. Rafe's tenderness as he'd shown Haroon how to hold his baby son beat any number of sun loungers and waving palms.

'Well, the good-looking part will have to wait until I'm less busy. I'm just hoping that Rafe can navigate his way through to getting the baby whatever he needs. He seems to have some influence here.'

Maddie grinned. 'There you go. Not just gorgeous, he's a knight in shining armour as well...'

The screen froze again, and then the call dropped. That might be just as well. There wasn't the bandwidth available to accommodate Mel's thoughts about Rafe. Her phone beeped and a message from Maddie flashed up on the screen. Mel waited while it downloaded, and found it was a checklist that Maddie obviously kept handy for students and general practitioners.

Thanks, Maddie. Perfect, I appreciate it.

Mel added a couple of kisses to the message and sent it. Then she sent another.

Re knight in shining armour. You have NO idea...

That would get Maddie's imagination going. She'd wondered aloud whether a tropical holiday retreat might contain any suitable love interests, and it seemed that Mel would at least have a few stories to tell about that when she got home, courtesy of the storm.

Her phone beeped. Maddie had sent a line of smiley faces, along with a comment saying she couldn't wait to hear all about it. Mel sent kisses and an acknowledgement and put the phone back down again. She couldn't wait to find out what might happen with Rafe either, and she still wasn't convinced that any possible outcome would be good. Give in to the obvious chemistry that bubbled between them and then watch him walk away. Or resist it and keep wondering. Neither sounded particularly ideal and whenever she thought about it she felt her heart thump.

The door opened by an inch and she jumped. 'Okay. You

can come in.' She'd imagined that Rafe might be waiting somewhere for her to finish the call.

'Got all you needed?' The door swung open.

'Yes, I've got Maddie's checklist and the line stayed up long enough for me to ask her a few questions as well, so I've got a good idea of everything we need to check before we refer the baby on. But if we're right then the baby's going to need hospital treatment. What's the state of play there?'

Rafe's brow creased. 'Maldives has made great strides in making medical treatment available to all of its population, but the very geography of the place poses unique difficulties. There's a scheme which arranges for any Maldivian who needs medical treatment not available here to receive treatment abroad in partner hospitals.'

Mel nodded. 'Any idea what's going to be involved if Zeena's baby needs surgery?'

'I gather that nearly half the surgery for adult cataracts is done abroad.' Rafe shrugged. 'So I imagine that might be the case for the baby. But the hospital I work with in Colombo does this kind of surgery, and is approved as a partner hospital. I've sent a few messages and I'll know more in the morning, but don't worry about that. Whatever Zeena and Haroon need, I'll get it.'

Knight in shining armour. In truth, Rafe didn't look much like one at the moment. He looked tired, and more than a little rumpled. Better, actually, than a knight in shining armour could ever be. As if the smell of soap and a baby, combined with his own warm scent, could be just the thing she wanted to surround her.

'Okay, so medically speaking, there isn't anything that Maddie can suggest right now. If the baby has cataracts then our job is to pick that up, do a little groundwork on what the cause might be, and refer him on to a specialist.'

Rafe nodded. 'So I guess that tonight we could just respond to any questions and let Zeena get some rest. Then speak to them both in the morning?'

'That sounds good.' Mel couldn't help smiling at the way he'd suggested, rather than just told her what they were going to do next. 'Although I'd like to take another look at the baby, just to make absolutely sure that there are no signs of any other underlying condition.'

'Sounds good too.' The smile playing around Rafe's lips told her that the novelty of this joint decision-making process wasn't lost on him either. 'We can just whisk him away for a moment and give him a thorough checkup. That's standard.'

'I agree. Let me just read through Maddie's checklist, so that I don't miss anything.'

He nodded, sitting back down on the bed next to her. It was very difficult to read with him so close and Mel wondered if she should push him away. Find something else for Rafe to do...

Maybe, since he was a king of the jungle, he could think about taking his top off. That would be enormously gratifying. Mel supposed she could use the excuse of wanting to check his stitches, but that would be mixing business with pleasure. She dismissed the thought, trying to focus on the words in front of her.

'Anything else we can agree on while we're about it?'

Yes! Actually, no. The only thing that Mel could think of that they might agree on was going to get her into deep, deep trouble, even if it would give her something to tell Maddie when she got back to London.

'I... Why don't I send you the checklist?' Having him close enough to read over her shoulder meant that she wasn't doing much reading.

'Yeah. Thanks.' There was a note of disappointment in

his tone, which matched the sinking feeling in her heart. Mel ignored it, and forwarded the checklist on to him. Then…*then*…just when everything was going so well, and she had herself under control, she made the mistake of looking up at him.

Those eyes. If the king of the jungle had been telling her that he wanted wild sex in any number of different positions, right here in the doctors' ready room, the message couldn't have been much clearer. But there was a trace of the knight in shining armour in the look on his face. As if he would ask for only one touch of her hand, as a mark of her favour.

Mel wondered if he'd ask. Then his gaze dropped to his phone.

No, no, no… If she'd learned one thing in the last twenty-three years, since Michael had left, it was that there was nothing wrong with saying what was on your mind. It was the things that remained unsaid which had power over her, and it was the wrong kind of power.

'It never stops being moving, does it? Seeing a new life come into the world. A new person with so much potential…'

He looked up at her, heat sizzling in his gaze. Maybe he saw the same heat in hers, but Mel guessed that would never be enough for Rafe. He'd never act on an assumption. He needed more than that. She did too. One of the enigmas that accompanied the passing of the years. It became easier to talk about things, but also a bit more necessary.

'It's moving. I thought you handled the whole thing very well.'

'You provided the framework. I felt confident in doing what I felt was right for Zeena.'

He nodded. The silence between them sizzled with electricity, as lightning flashed outside, and Mel instinctively moved closer to him.

'I suppose that the storm adds an intimacy to it all.' Rafe seemed to be going through the whole gamut of reasons why they should feel this way, and carefully avoiding the one thing that would explain all of it.

'Suppose so.'

There were any number of smiling, tactful ways that she could stop this. None of them were going to happen. They'd both gained enough experience of the world to be walking into this with their eyes wide open, and that was what would stop them from going too far. Not self-control, because there was no way that anyone could defend themselves against the melting look in his eyes.

'I'm…um…a bit out of practice with this. But I'd like to ask you something.'

Delicious shivers of anticipation ran down Mel's spine. 'I'd like it very much if you asked me something.'

Rafe smiled. 'We've only known each other for twenty hours. But that seems to be enough to make me want to kiss you.'

'I'd like it very much if you did that as well.'

He hesitated. No, Rafe didn't hesitate about anything once he'd committed himself to an idea. He was showing her that this meant something and it wasn't just a passing whim, which was all good because it wasn't a passing whim for Mel either. Then his fingers touched the side of her face, so gently that they made her shiver. His lips touched hers in the gentlest, most devastating kiss she'd ever experienced.

It took a moment to gather her senses. Rafe had moved back a little, but he was still gazing into her face. Still there, with no trace of regret for what they'd done.

'Nice.' She reached forward, her fingers brushing the

material of his scrubs top. Closing and bunching the material in her grip. 'You want to do that again, as if you mean it?'

'You think I didn't mean it?' His mouth curved at the challenge.

And then, suddenly, there was no question about what Rafe meant, or about what he wanted. When he pulled her close and kissed her, each breath, each heartbeat depended on Rafe's demanding, searching presence.

Even when he pulled away from her he still held her in his thrall. He was staring down at her, naked hunger in his eyes. She'd known him for barely a day, kissed him once and she was his.

That kind of thing just didn't happen. It was something else… Mel couldn't think what, but something. This one kiss had triggered more passion than all of the polite, uncommitted affairs that she'd contented herself with over the years.

A knock sounded on the door and they jumped apart guiltily. Rafe was on his feet in a second, man of action as ever, striding across the room to open the door. There was a quiet conversation with one of the women who'd been Zeena's birth partners and he turned to Mel.

'She says that Zeena's settling down to sleep now. This might be a good time to check on her vitals and do our post birth checks on the baby?'

Mel nodded. Her mouth wasn't up to words just yet.

'Okay, I'll bring him down to the consulting room and meet you there. When you're ready.'

Mel nodded again and he grinned, walking through the open door before turning as if he'd just forgotten something.

'By the way. I meant it…'

'Yes.' The word came out almost as a squeak, which

was unlike her. Mel was always in control of any relationship, and knew when to stop and exactly how to walk away without causing any damage to anyone.

But she was rapidly realising that Rafe was different. He gave her a smiling nod and then turned, closing the door quietly behind him.

Every nerve-ending was tingling. Nothing hurt. Rafe couldn't feel the scrape on his arm any longer and the cut that Mel had stitched for him had stopped throbbing. He felt as if he'd just been struck by lightning and then risen to his feet, the possessor of superpowers.

It was all nonsense, of course. Rafe knew full well that it was possible to fall in love after a first kiss, he'd done so with Annu, but their first kiss had taken considerably longer to get around to. Twenty hours was a different matter. How could you love everything about someone when you knew almost nothing about them?

But the feeling just wouldn't listen to sense. He felt like a man who could defy the usual laws of science, or human psychology, or love, or whatever else was involved in what he and Mel had just done. That kiss was the only true thing, the only absolute that he had to rely on.

Zeena was so dozy now that she hardly responded when he took her blood pressure, opening her eyes only when the cuff tightened on her arm. Haroon was almost asleep too, and Rafe operated the controls on the reclining chair by the bed, telling him to get some rest while his son was being weighed and examined.

While he was waiting for Mel, he flipped through Maddie's notes. Clear and concise, they covered all of the things that an ophthalmic surgeon might want to know from a referring doctor.

'How are you with examining for cataracts?' Mel's

voice interrupted his reverie, her soft-soled shoes not making a sound on the tiled floor.

'Fair to middling. In the course of my general practice I've seen quite a few kids with cataracts.'

He couldn't help staring at her. Mel had re-fixed her hair and was pulling on a disposable apron and gloves, ready to work. Her eyes seemed a little wider and her mouth a little redder. If it was at all possible she was a little more beautiful, and Rafe couldn't help but notice every last thing about her. The way she moved. How she smiled down at the baby in the cradle, her finger gently brushing his cheek.

'That trumps my experience. I tend to concentrate on the mothers.' Mel was somehow managing to look at him without directly returning his gaze. It was a talent he should try to emulate.

'Okay, so you'll hold him while I do the examination?'

She nodded, picking the baby carefully up from his cradle, shushing him and rocking him gently when he started to fret. Rafe took the ophthalmoscope from its case, dimming the lights.

'Okay, little man. Open your eyes for me…' Mel moved the baby into a vertical position against her body, and he saw the shadow of her smile in the darkened room. 'There he goes.'

It was tricky to find the right angle without getting too close to her and in the end Rafe gave up, and found his cheek resting against her shoulder. But Mel didn't seem to mind, and he could see what he needed to see, all thoughts of pleasure banished from his head as he carefully examined the baby, noting all of his observations.

Finally Rafe turned the lamps back up again. He didn't have the heart to tell Mel that she could put the baby back into his cradle now, and she sat down with him still in her arms, his eyes closed again now and his little body snuggled against her chest.

'What did you see?'

'The red reflex definitely shows a cataract in his left eye, and there seems to be a slight reduction in the reflex in the right eye as well.'

'Bilateral, then.' Mel's brow creased. 'Then it's most likely to be either congenital or the result of an infection while in the womb, such as measles or rubella.'

'Could be rubella. There's a lot of work being done to eradicate rubella here, but it's still more common than in England.'

'So the next thing to be done is to check whether Zeena had any infections while she was pregnant. Or whether she or Haroon had cataracts themselves when they were children.'

Rafe nodded. 'Yes, I think it'll be better to do that in the morning, when they've both had some sleep.'

'Agreed. I'll sit with them until the morning...' Mel stifled a yawn, as if the mere mention of it was making her feel tired.

'No. You go and get a few hours' sleep. I'll do it.'

'But you're tired too...' Mel protested and Rafe silenced her with a frown.

'That's not up for discussion. I'm back to my autocratic ways. Put the baby down now and I'll check him over quickly for any signs that there are underlying conditions that might have caused the cataracts.'

'It's unlikely. I don't see any signs of Down's Syndrome.'

'Neither do I. Just roll with it, Mel, and let me check.' Mel's obvious dismay at being sent back to bed to get some much-needed sleep was delightful.

She rolled her eyes. 'Leopards never really change their spots, do they?'

'I wasn't even aware I had spots. I think you'll find most leopards feel much the same.' He gave her a grin as she laid the baby back into the cradle. 'Go on, then. I'll come and wake you at about nine o'clock.'

'Eight. I'll take over and let you get a couple of hours' sleep, and then we'll talk to Zeena and Haroon together.'

'Whatever. Go to bed, Mel.' It was just as well that they were taking turns to sleep, because Rafe wasn't sure that he could go back to the ready room and stay in his own bed if Mel was there, however tired he was. The thought of holding her while they both drifted off to sleep was far too compelling.

CHAPTER TEN

RAFE HAD ALMOST dozed off a couple of times, and his arm was beginning to throb uncomfortably. He'd put off going to wake Mel, but she'd obviously set an alarm for herself because she came to relieve him at ten past eight, looking as fresh as a daisy.

'The storm doesn't seem to be moving away yet...' she whispered to him as he met her in the doorway.

'No, I checked the radio and it'll probably last for the best part of another twenty-four hours. You got some sleep?'

'Yes. Go and do the same.'

He was too tired to argue. Rafe almost stumbled to the ready room, where a feeble grey dawn was doing its best to penetrate the shutters over the windows, and not succeeding all that well. Unlacing his boots and pulling off his clothes, he fell onto the bed, half asleep before his head even hit the pillow.

He woke to the smell of bacon and coffee. Reckoned it must be a mirage, and then sat up straight in bed when he heard Mel clattering around in the small kitchen. As far as he knew, mirages didn't come complete with sound-effects.

'You haven't been switching anything on, have you?' he called in to her.

'No. They've got a barbecue going in the kitchen, and

I asked them to make bacon rolls. If you don't like them, I'll eat yours.'

'Nice try. I'd walk many miles for a decent bacon roll.' Rafe realised that he was naked apart from his underwear under the sheet that covered him, and quickly pulled on his jeans and shirt.

'These look at least a nine and a half out of ten. Lightly toasted rolls, and crispy bacon with your choice of condiments. Fresh coffee...' And the scent of roses as he walked into the kitchenette, to find that Mel had set a plate with two bacon rolls out on the small folding table, along with a takeaway cardboard cup of coffee. She snatched up the bag that lay on the counter top, along with her own coffee.

'Where are you going? You're not going to join me?' Rafe stretched his arms, feeling the stitches pull a little.

'No, I've got some doctoring to do. There's another queue forming outside the consulting room. Join me when you're ready.'

'Okay. Anything serious?'

'Not from the looks of it. Everyone's chatting together quite happily, and when I looked out and asked if they were okay there for a few minutes they all said yes.' Mel flashed him a smile. 'I've got one of the concierges going down the queue and asking everyone what they want to see a doctor about. Zeena's fine and the baby's fine, so you can take your time over brunch.'

It might take him a few minutes longer to get going these days, but Rafe hadn't lost the ability to work through the night, and some sleep and then bacon rolls was a luxury. Mel was already out of the door before he could mention that, and Rafe turned his attention to finding his toothbrush before his breakfast started to get cold.

Twenty minutes later he was washed and ready to meet

the day. He set up in one of the spare patient rooms, helping Mel to cut through the queue of people outside.

She appeared in the doorway, just as his last patient was leaving. 'So. Two cases of indigestion, three sleepless nights and a couple of headaches. I did, however, get a broken toe, which provided rather more mental exercise.'

'I'll raise you a broken toe with a sprained ankle.'

Mel shook her head, grinning. 'No, breakages trump sprains every time.'

'Torn ligaments? They can take longer to heal…'

She raised her eyebrows. 'Someone's torn a ligament?'

'No, I just wanted to know where they came in the pecking order, in case I do come across one. And, of course, anything that needs stitches has got to rate higher than something that doesn't break the skin.' He gave her his smuggest look, knowing it would provoke Mel. 'I have stitches.'

'What? They're *my* stitches, I'll have you know!'

'I took a look at them this morning, and it's *my* skin. My body's my own…'

'Oh, no. Not when you're bleeding. That arm belongs to me.'

Rafe chuckled, leaning back in his seat. 'Just turn that around for a moment. What would you say if I told you that any part of your body belonged to me?'

They were teasing, flirting. Maybe it was a way of keeping that kiss under some measure of control, telling themselves they could handle it. Maybe a way of forgetting that there was still a storm raging outside, or that they'd be talking to Zeena and Haroon about their little boy's eyes soon.

Or maybe they were just enjoying it. Rafe definitely was. Whatever. They had things to do this morning. He took his phone from his pocket, calling up the messages he'd received.

'The doctor who usually covers this area has been in touch. She says that she's spoken with the people I suggested and agrees that transferring the baby over to Colombo is going to be the best option, particularly since the storm's going to be putting extra pressure on the hospitals in Male'. So she's going to try to put things in motion from her end. I've alerted the hospital director, and a few other people who can help with getting them over to Sri Lanka once the storm's lifted, so hopefully there shouldn't be any difficulties there.'

Mel nodded, appearing to forget all about which of them his body belonged to, which was something of a disappointment. He could stand having that conversation with her...

'That's great. Now all we have to do is speak to Zeena and Haroon.'

Telling new parents that there was something wrong with their child was always a difficult conversation. Implying that it was something inherited added a second layer of awkwardness. No one could help their genetic make-up, but people did tend to ascribe blame for such things.

Rafe went through everything coolly and calmly. His positive attitude, which Mel had described to herself as overbearing more than once, was actually something of a bonus. Neither Zeena or Haroon questioned his reassurances that medical science could help their baby, or that the treatment he needed would be available to them.

He asked whether Zeena had fallen ill during her pregnancy, and both parents shook their heads. So Rafe gently introduced the idea that the condition might be inherited. Zeena's previously serene acceptance of the situation crumbled, and tears formed in her eyes. This was just what they'd been trying to avoid.

'We can test your eyes now, to find out if either of you have small cataracts that haven't impacted on your vision. It's good if we know the situation for the sake of other children you'll be having in the future. They can be monitored carefully—' Rafe was being positive and reassuring, but a tear rolled down Zeena's cheek.

Mel squeezed Zeena's hand but before she could say something to comfort her Haroon spoke.

'Zeena, you are my wife and I do not want you to be tested. If Dr Davenport will be kind enough to perform the test on me, then that is all we need to do.'

'Yes, Haroon. Thank you.'

The silence in the room was broken by a roll of thunder. Rafe sprang to his feet, smiling at Haroon. 'Very well. If that's what you want.'

What? Wait… Then Mel saw it. Rafe wasn't just going along with this. He'd be talking to Haroon when he got him on his own and finding out what was going on. She held her tongue, and Rafe ushered Haroon out of the room.

Zeena had stopped crying now, and was nervously reaching for her baby. Mel lifted the small boy from his crib, delivering him into his mother's arms.

'Now that it's just you and me, Zeena, may I ask you something?'

Zeena was looking at her speculatively, clearly sensing Mel's disquiet. 'Haroon can be a little bossy at times, can't he.'

'Was he telling you that you mustn't be tested? Because that's really up to you.'

Zeena smiled suddenly. 'Did you know divorce is very common here in Maldives?'

'I remember reading something of the sort. Maldives has the highest divorce rate in the world, doesn't it?'

'Yes. My mother was divorced three times, which is

not unusual. My stepfather was not a kind man, and would beat us. Haroon knows this.'

'I'm so sorry that happened to you, Zeena. But I'm not sure what you're telling me.'

'When I married Haroon, he told me that he would be my only husband. That he would always be a loving husband to me and never allow what happened to me to happen to our children. He has kept his promise, but sometimes I am fearful. When Dr Rafe said that there was something wrong with our baby...' Zeena bent, kissing the little boy's forehead.

'I can understand that. I'm fearful too, about things that have hurt me.' Mel thought for a moment. 'So this is Haroon's way of letting you know that he won't leave you? Telling you that you don't need to be tested.'

Zeena nodded.

'But you know that this really isn't a matter of fault. We just want to know what's happened so that your baby can be given the best treatment possible.'

Zeena smiled. 'Haroon knows this and so do I. We learned about genetics in school. I cannot help my fears, though, and I have Haroon to protect me from them.'

'But what happens if Rafe doesn't find any cataracts in Haroon's eyes?'

'Then I will talk to him and he will be persuaded when he sees that I have thought about things and I am no longer afraid. Can you understand this?'

All too well. Mel could understand how much it would have meant to her to have a man who would calm her fears, instead of whipping them up to a fever pitch. Someone who would take care of her and Amy.

'You're telling me that Haroon's a good man, aren't you? And that I'm not to worry about you.'

Zeena nodded. 'Yes. Exactly.'

The wait still seemed interminable, though. Rafe was obviously checking carefully, knowing that this test meant more than just filling in the medical facts. Finally Haroon appeared in the doorway, holding a piece of paper which bore Rafe's handwriting.

He walked over to Zeena, sitting down on the bed. 'Zeena, I am sorry. The doctor has found small cataracts in both my eyes, and it seems I may have passed this condition to our son.'

Zeena nodded. 'Then our son is also lucky, that he will be strong and brave like his father.'

Mel glanced at Rafe, and he gestured a signal that they should go now. She followed him outside, leaving Zeena and Haroon talking quietly together.

'If you're going to give me an earful for not saying something about Zeena's right to make her own medical decisions you'd better do it now.' Rafe had walked to the doctors' ready room, closing the door behind them.

'You were right.'

He raised his eyebrows. 'You never cease to surprise me, Mel.'

'You made a call, based on your knowledge of the area and the fact that you'd be asking Haroon a few relevant questions before you examined him.'

'You were listening at the door, were you?'

'No, I was asking Zeena the same questions and probably getting much the same answers. It turns out that she has her own, very reasonable, fears that stem from her experiences as a child. And that Haroon was reassuring her that things are different now.'

Rafe nodded. 'That's pretty much what he said. So... we're trusting each other now, are we?'

It certainly looked that way. Mel had trusted Rafe to

ask the right questions, and he'd trusted her. 'Any problems with that?'

He chuckled. 'Not one. As long as you tell me that you would have come out fighting if you'd found that Haroon was making medical decisions for Zeena that she didn't agree with.'

'What do you reckon, Rafe?' Mel looked up at him, and suddenly found herself caught in his gaze. For all the pretence of being at odds with each other, they had more in common than either of them dared to admit.

'Just checking. A storm like this can get to you in all kinds of ways. I'd hate to think that you were losing your grip.'

'Think again.' Mel looked at the shuttered windows, wishing she could see what was going on outside, if only to reassure herself that all that banging and crashing didn't mean that the whole island was sinking into the sea. 'Although I'll admit that the storm's beginning to get to me.'

'Yeah, me too.' Rafe wiped his hand across his face. 'Shall we try the radio again, see if we can find out what's happening…?'

The news from the radio had been good. The storm was expected to pass in the early hours of tomorrow morning, and blow its fury out over the ocean to the west of the islands. It wasn't quite done with them yet, because when Mel checked her phone there was no signal, and Rafe could get nothing on his either. But Mr Manike had been busy, organising both staff and hotel guests to keep everyone occupied, and that afternoon there was a general atmosphere of quiet camaraderie and the feeling that they were over the worst without any significant damage.

They slept in shifts again, although it wasn't strictly necessary to sit up with Zeena and the baby because they were both doing well. But when Mel felt Rafe's hand on her shoulder, rousing her from sleep, the necessity was all too obvious. Pulling him into the narrow bed to feel his body pressed tight against hers was the first thing she thought about, and she sat up quickly, getting out of bed and grabbing a dressing gown to put on over the long nightshirt she was wearing, before she could act on the impulse.

'It's quiet…' She looked around, almost missing the sound of the wind.

'Yeah. I don't think you really need to get up. Everyone's asleep.'

Everyone but her and Rafe. 'That's okay. Get some sleep. I'll see you in the morning.'

She watched the light filter through the shutters in Zeena's room as dawn broke. Listened to the silence, broken only by steady breathing and a fretful sound from the cot that promised that everyone would be awake in a moment, and that Zeena would get a chance to consolidate her progress in feeding her new baby.

An hour later, she heard the sound of activity. Rafe was obviously up and around, and indulging in what seemed to be an inexhaustible need for action. She slipped out into the corridor and saw that the door to the consulting room was open.

'Shush!' She found Rafe talking intently to Mr Manike. 'We've only just got the baby down to sleep again.'

'Sorry…' Rafe gave her an irrepressible grin and Mr Manike added his own mouthed apology. 'Just deciding whether it's safe to go out and assess the damage.'

Mel closed the door behind her. 'And…?'

'Mr Manike is sending a few scouting parties out first. When they report back, the guests will be advised accordingly.'

Mr Manike nodded. 'One of our first priorities is to see

if we can repair the mast, so that we can find out what's happening with regard to the baby that needs medical care.'

That would be good. From the look on Rafe's face, it seemed that he considered it a superlative move. 'I'm going to check the plane out, and then go and see if I can help out with the mast. Want to come?'

There was no real reason why she shouldn't. The baby was feeding well, Zeena's confidence was growing and she was recovering from the birth. It was time to let go a little and let her get into her own rhythm.

'Yes, okay. When are you thinking of going?'

'I'm going to fetch breakfast. Then we can get started.'

Mel's stomach was full and she'd laced her walking boots tightly. Even though it was hot, she wore jeans and a jacket to protect herself from the mess made by the storm, and Rafe had found a pair of thick work gloves for her. He appeared holding a large bottle, which contained the gecko that he'd rescued from Terri's room.

'You're letting her go?' Rafe had assured Mel that the tiny creature was female', but drawn the line at giving her a name, on the basis that they might get too attached. Mel took that to mean that he was getting as attached to the gecko as she was.

Rafe chuckled. 'She's a wild animal, not a pet. Neither of us are going to take her home with us, so yes, I'm letting her go. Sooner is better than later.'

He was right. It was easy to feel that the gecko's smile was the result of some recognition, but that was just the shape of her mouth. And the truth was that they would both be going home soon enough. Mel pulled on her gloves, trying not to think about the realities of their homes being on opposite sides of the world.

It had seemed odd to put sunglasses on with a jacket

and boots, but when they stepped outside she needed them. The sky was a cloudless blue, merging into a sapphire sea. The sun shone and, apart from driftwood and branches piled everywhere, and the rather raggedy appearance of the water cabins, everything seemed surprisingly normal.

'It doesn't seem too bad…' There was a lot of mess and water around, and the outside of the hotel no longer looked as pristine as it had, but there was nothing that couldn't be cleared up.

'Yeah. I hope the plane's not been damaged.' He seemed suddenly intent and purposeful and Mel followed his long strides to a large outhouse. The gecko's bottle was thrust into her hands, and Rafe cleared the branches away from the entrance, taking down the shutters and producing a key from his pocket to unlock the door. He hurried past the neatly stacked marine equipment to the far end of the space.

Rafe walked around the aircraft, checking the bindings that held it in place, and looking underneath the fuselage for any signs of leakage. Then he swung himself up onto the top of the float, opening the door of the cabin and getting inside.

'All right?' Up close, the sea plane seemed rather more exciting than it had at a distance. Or maybe it was Rafe who seemed more exciting, his movements so sure and graceful now.

'Yeah, she looks fine. Want to come up and take a look?'

Yes, but the cabin seemed a little cramped. It would be better to stay in the open air with Rafe. They'd already found out what happened as a result of having been thrown together.

'I'd love to later. But the mast…'

Rafe nodded. 'Yeah, you're right. First things first. I'm rather hoping I have a few messages.'

He locked the door of the outhouse, putting the shutter back in place. Taking the jar from her, he indicated some rising ground to the left, saying that was the easiest route to the mobile phone mast which towered above the island. Then he set off in that direction.

Rafe was still a fast walker. And he still preferred to walk in a straight line instead of taking the path, but that didn't seem quite so counterintuitive at the moment, since the path had disappeared under piles of leaves and broken branches. The ground sloped gently upwards and Mel was out of breath before they were even halfway there. Suddenly he stopped.

'This looks like a good place.'

It didn't actually look any different to any of the other places they'd walked past. Was this a trace of consideration for her, tempering Rafe's desire to get to his destination?

'You think so? I could do with stopping for a minute…'

That was odd too. Admitting her weakness, instead of just gritting her teeth and pushing on.

'Right then…' Rafe seemed to have forgotten all about his assertion that the gecko wasn't a pet, and was grinning at the creature. 'You'll be happy here, doing your own thing.'

He stooped, laying the bottle on its side and taking the stopper out. 'Keep your eye on her. She'll take a minute to find her way out, but when she goes, she'll move fast.'

They watched, both bending over the bottle and waiting. The gecko slowly seemed to get the idea, nosing her way towards the neck of the bottle and pausing, seeming to sniff the air. Then she was off like a flash, with only a small disturbance of the undergrowth to track her path.

'Bye… Take care of yourself.' Mel straightened up, waving after the creature.

'She's where she ought to be.'

'I know. Look after them, love them the best you can, then let them go.' Mel was still a little sore from having done that with Amy so recently.

'Yeah. I still miss Ash, running into my bedroom and jumping up and down on the bed to wake me up.' Rafe turned the corners of his mouth down. 'That's a while ago now.'

'You never quite lose it, do you? That feeling that you want them to be six years old again.'

'No.' Rafe seemed lost in the past for a moment, but when he looked down at her he was right back in the here and now. 'Probably best not to dwell.'

'Mm-hm. No more dwelling.' She looked at the rough ground, sloping gently upwards between them and the mast. 'We've still some way to go.'

Rafe held out his hand, almost bashfully. And, almost apologetically, Mel took it.

It was hard going, through undergrowth that was still wet and had been ravaged by the storm. Once she almost slipped, grabbing hold of Rafe tightly as he steadied her. But soon they were in a circle of cleared ground, the mast looming above their heads. They walked towards a small building which must house the generator and electrical equipment associated with the mast, and where a group of men were talking.

'Dr Davenport.' One of them grinned at him. 'You want your phone working again?'

Rafe nodded. 'Yeah, I'm expecting a few messages. What's the prognosis?'

'Everything's good. But the antennas have blown down in the storm.' The man indicated a flat, rectangular antenna, which was lying on the ground next to them, and two more which seemed to be lodged in the struts, half-way down the mast.

'So it's just a matter of fixing them back up?' Rafe shadowed his eyes, looking up. 'You have safety harnesses?'

'Yes, of course. We're drawing lots to see who will go.'

Mel kept her eyes fixed on the ground at her feet. She knew exactly what was coming next.

'Well, count me in.' Rafe turned to Mel. 'I'll bet the view's spectacular up there.'

Was he *asking* her? It was difficult to tell, and Mel suspected that Rafe wasn't going to be dissuaded from climbing the mast. It actually didn't look that difficult. In the centre of the network of struts was a ladder with a circular safety cage around it, running right to the top.

'I imagine so. Getting up there looks pretty straightforward.' It was difficult to inject any enthusiasm into her words.

'Right then.' He produced his phone from his pocket. 'Keep an eye on this, will you? Hopefully, we should start receiving messages when the antennas are back in place.'

As she watched the men get into their safety harnesses and go through the safety procedures, Mel couldn't help a flutter of anxiety for Rafe. What if something broke? If one thing broke, that wouldn't be too bad, but three things breaking simultaneously would send him hurtling to the ground.

Or what if the tower had been weakened by the storm, and just fell over? She walked across to one of the four large feet, planted on slabs of concrete, the huge metal fixings that held them down bigger than the length of her foot. Surely they would hold?

The problem was that she just didn't know. She couldn't measure the odds or assess probabilities, and so fear was beginning to tear at her heart. Maybe it would be best if she went and sat down at the edge of the clearing, so that Rafe wouldn't notice how apprehensive she was.

'Hey.' She jumped as she heard his voice behind her. Mel composed herself and turned to face him.

'Hi. All ready to go?'

'Yeah. The structure's solid, and it's safe to climb. These guys wouldn't be going up there if they thought otherwise.'

He saw straight through her. Mel nodded.

'Two will be going halfway, to retrieve the antennas that are wedged in the structure. That's actually the trickiest part, and I'll be doing the easy bit and going to the top with a fourth man. The antennas will be hauled up to the top on cables, and then we'll fix them.' He showed her the two large clips attached to his harness. 'All the while, we'll be using these to make sure we don't fall.'

'Okay. Good, thanks.' She was feeling calmer now. The first best option was for him to stay with his feet on the ground, but that wasn't going to happen, and so the second best was for him to just do it, while she stayed at the bottom and pretended it wasn't happening.

Rafe hesitated. 'Why don't you go and stand with the others at the bottom? They can do with all the help they can get to haul the antennas back up. You might even get a cup of tea.'

He was involving her. And suddenly Mel felt equal to the task of watching him go.

'Okay...yes, okay. I may as well make the tea. They're busy.'

Rafe gave her a melting smile. 'I'm sure they'll appreciate that.'

CHAPTER ELEVEN

IT WAS ODD. Or maybe it wasn't odd at all. Rafe's first instinct had been that there was a job to be done and that he wanted to help with it. That was always his first instinct. But when he'd seen Mel walking away to the edge of the clearing she'd suddenly become his only priority.

He'd worked and he'd built a life. But the only person who'd made him think twice about stepping forward to take on each difficult task ahead was Mel.

He climbed halfway up the mast, stopping for a rest as had been agreed. Rafe looked down and saw Mel, standing with the other men, sipping tea. By some instinct, she seemed to realise that he was watching her and she looked up and waved.

'No looking down.' The man climbing with him gave the smiling advice, and Rafe nodded.

He waved back to Mel and then turned his attention to the top of the mast. It seemed to sparkle in the sun even more brilliantly because he knew that Mel was on the ground, waiting for him.

Mel had insisted on making the tea, and waited with the others. The two antennas were retrieved and examined, pronounced a little battered but good enough for use and then fixed to a pulley to be sent up to the top of the mast.

Mel took her work gloves from her pocket, hauling on the cable with the work crew.

Rafe and the man with him were working steadily and deliberately. The first antenna was fixed and everyone took their phones out of their pockets.

'Nothing?'

Nothing. Everyone shook their heads and waited.

Rafe and the other man were working separately now, each fixing an antenna to the top of the mast. There was a pause while they connected them, everyone staring upwards.

'I have two bars…'

'I have three!'

Mel took her phone and Rafe's out of her pocket. They were both vibrating, messages pinging in one after the other. She turned, smiling to the foreman of the work crew.

'I've got messages.'

'Good. Very good…' He began to wave to the men at the top of the tower, yelling at the top of his voice. 'We have messages!'

It was a long climb back down to the bottom of the tower, and Rafe and the other man stopped halfway to rest, as they'd done on the way up. Mel checked his phone, seeing a whole list of messages on the screen, and then put it back into her pocket, turning her attention to her own messages.

He reached the ground, disconnecting his harness and walking swiftly towards her. 'So it worked…'

'Yes, you have lots of messages.' She handed his phone to him and he disengaged the lock screen. Someone handed him a cup of tea and they stood in the sunshine, both scrolling through the all-important news that had been sent.

'Maddie got the photos I sent, of Haroon's and the baby's eyes…'

'Yeah? What does she say?' Rafe looked up from his phone.

'The baby definitely has all the signs of cataracts and he should be referred to a specialist straight away. It's a bit more difficult to tell with Haroon but she says that she'd be wanting to investigate further on the evidence of what we've described.'

'Great. That's very useful. Can you send it on to me and I'll forward it to the doctor in Male' who's arranging the treatment?' Rafe paused for a moment, reading through something. 'It looks as if the transfer to Colombo will be authorised. My colleagues there have managed to expedite that.'

'Good. Will you be going with Zeena and Haroon, back to Colombo?' Mel felt her heart beat a little faster. This was all good news but it meant that she was losing Rafe.

'Um…' He was scanning another message and then he looked up, grinning at her. 'Apparently not. I've been asked to stay here for a while and set up a medical hub for the surrounding islands. Anyone who's been hurt in the storm, or in its aftermath. The hospital in Colombo will be sending someone over to accompany Haroon and Zeena as soon as the transfer's been authorised.'

'Really?' Mel couldn't conceal her delight.

'Yes, resources are stretched at the moment and the doctor who usually covers this area is needed elsewhere. The sea plane means that I can get around, and the hotel's clinic facilities are ideal.' He looked up at her. 'Are you in?'

'Yes! I'm in.'

'You don't want to relax and finish your holiday?' He was teasing now. He knew full well that she didn't.

'Be quiet, Rafe. This is much more interesting than a holiday.'

He grinned, typing a reply on his phone. It buzzed again, as if someone had been waiting for his reply. 'Looks as if we're up already. They want me to visit one of the neighbouring islands as soon as I can.'

They made a hurried farewell to the work crew, who were packing up their things ready to go back to the hotel. Rafe was making no concessions in his pace this time, and Mel was glad of his guiding hand, and the downward slope between them and the hotel.

His first task was to speak to Mr Manike. Then everything else started to fall into place. Work parties were quickly arranged and Mel saw guests, along with staff, helping to push the sea plane back into the water under Rafe's careful supervision, then bringing out the metal-edged boxes of medical supplies that he'd brought with him.

Rafe hurriedly showered, washing off the grime from his foray up the phone mast, and Mel climbed into the seat next to him. An hour had passed since Rafe had received the message, and they were ready to go. A group congregated on the beach to watch the sea plane taxi across the water and as it gathered speed plumes of spray rose on either side, obscuring Mel's view. Then suddenly they were in the air.

'Oh! It's beautiful!' She couldn't help catching her breath at the serene blue of the ocean and the paler ring of shallow water around the island. The white beach surrounding a heart of green.

'Yeah.' Rafe seemed a little tight-lipped, concentrating on the task ahead of them. That, above everything else, even her own fears of the unknown, made her suspect that it would be a challenge.

The sea plane flew low and when Rafe circled their small island destination to find a good landing area the difference was obvious. There was a sprawling hotel on one side of the island, and from the air she could see that it hadn't fared as well as their own. There was evidence of damage, and the people who had straggled out onto the beach seemed dejected and aimless. Rafe landed the plane, taxiing carefully to a small jetty where they could disembark and unload whatever medical supplies they needed.

Rafe and Mr Manike's careful preparations for the storm became a great deal clearer to Mel now. These people had no support, the hotel was a shambles and no one seemed to be doing anything about it. It was a far cry from the quiet optimism that she'd seen after the storm on Nadulu.

Rafe turned to her. 'Mel, I'm going to say something that might not make you feel any better.' The look on his face told her that it definitely wouldn't.

'Okay, fire away. Whatever's happened here can't be worse than what's in my head at the moment.'

His lips twitched in a smile. 'I've already got that message. I need you to be careful and stay watchful. I'll be issuing a few orders, and it would be great if you could tell me your objections in private.'

'I get it. These people need direction, and it's nothing personal.'

'Yeah. Exactly.'

She nodded, undoing her seat belt, and Rafe got out of the cockpit and helped her across the float and onto dry land. The crowd milled around them and she saw that several people had untreated cuts on their faces and arms. Some were shouting.

'Can we have some quiet?' Rafe's voice rose above the rest, and demanded acquiescence. 'I'm Dr Davenport and this is Dr Murphy. Is the manager here?'

'Yes!' A smiling man in a casual white shirt and trousers stepped forward. 'I'm the manager.' Very different from Mr Manike. Mel was beginning to appreciate his formal, rather authoritarian manner.

'Right. I need these people back in a safe place in the hotel, and two of your staff here with the plane. We'll also want space for triage and treatment of patients.'

The manager looked around and, before he could decide what to do first, Rafe had already beckoned to two young men, who had been trying to marshal and calm the others.

'Will you stay right here, please, and make sure that no one touches the plane?'

'Yes, Doctor.' One of the men almost sprang to attention, and he and his colleague moved to a spot between the plane and the crowd, shooing everyone back.

'Everyone move quietly back to the hotel. You'll be given further instructions there.' The press of the crowd became less insistent as people started to turn and walk back up the beach.

'I have the perfect place for you.' The manager was obviously falling into line too. 'Follow me.'

The crowd parted to let them through and Mel stayed close to Rafe as he marched up the beach towards the hotel. She nudged him and he looked down at her.

'Your bossy side is surprisingly useful at times.'

Rafe grimaced. 'I thought you were going to give me a break?'

'This *is* me giving you a break.'

'Ah. Good to know.' She felt his fingers brush the back of her hand. They were going to get through this chaos.

They'd worked through a whole roomful of people with minor injuries, mostly cuts from flying glass, and returned to Nadulu with a full complement of passengers. Dave had a cut on his leg that had become infected, and he was already running a slight fever. Mel had administered intravenous antibiotics and decided that the medical suite was the best place for him for a couple of days.

Izzy had torn at both of their hearts. A seven-year-old girl who had been blown off her feet when a branch crashed through the window of her parents' hotel suite. She'd escaped with only minor cuts but had broken her wrist and been in severe pain since yesterday. Rafe had applied a splint and asked if she'd like a ride on a sea plane, and the little girl had managed to give him a smile.

Izzy's parents and Dave's wife had filled the other seats for the short flight. Hotel staff were waiting for them, and helped transfer Izzy and Dave to beds in the medical suite. Izzy's mother had looked around her and burst into tears of relief.

Two more patients had arrived by boat from one of the other islands, battered and bruised after falls during the storm. Mr Manike had settled them into beds in the doctors' ready room, and rather apologetically told Mel that one of the female' concierges had gathered her luggage together and transferred it to a premier suite on the top floor of the hotel.

'Mr Manike, you're a wonder. Keeping all of our patients in one place is perfect, thank you.'

'All part of my job, Dr Murphy. Nothing is too good for our doctors.' Mr Manike gifted her with a rare smile, which made it all the more special, and walked away.

She saw Rafe heading towards the consulting room and hurried after him, hoping that he knew where the key was for the medicines fridge that he'd brought with him when he'd first arrived on the island. Mel slumped down into the chair behind the desk.

'Those poor people, Rafe. I could hardly bear to leave them.'

'Yeah. But we did the best we could. We triaged and

then treated everyone in order of need. There are boats on the way from Male' to take everyone off the island this evening.' Rafe had put in an urgent call with the travel company that ran the hotel, insisting on medical grounds that the evacuation take place today.

'I know, but I wish we could have done more.'

'Hey. How many cuts did you stitch?'

'I've lost count.' Rafe's apparent obsession with helping to fix window shutters seemed entirely reasonable to Mel now that she'd seen the results of badly fixed ones at first hand.

'Too many to count is a respectable total. You can never do as much as you want in these situations.'

'I'm just realising how lucky I was to be here, where things were better organised.'

Rafe nodded. 'Makes all the difference. Mr Manike can take a lot of credit for that, although I don't suppose he will.' Rafe had been fiddling with his key-ring and finally managed to detach the key for the medicines fridge. 'There you go.'

'Thanks. You couldn't put it back on the key-ring and then take it off again, could you? I'm not sure that I can stand up right now.'

He chuckled, bending down to wrap his arms around her and pull her to her feet. Mel was wide awake now. All it took was the brush of his cheek against hers.

'Right. Thanks.' She pulled her scrubs top straight. 'I suppose I'd better get on.'

There was still more to do. Mel had left Dave's wound open to allow the infection to drain and it needed careful monitoring, even though Dave had expressed the opinion that a little walking around would probably do wonders. His wife Beverley had had the last word on the matter, telling him briskly that he was to stay exactly where he was and do as he was told. Mel knew an ally when she found one, and had carefully gone through everything that Beverley should bring to her attention.

Izzy was a joy. Mel had found Rafe in her room and, while he finished talking to her parents, Izzy had proudly showed off the temporary cast on her arm, whispering to Mel that she could sign her name next to Doctor Rafe's.

Their other patients, two young men, looked as if they'd been beaten up, after having ventured out of their hotel during the storm. One had been slammed against a sea wall and the other had been trapped under a tree that had been uprooted by the gale. The hotel's first aiders had given them a thorough going-over when they'd arrived and they'd been under their watchful eyes ever since. Rafe examined them both and confirmed that there were no broken bones, which was a minor miracle considering the number of bruises they both had.

'Guys, I'm not going to ask what you thought you were doing.' Rafe shot them both a pained look. 'But would it be safe to say you'll think twice about going out in a tropical storm in future?'

'Yeah, definitely.' Robbie was the more cheerful of the two. 'There were six of us and we had this bet—'

'No, don't tell me.' Rafe held up his hand. 'Seriously, I don't want to know anything other than you're not going to do it again.'

Robbie grinned. 'Fair do's, chief. Never again, eh, Brian?'

His friend stirred in his bed, wincing as he did so. 'Are you kidding, mate? Of course never again.'

Rafe walked out of the room and closed the door behind him. Then he leaned against the wall, closing his eyes.

'What?' Perhaps he'd finally ground to a halt after a

day's unremitting work and couldn't find the energy to take another step.

'I went out. In a tropical storm. On my own.'

Mel laughed. 'Oh, and you want to know whether I think you're as much of an idiot as those two in there?'

'Don't beat about the bush. Just tell me.'

'Yes, Rafe. You're an idiot. But you had very good reasons. You were trying to keep everyone together and out of danger. I didn't really realise how important that was until today. And you were quite right when you said that there were only two doctors and it didn't make sense for us both to take the risk.'

'Okay.' He put his hand against his chest, his eyes still closed. 'That didn't hurt too much.'

'There was a trace of machismo there, though. That thing of wanting to be the one that goes, so the woman doesn't have to do it.'

'That hurts.' He opened his eyes. 'I trust there was a bit more than just a trace.'

'Oh, so you admit it?' Mel put her hands on her hips.

'Yeah. Beat me up for it if you like. I'm far too tired to feel it.'

He was incorrigible. Not at all the kind of guy that Mel would usually have fallen for... But then those discreet relationships with friends seemed unbearably polite now. The kind of man who would never challenge her and make her feel the way Michael had. But challenge was what she lived for in most other parts of her life and Rafe was beginning to show her that she was equal to that challenge in a relationship as well.

'Come to my room.'

He raised his eyebrows. 'So you can beat me up in private? Or is that a proposition?'

Mel smiled. One thing about Rafe, she never had to worry about him not saying what was on his mind and that meant she didn't have to stop and wonder what the most tactful way to say anything was.

'Neither. I'm far too tired. But I could watch a sunset and there's no one else around to do it with.' Or to understand. All of the frustration and all of the little victories they'd won today.

Rafe thought for a moment. 'Sounds good. I just need to hand over to the hotel first aider first. I'll see you up there?'

'All right. See you there.'

She took the lift to the top floor of the hotel, checking the room number on the card in her hand. It would be okay to leave the door open for Rafe. He wouldn't be long. The hotel's first aiders were both very competent and knew when they should call for a doctor.

The sun was sinking towards the sea, already sending golden ripples through a backdrop of blue. And this was just the place to watch it, big floor-to-ceiling windows and a couple of very comfortable-looking sofas. The coffee table in between them held a large display of flowers and a bowl full of tropical fruits. Mel looked at the note which accompanied the flowers.

To Dr Murphy. With heartfelt thanks, J Manike

Mel smiled. Less was most definitely more where Mr Manike was concerned. She walked over to the folding doors which separated the bedroom part of the suite from the living area and found that the same floor-to-ceiling windows gave the same stupendous view. All of her things had been arranged neatly and her empty suitcase stowed away next to the wardrobe. In the adjoining bathroom there was a gift box containing scented soaps and moisturisers. Mel squirted a dab of the handcream onto her hand and it was thick and luxurious.

'Hey. This is *nice.*' Rafe's voice floated through from the living space.

'Isn't it? I should be wearing a beautiful dress before I even think about watching the sunset.'

'You don't need the dress. And scrubs are a much more telling badge of achievement.'

Rafe said the nicest things. As if they were just matters of fact and not compliments at all. It made her feel that she didn't need to thank him for making her feel good, as if it was a pleasure she didn't wholly deserve.

'What's that?' She nodded towards the bottle and two heavy cut-glass tumblers that he was holding.

'You said that you'd be ordering a single malt Scotch when the storm was over. I guess it's over now, even if there is a lot more for both of us to do.' He put the bottle down on the table and Mel squinted at the label.

'You have good taste. That's expensive Scotch.'

'Blame Mr Manike. I found it in my room instead of flowers and fruit.'

'No, you don't get away with that. I blame *you* for remembering.' Mel sat down on the sofa and Rafe took the opposite one, pouring a splash of Scotch into each of the glasses.

'Ice?' he enquired innocently.

'I'm not watering this down.' Mel picked up her glass. 'What shall we drink to?'

Rafe considered the question for a moment. 'Getting through?'

'Is that *all* we did? Just get through?'

He chuckled. 'Getting through together then. That was a bit more challenging at times.'

Mel chinked her glass against his. 'Getting through together.'

His gaze held hers in an embrace as they drank. Mel leaned back on the sofa, closing her eyes to try and keep that image in her head for as long as possible.

'I think I'm too tired to watch the whole sunset.'

'Yeah. Me too...'

CHAPTER TWELVE

MEL WOKE UP. The sea was sparkling in the early morning sunlight, and she was lying comfortably on the sofa. This was a great sofa, she'd have to get one like it at home. These peaceful, bright mornings were something she'd like to take home with her as well. The scent of flowers and the sound of Rafe's breathing...

What?

She rubbed her eyes, looking across at the other sofa. Rafe was fast asleep, his lips curved in a slight smile as if his dreams were good ones. And she couldn't remember for the life of her how she'd got here. She'd been sipping Scotch...

That wasn't to blame. Most of her drink was still in the glass on the table. Her sneakers were under the coffee table but she recalled slipping them off when she'd sat down. And she had her socks on. No one had sex in their socks, did they?

'Rafe! Wake up!' Her tone must have been more urgent than she'd intended because he sat up suddenly.

'What is it?'

'Um...nothing. You were just asleep. And it's morning now.' Mel gave him an embarrassed look.

'Ah. Yeah, okay. Thanks for noticing.' He looked

around, clearly wondering the same as she had. 'Yester-day was a tiring day, wasn't it?'

'Yes, it was. I didn't stir all night.'

'Me neither.' He frowned. 'Actually, I did. I woke up and ate one of your rambutans.' He nodded apologetically towards the fruit bowl.

'That's okay. Help yourself.' This was just excruciat-ing. It would have been much better if they *had* had sex last night. At least the endorphins would help with the morning after.

'Right then. Well, I'd better be going.' He looked at his watch. 'Six o'clock. Early breakfast in an hour?'

'Yes, I'll look forward to it. Don't forget your Scotch...' Rafe was already halfway towards the door.

'Uh...hold onto it, will you? We can try again with the sunset...'

'Try again?'

He stopped suddenly, turning around. 'There's going to be another one this evening and I'd like to watch it with you. Maybe we could do it without the scrubs and the ex-haustion this time.'

Mel's heart began to beat a little faster. 'You mean a date?' The words slipped out before she could bite her tongue. She should have just said *yes* and left it there.

'We could call it that...' He turned and suddenly all of Rafe's charm and adventurous certainty seemed to drain away. This terrified him too.

'Mel, I'm not asking you for a pleasant evening that may or may not turn into a very pleasant night. Will you come on a date with me?'

There was a world of difference. She'd spent a lot of years convincing herself that a nice meal followed by sat-isfying sex that didn't leave you wanting to go back for more was enough. This was uncertain and delicious, and didn't have a sell-by date stamped on the wrapper.

'I...haven't been on a date for a while.'

'Me neither. Are you okay with the idea?'

No. Not even slightly okay. But she wanted it.

'If you are...?'

He thought for a moment. All of Rafe's defences were down and he was taking this seriously. 'Yes. I'm definitely okay with it.'

'Me too.'

He gave a nod, as if his throat was as dry as hers and words were just as impossible. Then he turned, his pace brisk again as he walked out of the room.

Mel flopped back onto the sofa, looking up at the ceiling. The storm had been a hard taskmaster, constantly pushing them together and pulling them apart. But she'd already proved that she was a lot tougher than the things that life could throw at her. There would be another sunset and she and Rafe would be there to watch it.

By the time they met in the restaurant for breakfast Mel had stood under the shower for long enough to calm herself. Rafe obviously had as well because he was smiling and relaxed, ready to talk through the things that needed to be done today.

Their patients were their first concern. Mr Manike had extended an invitation to both Dave and Izzy's families to stay at the hotel until they were fully recovered and ready to travel. Brian and Robbie were bruised and aching but well enough to return to their hotel and Rafe would fly them back there this afternoon. Zeena and Haroon would be leaving for Male', to catch a flight to Colombo later this morning.

They spent an hour with the couple, discussing what

would happen next. Zeena and Haroon seemed even closer, even more in love with their baby son if that was at all possible. Mel's own experience after Amy's birth was so different, and it was touching to see them together. As they were going through the notes, making sure that they were all in order before they were handed over to the doctors in Colombo, Rafe's phone buzzed.

He picked up his phone and smiled. 'Looks as if we have a visitor…'

Mel followed him out of the hotel and down to the beach, wondering how *they* could have a visitor when their circle of friends and acquaintances was entirely separate. A white speedboat was nosing its way into dock, against the newly swept jetty, and Rafe started forward suddenly as a young man climbed out.

Even from this distance, she could see who it was. Their visitor was familiar from the photographs that Rafe had shown her and he had his father's easy way of moving. The two men met on the jetty, giving each other an unashamed hug, warmth of a kind that you couldn't manufacture. Then they began to stroll towards her.

Ash. Rafe was always happy to see his son, that went without saying. The slight reservation that nagged at the back of his mind was over something that hadn't even happened and probably never would.

That wasn't the point. When Ash had been old enough to ask, Rafe hadn't denied that he'd had a few 'women friends' since Annu had died. As Ash had got older he'd assumed that might involve sex, in the same way that Rafe had assumed that when his son went away for the weekend with a girlfriend they might or might not be sleeping in separate rooms. But the one thing that Ash knew for sure, and had always known, was that there had never been anyone who could replace his mother.

Mel had asked Rafe to kiss her as if he'd meant it. And he had. He'd *really* meant it, and that was a first for him. It made very little difference that they hadn't done anything more, because Ash was smart enough to see that Mel was different. Rafe wasn't sure how he might feel about that.

'It's been a great help to have another doctor here.' Mel was hanging back, watching them as they strolled towards her, and Rafe decided that telling Ash who she was would be the most natural thing to do.

'You've not been running her too ragged, have you, Dad?' Ash grinned at him.

There was no good answer to that. 'Not as far as I'm aware.'

'Okay. Don't tell me then.' Ash grinned at him, striding forward to shake Mel's outstretched hand and introduce himself. She was smiling and a little pink-cheeked in the sunshine, as if she too felt the awkwardness of the situation.

'So what brings you here, Ash?' Mel asked.

'I'm here to collect the family whose new baby has cataracts. The hospital said they'd send someone, and I volunteered. Thought I'd check up on what Dad was up to while I was here.'

Mel looked as taken aback by the thought as Rafe was, and he decided to change the subject before she felt impelled to answer.

'I imagine that Zeena and Haroon will be spending much of their time at the hospital, but if they need somewhere to stay you've got the keys to my guest house, haven't you?'

'Yes, I'll sort that out. I hear you're staying here for a while, island-hopping.'

Rafe smiled at his son. 'Do me a favour and try to make it sound as if I'm doing *some* work, or I'll be answering to the hospital administrator when I get back.'

'Unlikely, Dad. She told me to remind you to leave a little something for the other doctors in the area to do.'

They strolled to the medical suite together, chatting amiably. When Ash sat down to read the notes, Rafe decided it would be okay to leave him alone with Mel for a few minutes while he got coffee.

When he returned, balancing three cups on a tray, he heard Ash's voice floating through the open door of the consulting room.

'I'm specialising in surgery. My ambition is to help bring simple surgeries to rural populations in Sri Lanka. We can help change a lot of lives…'

He shouldn't eavesdrop. But he was so proud of Ash. Then Rafe heard Mel's voice.

'That's an admirable goal. I know that progress is being made, but that there's still a lot more to be done.' Mel's tone was interested and encouraging.

'That's right. New techniques are being developed all the time and I really want to be a part of that. Not just a part of it, I want to be on the cutting edge. I know it'll take a lot of hard work…'

Rafe couldn't resist stepping forward, and Ash and Mel both looked up at him at the same time.

'He's not afraid of that.' He gestured towards the file that lay on the desk in front of Ash. 'Read the file. You want to get a good practical solution of how to get specialist help in an isolated situation then it's right there. Along with a few very good examples of the right questions to ask and the right way to answer them.'

Rafe set the tray down, putting Mel's coffee in front of her, and she looked up at him. Just the hint of a smile and the hint of a blush. She waited for Rafe to sit down and then turned to Ash.

'I'm very interested in what you've been saying about your own career. You might find it useful to be in touch with some of my contacts in London. Perhaps I could take your phone number?' She flashed Rafe a querying look and had obviously been waiting for his return before she broached the subject.

Ash hesitated. 'It's kind of you, but I wouldn't want to put you to any trouble.'

Rafe leaned back in his seat, grinning. Mel's contacts would be a good addition to the resources at Ash's disposal. He'd worked hard and gained the respect of the people around him. It was time for him to start spreading his wings.

'If a doctor of Mel's seniority and experience offered to take my number I wouldn't hesitate.'

'You don't need my number, Rafe. I'm sitting right here.' Mel rolled her eyes but looked pleased at the way he'd emphasised the words *seniority* and *experience.*

Ash took the blatant hint and grinned, handing over his phone so that Mel could save the number on hers.

They'd said their goodbyes and Mel had hugged Zeena, planting a kiss on the baby's forehead. She shepherded the couple along the jetty and Rafe hung back to give them some final time alone.

'Mel's really nice.' Ash was standing beside him, watching her.

'She's a good doctor.'

'Not what I meant, Dad.'

'Yeah. I know.'

His son fell silent for a moment, and Rafe reckoned he'd said enough. He should probably work out exactly what was going on between himself and Mel before he said anything to Ash.

'Dad, I didn't ever get the chance to talk with Mum, but you and the family brought me up to know what her values were, right?'

'Yes. Your mother was a good woman, and she'd be proud of you.'

'I know. I can't speak for her, but I think I understand the way she might have thought. She'd be proud of you too, and want you to be happy.'

Rafe considered the question. 'I'm glad you think so. But I *am* happy with my life, Ash.'

'Happier, then. Look, Dad, I know you loved Mum and that your relationship with her was something special. Having something else that's special doesn't wipe all that out, does it?'

'We're at the stage where you start giving me advice, are we?' Rafe didn't mind that at all, and he'd wanted to hear what Ash had just said, more than he was able to admit.

Ash rolled his eyes in exasperation. 'Dad…!'

'Sorry. I'm listening. I just don't have an answer for you right now.'

'You'll think about it, though? I'm not telling you what to do.' Ash was smiling now. 'But…you know…'

'I know.' Rafe gave his son a hug. 'You're telling me that whatever I do is okay, and I really appreciate that, and that you took the time to say it. Thank you, it was a good talk.'

'Any time, Dad.' Ash looked a little relieved that Rafe had drawn the talk neatly to a close.

'You've got a patient waiting for you. Go and get on the boat.' Rafe grinned, nodding towards Mel, who was holding the baby while the pilot helped Zeena to her seat.

'Yeah. Don't worry, I'll look after them. See you soon…'

Ash hurried away, smiling at Mel as he took the baby

from her and got carefully onto the boat. She waved, calling something that was lost in the sound of the engine, and Ash waved back. As the boat drew away, she watched it go and then walked back to Rafe.

'You're right to be proud of him, Rafe. He's impressive.'

Rafe turned, not wanting to watch while the boat disappeared over the horizon. Goodbyes weren't his thing. 'It was good of you to take his number.'

'My pleasure.'

They started to walk together across the sand to the hotel. Finally Rafe summoned up the courage to ask the question he really wanted to ask.

'So could *I* have your number?'

Mel thought about it for a moment and then smiled. 'Yes. You can have my number.'

CHAPTER THIRTEEN

THEY'D FLOWN TOGETHER AGAIN, taking Robbie and Brian back to their hotel and making sure there was no one else who needed them. Calls to the other four islands that Rafe had been asked to look after produced no other patients, and on the way back Rafe had dipped and wheeled, putting the sea plane through its paces and Mel's heart into her mouth.

Dave and Izzy were both progressing well, and the medical suite suddenly felt very empty. Rafe had disappeared on an errand somewhere, and the sunset was only four hours away. Mel went to the consulting room and opened the condom cupboard, surveying its contents. She wasn't taking anything for granted, but there was no harm in being ready. There were so many difference choices, though...

'You found them, then.' Rafe's voice sounded suspiciously cheery and Mel slammed the cupboard door closed, looking round to find him leaning in the doorway.

'No. I can't think where they've put the plasters.'

'Plasters are over there. That's the condom cupboard.'

'Right. I wanted plasters.' Who was she trying to kid? Rafe didn't look even slightly convinced. 'Okay. How did *you* know that was the condom cupboard?'

'I came across it when I was looking for plasters. They've got a dazzling selection, haven't they?'

Mel sighed, opening the cupboard again. She'd been caught in the act and denying it was only going to be even more embarrassing.

'Yes. It's pretty impressive.' She heard his footsteps and looked around the door to find him standing next to her. Maybe choosing their favourite condom would break the ice that seemed to be forming around her.

'What do you say we forget all about that?' Rafe took her hand, pressing it to his lips, then closed the cupboard door. 'This is something different for both of us.'

'Yes.' Mel's throat felt suddenly dry. A date really was more challenging than any of the other relationship options available.

'Would it help if I said that I don't think I'm the guy that brings condoms with him on a first date?' He shrugged. 'Not as far as I remember, anyway.'

The panicked feeling lifted suddenly. 'It helps. As far as *I* remember, I appreciate the gesture.'

'You like picnics. And swimming?'

'Yes.'

'Then I'll see you in half an hour.'

'That sounds perfect.' She reached for him, suddenly unable to let him go. 'Are you open to—?'

'Yes.'

She pulled him close and he backed her against the door and kissed her. Great kiss. Then he kissed her again. Even better. More head-swimmingly, heart-stoppingly delicious.

Just as she was about to leave him wanting more, he left her, wanting so much more that she could hardly bear it. She pulled him back, kissing him one more time.

'Half an hour.' He whispered the words against her ear.

'Yes.'

'Don't bring condoms.'
'I wouldn't dream of it.'

This was the first time in Rafe's life that *not* having a
packet of condoms on hand had opened up the number
of options available. It wasn't that he didn't want to have
sex with Mel. He wanted it so much that he was having
trouble stopping thinking about it. But it was complicated.
They both needed to take their time and be sure of what
they were doing.

And this *was* something different. Physical intimacy
no longer felt like the betrayal it once had. But becoming
involved with someone, the way he was with Mel, was entirely different. His belief that true love could happen only
once had been fuelled by the idea that maybe heartbreak
would only happen only once as well.

He knew all about risk, how to calculate and minimise
it, and Rafe understood the risk involved here. Mel had put
her life back together after a disastrous relationship and
she had peace now. He'd grieved and then found a way to
make his life mean something. They were neither of them
perfect, but they'd found a way to live with their imperfec-
tions. It didn't sound much, but experience told Rafe that
that was one hell of an achievement.

And, on top of all that, they lived on opposite sides of
the globe. Compromising with each other was a commitment which wasn't to be taken lightly.

He still wanted her, though. And wanting her made him
selfish enough to contemplate the risk. When they met in
the reception area of the hotel, packed sandwiches and
fruit from the kitchen in the bag slung over his shoulder,
she seemed to glow. And when they walked together into
the sunshine, Mel sparkled. Rafe wanted her smile, and
the scent of roses that she always seemed to carry with her.

Hand in hand, he led her to the place he'd selected for them to swim. A small cove on the other side of the island, which none of the other holidaymakers seemed to have found yet because it was deserted. Ahead of them the sand merged into sea in a wash of colour and behind them a gradient in the land afforded a sense of privacy.

'This is gorgeous!' Mel clapped her hands in delight. She wore a bright sarong over her bathing costume, her hair tied up. Rafe had been concentrating on admiring the curve of her shoulder all the way here.

'I think so.' She *was* gorgeous. 'Shall we swim first?'

She smiled up at him. 'It would be wrong not to.'

This moment was all about a sheer love of life, that feeling of freedom that he always felt when Mel was smiling at him. The breeze against his skin as he took off his shirt, and the feeling of his limbs moving as he broke away from her, running to the massive trunk of a palm tree that bent over the water.

'Rafe!' The note of panic in her voice made him stop, but when he turned she was smiling. 'Tell me you're not going to break your neck.'

'I'm not going to break my neck.' That seemed enough for her and he heard Mel's laughter as he scrambled up the trunk, launching himself into the air in an expression of the joy that life seemed to hold at the moment.

There was a satisfying splash as he hit the water and he saw bright flashes as startled fish shot out of his way. Then he hit the surface, feeling the rush of adrenaline pulse through his body and the sun on his back.

If only she'd let go of her fears and experience these simple pleasures. But what was pleasure to him was an agonising *what if?* to her. He waved, beckoning to her to come into the water.

She hesitated. Rafe could almost see the cogs turning

in her head, weighing up all of the possibilities. And then she did it. Mel walked over to the palm, climbing onto its trunk and slowly straightening to stand. Arms out at either side of her, she started to walk slowly out over the water.

'Be careful…'

She wobbled slightly and he caught his breath. At least he'd taken advantage of a few handholds to make his way along the trunk, but Mel's back was completely straight, her steps slow and controlled like a ballerina.

'You're telling *me* to be careful?'

'I couldn't balance like that.' Any minute she was going to go headlong into the water.

'Does that make me more foolhardy than you?' There was a look of intense concentration on her face.

'More accomplished…' More beautiful, more graceful. Maybe a little less willing to hurtle her way through life and just feel the wind in her hair, but he was realising that Mel had nerves of steel.

He watched as she walked carefully, never putting a foot wrong. The pliable trunk bent a little beneath her weight and Rafe found himself trying to solve impossible calculations of angle and height. Then she turned, looking down at the water before she jumped in.

She landed a little way away from him, the water pluming up around her. For a moment he couldn't see her and sudden fear made Rafe strike out towards her. Then Mel's head broke the surface, and she was grinning at him.

'Nice one.' He wanted to draw her a little closer but he didn't dare.

'You want to try it my way?'

'I'm not sure that I could.'

'If you try mine, I'll try yours.'

That was a challenge he couldn't pass up. It had the hint

of a lover's dare about it, and Mel's lips held the hint of a lover's reward if he could pass the test.

'You're on.'

He swam back to the beach, pulling himself up onto the trunk and standing. This wasn't as easy as Mel had made it look. Twice he stumbled and stepped down into shallow water, and then he got a little further and splashed down into the water next to her.

'Don't look at your feet. Look at where you're going.' Mel offered the advice and Rafe wondered how that was going to work if he couldn't see where he was putting his feet.

Okay. Try again. This time he reached the end of the trunk and dived into the water. He surfaced to the sound of Mel whooping and clapping her hands above her head.

'Now you…'

She looked speculatively up at the trunk. 'Any advice?'

How on earth did one advise on spontaneity? 'Uh… No, not really. Run with the wind.'

'Okay, that's helpful.' Mel got out of the water and took a tentative run at the trunk. She missed her footing almost immediately and stumbled back onto the sand.

Maybe this wasn't such a good idea after all. She was going to hurt herself if she tried that again. She was far too hesitant and not letting her own instinctive ability to grab at a few handholds take over. Rafe swam back to the beach, but not in time to stop her from jumping up on the trunk and trying another run.

But, moving fast, he was just in time to catch her. She slipped just as she was over the water's edge and Rafe managed to scoop her up before she hit the ground, holding her tightly as his heart beat fast.

'Maybe it's not such a good idea after all.'

'What?' She wriggled free of him. 'You can do it, but I can't?'

'It's not a matter of who's allowed to do what. I don't want you to hurt yourself…'

She was backing away from him now. And then suddenly mischief showed in her face. Mel started to run across the beach.

'No, no, no…' She veered closer to the foot of the palm trunk and he started to run after her. 'Don't do it, Mel.'

He reached forward, just missing one of her flailing arms. She got away from him, describing a wide circle on the beach, her laughter serving only to encourage Rafe in trying to catch her. Before he knew it she was scrambling up the trunk, and he followed her as she sped nimbly along it.

He caught her, just as she reached the point where he'd launched himself into the water. Curling one arm around her waist and hanging onto the broad base of a palm frond with the other, he pulled her close, never caring that they were touching in ways that he'd dreamed of, just feeling the balance of her weight against his.

Mel was laughing, and trying to wriggle free of him. A sudden madness took over, and Rafe let go, holding her against him as he jumped. They hit the water together with an almighty splash, and she was still in his arms as he surfaced.

'I've got you…'

She gave him a bright smile, winding her arms around his neck. 'I thought I had you.'

'Yeah, I guess you do.' All he could think about at the moment was that they had each other. And, if he wasn't very much mistaken, she wanted that as much as he did.

One kiss. It was more of a peck really, but it shook him o the core.

But, in the curious paradox of a first date, wanting more was enough. He took his arm from around her waist and she let him go. The bright prospect of spending time with her seemed to glisten like the sunlight on the water, and that was all that mattered.

They'd had a great time. They'd swum and eaten their picnic. Baked in the sun a little to dry off and then wandered back to the hotel, hand in hand. Rafe had kissed her hand in a quiet gentlemanly touch, the look in his eyes that accompanied it telling her that he'd rather she didn't go to her room alone. Mel would rather not as well, but this relationship was worth spending a little time on, and doing it right.

She sat alone, watching the sunset. Wishing he was there to watch it with her and yet something told her that he'd be watching it too. Alone, but thinking of her. Rafe had been right. It would take time for them both to find the moment when they could finally give themselves to each other. And his willingness to wait, to take nothing less, touched her in a way that no other man had done before.

She smiled as the bright display of amber and red began to spread across the sky.

'I did it...'

She'd been afraid to climb up on the palm trunk, and almost baulked at the idea. But she was even more afraid of going back to a life where anxiety shackled her. She'd learned how to push through the big things, changing jobs, signing the agreement to buy her house, determined to make a good life for Amy and herself. But somewhere along the way she'd neglected the little things. Those simple pleasures, the thrill of making it to the end of the palm trunk and the rush of water against her skin when she'd jumped in became things of great value when she was with Rafe.

She should think about going to bed, to sleep. There would be a lot to do tomorrow and... But she wanted to wait a while and watch the bright array of stars as it appeared in the sky. On a clear night they were so much brighter than they were at home, and she should take this pleasure while she could.

'Ugh. Not again...!'

So it was a comfortable sofa, she'd already established that. Mel hadn't meant to sleep on it for a second night in a row, but she'd been watching the stars. And it had been well worth it, even though her neck was a little stiff.

That eased when she carefully massaged the muscles under the hot water of the shower. When a waiter arrived, with her early morning wake-up call and a large cup of coffee, there was an envelope on the tray.

Mel took a gulp of the coffee, tearing the envelope open and smiling when she saw Rafe's handwriting.

I loved every moment of our date together. May we do it again this evening?

One more pleasure that had been lost. The frisson of anticipation, of not quite knowing what would happen next and allowing Rafe to surprise her. Mel had come to feel that surprise wasn't necessary when it came to relationships.

But she couldn't keep still now. She picked up her coffee, making her way down to the medical suite. Rafe was sitting in the consulting room, writing up notes in a patient folder.

'Yes. I had a wonderful time and I'd love to do it again.' Probably not the most well thought out of replies, but that didn't matter because Rafe's smile told her all she needed to know.

Mel sat down, taking a sip of her coffee and then handing it to him. He turned the cup, drinking from where her lips had touched it, and then handed it back.

'Say…six o'clock?'

'Six is great. Where are we going?'

'Somewhere nice.'

Okay. A surprise then. 'What should I wear?'

He grinned. 'Whatever you like. I have one decent shirt, which is currently being laundered, so I don't have much choice in the matter.'

'Okay. I have a choice, so I'll think about it.'

'I'll wait to see what you decide on then.' He leaned back in his seat. 'And, meanwhile, we have Izzy and Dave here, and there have been some calls from a couple of the other islands, so I think I'll need to visit. Would you like to come?'

'Yes, I'll come. I want to make sure you'll be back for six.'

The sea plane had touched down at five o'clock. There had been more to do than they'd thought and Mel might have been tempted to sit down and put her feet up, but she was too excited for that. They'd parted in the reception area, Rafe going back to the medical suite to check on Izzy and Dave, and Mel going to her room.

She knew just what she was going to wear. She'd brought a dark blue dress with her that was cool and comfortable, and yet still dressy enough for the evening. The jagged hem was filmy around her ankles and she had one pair of high-heeled sandals to go with it. Mel showered and took time over her hair and make-up, smiling at herself in the mirror. Since Rafe hadn't told her what he had in mind for tonight, there was no need to agonise about whether this was appropriate or not. She could dress to please herself, or to please him if she wanted.

The look on his face when she met him in the reception area told her that this *did* please him, very much. And Rafe had obviously made an effort too, his white shirt and chinos neat and freshly laundered. He whispered a compliment in her ear and she whispered one back, before he led her outside to one of the buggies that guests used for getting around the island.

He took the wide path into the trees, turning into a part of the forest that Mel hadn't seen before. She could see a light glimmering up ahead and when he stopped the buggy she saw steps leading around an enormous trunk and into a pool of light that emanated from the heart of the tree.

'I thought…' He seemed suddenly unsure of himself. 'Since I promised you a sunset, this is the best place to see it from. If you don't want to climb up there we could go somewhere else.'

'It's wonderful, Rafe. However did it survive the storm?'

'The steps and the platform at the top all come apart surprisingly easily. One of the work teams put it all back together again as part of the clean-up operation. I went up there myself last night and checked that they hadn't missed anything.'

Right now, Mel felt she would be safe anywhere if Rafe was with her. 'So you were watching the stars too?'

He chuckled. 'I may have taken a few moments out to do that as well.'

Rafe took her hand and they walked up the spiral steps. At the top, a sturdy platform with rails around the edge and a canopy above their heads. It was lit by lanterns and at the centre of the platform a table was set with a snowy white cloth and covered dishes.

'Oh!' Mel walked to the guard rail. 'You can see some of the other islands from here.'

'You like it?'

'I love it, Rafe. Thank you so much. This is so beautiful.'

He smiled. 'Sorry, can't see it. I have something more beautiful to look at.'

'Stop!' She nudged her elbow against his ribs. 'You've been looking at me all day. This is only ours for tonight.'

All the same, staring at him as he popped the cork of the champagne that was waiting on ice, and while they ate what Mel could only describe as the most luxurious picnic she'd ever seen, did seem even better than the view. Surrounded by the sounds and the scent of the forest, in their own small world. As the sun began to go down, he refilled their glasses and they walked back over to the edge of the platform to watch.

Tonight, it seemed as if even Mother Nature had pulled out all the stops for them. A magnificent sunset that filled the sky and sent shimmers of gold across the sea towards them. Mel leaned in against his chest and felt Rafe's arm around her shoulder.

'There's something I want to say, Mel. The one thing you haven't asked me about...' He fell silent, as if waiting for her permission to speak.

'Say it.' Mel had a good idea what he meant, and she did want to know.

'You've never asked me whether I still love Annu. And the answer is yes, I do and I always will. But that relationship is in my past now and what I feel for you belongs to us alone, no one else. You've helped me to believe that anything and everything is possible.'

'Thank you. I did want to know and... I couldn't have had a better answer. I don't know what's going to happen next, and I'm still afraid. But I want to be with you more than both of those things.'

He nodded, turning towards her. 'That's how I feel too. Maybe we could take one day at a time, and find out where it all leads?'

'Yes. That sounds like a good plan, Rafe.'

He kissed her. Softly at first, and then as if he really meant it. They held each other tight as the sunset covered the sky with brilliant colour. As it faded in the sky he led her down the steps to the ground.

The evening had started off at an exquisitely leisurely pace, but now they couldn't wait. When they got to Mel's room Rafe kicked the door closed behind them, taking her into his arms and kissing her.

They stumbled together into the bedroom.

'I have condoms,' Mel gasped as he kissed her again. 'I thought that was okay for a second date…'

'So did I.' He started to pull the zip at the back of her dress, and it fell from her shoulders.

'So, so glad we don't have to go all the way downstairs…' She shivered in the warmth of his gaze.

'Marvellous thing, forethought…' Rafe tore off his shirt, embracing her again.

Her dress fell to the floor at her ankles. Rafe stripped off her underwear and then the rest of his clothes. She felt her back hit the mattress and his body covered hers, strong and unyielding. He smelled of the sun and the forest.

'You're sure?'

He knew she was. But Mel knew that he needed her to say it. The thought that one word from her could let loose something momentous was exquisite.

'I'm sure, Rafe. Are you?'

'Beyond sure…'

One more moment of exquisite stillness. They both wanted the same thing, but there was no rush now, no danger of it slipping away. The one thing stronger than physical pleasure, the knowledge that tonight wasn't just about sexual satisfaction and had everything to do with the look in Rafe's eyes, made her shiver at the lightest touch of his fingers.

He felt it too. When she brushed a kiss against his lips he let out a groan. Each action provoked a deliciously intense overreaction. Rafe's gaze held her tight, in the most erotic of embraces. He saw her. She saw him.

Unable to wait any longer, she took his hand, guiding it downwards. Felt him gently pushing her legs apart, his fingers probing and arousing, making certain she was ready. Mel was *so* ready. And then she realised that no one could ever be completely ready for something like this. He pushed inside her and something seemed to ignite. Rafe moved again, and intense feeling washed over her, completely out of control.

'Mel…?' He hadn't expected this either, but she wrapped her legs around his hips, begging him not to stop. Rafe knew just what to do. He held her tightly, thrusting again, and she cried out. She felt the beginnings of something building between them, something that she couldn't have slowed down even if she'd wanted to. Then, like a bolt of lightning out of a clear blue sky, she came, her body arching and shaking uncontrollably. She felt Rafe's body stiffen against hers and knew that he was sharing these long, exquisite moments of release with her.

It was a while before she could let him go, the moments measured by their pounding hearts. When she finally loosened her arms from around his neck he lifted his weight from her, rolling over onto his back and holding her against his chest.

'Maybe I need to work on my timing...' He sounded almost apologetic.

'Your timing is wonderful. I was ready for everything and you gave me everything.'

He pulled her close, kissing the top of her head. 'I was hoping to give you everything for a little longer.'

'I don't think that would have felt so good...' Doubt crept through the corners of her mind. Maybe Rafe hadn't experienced what she had. The sudden, unyielding passion that wouldn't be moulded or prolonged, in just that same way that an explosion couldn't be contained.

'It was exquisite. Amazing. You felt it too?'

She leaned over to kiss him. 'From my head to my toes. One whole night rolled up into the most incredible feeling...'

He chuckled. 'A whole night? You're sure about that?'

'I'm not sure about anything. I'm just waiting to see what happens next.'

'Me too. Since we didn't have time for it the first time around, would you like to play a little?'

That should be impossible, after what had just happened between them. But just the thought of it prompted a tingling reaction that told Mel that nothing was impossible.

'I thought you might want to rest a bit.' Mel kissed him. 'You can rest if you want.'

'No, I can't, not when you're kissing me like that. And I want to get to know your body a little better.'

That sounded just delicious. 'Mmm... I'm looking forward to getting better acquainted with yours too...'

CHAPTER FOURTEEN

MEL WAS PROPPED up on one elbow, watching Rafe sleep in the early morning light. Getting to know each other a little better had turned into a delicious, drawn-out conversation, his body speaking to hers in ways that she hadn't felt possible. Talking and making love into the night, until they'd both fallen soundly asleep.

'You're watching me.' Rafe's sleepy voice disturbed her reverie.

'Yes. Do you mind?'

He chuckled, rubbing his hand across his chest. 'I'm not quite sure whether I should be questioning your taste.'

'I have excellent taste.'

He pulled her down, kissing her. 'And you make me feel good.'

She was leaving it all behind. It was just a matter of keeping her nerve, and not looking down. If she did that, she'd only see how far she could fall.

'Shall I order breakfast?'

'Don't you want to be a little more discreet than breakfast for two?'

No, she didn't want to be discreet, or polite or to keep her distance. Mel had done all that and it bored her. She wanted Rafe's passion, the way he didn't care too much what anyone else said, and the way he swept her off her feet.

'Do *you* want to be discreet?' The thought that maybe he wouldn't want to own up to this affair with her snagged suddenly in the corner of her mind. Without that, he could say as many pretty things to her as he liked, there would still be that nagging doubt.

He wrapped his arms around her, kissing the top of her head. 'I would like to climb the mast again this morning. String up a banner saying *Dr Mel Murphy thinks I'm good enough for her.* Would that be okay with you?'

'No, it would not. It's an unnecessary risk and you might fall.'

'Okay…how about sky-writing?'

'No! It's a waste of fuel.'

'True. How about writing it in the sand then? Big letters.'

Mel smiled. 'It'll be gone in a couple of hours, everyone will have been walking all over it.'

'Right then. Breakfast for two. And just in case the waiter doesn't pick up on the signs and go straight back down the kitchen and start spreading rumours, I'll phone down and order a second pot of coffee.'

'Hmm. That should do the trick.' Mel reached for the phone.

Breakfast for two never arrived. Rafe was still in the shower and Mel opened the door to her room, wondering why the waiter was hammering on it so insistently.

'Dr Murphy… I am looking for Dr Davenport, but I cannot find him…'

'Slow down.' She stepped back from the doorway, beckoning the concierge inside. 'Dr Davenport's here. What's happened?'

'One of the outdoor barbecues was damaged by the storm, and no one noticed. The cook has been burned.'

Rafe appeared, dressed in one of the hotel bathrobes,

and the concierge's eyebrows shot up. 'You go, Mel. I'll get dressed and be right behind you.'

The flash from the exploding barbecue had singed the cook's eyebrows and he had a burn on his arm, which was thankfully minor, although it would be painful for a couple of days. When she saw that his injuries weren't significant, Mel suggested that Rafe stopped cooling his heels in the medical suite and that he go and find out what had caused the barbecue to flare up so dangerously.

He returned with Mr Manike as Mel was dressing the cook's arm. After solicitous enquiries as to his employee's well-being, Mr Manike took the man off, leaving Mel and Rafe alone.

Rafe's hands and arms were covered in soot and he was leaning in the doorway, trying not to touch anything. Mel had been trying not to distract herself by looking at him.

'Did you find out what happened?'

He nodded. 'Yeah, one of the valves had started to leak. It's one of those accidents that can happen at any time. The barbecues were all covered and checked after the storm.'

'So no one missed anything?'

'No. Mr Manike's obviously not all that pleased, since he does his best to make everything safe and he doesn't want anyone hurt. But he knows he did all he could to prevent it.'

Sometimes you just had to let these things go. It was a lesson that Mel was learning. All of the checks and balances in the world probably wouldn't have averted this. Suddenly Rafe's attitude seemed a great deal more reassuring. He didn't try to quantify all of the things that might go wrong. He went out and got to grips with the cause of a problem and fixed it.

Maybe that was why she couldn't help but feel safe

when she was in his arms. Couldn't help but smile when she saw him rumpled and covered in grime from whatever task he happened to have got himself involved with.

'What?' He spread his arms, looking down to see if he'd got any soot on his clean shirt.

'Nothing. I was just thinking that you're very reassuring.'

He raised his eyebrows. 'That's nice to know, but I thought you found me reckless. I've been working on it.'

He had. Rafe had been telling her what he intended to do next and making decisions with her. She still didn't feel completely at ease with some of the things he did, but Rafe wasn't reckless.

'I've been working on things too. I have a feeling that being ready for anything is a lot more effective than making a list of what everything might include.' She smiled. 'Not that I'm completely convinced yet.'

He smiled. 'You shouldn't be. Lists are good too.'

They were starting to grow together. Learning to accommodate each other's way of doing things, taking the best and leaving what didn't work. Still different, but that didn't seem to grate any more.

And this was a new pleasure. Smiling at him across a room, the intimacy of last night still humming in her veins. Knowing that it was still a part of him too.

'I guess we've really done it now.' She held his gaze, looking for any sign of regret and saw none.

'Guess we have. I could probably justify taking you to dinner to watch a sunset, but I can't think of any good reason for being in your room first thing in the morning, dressed in a bathrobe.' He shrugged. 'Other than the truth, of course, which I don't have a single regret about.'

She had no regrets either. Maybe a few worries, but that was natural when you were embarking on something new. Mel was beginning to understand that her aim of leaving a lover without any questions in her mind at all had limited her choices. Caring what happened next was one of the things that had made last night so explosive.

'I don't either. And I'm happy if everyone knows.'

He grinned broadly. 'Really? Because we could send a much more obvious message...'

What was he up to now? Mel felt a tingle of excitement as he strode towards her. Soot on his hands, a smear on his brow...

'No! Rafe, no handprints!' She crossed her arms against her chest, backing away from him, laughing.

'Shh.' He put his finger against his lips, leaving a smudge. 'Anyone might be listening.'

She couldn't resist his teasing. When he reached for her, tracing his fingers against her cheek, she knew he must be leaving evidence of his caress. When he kissed her there would be more.

Who cared? What was soap and water for, anyway?

They'd been working together for over a week now and sleeping together for the last four nights, and it seemed odd to see Rafe flying away alone in the sea plane. But he had islands to visit, and Mel had patients here to deal with.

But when he came back again she could watch him shower. Today there was rather more mud than water streaming off his body, and the soap he was rubbing along his arms was developing a greenish tinge.

'What did doctoring include today then?'

'You're not going to believe a particularly muddy patient?' he enquired and Mel shook her head. 'Blocked water channel.'

'And dirty water means sick people.'

He grinned, nodding. 'Not yet, thankfully. Call it preventative medicine. What have you been up to?'

'I saw Izzy and her parents off on the boat to Male', along with a letter and the X-rays for her doctor at home. The two patients we brought over here yesterday are much better and I reckon we can discharge them tomorrow. And I went and spoke with Mr Manike this afternoon.'

'Yes? What did he say?'

'It was as we thought. He hasn't been sleeping. He's been doing so much to keep everything running smoothly, during and after the storm, that he just can't switch off at night. We had a long talk and he opened up about some other problems he's been having. He's on the brink of clinical exhaustion.'

'You told him that?'

'I told him that we were both very concerned about him and that he must try to slow down, before he becomes seriously ill. I went through all of the things that can help him, exercise, dietary changes and allowing himself time to wind down as much as possible before he goes to bed. If he still can't sleep I'll prescribe a mild sleeping tablet, but for starters I tried hot chocolate and bridge.'

'Bridge?'

Mel grinned. 'Yes, apparently he's a bridge player. So I rounded up a couple of the guests who play and managed to get him out of his office to make up a foursome. Then I sent him off home with instructions not to come back until tomorrow. Hopefully he'll get a good night's sleep and we can start getting him into a more healthy routine.'

The water was running clear now and Rafe stepped out of the shower. Mel wrapped a towel around his waist, stealing a kiss at the same time.

'Good thinking. Have you played before?'

Mel reckoned that Rafe probably had. His capacity for

just rolling up his sleeves and trying things out meant that he'd done a lot of things.

'No. Mr Manike explained all the rules very carefully, but I still ended up losing all my matchsticks and four ly-chees.'

'Maybe I'll challenge you to a game then.' He tugged at the fastening of her wraparound skirt. 'You could lose that instead of matchsticks and lychees.'

'Careful. I might improve suddenly and you'll be the one losing your shirt.' She tugged at the towel and Rafe grabbed at it.

'I'll take my chances. I might see if Mr Manike's up for a game tomorrow afternoon, to brush up my skills.'

Mel sat down on the side of the bathtub. Rafe was expecting her to leave him alone to dress, but that was one hundred and twenty seconds of pleasure that she wasn't going to get again.

'You don't like me watching you, do you?' She smiled at his hesitation in losing the towel. Rafe had no difficulty with nakedness when he was doing something, showering, swimming, making love. When she drew attention to it by watching him, he became uncharacteristically shy.

'I…don't get the appeal of it.' His hand went to his chest in the diffident gesture he always made when he caught Mel admiring his body.

'But you understand the other things I like so well…'

'That's not the same thing. I have my mind on you then.'

Mel focused on his face, reaching up to stroke his cheek. Passion ignited in his eyes, but that wasn't what she wanted at the moment. She wondered whether she could ask even more of him.

'Let's do something different, Rafe.' She knew that he couldn't resist *that* challenge.

* * *

This was hard. They'd undressed and Mel had propelled him into the bedroom, reclining on the opposite side of the huge bed. That was tough for starters, because he wanted to touch her. Then she'd taken the game a little further, and it had suddenly seemed as if it wasn't a game at all.

He'd been getting used to her watching him. Having her tell him everything she liked about his body was unexpectedly difficult. It was a workhorse, a machine. A means to an end that he fuelled regularly and took good care of. But in Mel's eyes he was a work of art, and that didn't sit too easily.

'I don't think I'm vain enough to believe you.'

'I don't think you're honest enough to believe me.'

Rafe couldn't help smiling. Mel's habit of saying what was on her mind was all the more appealing when she was naked. 'Cut to the chase, why don't you? I can think of far more things to say about you.'

She grinned. 'Go on then. I can take it.'

He let his gaze slip over her body. She didn't even flinch. 'You're in amazing shape. You've been working out pretty regularly, haven't you?'

'Yes, I have. I'm gratified you noticed. Makes it suddenly worth the effort.'

Okay. This he could do. 'And you don't dye your hair. You have a few strands of grey, but I really like that.'

'I'll have a few more before long. Grey seems to be all the rage these days.'

'You carry the look well. You carry your laughter lines well too.' He touched the side of his own eye and thought better of it in case Mel noticed *his* wrinkles.

'Yours give a lot of character to your face.'

Rafe shot her a reproachful look. 'It's my turn, isn't it?'

'Just saying. I can't help noticing these things.'

'I'm noticing that one of the things that makes you so stunningly beautiful is that you're comfortable in your own skin. You know who you are and what you are, and that's an incredibly sexy thing in a woman.'

'That's an amazing compliment, Rafe, thank you.' The slight flush in Mel's cheeks told him that she'd really liked what he'd said, even if he had only spoken the obvious truth.

An obvious truth that might well have some relevance to his own life. He'd run from his grief and, even though he didn't feel its sting any more, he still had the feeling that the passage of time wasn't necessarily a good thing. That leaving the past behind and living for today, meant that he'd lost the youth who had left England and fallen in love with Annu, and he was only just learning to value the man who was falling in love with Mel.

'Mel, can we stop this? I really want to touch you.' He *did* want to touch her, so very badly.

She nodded, her eyes darkening suddenly with desire. 'I can't resist you, Rafe…'

'Do you want to?' It occurred to him that on some level they were both resisting each other. Both realising that the other challenged the hard-won peace they'd found in their lives. He had a full and happy life here in Sri Lanka, and she had the same in England. Different lives, not just different places.

'No, I don't think I do.' Her gaze slowly moved down from his face, and he felt a throb of arousal. Rafe's hand moved instinctively to cover it and then he stopped himself.

'How about a compromise? You can watch me making love to you.'

He moved towards her on the bed and she reached for him. It seemed that she liked the compromise as much as he did.

CHAPTER FIFTEEN

IT HAD BEEN more than two weeks since Rafe had first met Mel. A relationship that had started in conflict and ended in perfect accord. Rafe woke in the bright clear light of early morning. Last night had been electrifying, and his body was still buzzing pleasantly with its memory.

With three days to go before Mel was due to leave and nothing really settled between them, it seemed that the physical was taking charge and showing them what they needed to know. How to beg a little. When to bend and when to break. How wanting something enough meant that it was possible to give up everything and still feel that you'd lost nothing. All of those strange contradictions that only made any sense when you admitted that you were in love.

And, despite his belief that loving and being loved happened just once in a lifetime, and then only if you were lucky, Rafe had to admit that he loved Mel. And that he was pretty darn sure she loved him back. The feeling that love might turn into loss had held him back, and he still didn't want to think about it. But he had to get a grip and hold onto this new and unexpected happiness. He reached for her, wondering if it was at last time to tell her, and found only an empty space in the bed, still warm from where she'd been lying.

The idea swirled in his head. New and precious, like an orb of light that seemed to reach every part of his being. Rafe got out of bed, throwing on his clothes. He knew exactly where Mel would be.

Mel saw him, walking along the beach towards her. Barefooted, his cream-coloured casual trousers rolled up to save the hems from the spray of the sea. Broad-chested, his polo shirt taut in all the right places. Still a little tousled from sleep and the morning breeze. Rafe was everything her heart wanted.

'Good morning.' She waited for him, greeting him with a kiss.

'I missed you.' He put his arm around her shoulders and they began to walk together in the surf. 'Looking for new horizons already?'

She'd been thinking about them. Wondering what they might be, and whether Rafe would be a part of them. The future had seemed incompatible with their hedonistic enjoyment of the moment, but more and more it seemed that there were promises to be made. Those promises had been on the tip of her tongue more than once in the last few days, and she'd seen them in Rafe's eyes too.

'I was considering them.' She still didn't quite know how to put it all into words. Ever since Michael had smashed her horizons to pieces she'd carefully removed them from any man's grasp.

'Me too. I…' He stopped suddenly, taking her hand and raising it to his lips. 'Mel, I can't imagine a time when those horizons don't include you.'

She caught her breath. This was everything she'd been wanting Rafe to say to her, and yet now that he'd said it she was afraid. Maybe fear was a good thing. It sharpened the mind and helped you get things right.

'I can't imagine that either.'

'This is a hard thing for me to ask but…would you consider staying on for a little while? A few weeks. Months maybe, if you could take that amount of time off work.'

Months. Maybe. Disappointment made her pull away from him.

'Rafe, I… I can't do that. I mean I probably could. I'm self-employed and I've deliberately set my work up to be flexible. But how can I spend just weeks with you and then go home again?'

He pressed his lips together, and for once Mel couldn't see what he was thinking. 'I thought…if you came to Colombo with me, then you could see how things work at the hospital there. See my home…'

'And then go back to London?'

'I didn't say that. Then we do whatever we want to do.'

Go with the flow. Swim with the tide. Rafe could allow things to work themselves through without being crippled by anxiety. Mel had learned to live with that, enjoy it even, but now that they were about to take the next step in their relationship her fears resurfaced, hitting her hard. What if she fell back into that downward spiral of anxiety, which would leave Rafe's own adventurous spirit no room to breathe?

'I can't do that, Rafe. I'm sorry. I really need some kind of plan.'

She could see the hurt in his eyes. Feel it in her own heart. And then he backed away from her, shaking his head.

'I'm sorry too, Mel. I love you, and I don't want you to be uncertain about the future. But I need more time and a little more space to come to terms with the idea that committing myself for a second time won't ultimately lead to loss. If you could just trust me…'

'You can't leave it behind, can you? The past…'

'No more than you can. But give it time. I really believe that we can get there.'

Could she accept Rafe's commitment to today, without knowing what the future held? Mel wanted to share his sure belief that the future would take care of itself and that it didn't need to be planned out, but the wash of anxiety at the thought told her that this was a step she couldn't take.

'I know it's a great deal to ask, particularly since we haven't known each other for very long. But how can you believe in something so fully, when you still don't know how and when you're going to do it? If you're going to do it, even.'

'Because…' he shrugged '…I just do. I know that I love you.'

'Then talk to me. We'll both put all of our cards on the table and we'll figure something out. We've worked out how to make decisions together already, and this is just a bigger, harder decision.'

'One that we can make when we're ready. Give it a little time.'

This couldn't be happening. Not like this. Mel had known it would be hard, but surely it wasn't impossible. Rafe wasn't asking so very much of her, and she wasn't asking much of him. It was just the sting in the scorpion's tail, that neither of them could give what the other asked.

'I can't give you something I don't have, Rafe. I know myself, and I need to know what I'm going to do next. Without that, everything will just spin out of control and I'll let anxiety destroy everything we have.'

His face hardened. 'Then there's only one thing to do. We end it right now.'

The shock stunned Mel into silence for a moment. His

quicksilver, impetuous heart didn't know how to stop him from acting, once he knew what he had to do.

Rafe turned and walked away. And Mel couldn't stop him, because she knew in her own heart that he'd done the right thing.

Mel was packed and ready to go. She'd managed to get a last-minute seat on a flight from Male' to Colombo, and when she got there she'd hole up in an airport hotel for a couple of days until her holiday flight back to London. It wasn't going to be the best of journeys, but it was better than being here, on a small island with the man who had broken her heart.

She couldn't even bring herself to hate him for it. They'd been under pressure and their fears had reared up and smacked them both in the face. And Rafe had put an end to it all, before it could be taken from him. She'd seen the sea plane climb in the sky, and she had no idea where he was going or when he'd be back.

There was only one person she had to say goodbye to. Mr Manike was sitting in his office, and when she knocked and entered he sprang to his feet.

'Dr Murphy.' The formality belied the warmth of his tone. 'What can I do for you?'

'I came to say goodbye, Mr Manike. And to thank you for everything you've done to help keep us safe here. I know it's been a gruelling task.'

Mr Manike smiled. 'And you came to my aid when it threatened to overwhelm me. You are leaving so soon?'

'It's time, Mr Manike. I need to go home.' Mel almost choked on the words, blinking furiously behind her sunglasses. 'But I'll be writing to you as soon as I get back to London, to find out how you are.'

Mr Manike nodded an acknowledgement. 'May I dissuade you?'

'No. I just need you to get me a speedboat over to Male', by six this evening. I have a flight to Colombo at eight.'

'Without Dr Davenport?' Mr Manike pressed his lips together. 'Dr Murphy, I must tell you that sunglasses are a poor disguise for tears. And that, as manager of this hotel, I would not be doing my job if I did not know where all my guests are sleeping.'

He hadn't even hinted that he knew. Mel supposed that walking around the island holding hands was a pretty sure clue, and imagined that most of the staff and a few of the other guests knew as well. But Mr Manike always seemed so separate from everyone else.

There was no point in the sunglasses any more. Mel took them off and Mr Manike handed her a well-pressed cotton handkerchief from his pocket.

'It's not his fault, Mr Manike.'

'Not yours either, unless I am very much mistaken.'

'No. We're just different. And I don't want to be here for another three days just being angry with him over things that neither of us can change.'

Mr Manike took a deep breath, folding his hands together on the table. 'Dr Murphy, I owe you a great debt. You have used what should have been a holiday to take care of others here, including myself.'

Mel smiled. 'Yes, I'm going to be checking on whether you take the holiday you promised to. And you owe me nothing. The fact that you're looking much better now is reward enough for me.'

'You are very kind. Mushan will be waiting to escort you to Male' and safely onto your flight, as soon as you are ready. You have a reservation for a hotel in Colombo?'

'I can stay at the airport hotel...' Mr Manike had put

two and two together and guessed that she'd be waiting for her scheduled flight home.

'I will arrange your reservation.' Mr Manike opened his desk drawer and drew out a thick card, embellished with the name of a hotel. 'The manager is a personal friend and I will call him now.'

'Thank you...' Maybe this was all getting too real, and the idea that she was leaving Rafe was finally sinking in. Maybe Mr Manike's kindness. Mel wiped the tears from her eyes.

'Dr Murphy. I would like to ask one more thing of you.'

'Of course...'

'Dr Davenport is a good man. Please consider the past, but do not allow it to rule you.'

Rafe had returned to Nadulu and found Mel gone. Hadn't that been exactly what he'd wanted her to do, to go before he had a chance to beg her to stay?

All Mel had asked him for was some kind of plan. He could have stopped all of this and made one with her, but he wouldn't lie to her and he knew she would have seen through his deceit anyway. She knew that she loved him, but that he needed a little time to drill it into his thick skull that love didn't always mean loss.

They'd been blinded, by passion and the belief that somehow they could both change. Maybe they could, but they just hadn't had the time to do it. The best thing he could do now was to face it, and to leave before he hurt her any more than he already had.

All the same, he'd been tempted to take the sea plane and go after her, but it was late in the evening and sea planes were forbidden to fly after dark. Paralysed with fear, that Mel was lost somewhere, in an unfamiliar city and on her own, he went to find Mr Manike. If anyone

would know where she'd gone then he would, and maybe
Rafe could contact someone who would find Mel and make
sure she was safe.

'I understand your concern, Dr Davenport, and admit to
having shared it. I had Dr Murphy escorted to her aircraft
in Male', and she was picked up at the airport in Colombo
and taken to a hotel run by a personal friend of mine. She is
there now, and will be escorted onto her flight to London.'

Rafe breathed a sigh of relief. Mr Manike had stepped
into the breach and made all the arrangements needed.

'Tell me which hotel, Mr Manike.' He tried to keep his
voice level.

'No.' Mr Manike folded his hands on the desk in front
of him.

'You mean you don't know?'

'You insinuate that I would allow Dr Murphy to go to
an unknown hotel, Dr Davenport?' Mr Manike's tone be-
trayed his outrage at the thought.

'No…no, of course not. You're not going to tell me
though?'

'Dr Murphy asked me not to, and I will not break my
word.'

Mel had made the same decision he had. He'd walked
away from her, knowing it was the right thing to do, and
she'd packed her bags and done her own piece of walking.
He took a breath, trying to steady himself.

'Fair enough. You've acted in Mel's best interests and
I'm grateful to you for that. I'm sorry you had to get mixed
up in this…'

'It has been a matter of some regret to me too. I did
offer one thought…'

Rafe didn't want to hear it. There was nothing that
anyone could say which would make this any easier. He
needed time before he risked believing in a plan for their

future together and Mel couldn't give it to him. It was as simple as that.

'That's between you and Dr Murphy too. Will you do me a favour, my friend?'

'Of course.'

'You shouldn't be in your office this late. Shall I see if I can find another pair for a rubber of bridge before you turn in for the night?'

Mr Manike beamed suddenly. 'I think we might both benefit from that. I will order a nightcap...'

Mel had been back in England for three weeks. She wasn't exactly sure, but her impression was that not one day had passed without rain.

Not warm rain. Not heavy rain. The kind that soaked insidiously into your jacket, and trickled icy fingers down your neck. The kind that suited her mood completely, because without Rafe everything was grey and cold.

Ash was a problem. Mel had promised to call him and she didn't want to let him down, but she didn't want to put Ash in a difficult position either.

Maddie came up with the answer.

'I'll get in touch with him. I'll say you're out of town, and that you've passed his number on to me. I might even be a bit more use to him than you are. He wants to specialise in surgery, you say?'

'Yes, you're a lot more relevant to what he wants to do than I am. Do you mind?'

'No. I mind that you won't call his father.'

'We're done, Maddie. Rafe's a great guy but we're not compatible. I made the right decision.'

'Which is why you're so happy about it.'

Mel stared miserably at the table between them. Maybe

she shouldn't have suggested this coffee shop. The music was making her want to cry.

'Why does this place always have to play these…songs?'

'You never minded it before.' Maddie took a sip of her cappuccino. 'And that's a case in point, Mel. If you can't stand an ever so slightly sad song about love, then that says it all. Trust me, I know these things.'

'Maybe I should call Rafe. Just apologise to him and end things properly.'

Maddie rolled her eyes. 'No! If what you want is to end things, then it's already done. Finished. You either let it go or you call him and tell him you want to start things up again. Apologise if you like. I don't think that matters one way or another.'

'It matters. I just walked away.'

'If someone had asked me to give up my job and go on a three-month jaunt around Sri Lanka I'd have thought twice about it as well.'

'He didn't exactly say that.' Mr Manike's words echoed in Mel's head. Consider the past but don't allow it to rule you.

Maddie puffed out a sigh. 'Okay, well, you know what I'd do?'

'No.'

'You're trying to find a way to end well, and there isn't one. Accept that you're not done with the guy yet, and decide where you want to go from there.'

Rafe arrived back from Nadulu, slinging his bag down in the hall. Everything was going well in that part of the world. Everything seemed to be going well back in Colombo. There were no messages for him at the hospital, no requests for urgent medical help. He slumped down onto the sofa. Everything was going so well that he just might drown his sorrows and get very drunk tonight.

His phone rang, and he answered it. *Please* let this be someone who needed his urgent and single-minded attention. Someone who would stop him feeling the grief over losing Mel.

'Rafe Davenport.'

'Hello…?'

The caller didn't need to introduce herself. He knew exactly who it was. Rafe sprang to his feet.

'It's Mel.'

'Mel. How are you?'

'Good. You?'

'Yes, I'm good too.'

Silence. Was this what Mel had called for? Had she hung up? Terror at the thought made him blurt something—anything out.

'Mr Manike's well.'

'Ah, good. He's been getting some rest, has he?'

'Yes, and he's spoken to the owners of the hotel and told them he needs an assistant. They agreed immediately. They know that he runs the place like clockwork. He's far too valuable to them to lose.'

Three whole sentences. Rafe congratulated himself.

'That's great. I got an email from him the other day, and he said that he'd been well.'

So Mel wasn't phoning about Mr Manike. Rafe searched his mind for something else to say.

'Ash got a very nice message from your friend Maddie the other day.'

'Ah, good. He didn't mind me passing his number on?'

'No, he's grateful for her help. I appreciate her time.'

'She's more than pleased to do it.'

Another silence. Rafe decided to wait this time, to see if Mel would say something.

'I'm glad you're well, Rafe.'

'Thanks. I'm very happy to hear that you're well.'

'I'll…um… I'd better let you go.'

'Yes…' Rafe grimaced. He hadn't meant that. He'd meant, *No, don't go, because I need to talk to you.*

'Right, then. I'll… Nice to speak to you, Rafe.'

The line went dead. Rafe stared at his phone.

'Hello…? Mel…?'

What was that all about? Suddenly Rafe knew exactly what it was about. Mr Manike hadn't been the only person at the hotel who had wondered aloud whether Rafe would like to talk. Ash had made a point of taking him for lunch when he'd arrived back at the hospital and talked.

Mel had friends. Maddie must know what had happened, and in Rafe's experience that meant talking. Everyone had been talking apart from the two people who really needed to talk, because they'd broken each other's hearts.

And that was going to have to change. Right now.

CHAPTER SIXTEEN

RAIN. AGAIN. IT had been almost two days since Mel had called Rafe, and all she'd been able to think about was how she'd made things worse. She hadn't ended well, or opened a line of communication. She didn't even have the consolation of having said what she wanted to say.

Maybe she should call again. Maybe she should just let it alone. There must be a third option because the first hadn't worked so well and the second was utterly impossible.

The doorbell was a welcome diversion. It would take at least a minute to take a parcel in for next door, and that would be one minute that she wasn't thinking about Rafe and wondering what to do next. Only when she answered the door it appeared that finally stress had got the better of her, and she was now hallucinating.

'Mel.'

'Rafe.' That was all Mel could think of to say.

'Mel, you were right and I was wrong. I walked away when you needed me the most, and I let you think that I didn't care enough to work things out. But I love you, and I'll go down on my bended knees and ask you to forgive me, and to marry me. And…live with me, wherever you want to live. Have sex with me whenever you're so inclined.'

Mel stared at him. Clearly he hadn't planned what he

wanted to say to her. He'd just been the Rafe that she was irreversibly in love with and gone with the flow.

'Do you want to come in first?'

He looked around at the wet garden and dropped his holdall on a dry spot in the porch. 'I could do it here…'

'Rafe! This is England, not a tropical island. People don't just fall to their knees proposing all over the place.' She reached forward, grabbing the front of his jacket and pulling him inside. Rafe staggered over the step and into the hall, managing to catch up the handles of his bag as he went.

'Here, then.'

'You're serious?' Bright warmth had suddenly flooded into Mel's world, and she wanted nothing more than to feel Rafe's arms around her.

He held his hands out in front of him. They were shaking. 'Mel, I've never been any more serious about anything. When you called me I knew that it wasn't over between us. And I knew that we had to stop talking to other people, and talk to each other.'

'In that case…' Rafe was clearly in a bad way over this and there was only one thing to be done. Only one thing she wanted to do. Mel stood on her toes, wrapping her arms around his neck and kissing him.

'Mel…stop.' His whole body was shaking, but he kissed her with the same hunger that he'd always shown. 'You deserve an explanation.'

'I know what happened, Rafe. We loved each other and it just became too hard to bear. It was too much for us to realise that this was something different and that it wouldn't end the way everything else has for us.'

He nodded. 'That's fair. But I was the one who acted badly.'

'We both acted badly. And now we're going to repair

that. Because, for the first time in our lives, we're in a place where we can.'

He was staring at her, obviously considering what to do next. Mel knew. It was what she always should have done next. She pulled off his jacket, hanging it on a peg in the hall. Underneath he was wearing a thick sweater and a shirt. Maybe a T-shirt underneath that. Layers of clothes were a new experience and for a moment she savoured the thought.

She started to back up the stairs. 'Rafe, if I get to the top and you haven't got me in your arms, I'm going to order you out of this house…'

Suddenly he was all motion and action. The man she loved, sweeping her off her feet and carrying her upstairs. He made a lucky guess that her bedroom was the one at the front of the house and nudged the door open with his foot.

'Nice bedroom…' He pinned her against the wall, kissing her.

'Clothes, Rafe. Get your clothes *off.* You can admire the decorations later.'

Making love with Rafe was never going to be a hurried affair. It was almost dark by the time they'd got out of bed, and Mel led him downstairs and into the sitting room. She left him looking at the titles on her bookshelves while she went into the kitchen to fetch a bottle of champagne that had been sitting at the back of the refrigerator for months.

He grinned when he saw the bottle and two glasses, wresting the cork from the champagne with practised ease. 'Before we have too much of this, there are some things we need to discuss.'

That was okay now. They were both ready to move forward and make a life together. Mel sat down on the sofa and when Rafe joined her she tipped her glass against his.

'Here's to finding the right path, then.'

He nodded, taking a sip from his glass. 'You have a lovely home, Mel. You have a great career and a life. I understand that you've worked hard for that, and for your peace of mind, and I never want to take that from you.'

'If I couldn't leave then it would turn into a prison, however comfortable it is.'

He kissed her forehead. 'Being able to leave it all behind isn't a reason to actually do it, Mel. Why don't I start with my plan, and then we'll negotiate?'

'Okay. Sounds fair.'

'I want you to marry me. We can keep the house in Sri Lanka on for the time being, because it would be great to be able to go and visit Ash from time to time, but I'll give up my job in Colombo and find one here. We'll be together, and we can either stay in this house or get another one between us. Whatever you want.'

'Hmm.' Mel pursed her lips. 'I like the being together part, very much.'

'That's a good start…' His eyes flickered with humour. 'And the rest?'

'I see us spending the winter in Sri Lanka. Then coming back here to London for the summer. You can show me all of the things you love about Sri Lanka, and I'll reacquaint you with all of the things you used to love about London.'

Rafe thought for a moment. 'I can organise a six-month break from work if you can. And I'm sure there's plenty to keep someone of your expertise busy in Colombo if that's what you want.'

'Likewise, London needs your talents too. So that's settled?'

'Yeah, it's a really good plan. Where would you like to get married?'

'I'm…thinking we won't get married. Not just yet, anyway.'

He stared at her. 'Okay, I'll be honest with you. That's a disappointment. May I ask why?'

'It's not that I don't want to marry you, Rafe. I just want a little time for us to live with our promises. I love you, and I trust you. That means that I can walk away from the past, and my anxiety about the future. I want to show both of us that I can.'

He nodded. 'I think I understand that. In that case, I'll promise you right now that I will love you the way you should be loved, and that I won't leave you. You have my word, and everything that I am, on that.'

'I promise you too, Rafe. I'm going to love you well, and I'm not going to leave you.' She flung her arms around his neck, kissing him. 'I'm so happy. You've made me so happy...'

'May I ask one more thing of you?'

'Yes, of course.'

He got to his feet, walking out into the hallway and feeling in an inside pocket of his jacket. When he returned, sitting down next to her on the sofa, he slipped a ring box into her hand, curling his own hands around hers.

'I know you don't want to get married right now. I respect that, and I think we both need some time to understand that the promises we've made are real and lasting. But will you take this, as a symbol of those promises? You don't have to wear it, just keep it safe...'

'I'd like to wear it.' Rafe's sudden smile told her that he'd like that too.

He took the ring from its box. A clear blue sapphire mounted on a plain band. The stone needed nothing else in the way of adornment, and when he slipped it onto her finger it flashed in the lamplight. Mel caught her breath.

'Rafe! It's beautiful. Whenever did you get the time to buy this?'

He pressed his lips together, looking almost apologetic. 'On the way to the airport. I'd been trying to live without you, telling myself that it was best for both of us, and then you called. I knew I had to come and…'

Mel was laughing now. 'So you dropped everything and went to the airport, buying a ring on the way?' It was the nicest thing he could have done. So like Rafe, and his love of movement and action.

'Almost. I called the hospital first to tell them I was going to England on an urgent personal matter. And I know a little jewellery shop where I was bound to get something nice, which does just happen to be on the way to the airport—' He fell silent as Mel laid her finger across his lips.

'Stop. I love that you decided to come and just did it. And I love the ring as well. It's perfect.'

'I'll make an effort to plan things a little more in the future.' He smiled down at her.

'Don't. Please don't change, because you're the man that I'll always love, just as you are. The one I'm *going* to marry.'

He picked up the two champagne glasses, handing Mel's to her. 'Take all the time you want to think about it. Because persuading you is going to be my greatest pleasure.'

They'd spent six months in Sri Lanka, living in Rafe's house in the hills and working out of the hospital in Colombo, travelling together to the parts of the island where they were most needed. Rafe had been proud of Mel's determination to make the most of her stay, and his adopted country had given her so much in return. Then six months in London. He'd forgotten how much he loved London in the summertime, and Rafe had rediscovered the pleasures of living in the city where he was born. Ash had been staying with them for the last three weeks, and Mel had introduced him to several very senior surgeons from her contacts list, who had been pleased to chat with a young doctor about ways he could pursue his ambitions.

He and Mel had kept their promises. They'd loved each other sincerely and completely, a love that had grown deeper every day. And then Mel had said the one word that had made them consult the map again.

Yes.

It appeared that getting married was far more complicated than just finding a presentable suit, a fabulous dress and someone to marry them. In the end, as they were drinking coffee on the patio after a leisurely Sunday lunch with Ash, Amy and her husband Ben, the matter came to a head.

'We're staging an intervention.' Amy had clearly been elected to speak for all three of them.

'Really?' Rafe suppressed a smile as Mel made a very good job of feigning surprise.

'Yes, really, Mum. You and Rafe are going to make a decision about your wedding.'

'Ah. Well, now you mention it, we really should come to some decision, shouldn't we, Rafe? Let's hear it then, darling.'

'I've canvassed your friends…' Mel's eyebrows shot up at the thought, and Amy started again. 'Actually, I just called Maddie, and she said she'd love an excuse for a holiday in Sri Lanka and she was sure a few other people would as well.'

'But what about Gramps and Grandma?'

'We talked about it when I took Ash round to see them the other day. They say they're up for it, and Ash says that they'll have no shortage of invitations for trips out from the family.'

Mel looked up at Rafe and he nodded.

'No shortage at all. But we're not getting married without you three.'

'Well, then, that's perfect, because Ben and I would really like to go to Sri Lanka and I'm dying to see your house there after all of those gorgeous photos that Mum brought back. Ash says he'll show us around while you're off on your honeymoon.'

'Yes, I'll take them to Kandy, and the rock fortress at Sigiriya. Maybe Yala National Park,' Ash broke in. 'As long as you don't have any of those places in mind. We wouldn't want to crowd you.'

'That all sounds lovely. What do you think, Rafe?' Mel nudged him in the ribs.

'They seem to have everything covered. The guest house is plenty big enough for your parents along with Amy and Ben, and we can put everyone else up in the house. Have the reception in the garden, maybe put up a tent.'

'A marquee.' Ash clarified the arrangement for Amy and Ben's sake. 'It's a very big garden.'

'So what do you say?' Amy beamed triumphantly, and Rafe shot Mel a grin.

'Well, if Mel's happy with the idea I certainly am. Thanks for the intervention, guys. That was really helpful.'

Rafe put the coffee cups into the sink and turned to put his arms around Mel. 'Looks as if we're going to Sri Lanka, then.'

'So it does. Only Amy forgot Mr Manike.'

'That's okay. I'll give him a call tomorrow, and ask him to come across for the wedding. Well done, darling.'

Mel laughed. 'I knew that Amy wouldn't be able to resist stepping in if I told her we just couldn't make a decision. It makes everything so much easier if they think it's their idea.'

'What's next then? After the honeymoon.'

'We've both got a few job offers, here and in Sri Lanka. What do you say we just go with the flow and see where life leads us?'

Rafe kissed her. 'That sounds like a great plan. We'll do that.'

* * * * *

ONE-NIGHT FLING IN POSITANO

ANN McINTOSH

MILLS & BOON

For all who long to wander,
but have found their way impeded.

And for Nic, whose unfailing belief in me
means more than she can ever know!

CHAPTER ONE

THE PATH TO Spiaggia Tordigliano wasn't easy to find, but luckily Kendra Johnson had help in the form of Lejla and Ahmed Graovac, who knew the beach well.

"The top of the trail isn't on most maps," Ahmed explained, as they made their way down the narrow, stony path. "It's more of a local beach, popular especially with boaters, and not that many tourists come here, even in the high season."

That was exactly the type of place Kendra had asked the Graovac siblings to tell her about after meeting them in Naples and striking up conversation. In her experience, it was far better to go to the places the locals did. That was when you got the real flavor of an area or country.

What she hadn't expected was that the siblings would take the day off in the middle of the week to take her sightseeing.

"There isn't much to do right now," Lejla explained, when Kendra asked if she didn't have to be at work. "The owner of the café where I waitress will probably be happy not to have to pay me. Once the tourists start coming, though, I'll be working nonstop."

"And I want to practice my English," Ahmed interjected, sending Kendra a brilliant smile. "If I make it better, it will be easier to find work."

"How about you speak English, and I'll answer in Italian," she suggested, grinning back. "I need to practice for my upcoming job."

Which was how she ended up on the small path winding down from the main road toward the sea, tall grasses on either side brushing her legs and a fresh spring breeze blowing up from below.

"Tell me about Canada," Ahmed said, slowing down so that Kendra caught up to him.

"Don't mind him," Lejla interjected. "He's obsessed with North America. Keeps talking about going there to live."

"Not North America. Canada," her brother replied, sending her a scowl. "I heard that Canada is a polite, beautiful place, and one day I want to see it for myself. All of it. Polar bears. Everything."

Kendra chuckled. "That would take you a very long time. Canada is a huge country."

"Maybe so. But I hear from my friend's cousin who lives there that it is wonderful. Full of opportunity."

Not wanting to burst his bubble but trying to be honest, Kendra replied, "It's not that different from other places I've been. There are all kinds of people everywhere, and opportunities for some, but not always for others."

In a way, she could understand Ahmed's enthusiasm for somewhere he'd never seen. Wasn't that the same impulse that kept her traveling from place to place, and made her a bit indifferent to her homeland?

Much of the last six years had been spent traveling to different countries, working a few months here, a few there, immersing herself in the various cultures. The worldwide pandemic had put her plan of working her way around as much of the world as possible on pause.

She'd been in Dubai when the worst of the virus hit,

and luckily enough her contract teaching English had been extended, becoming a remote job. However, even with her students to talk to during the week, weathering the isolation had been difficult. Oh, she liked her alone time as much as the next person—probably more—but it had been the one time she'd wished she'd been back in Toronto. There, at least, she could possibly have formed a bubble with her aunt and cousins, or gone back to hospital work, doing her part to fight the virus.

Dubai was supposed to be just a short stop in a place she'd heard so much about but never visited. Planning to stay only a month or so, she hadn't applied for a work visa, or for a nursing job. Being offered the teaching position had been happenstance but she'd seen the four-month stint as a way to save up a bit more cash, and taken it. Instead, it had turned into almost total solitary confinement, lasting more than eighteen months.

How glad she was to be on the move again!

The job in the village of Minori, on the Italian Amalfi Coast, had come through at just the right moment. She'd gotten to Italy at the beginning of May, and her stint at the clinic was scheduled from the beginning of June to the end of October. Spending six months exploring this lovely country felt like heaven, and looking around at the bright springtime sky, Kendra couldn't help grinning.

Maybe it was the enforced confinement she'd just escaped that made her think it was the most beautiful day she'd ever seen.

"Italy isn't to my liking," Ahmed said, his nose wrinkling slightly. "Our parents should have tried to get to Canada when they fled Bosnia."

"They didn't have that option, Ahmed." If Lejla's tone was any indication, this wasn't the first time she'd heard her younger brother say so. "Don't be a brat."

Ahmed huffed, and sent his sister a glare. "We'd be better off if they had. And if I lived in Canada I would never want to leave, the way I want to escape Italy."

Just then they turned a corner in the path and the vista below opened up.

Kendra stopped, her breath catching in her throat for a moment as a wave of emotion overtook her, causing the sound of the argument going on behind her to fade into insignificance.

The land and seascapes were a study in greens, grays and blues, bordered by the darkness of the rocks and sand, elevated to almost mythical splendor by the glint of sun on the water. Outside of the cove, on the open water, a fishing boat went by at what seemed a leisurely pace, the bright red of her hull adding the perfect splash of contrasting color. A little closer to shore a small sailboat tacked, the white of its sail like a friendly flag, waving.

There was no real comparison between the scene below and the coast of Nova Scotia, where she'd lived until she was ten, but a wash of longing made her eyes prickle anyway.

Open water, especially the sea, always spoke to her, no matter where she was. It was the voice of her childhood. Whatever mood it was in, whether murmuring, splashing or roaring, it took her back to a time of peace, contentment and joy. More than anything else, it made her think of Dad. Of his laughter, booming voice and sudden rages that never scared her because they were so transient—gone in a blink—with the laughter coming back right on their heels.

She'd gotten that from him. Both the temper and the tendency to laugh often, and she was glad of it. He'd been wonderful, and she missed him every day.

Losing him so young, she knew her memories were probably skewed, but no less precious for that fact. And the sea was equally precious, since it invariably brought those reminiscences back.

"And if I lived here," she whispered to herself, thinking about what Ahmed had said moments before, "I might never want to leave."

Still arguing in what she assumed was their native language, the Graovacs passed her and went down the path toward the beach, but Kendra wasn't ready to follow yet. Held in place by the stark, almost harsh beauty spread out before her, she took a deep breath of salty air and simply allowed herself to *feel*.

The cool, briny breeze against her face, overlaying the warmth of the sun.

An almost spiritual call of rocks that looked as though carved with a serrated blade, set against the dazzling blues of the water and sky.

With the stony grays and black sand, it should have been a dour scene, but it wasn't. Instead, for Kendra, it evoked a strange, joyous recognition, although she'd never been here before.

The slap of the waves breaking, the rustle of the wind through the grass and the trill of a bird were the only sounds, now that her companions had moved out of earshot. A complete contrast to the fervent rush and noise of Naples, with its constant motion and chatter. While the city had provided all the friendly faces and excitement she'd been missing, the peace and tranquility here spoke directly to her soul.

"Mi scusi."

The deep voice, coming from directly behind her, startled Kendra out of her trance.

"Oh," she said, turning. But the apology she planned to proffer died on her tongue, as she looked up into a pair of midnight-dark eyes, and was once more washed with a nameless, unrecognizable emotion.

He wasn't really handsome. His face was too broad, his nose too beaky and his lips a tad too thin for him to be considered classically good-looking. His hair was as dark as his eyes, curling wildly in the ocean breeze, giving him a tousled, just-out-of-bed look. He was also tall and broad—barrel-chested and thick of trunk—but not, she thought, fat. Just a large, solid type of man, his shape very different from the body types worshipped in the fashion magazines or on the silver screen. The kind of man who would make even a woman as big-boned and hefty as herself feel feminine and, if not tiny, then perhaps *dainty*.

Effortlessly elegant, even in casual clothes, just one glance at him set Kendra's heart racing in the silliest way, and left her completely, utterly tongue-tied.

So, instead of trying to say another word, she stepped aside to let him pass.

With a murmured *"Grazie,"* he strode off down the path without a backward glance, while she stood there watching him until he disappeared.

Wondering when, if ever, her heart would return to a normal pace, and this sensation of light-headedness would go away.

"Kendra. Aren't you coming? We still need to get over to the other side where the beach is nicer."

"I'm coming," she called back to Ahmed, forcing her legs to move, when they really didn't feel strong enough to hold her up.

It was just the surprise of having that huge man sneak up on her, she told herself, as she followed her friend toward the rocks on the right-hand side of the beach.

Nothing more.

Although, she had to admit she'd been drawn to him in

the weirdest way. That in itself was amusing, since on the whole the Italian men she'd met so far really hadn't piqued her interest. Not that there weren't some who were attractive. Even some whom she could honestly say were almost stunningly handsome. Yet, although she'd so far enjoyed the man-watching, not one pair of slumberous eyes or a wide, bright smile had given her pause.

Until now.

Mind you, with the way she was feeling, she wouldn't mind indulging herself with a night or two of passion. The last time she'd had sex...

She actually had to stop and think about it, to figure out how long it had actually been.

Maybe Mick, in Hong Kong?

He'd been a good, if uninspired, lover, who'd wanted her to stay there even though she'd been up-front with him about her plans to move on. It had certainly soured her last couple of weeks in the special administrative region of China, and she and Mick had parted on rather frosty terms.

At least on his side.

She didn't have the time or the energy to get upset with people, especially since she knew she wouldn't be around long enough for it to make a big difference in her life. However, she also wasn't in the habit of jollying people out of their snits.

That was all on them, and above her pay grade.

Climbing a ladder, and then scrambling over the rocks, revealed the other side of Spiaggia Tordigliano. And there, already about halfway down the beach, was the man from the path, sitting on the sand, an open book on his lap.

Maybe if she wasn't with Ahmed and Lejla she'd have been tempted to mosey on down that way and interrupt his reading. Just the thought made her smile to herself. Daydreams and lust from a distance were all well and good, but she was wise enough, and careful enough, not to give in to that kind of impulse.

After all, he could be a wandering serial killer, for all she knew!

"What are you smiling about?" Ahmed sent her a curious look, as he held out a hand to help her down from the last rocky ledge.

Ignoring his silent offer of help, Kendra hopped down on her own, grinning back at him.

"Nothing really. It's just so beautiful here, I can't help smiling."

He cast his gaze around, and then shrugged slightly.

"It's okay, and I like that it's rarely full of people, but I'm sure you've seen more beautiful places."

Lejla had brought a blanket for them to sit on, and they spread it on the sand. Kendra kicked off her shoes and sat, then lay back, reclining up on her elbows so she could take in the ocean view and watch the sea ebb and flow onto the shore.

Three small motorboats were anchored in the bay, and the music and laughter of their inhabitants carried across the water. Ahmed was once more asking about Canada, and Kendra answered his questions while watching the waves. The sailboat she'd noticed earlier came back into view, closer to shore now, and she could see what looked like a man and a child in the vessel. Farther out at sea, a large luxury yacht was just disappearing around the headland.

The sailboat tacked again and then, as Kendra watched, the child moved from the bow and scrambled to where the man sat in the stern, and they began to switch places.

Probably a sailing lesson, she thought, smiling as she remembered going out with her own father for just the same purpose, and performing the same maneuver.

The child was in position, the man just turning to sit in the bow, when the boat rocked violently and the boom swung. Instinctively, she shouted a warning, watching in horror as the man was struck on the side of the head, and went over into the water.

Kendra was already on her feet, dark glasses tossed aside as she pulled her shirt off over her head.

"Kendra, what...?"

"Try to get someone to help the child in the boat," she said, making it an order, rather than a request. Lejla jumped to her feet and gave a strangled cry, obviously realizing what was happening, and pointed to where the sailboat headed out to sea, the child in it screaming for his or her father.

Kendra had her shorts off already and ran for the water, adrenaline pumping so her heart hammered and her focus narrowed to the last point where she'd seen the man.

The frigid water hardly registered as she ran in and then did a shallow dive. Her strong arms and legs, along with her training in water rescue, served her well in getting her out to where she thought she needed to be, but there was no sign of the boater.

Taking a deep breath, she dived, searching beneath the waves, turning in a circle, aware of the current wanting to pull her farther down, and away.

Nothing.

Stroking strongly to the surface, she took another breath, and dived again, now letting the current guide her, hoping it would drag her in the right direction.

There.

A shadow, sinking, floating away.

No time for another breath.

Swimming down, down, grabbing hold of an arm,

then making for the sunlight that suddenly looked to be miles away.

When she finally broke the surface again, Kendra gasped in needed air, even while tugging the man's head above water, and arranging him in a rescue hold.

Then she was flutter-kicking, as hard as she could, back toward the shore, ignoring the almost sickening pounding of her heart, the ache in her lungs, her full concentration on keeping the man's face above water and getting him to dry land.

Something brushed against her arm, but before she could even think to be scared, a dark head hove into her line of sight. Surprised, Kendra's gaze collided with a pair of black, fathomless eyes set in a strong, square, instantly recognizable face.

There was no time to register much more than that, before that deep voice said, "Let me take him."

It took her a moment to interpret his words. Her Italian was passable, but she'd never considered having to use it under quite these circumstances, with her nerves jangling and her heart pounding so she could barely hear him.

"No."

She made her voice firm, adding a quick shake of her head for emphasis, and was pleased when he took her at her word. Rather than insist, he simply kept pace with her until she got to the shallows. Only then did he move to assist her to carry the man up onto the shore and place him on the ground, out of the way of the surf. Now Kendra could see the bruise to the boater's temple, and registered the fact that he didn't seem to be breathing.

She reached for the unconscious man's neck to feel for a pulse, but the man who'd swum out to assist her got to it first. Their hands brushed, and Kendra drew hers back quickly.

"I'm a doctor," the man said brusquely, not looking up from where he was focused, his long, thick fingers pressed against the other man's carotid. Bending, he put his ear close to the boater's face for a long moment.

"The ambulance is on the way," Lejla said, from behind Kendra's shoulder, her voice choked and scared. "And one of the motorboats is helping the child in the sailboat."

The doctor didn't answer, but positioned himself to begin chest compressions.

"I know CPR," Kendra said, realizing he had the situation well in hand, so there was really no need to tell him her own credentials as an RN. "I can help."

His gaze flashed up to her for an instant, and Kendra shivered.

"Grazie."

But there was little to do but watch as he set to work, performing the chest compressions with calm competence, counting as he did. Periodically he paused, and once more put his ear to the other man's face. Then he was back to it.

Kendra could hear the wail of sirens in the distance, just as the patient began to cough violently, and his child ran across the sand, shrieking, "Papa! Papa!"

It was a relief to be able to take hold of the little girl— as it turned out to be—and tell her, "Your papa is going to be all right. What is your name?"

"Isabella," she gasped out through her sobs.

It took a while for the ambulance attendants to get to the beach, but sooner than she'd expected, considering the route they had to take, they were running across the sand toward them.

The doctor looked up at Kendra to say, "I will accompany him in the ambulance." Turning his attention to Isabella, he said, "You will come with us too. We will take your *papa* to the hospital, and make him all better."

The gentleness of his tone when speaking to the child made a shiver run along Kendra's spine. Getting up to make way for the ambulance attendants, still holding Isabella close to her side, Kendra watched as the doctor also rose. He was giving the attendants their patient's information, but Kendra didn't hear any of it.

All she could do was stare at him, and the pounding of her heart now had nothing to do with her prior exertions.

He was a magnificent sight, his heavily muscled body moving with surprising fluidity as he jogged over to a pile of clothing dropped haphazardly on the sand. All he was wearing was a pair of boxer briefs, which, being wet, were molded to every plane and bulge of his lower torso and upper thighs.

Every.

Single.

Bulge.

All of which were impressive.

When he started shrugging into the blue, long-sleeved shirt, Kendra shivered again.

Why didn't I go and speak to him when I had the chance?

But having the crying little girl clinging to her side made most of the regret fade away. If she'd been concentrating on flirting, she probably wouldn't have seen the accident occur, and maybe the man now on the stretcher wouldn't have been saved.

Tearing her gaze away from where the doctor was struggling to put his pants on over his wet skin, she gave Isabella a tighter squeeze. Running her hand over the little girl's head, she made soothing noises, not trusting her befuddled brain to find the right words in Italian. Her insides were quaking like jelly, the combination of coming down from the adrenaline and her strange, visceral reaction to the man now striding toward her across the sand.

Their gazes met again, and those seemingly bottomless eyes made the vibrations in her belly intensify, until she knew if she didn't look away once more, her legs might just give out.

Taking a shaky breath, she turned to watch as the paramedics began to carry the stretcher over the sand.

"Come, little one." The deep rumble of his voice shot through Kendra's veins, disturbing her equilibrium even more. When he held out his hand to the little girl, Kendra clenched the fingers of her free hand, so as not to reach for it herself. "As for you," he said to Kendra, with not a hint of the tenderness he'd had for Isabella. "You need to get dry. You're shivering, and we already have one patient. We don't need another."

Kendra nodded, not willing to trust her voice, lest she tell him that just looking at him made her hot all over, and she didn't need a towel.

Then, at a shout from the ambulance attendants, now almost to the rocks, the connection between them was shattered, and Kendra took in a deep breath. The doctor picked up Isabella, and with one last nod started at a trot across the sand after them, and in moments was gone from sight.

But the memory of him lingered long after, leaving Kendra with a strange sense of life having changed, and a host of questions that started with, *What if...?*

CHAPTER TWO

DR. MASSIMO BIANCHI had a theory that Fate had a diabolical sense of humor. One that he didn't appreciate.

It really liked dangling things in front of him, only to yank them away again.

Which is why, as he looked across the café in Positano at the woman in the midst of a raucous group of people, he made no effort to go over and speak to her.

The last thing he needed was to stand there, tongue-tied, while everyone else around him chatted and laughed.

Only too well did he know what it felt like to be the odd man out—the one everyone else ignored. After all, he'd just left his parents' home, where all his ebullient relatives had laughed and chatted and shouted, not even trying to include him. That he was used to. He'd lived it most of his life. Being the middle child of seven and the only introvert in a large, extroverted family—the one teased for being studious instead of rambunctious—he knew when to keep to himself.

So, instead of exposing himself by going over to where the woman stood, he turned his attention back to the view spread out before him. Trying to achieve the peace sunset on the Amalfi Coast usually brought to his heart.

In his estimation, there could be nowhere as beautiful as the rugged coast, with the mountains and terraced farms above, and its tenacious villages clinging to the slopes. With both land and sea bathed as it was now in the golden glow of the sun sinking toward the horizon, it was the epitome of everything lovely.

Massimo found himself glancing back at the woman on the other side of the bar, and quickly pulled his gaze away again.

It was the second time he'd seen her in as many days, and he couldn't understand his reactions. Just looking at her made his muscles go rigid, his heart race and tumble.

He'd been testy for the last two days, ever since that first sight of her, at Spiaggia Tordigliano.

All he'd wanted was a quiet day away from the tension he always felt when visiting his family in Napoli. That sensation of being out of step with everyone. But instead of a relaxing beach visit, what he'd gotten was a jolt, akin to a punch straight to the solar plexus, which left him winded and confused. So much so that rather than stay at his parents' home until after the weekend, as originally planned, he'd felt the intense need to get away by himself for the rest of his vacation.

Suddenly the constant noise and hoopla in the house, the cacophony of cars and people in the city, had been too much to bear.

He was honest enough with himself to know the change from routine trip to the beach to emotional whirlwind had happened long before the drowning incident. In actual fact, it had started on the trail down to Spiaggia Tordigliano, when he'd come up behind that woman standing on the path.

Something about her straight-backed posture, the air of almost palpable joy in her stance, had kept him rooted where he stood. He'd almost expected her to throw open her arms, as though to embrace the scene before her, although she didn't move at all.

Her immobility had given him the opportunity to take in as much of her as he could see.

She was fairly tall and solidly built, with a beautifully shaped skull, broad shoulders and a torso that tapered in before flaring into wide hips. Smooth skin, chestnut-hued in the sun, reminded him of the finest silk. Her hair, an unusual shade of mingled walnut and honey, hung in a thick plait along her spine, and his fingers itched to touch it, and discover its texture. Long, strong legs and arms completed the picture, and although Massimo had always in the past been attracted to petite, willowy women, he'd found himself fascinated.

He'd very much wanted to see her face.

Making her aware of him elicited a sound of surprise, and she'd turned to look at him…

Cavolo!

Just the memory of seeing her face for the first time had Massimo muttering the oath under his breath, although at the time he'd bitten it back.

Her face was broad, with high, sharp cheekbones, and eyes of medium brown with an unusual shape—not quite oval but with a little droop at the corners that made them unbearably sexy. Those eyes had widened as she looked at him, and in them gleamed what appeared to be the same surprised recognition washing through his veins.

Yet he knew, without doubt, they'd never met before.

Then his gaze had fallen to her lips, which were lush— delicious—and slightly parted, as though she were about to speak, although she did not.

His entire body went hot, and tightened in a rush of need so intense he felt ever so slightly dizzy, and the shock of it had him hurrying past, when everything inside him shouted for him to stay. To ask her name.

To kiss that luscious mouth, even if to do so would land him in all kinds of crazy trouble.

He was not a man given to impulsiveness, so just having those thoughts even cross his mind propelled him to walk faster, so as to get away from the temptation she presented.

Yet, his mind had remained there, with her, and when the young man she was with called to her, Massimo's brain insisted on taking note of her name.

Kendra.

It suited her, but then his brain had so many questions that circled and whirred in his head.

Did she live in Italy, or was she a tourist?

If she were a tourist—and it was difficult to tell, since she'd answered her friend in fluent, if accented, Italian— where was she from?

And, as for the young man with her, was he her boyfriend, even though it was none of Massimo's business whether they were a couple or not?

All of those conflicting feelings had made his quiet day implode on itself, and although he'd pretended to be reading, his gaze had kept straying up the beach.

To her.

Which is how he was instantly aware when she shouted and jumped to her feet. As she stripped off her shirt and shorts, his brain could make no sense of any of it, until he heard the screams coming from the sailboat, and realized what must have happened.

By then Kendra was already running toward the water, dressed only in a sports bra and barely there panties.

Now that was an image seared into his mind for all times. One that he'd had to push aside while he tore off his own clothes and went into the sea after her.

He may as well not have bothered, since she was already on her way back to shore with the boater by the time he was halfway to the scene. Her cool, calm demeanor was truly impressive, as was her sheer physical strength.

It wasn't something he thought he'd ever find alluring, but there was no mistaking his feelings for anything but attraction.

Of course, all of that had to be put aside so as to help his patient, and there had been no time to do anything other than dress and, taking the patient's daughter, go after the paramedics. But it was impossible to forget the sight of her body, in no way concealed by her wet underwear.

Lovely full breasts and pebbled, dark nipples clearly visible through her bra.

Rounded, smooth belly, with the indentation of her navel begging to be laved by his tongue.

Those long, strong legs ending in tight, high buttocks that he wanted to palm. To squeeze.

The enticing mound, where a line of dark hair showed beneath her cotton panties.

Once more he'd wanted to kiss her, touch her, take her away to the nearest bed and discover what it would take to satiate her, over and over again.

While Massimo was glad the man rescued from the sea, Fortuno Demarco, was alive and doing well in the hospital, there was a part of him that had regretted the missed opportunity.

And now, there she was again.

But still he resisted the temptation.

His was not the type of demeanor suited to flirtation, and although there was no escaping her allure, he also was quite sure this was another of Fate's annoying little tricks.

Nothing good could come from speaking to her.

Then, as he was taking a sip of his *aperitivo*, there was

a light touch on his shoulder, and a warm, slightly husky voice said, "*Dottore*, how is your patient?"

And he realized Fate was trying to bamboozle him once more.

How often did life give you a second chance?

Not nearly often enough in Kendra's book.

So, when it did, she was always the first one to jump all over it.

Risk-taking didn't bother her in the slightest. In fact, she often thought it was encoded in her DNA.

Yet, when the seated man put down his glass and turned those midnight eyes on her, something inside shivered out a warning.

"He should have been discharged from the hospital in Napoli today."

At the sound of his deep, quiet voice her mouth went dry, and her knees felt shaky. She licked her lips and, pulling out the other chair at the table, sat down. But she kept the smile firmly on her face, not wanting to reveal the strangely magnetic pull the doctor was exerting on her senses.

"So, no complications?"

That earned her a slight headshake, but his gaze never left her face. "None. In fact, after he was reassured of his daughter's safety, he immediately asked about his boat."

Amusement rippled through her, bringing a gust of laughter.

"Boys and their toys," she said in English, not able to translate it in her head into Italian.

The doctor smiled slightly, and the twinkle she saw in his eyes made a shiver of awareness trickle down her spine.

"*Sì.*" He nodded. "Boys and their toys."

The sound of that alluring voice speaking English with

a delicious Italian accent turned the shiver into a tremor of need deep in her belly.

"Are you a tourist?" he asked. "Or do you live in Italy?"

She knew better than to divulge information about herself to strangers, so, smile still firmly in place, she replied, "Oh, I'm just traveling through."

It wasn't a lie, really. She was traveling through Positano on her way to her new job, but he didn't have to know that detail.

"What other parts of Italy have you seen?"

He'd reverted to Italian, and Kendra did too.

"I've been to Rome, Venice and Florence, but didn't get to spend as much time as I'd have liked to. One day I'd like to go back and see more of them."

His gaze dropped for a moment, and Kendra realized he had the most amazingly long, thick eyelashes, which she'd somehow not noticed before, caught as she was by his dark, mysterious gaze. Why seeing those lashes made her breath hitch for a second, she wasn't quite sure.

"You liked Roma?"

There was something in his tone, a curious inflection she couldn't understand and found herself wanting to, but she answered honestly anyway.

"It certainly was vibrant and beautiful. And when you come from a country where people consider a three-hundred-year-old building a landmark, seeing the really ancient buildings and artifacts was stunning."

The corners of his mouth lifted, and Kendra lost her ability to breathe when she saw him smile fully for the first time.

He went from passably good-looking to sinfully handsome with that simple act, which caused deep slashes, like elongated dimples, in his cheeks. And she knew, right then, that she absolutely, positively wanted to have sex with this man.

How to initiate that, though, was the question.

"I can see how that may be true," he said, twisting his glass back and forth between his fingers, his gaze once more fixed on her face. "We tend to take such things for granted here."

Pulling herself together, keeping a slightly amused expression on her face, she nodded. "Seeing ancient sites reminds me of how fleeting life can be, and prompts me to keep enjoying the brief time we all have."

His eyebrows rose slightly. "You've seen many such places?"

Now this was a safe enough subject, and she leaned back into the chair, relaxing.

"Not all as ancient as the Colosseum, but I've been to Angkor Wat and Lalibela, as well as a host of other places, like the Valley of the Kings and the Pyramids."

He tilted his head, the intensity of his gaze deepening. "You have traveled extensively."

"Yes. First for my job, and then because I wanted to."

"How many places have you visited?"

She could hear the curiosity in his tone, and it amused her. No one believed her when she told them the actual number, so she said, "Too many to count. Several African and Asian countries, Australia and New Zealand, and now I'm working my way through as much of Europe as I can manage."

"La voglia di girovagare."

It took her a moment to parse that out in her head, and then she laughed. "Yes, you're right. I do have wanderlust. Or perhaps more the desire to simply be a vagabond, never settling anywhere."

"What are you looking for, when you travel?"

The question took her aback. His tone gave it a meaning beyond the obvious, and opened up a space inside her she didn't want to explore. A sore spot on her soul.

Now it was hard to keep smiling, but she somehow achieved it.

"Adventure. Freedom. A wider worldview than the one I grew up with, I think. It's in my blood, somehow, and I don't see any good reason to resist it."

"Fair enough." He tipped the rest of his drink into his mouth, giving her a lovely view of his strong neck, the motion of his Adam's apple giving her an awful thirst she couldn't deny. Putting down his glass, and as though hearing and misunderstanding her thought, he asked, "May I offer you a drink?"

She hesitated, turning the situation over in her mind, figuring it out to her satisfaction.

If the chance arose, she would make the first move to become intimate with him, and have no issue with doing so. But that wouldn't happen here, surrounded by other people, overlooked by the crowd.

Getting him alone might prove to be difficult, but she'd give it her best shot.

"Actually, I was going to go down on the beach to watch the sunset. Would you care to join me?"

It was his turn to hesitate, those bottomless eyes giving nothing away, but searching her face, as though trying to figure out her true intention for asking.

Then he nodded, just once, and pushed his chair back from the table.

"It would be my pleasure to accompany you, on the condition that you allow me to buy you dinner after."

Kendra gave him her best and widest smile, and, as he eased her chair out from behind her and she stood, she suspected he was contemplating the same outcome to the evening she was.

"I'd love to."

CHAPTER THREE

MASSIMO SMILED AT the squirming, fussing toddler and hummed a little tune to distract him. The tactic worked, as it often did, and little Tommaso calmed a bit, his bright gaze affixed to Massimo's face. When Massimo began to sing a ditty popular with the two and under set, Tommaso actually laughed, and totally missed the fact he'd been inoculated.

"You're so good with the little ones," Mrs. Tarantella said, while Massimo was filling out Tommaso's vaccination form and she fought for supremacy over her son, who was once more wriggling, wanting to be put down. "When are you going to start a family of your own?"

It wasn't the first time he'd been asked such a question and, as he always did, Massimo just smiled, and replied, "Have you been speaking to my mother? She too is always asking."

He couldn't help hearing the little cough of laughter Fatima, the nurse assisting him, gave. Nor was it possible to avoid seeing the speculative gleam in Constancia Tarantella's eyes, as though she were mentally listing all her available female relatives. But, before she could continue that line of questioning, Massimo turned the conversation to Tommaso's next wellness visit, set for two months hence.

Mrs. Tarantella frowned.

"August is the busiest time of year for us," she said, shaking her head. "I might not be able to bring him then."

"Make time, please." Massimo made his voice firm, but softened the demand with a smile. "While Tommaso is doing well, because he was premature and had complications with his lungs it's important that we monitor him even more carefully than usual. He's still on the lower end of the height and weight percentiles, and there are milestones I want to make sure he is hitting as he grows."

With a marked reluctance, Mrs. Tarantella agreed to make the appointment, and soon after departed, her son straddling her hip and waving gleefully at Massimo and Fatima.

As he made the last of his notes, Fatima cleaned and sanitized the room in preparation for their next patient, humming the same tune Massimo had sung for Tommaso.

"Porca vacca," the nurse said, her tone somewhere between annoyed and amused. "Now that tune will be stuck in my head all day."

Massimo didn't comment, and Fatima probably didn't expect him to. Everyone at the clinic was used to his quiet ways.

"You must be tired of everyone trying to marry you off," the nurse said, as she sprayed down the examination table and began wiping it down. "Every woman who comes in here seems determined to find you a match. I'm sure Mrs. Tarantella asked you the same thing last time she brought Tommaso in."

What could he say to that? Even if he were inclined to comment, to say what he really felt about it would be far too revealing.

He no longer believed in the type of love he once dreamed of. The kind that was inescapable, all-encompassing and struck like lightning, sweeping all away in its path. Love that lasted eternal, and was reciprocated. Once upon a time he'd felt that thunderstruck sensation, and believed he'd found his one.

Therese had cured him of that notion, with one vicious indictment of everything he held dear.

"You're a stuffy old man already, Massimo, and not yet even thirty-five! How could I bear to spend my life with you, moldering away in this hole of a village?"

She hadn't cared that he loved Minori and the Amalfi Coast. Or that he felt he was doing the work he was meant to. He didn't need—or even like—the bright city lights, preferring a quieter existence. Nor did he feel working in a small clinic was less important than working in a large hospital, or doing major surgeries.

In fact, the job he did was, in his view, equally important, since it served people sometimes an hour away from a hospital, or elderly folk who had difficulty getting around. If clinics like the one here in Minori didn't exist, what would those people do? And when they all flocked to Napoli or one of the other cities for treatment, those places would be overburdened.

But, for all that, he might have given in and gone with her, if it weren't for Nonna, whom he'd promised to help convert her small farm into an *agriturismo*. He'd given his word that he'd supervise the building of three villas on the property, and assist her to get the venture up and running, and his word was his bond, always.

Again, Therese hadn't cared.

"You're allowing that old witch to use you. You have six brothers and sisters. Why can't one of them come and help?"

If anyone ever asked him if he could describe love dying a horrible death, he'd reach back for the memory of that moment, and hearing those words. And, even if unable to articulate it, would still feel that sick, bottom-dropping-out-of-his-world sensation.

Could still feel it even now.

He could forgive her for all the things she'd said about him. He'd heard variations of that theme even from his own father most of his life. That he was boring, too cautious, too rigid and—on one memorable occasion—insipid when compared with his more colorful brothers and cousins. But what was unforgivable was Therese's attack on an elderly woman who'd done nothing but try to be good to her grandson's fiancée. In that moment, she'd shown the true ugliness that lay beneath her stunning exterior.

"It was just infatuation," Nonna had said, with a definitive nod. He'd never told her why the relationship had ended, too hurt and angry, and not wanting to cause her any pain. "One day you will discover the difference."

But his meeting and courting of Therese had been born of love, he was sure. Growing up on the stories of his parents' first encounter, Massimo had expected that rush of attraction, the falling sensation on first sight. Therese's sultry beauty, her come-hither eyes and sensual persona, had felled him in an instant, and he'd had the surety that this was the person meant to be his, forever. Having experienced *amore a prima vista*, and seeing it go so terribly wrong, he no longer believed love at first sight was the answer. Or perhaps even true.

For an instant, memories from just days ago rushed into his head...

"Ah..."

The gasp was followed by husky laughter, and a circling motion of the hips that made Massimo have to call on every ounce of control he had, so as not to explode in-

side her. Then she tightened her long, strong legs around him, as though to immobilize him.

"Wait. Wait. You're going to make me come too soon."

Her words made him freeze, and although still buried to the hilt inside her, they also took the edge off his own incipient orgasm.

"Isn't that a good thing?" he asked, looking down into her brown eyes, now dark with the same lust burning through his body.

She chuckled, then licked her full lips, making him want to kiss her until she gave another one of those pleasure-drunk groans.

"Orgasms are always better when delayed," she said, her deep, sexy tone making him shiver in reaction.

It was then he recognized how she'd controlled the way he touched her, and the length of time he'd stimulated the various parts of her body. While he'd been intent of giving her that ultimate pleasure, she'd been holding it off, turned on not just by what he was doing, but also by gratification deferred.

"Why didn't you say so before?" he asked, his body reacting in a way he hadn't expected, hardening even more, excited by the prospect of teasing her over and over again. So much so that he eased away from her, feeling only a small pang of regret as they uncoupled. "Let me..."

He flipped her over onto her stomach and was rewarded by another gust of delighted laughter, which quickly turned into murmurs and sighs of incipient ecstasy...

Massimo forcefully pushed the memories away, but not before his blood started to heat the way it had every time he'd thought about her, or been in her presence. The woman on Spiaggia Tordigliano, with her dark honey skin and striking brown eyes, had given as much pleasure as he'd tried to give her, but his reactions to her meant nothing.

Nothing.

And the night they'd spent together in Positano meant even less.

It was just the sort of encounter he felt comfortable having, and perhaps would seek out again in the future.

Little better than anonymous. No confidences shared. No baring of souls. Only an intense physical attraction brought to logical—explosive—conclusion.

While his mind kept turning to that wondrous night, and his body refused to let him truly rest because of the memory, it was perfect just the way things ended.

She'd moved on, and he was exactly where he was meant to be. Where he was happiest.

"Did you see the email about the new nurse while you were on vacation?" As he expected, Fatima had moved on to a completely different subject without waiting for a response. "Will you be at the welcome get-together later?"

"No."

He'd gone no-contact from work during his two-week vacation, and didn't have time for office parties. Just the thought of standing around while everyone made small talk around him was distasteful. Besides, now that Nonna had taken in a foster child, she needed his help more than ever.

Pietro was still getting used to being a part of a household, rather than one of a hundred children in a home for orphans and abandoned children. He needed a certain level of continuity, which had been disrupted when Massimo went on vacation.

"Mrs. Ricci has rented her a room for the five months she'll be here," Fatima continued, which actually surprised Massimo enough that he looked up. The nurse nodded, as though he'd asked a question. "Her *pensione* needs repairs, and she couldn't afford them, so she can't rent out rooms to tourists this year. Her son has promised to send her money from America to get the work started, but that hasn't happened yet."

It had been a lean couple of years on the Amalfi Coast for anyone involved in the tourist trade, so Massimo wasn't too surprised to hear that, although it did make him sad. Nonna had the same problem but, luckily for her, she had Massimo on hand to help her keep things afloat. Mrs. Ricci's roof had been damaged during the bad storm they'd had the year before, and it was a shame she hadn't gotten it repaired, but not surprising. Renting rooms to tourists had been her main source of income. No tourists equaled no money.

When he considered it that way, it made sense that she'd rent out a room to an itinerate worker, just to try to make ends meet.

"Are you all finished cleaning?" he asked Fatima, as he reached for the patient list she'd put on the small desk.

"Yes," she replied, pulling at the roll of paper affixed to the end of the examination table, and spreading the resulting sheet out with a flourish. "I believe it's Mrs. Giordano, next. I hope you're feeling in good voice. She seems to get deafer each time she comes in."

Massimo couldn't help smiling at that statement. It was all too true. Sometimes, between Mrs. Giordano's bellowing and his own, by the time the examination was over he felt as though his ears were ringing.

He was still smiling when he got to the door and, opening it, urged Fatima to precede him through with a slight touch on her shoulder.

Then he heard a sound that froze him in place.

A woman's laugh; as rich and deep and sweet as limoncello.

A sound he knew well. Even intimately. One he'd heard as they walked along the beach at Positano. Then again after they'd kissed for the first time and, most thrillingly, heard frequently as he and Kendra rolled about in bed, seeking and finding the ultimate delight in each other's bodies.

He'd never been with a woman who'd so frankly shown her pleasure when it came to sex. Whose unfettered joy and unrestrained search for her own unique brand of ecstasy seemed as natural as the sunrise, or a storm rushing in from the sea. And the audible evidence of her joy added another level to his own desire, elevating it to previously unknown heights, so the climb to orgasm was as thrilling as the moment of culmination.

But it couldn't be her, could it?

Feeling like a child, Massimo edged into the doorway to peer around the doorjamb. Then he drew back quickly, his body, which had already been humming as though electrified, suddenly ablaze.

It *was* her, walking with the clinic coordinator, Alessio Pisano, who was looking at Kendra as though she were a *torta caprese* and he had a taste for that decadent chocolate treat. Massimo ground his teeth, annoyed at the smarmy expression on the older man's face, and then forced himself to relax.

Encountering Kendra was inevitable, and while he wondered what she was doing here—whether she was ill and seeking treatment, or had some other reason to be at the clinic—he at least was forewarned.

Her reaction to seeing him would be interesting to behold.

So he stepped out into the corridor as though nothing at all was amiss, straight into Kendra and Alessio's path. When he made eye contact with Kendra, he knew the exact moment she recognized him by the way her eyes widened, and her lips parted in shock.

"Kendra," he said, still keeping his gaze locked on hers. "What a surprise."

She didn't reply. Instead, Alessio was the one who said, "Massimo, you've already met our new nurse?"

"Our new *nurse*?" Well, that was enough to stop him cold, and he saw her expression change to devilish amusement, just before her chuckles rolled over him like a capricious wave.

"Yes, our new nurse. Who did you think she was? And where do you two know each other from?"

Gathering himself, trying to ignore the way his heart once more raced and sweat gathered along his spine, Massimo replied, "I was at Spiaggia Tordigliano when she saved a man from drowning."

"And the doctor performed CPR," Kendra tacked on, the amusement in her voice patently clear. "It was a brief encounter."

"But memorable," Massimo countered, unable to resist the double entendre. Letting her know, no matter how she classified what had happened between them in Positano, he hadn't forgotten even a second of it.

"Of course it would be memorable," Alessio said, with another of his smarmy smiles aimed at Kendra. "Saving a drowning man? How did you know what to do?"

"It was part of my training when I was with the Canadian Armed Forces," she replied, her smile still in place, but a slightly cooler edge to her voice. "It's not an instinct one ever forgets."

"Ah, yes, of course." Alessio beamed, and clapped his hands, as though in approbation. "Your military training was one of the reasons the directors decided to hire you. That and your command of several languages. As I'm sure you're aware, we get a variety of tourists of different nationalities visiting the area, and the summer months are extremely busy for us as we care for them, as well as the locals."

Just then Massimo heard Fatima coming back with Mrs. Giordano. Or rather, heard Mrs. Giordano coming, as the elderly lady's shouting couldn't be missed.

"Who am I seeing today? Dr. Bianchi, or Dr. Mancini?"

"Dr. Bianchi," Fatima bellowed back.

"Oh, yes. That nice unmarried one. I like him. I keep telling my niece about him, and saying she should come to the clinic and meet him, but she won't listen to me. These young people don't know good advice when they hear it."

Massimo didn't think he'd ever blushed in his life until that moment, and it wasn't the type of sensation he relished, at all. Heat gathered in his chest and then flooded up into his face until even his ears felt as though they might spontaneously combust.

Kendra bit her bottom lip, unholy glee lighting her eyes. Leaning closer to him, she stage-whispered, "Let us not speak of this again, *si*?"

"Concordato," he mumbled, still embarrassed, but now fighting the urge to laugh along with her.

Her amusement was infinitely appealing.

Yet he also heard the subtext of her words—the injunction that they not speak of their prior meeting again either. That they forget the night they'd spent in his hotel room, driving each other insane until the early hours of the morning.

Hopefully he'd be able to go along with her demand, and will his body to ignore her presence far better than it had just now, when all he wanted was to demand another round of passion.

"Dr. Bianchi. We're ready for you."

At Fatima's words, he excused himself and, with one last glance at Kendra's twinkling eyes, went off to deal with his patient.

CHAPTER FOUR

KENDRA STOOD AT the window of her room in Mrs. Ricci's *pensione* with her cell phone at her ear. It was just gone six thirty in the morning, and she was catching up with her cousin Koko who lived in Toronto. They tried to speak at least once every few months, and it wasn't always easy to set up a time convenient for both of them. But Koko was a DJ, and sometimes, like now, she'd call between sets. Although Kendra could hear the bass pumping, Koko must have found a relatively quiet place, because her voice came through clearly.

"So, besides the fact that the roof of your room leaks, how else has it been?"

It had been two months since they'd last spoken, when Kendra was getting ready to leave Naples and travel on to Minori. In between they'd texted, just to check in, which usually meant short messages like: Made it to Positano safely, or, You should have seen the club last night. It was jumping.

If either had anything important but not urgent to say, they saved it for their phone conversations.

"Well…" She stretched the word out, knowing Koko would be all ears. "It's been good. I've met some fun locals to hang out with, and the people at the clinic have been great. Even the doctor I slept with before I knew he was going to be a coworker."

"What?" Koko shrieked so loudly she completely drowned out the bass line behind her. "You slept with some random dude, only to find out you'd be working with him afterward?"

Kendra couldn't help laughing. "Right? Seeing him at the clinic was an awkward moment, to say the least."

"Spill. I want to know everything."

As she filled her cousin in about the near drowning at the beach, and the subsequent tryst in Positano, Kendra left out some of the juicer bits. Like the way Massimo had made her body hum, lighting her afire in a way she hadn't really expected. She was no innocent, but it was difficult to get past the memories of the night they'd spent together because it had, in a strange way, felt like an awakening of sorts.

He was the first man who'd seemed to instinctively understand that she wasn't the type to chase orgasms, as though they were the only prize available during sex. Instead, Massimo had embraced her desires, taking her close to orgasm, then letting the impulse wane just enough to keep her constantly—ecstatically—on the brink. And she'd had the chance to learn his body in intimate detail, with no holds barred. Together they'd lit the night afire, and the memories of his hoarse cries of pleasure still echoed in her head, whenever she gave them the chance to creep in.

But she didn't tell Koko any of that. After all, her cousin was always inclined to make more out of a situation than was warranted.

Instead, she told her about the shock of seeing Massimo at the clinic—her instinctive hope that he was just passing through, and sinking feeling when she realized they'd be working together.

"It was so cute," she finished up, after telling a hysterically laughing Koko about Mrs. Giordano's comments. "He blushed. Like went bright red. He looked mortified, and it took everything I had not to tease him even more."

"So," Koko asked, after she'd gotten a hold of herself. "It sounds like you had a *great* time with him. Are you still sleeping together?"

Kendra laughed.

"Nope," she said, making her voice firm and sure, even though it meant ignoring a pang of regret. Massimo really knew his way around a woman's body, and there were times she'd found herself watching him with the kind of deep hunger she couldn't deny but also couldn't afford. "You know I avoid those kinds of complications."

Koko was quiet for a second, and when she next spoke, she sounded as though she wasn't sure she should say what she was going to. "You laugh, like you always do when things aren't easy and straightforward, but not all complications are bad, Kendra."

Kendra made a rude noise. "Girl, you know I always have one foot out the door, wherever I am. That's a recipe for disaster with most men. It starts out casual and the next thing I know he's asking me if I don't want to stay." When Koko didn't reply, Kendra went for the ultimate excuse. "Besides, we work together. It would just make things…"

"Complicated?" Koko's voice was softer. "Yeah, you mentioned your aversion to complications. But most of life is a series of complications. It's just how it is."

"Not for me," she replied, putting all the conviction she could muster into her voice, lightening the conversation with her amusement, although it felt forced. "The biggest difficulty I want is deciding where I'm going next. Or having a flight canceled unexpectedly."

Koko snorted. "Okay. Okay. I hear you."

Then her cousin changed the subject, instead bringing Kendra up to speed on other family members' lives, passing on any tidbits of family gossip.

"Have you decided where you're going next?" Koko asked, near the end of their conversation.

"Not yet," Kendra said, and her heart gave a hard thump at the question. "I'm thinking I'd like to travel around Italy a bit more, before moving on. Then I'll find somewhere warm to spend winter, but I have time to decide."

And Koko seemed satisfied with that.

By the time they'd said their goodbyes and hung up, sunlight was spilling over into the narrow roadway—little better than a cobblestone path—outside the window. When Kendra had first arrived at the *pensione* she'd seen a cavalcade of donkeys passing by on their way to a construction site just up the hill, panniers on their backs filled with building materials. It had amazed her, but once she considered how narrow and steep the streets were, it made more sense. The donkeys even easily navigated the stone stairways in other parts of town, taking materials and equipment up and bringing rubble back down, the way it had been done for centuries.

Koko's question came back to her then, along with the strange sensation Kendra felt whenever she thought about leaving the Amalfi Coast. There was a timelessness to Minori that somehow soothed her soul. On her first day off she'd walked the Sentiero dei Limoni—the Lemon Trail—from Minori to Maiori, and the views and quietude had given her more peace than she'd felt for a long time. Somehow, it was a though her father walked with her, and instead of grief at his loss she'd felt contented.

And that sensation had persisted wherever she went along the coast.

In some ways it was frightening.

She was always interested in learning about the areas she visited and the locals she encountered, but something about this particular part of Italy threatened to take hold of her heart, and never let go.

Places didn't usually affect her this way. Even the people she met were viewed as transient in her life, only a select few gaining the appellation "friend." Moving on had never been difficult and in fact was something she looked forward to, but she wasn't sure it was going to be that easy leaving here.

However, that wasn't something she had to think about for a while yet, especially since she didn't always plan her adventures in advance. Her contract was from June until the end of October, which not only allowed the clinic to have coverage during the busy season, but also let the other nurses get some time off.

And, she reminded herself, for probably the two-hundredth time over the last weeks, just because Dr. Massimo Bianchi did funny things to her insides whenever she saw him was no reason to act on the attraction. In fact, considering all the other feelings she had about Minori and its surroundings, she was better off pushing that particular complication aside!

Yet, it had been a long, fraught couple of months. Each time their eyes met, she had to fight off the memories of being in his arms. Of the way he'd touched her—both tenderly and roughly, the juxtaposition more arousing than anything she'd felt before—and the intensity of the pleasure he'd given.

"Why didn't you say so before?" he asked, and before she could reply he'd levered himself up onto his knees and away, so that their bodies separated, leaving her strangely hollow. "Let me..."

Before she knew what he planned, he grabbed her and

flipped her over onto her stomach, the movement high-lighting his strength. Maybe it should be scary to have a man manipulate her body so easily but, instead, it height-ened her arousal.

And when he lay over her, keeping her immobilized by his weight, and began a leisurely trip down her body, all she could do was laugh, and moan, and sigh. From neck to feet, his hands and lips and tongue swept and dipped, finding new erogenous zones, taking her to the edge of orgasm before moving on, leaving her shaking with the need to come...

And now, when his hair flopped over one eye, she wanted to smooth it back, and feel it crisply curl around her fingers again.

He turned her over again after what felt like an ecstatic eternity, and looked down at her with that hot, hooded gaze.

"I'm ready now," she said, having to force the words out from a throat tight with need.

Massimo shook his head.

"I don't think so." It looked as though he was trying to smile, but it was more of a baring of his teeth. "You like anticipation, and I'm finding I like it too."

Then, before she could respond, his head was between her thighs, but his gaze stayed locked on hers, as he once more explored her with his tongue. Oh, and he knew what he was doing, stimulating every nerve ending but the ones that would take her over the edge.

Reaching down, she twisted her fingers into his hair, tugging—hard. All that did was make him chuckle, the vibrations firing into her flesh, almost undoing all the hard work he put in, causing her to arch and cry out...

If she walked up behind him at the clinic, she had to

fight the urge to run her fingers down the deep hollow over his spine, knowing it was, for him, an erogenous zone.

Halfway through the night they found themselves taking a break, both sipping from bottles of water from the hotel fridge. Massimo was sitting on the edge of the bed, while Kendra reclined against the headboard, and it gave her the opportunity to fully appreciate the width and musculature of his back. He really was marvelously built, and the sight before her once more awakened the desire he'd only just satiated.

Without thought, she ran a cold, damp finger down his back, and the resulting shudder and goose bumps firing over his skin were inspiring.

"You liked that," she said, stretching to put down the water bottle on the bedside table.

"I did," he admitted, seemingly about to change position.

Her hand on his shoulder stopped him, and he looked over at her, his eyebrows rising in question.

"Stay there." She moved behind him, kneeling so she could snake her tongue around his ear, which earned her another hard shudder, and a growl. "I want to..."

Then she showed him exactly how she, too, could find ways to let anticipation build. Taking her time, she traced each muscle with her mouth, while she ran her fingers along the dip over his spine again and again, until his breath came hard and fast from between his lips. Stimulating him, until she knew he was on the brink, the way she'd been for most of the night.

The difference, though, came when she reached around his body and took his erection in hand, and didn't stop even when he told her if she didn't, he'd explode.

The way he allowed her free rein over his body was an aphrodisiac...

And those lips that she'd once thought too thin to be attractive…

Kendra shivered, her body afire with the memories, and the rampaging desire.

"Wow, Kendra. No," she said aloud, hoping to diminish the waves of lust now pulsing through her body. "This is not how we want to start the day."

Especially when in a very short time she'd be back in close proximity with Massimo.

No, getting all worked up like this wouldn't do.

At all.

Massimo was in a foul mood, and he had no one to blame for that but himself.

His life—which had seemed so very perfect just months before—seemed to be going to hell in a handbasket, and he wasn't sure what to do about it.

Nonna was irritable since a couple of bookings had been canceled, and she was worried about the loss of income. Pointing out that the villas were almost fully booked from now until the end of the season didn't seem to lessen her anxiety.

Perhaps sensing her tension, Pietro retreated into silence at the slightest incident, hardly speaking at all, and only when pressed. Although the young boy did everything he was supposed to and never was rude, having him shut down that way was worrying.

And then there was Kendra Johnson…

The nurse had been nothing but pleasant and cheerful. She got on well with staff and patients alike, and treated Massimo with professional courtesy, mixed with her habitual amusement.

Yet, just seeing her put him on high alert. Hearing her laughter sent almost unbearable longing through his body.

And she expressed her amusement a lot, each deep peal bringing back those excruciatingly sensual memories.

She'd laughed breathlessly when he found a particularly sensitive spot on her body, when he asked if she liked what he was doing. Even through her eventual orgasms.

No wonder then that each time he heard that joyous sound at work, every hair on his body rose, and heat inundated his veins. How he's stopped himself from dragging her off into an examination room and ravishing her, he really didn't know.

There'd been no discussion between them, but simply a tacit agreement that they would not talk about their night of passion, nor would it be repeated.

Whereas in Positano she'd made her interest crystal clear, now she was equally clear about keeping her distance. It was maddening, since the more reticent she was, the more he wanted to know about her. Thank goodness for the village *nonne*, who didn't hesitate to ask all the questions he wanted to, and Kendra seemed quite willing to answer.

"Is it true…?" is how most of their queries started, showing that the village grapevine was working.

"Is it true you're Canadian?"

"…that you were in the army?"

"…that you speak five languages?"

As it turned out, the answer was yes to them all except the last one, where it turned out she spoke six languages, with a smattering of a few others.

One *nonna* went so far as to take Kendra's face between her palms and, after a long, searching look, said, "I did not know there were Black people in Canada. Did your family go there from somewhere else?"

He'd expected her to pull away from such an invasion of

her space, but, instead, she'd stayed absolutely still, looking into Mrs. De Luca's eyes.

"There are all kinds of people in Canada, but my father's ancestor fought for the British during the American War of Independence and earned his freedom from slavery. When it was over, in 1776, he and his family were resettled in Nova Scotia, on Canada's east coast, and some of their descendants have been there ever since."

As though somehow mesmerized, Mrs. De Luca didn't release Kendra's cheeks, but asked, "And where is your mother's family from?"

That was when Kendra gently pulled away and, although she was still smiling, her tone was a little cooler as she replied, "My mother was from Argentina."

Then she changed the subject, bringing the appointment back on track.

He'd noticed she did that sometimes—smiled and shut people down at the same time. It was subtle, but once you knew what to look for, it became obvious. There were some subjects that touched a nerve, and although she didn't overtly react, there were tiny signs she threw up that said, "Step back!"

"Porca miseria," he muttered to himself, realizing he'd just wasted fifteen minutes staring at the patient list, thinking about a woman who had no interest in him.

Kendra Johnson was so bright, so incandescent, she'd never consider a boring, laconic man like him for anything more than a spontaneous one-night stand. All he could hope was that she didn't regret their encounter, but could think back on it with some pleasure.

And, if their disparate personalities weren't enough of an impediment, there was the fact that she was the kind of woman he doubted would ever settle down in one place. A vagabond, as she herself had said.

Massimo knew he'd never be completely happy away from where he was—here on the Amalfi Coast. Perhaps that made him stodgy—an old man, as Therese had accused—but he was content with his life.

At least, he usually was.

Getting up from the desk, he made his way out to the reception area, determined to keep his mind firmly on his job, and nothing else. Of course, as soon as he opened the office door, he heard Kendra chuckle, and every muscle in his body tightened. Which meant he was scowling when he reached his destination.

"Fatima. I've been asked to make a house call to Mrs. Lionetti this evening. Are you available to accompany me?"

Giving him a somewhat startled look, which told him he was being even curter than usual, Fatima shook her head.

"No, Dr. Bianchi, I'm sorry. I have to take Marina to Salerno to meet with the ophthalmologist right after work."

Marina, Fatima's youngest daughter, had strabismus that was resistant to nonsurgical intervention.

"I can go with you, if you need a nurse," Kendra interjected.

It was on the tip of his tongue to say it wasn't necessary, and he'd go by himself, but it was clinic policy that no doctor do a nonemergency house call alone. Biting back a snort of annoyance, he nodded.

"Fine. Be ready to leave at four thirty, please. Fatima, if you'd give Kendra the file so she's aware of Mrs. Lionetti's situation, I'd appreciate it."

Then, caught somewhere between anger and anticipation, he strode back to his office, trying his best not to stomp like a petulant child as he went.

And when he heard that bedeviling laugh again, he couldn't help the little groan that rose in his throat.

She was going to make him insane, if he didn't get his reactions under control!

CHAPTER FIVE

MRS. LIONETTI WAS diabetic and blind, and had limited mobility because of nerve damage in her feet, which was why she was one of the patients who always had the doctor go to her.

She also happened to live on the same street where Kendra was staying, just a little lower down, but when Kendra pointed that out, all Massimo said was, "I know."

His grumpy demeanor was beginning to grate, but, at the same time, she wasn't willing to delve into why he was behaving that way. Maybe it had something to do with her, or maybe it didn't.

There was definitely a part of her that hoped it was because he was still attracted to her, but also was unwilling to do anything about it. After all, misery did love company, and this constant hum beneath her skin whenever they were together was driving her bonkers.

So, as she always did when in any way unsure, she chuckled and said, "I don't think I've been as closely monitored as I am here since I left Nova Scotia when I was ten. Everyone seems to know my business."

That gained her a sideways glance, just short of a glare, which she proceeded to ignore. If he was going to be unpleasant the entire time, she wasn't going to jolly him along. That wasn't her way.

Even though, for once, she felt as though she wanted to.

Mrs. Lionetti was frail and querulous. Even when her son Tino told her who was at the door, she kept fussing.

"It's not time for me to see the doctor again. He was just here the other day."

"Ah, Mrs. Lionetti." Massimo's voice was soft, cajoling. "Didn't you miss me? It's been months since we saw each other."

"No, it hasn't, young man." Mrs. Lionetti's chin lifted belligerently. "You were here just a few days ago. And who is that with you?"

"This is Nurse Kendra Johnson."

"That strange foreign woman everyone has been talking about? Who likes to gad about at all hours of night? Going to the *taverna* and encouraging other young women into disreputable ways?"

Kendra had to bite her lip not to laugh. With a feisty matriarch like this, it would definitely set the wrong tone. And it didn't bother her in the slightest that her efforts to befriend the locals and enjoy her time in Minori were being classified in such a way. She'd developed a little cadre of ladies she usually had dinner with, and then they stopped off at one of the *tavernas* afterward. No doubt her being in the restaurants and bars late into the evening was seen as somehow questionable, despite being in the company of local acquaintances.

Ignoring the curious looks the two men were giving her, she said, "That's me, Mrs. Lionetti."

The elderly lady's eyebrows went up, and she gave a little snort, but said, "Well, come closer and tell me why you're here. I want to know who you are."

Kendra intercepted a glance from Massimo, who indicated he would be going into the adjacent room to speak to Mrs. Lionetti's son, and she nodded in understanding.

No doubt Massimo wanted to ask Tino about his mother's memory lapses, if that was what they were.

So, Kendra submitted to the third degree while taking the other woman's blood pressure and pulse, and listening to both chest and abdominal sounds. When Massimo came back into the room, she handed him the chart with her notations, and stepped back so he could begin his own examination.

From some of his questions, Kendra thought he might suspect Mrs. Lionetti of having a UTI, which could account for her confusion, but there were also other diseases and syndromes to consider. Non-24-hour sleep-wake disorder was one, since sufferers of blindness who tried to adhere to a normal schedule when their circadian rhythm was disrupted often exhibited signs of depression, and sometimes confusion. Insulin resistance in the brain or a small stroke were also possibilities.

Hopefully it wasn't irreversible dementia, or the onset of Alzheimer's disease, but she had no doubt Massimo would test for those too.

He was getting to the end of his examination when there was a huge, rumbling crash from outside, followed by a series of shouts and screams. Without thought, Kendra was on her feet and out the front door, looking first right and then left. To the left, farther up the hill, near Mrs. Ricci's house, she could see a cloud of dust, and some figures milling around, so she ran that way.

Then she came to a halt, staring for a moment at the devastation before her.

There was a pile of rubble almost filling the narrow street, right in front of Mrs. Ricci's house, and what was left of a house across the road from the *pensione* where Kendra boarded. Then she realized a group of men were frantically digging at the debris with their bare hands, tossing rocks away.

Running up to them, Kendra shouted, to be heard above the hubbub, "What happened?"

"Part of a building has collapsed. There's a man under here, somewhere."

She didn't hesitate, but set to work, grabbing pieces of stone, wood and other detritus, joining the effort to free the trapped worker.

"Guarda! Guarda!"

In the instant it took her to realize what the man next to her was saying, she heard a roar, as the pile shifted, beginning to collapse with an ugly groan, like a dying beast.

Before she could do more than take a step, someone grabbed her around the waist and swung her around, just as a building across from the original one damaged partially collapsed right onto where she'd been standing. Her rescuer hadn't been quite quick enough, as she felt a hard blow to her left arm.

A dust cloud descended over them, particles getting into her eyes making her tear ducts work overtime, and causing both her and her rescuer to cough.

It was only when she heard Massimo's voice, asking if she were all right, that she realized it was him, and that he had her securely—safely—held tight against his chest.

"Yes," she managed to say, between coughing fits. "But we need to get back and help the worker."

"Sì." But he was running his hands over her arms and back, as though checking for injuries, and it took everything she had not to gasp when he touched that tender spot on her outer bicep. "But that was too close for comfort. If I asked you to stay back, would you comply?"

Normally, she would have laughed, and told him no way,

but even with his face covered in dust and sweat, she could see the concern in his expression, and her heart clenched.

"Thank you for asking," she said, forcing herself to ease out of his arms, and shaking her head. "But no."

"*Eccolo! Eccolo!* I see him! Here! Here!"

And they were rushing back to the point where the injured man had been discovered, Massimo shouting orders, trying to tell the others not to move him, to be careful they didn't cause the pile to shift again.

"My bag," he snapped in her direction, and Kendra took off back to Mrs. Lionetti's house.

The elderly lady was clutching her sweater closed at the base of her throat, her eyes wide and her lips trembling as she called out, "What has happened? Where is Tino?"

"He'll be right back, Mrs. Lionetti," Kendra said, as she grabbed Massimo's stethoscope, and picked up his medical bag. "There's been an accident up the hill, but Tino's okay."

She hoped that was the truth. She hadn't recalled seeing the other man at the scene, but that wasn't surprising.

It was just total chaos.

Sprinting back, she found Massimo and two other men clearing additional rubble away from the patient.

Focusing on helping Massimo, she watched him check the man's vitals, while she found a neck brace, having it to hand when he needed it. Her arm was throbbing, but a quick look assured her there was no cut, as the light sweater she was wearing over her scrubs didn't appear to be torn, and there was no sign of blood.

"Concussion, and fracture of right radius and ulna," Massimo said, glancing up at the pile of rubble, which although now diminished still loomed above them in a menacing way. "No way to gauge spinal damage or internal injuries here. I'd rather not move him until we can get him on a back board."

"There's one at the clinic," she said. "Should I go get it?"

It would take her less than ten minutes to get there and back.

He shook his head, and she realized why when she heard, faintly in the distance, the wail of approaching sirens.

"The paramedics will soon be here. You should step back now. There's nothing more you can do."

She ignored him. The injured man had a free-bleeding laceration on his head and she'd already prepared a gauze pad to put on it. Applying pressure to the wound, she spared Massimo a glance, and found him giving her a glare.

"Guarda!" one of the men nearby shouted, causing Kendra to think the pile was shifting again and throw herself forward, trying to protect the patient. "Crazy woman! Get away from there!"

Realizing there was something else going on, she looked up, but it took her a few long moments to understand what she was seeing.

"That's Mrs. Ricci," she said, recognizing the older woman, who was standing looking out of a hole that had been punched in the side of a house. "What is she doing there? And why is she crying? Is this a relative of hers?"

"No," Massimo said. "The building collapsed right onto her house, and damaged it too."

It took a moment for that to sink in, then Kendra couldn't hold back the curse that issued from her mouth. "And that's my room in her house."

She didn't understand the sound Massimo made, until she looked at him and realized he looked—incongruously—as though he was battling both sympathy and amusement. Then she understood why as he dipped his head, drawing her attention toward a bright bit of lacy cotton sticking out between the rubble.

"I think that may be yours too."

She cursed again, wondering just how much of her clothes, especially her underwear, were buried under the pile.

And she could have smacked Massimo right there, in front of everyone, as he clearly struggled not to laugh.

Luckily for him, the ambulance attendants arrived just then, and she was forced to move out of their way.

Massimo made his report to the paramedics and assisted them to stabilize the patient for transport, before getting up and looking around for Kendra.

Now that the immediate danger was past, he was surprised at the anger pulsing through him.

He'd forever remember the moment when he'd seen the pile of rocks and debris tilt, sickeningly, above her while she remained unaware, having not immediately understood the shouted warning.

If anyone had told him he could move as fast as he had then, he wouldn't have believed them, but somehow he'd reached her side and yanked her away.

Even after that, when he asked her to move to a safe distance, she'd refused, splitting his attention between her and his patient. It had enraged him, even as he knew there was nothing he could do about it.

Now, she'd apparently disappeared, leaving him with no outlet for his anger.

"Massimo." He turned to find Roberto "Rosso" Gallo standing at his shoulder, staring at the devastation. Rosso was a local builder and businessman, and he was shaking his head. "I warned them this would happen if they didn't repair the damage caused to the foundation by the storm last summer, but they wouldn't listen."

"They didn't hire you to fix it, then?"

Rosso shook his head. "The owner of the house said I was too expensive, and I heard he'd given his cousin the job." He shrugged. "Instead of fixing the foundation, when I passed by last month, I saw they'd put on another room on top of the house. It looks like the foundation couldn't take the weight."

Massimo caught a glimpse of Kendra, who was hugging a crying Mrs. Ricci. Excusing himself, he walked over to them, just in time to hear one of the men standing beside them say, "No, no. You can't go back in there. It might not be safe."

"I have to." Kendra's voice was firm. "Everything I own is in that room. At least, whatever is left that isn't scattered down here."

"And if you fall to your death, what good will that do?"

Kendra shrugged. "Well, I won't need my stuff then, will I?"

His heart all but stopped. He was beginning to recognize the deep vein of independence that ran through this infuriating, crazy woman, and he wondered if he'd have to cart her away over his shoulder to stop her doing something stupid.

As though hearing his thoughts, she sent him a steely glare.

"Don't you start on me, Massimo." She said it in English and her voice wobbled slightly. In that moment, he realized that the fright was setting in, as the adrenaline in her system waned. "My passport, everything is in there, and I'm going in to get them."

It came to him, right then and there, that he couldn't let her do it, and there was only one way to stop her.

Turning away, he swiftly climbed the pile nearest the entrance to Mrs. Ricci's home and down the other side, glad to see the doorway was clear enough for him to make it through. Behind him came shouts, including from Kendra, but it was, he reasoned, already too late anyway, since he was partway up the stairs.

Judging from the configuration of the house in comparison with the street, it took him only a moment to find her room, and then he hesitated at the doorway. Even from there he could see how the floor sagged toward the broken wall, and, as though in warning, the house creaked, moaning as if in pain.

No time to lose courage now though.

Looking around, he spotted a battered knapsack at the foot of the bed, and a small duffel bag on the floor, close to a now dust-covered dressing table. There were a few bottles and tubes on the tabletop too, so, taking a deep breath, he made his way cautiously toward it. Again, shouts and screams came from below as he came into view from the street, but he ignored them as he grabbed the duffel, unzipped it and swept the bottles and tubes into it.

Then he swiftly pulled open the drawers and scooped their contents into it too.

The floor creaked. Something beneath his feet broke with a snap, and Massimo knew he'd tested his luck as far as he should.

Making his way as quickly as he could to the door, he snagged the knapsack on his way past, then a tablet from the nightstand, stuffing it into the duffel, and made it out into the small corridor.

It was only when he made it back down to the front door that he realized he'd been holding his breath almost the entire time.

There were men standing on the rubble, and they gave

a shout of satisfaction when he appeared, and the assembled crowd cheered as he passed the bags across, and then climbed back to safety.

All except the woman he'd done it all for.

As he approached, she hauled back a bunched fist. Luckily, he leaned away, avoiding the punch she aimed squarely at his chest. *Dio* only knew how much damage she would have done had it landed. At the same time she was shouting, "You idiot! You nincompoop! What the hell were you thinking?"

And, as everyone else stood there in shocked silence, and Kendra glared at him as though she wanted to murder him, Massimo found himself rubbing his chest, as though her blow had actually struck home, trying his best not to burst out laughing.

Her eyes narrowed, and her beautiful lips firmed into a straight, angry line. "Don't you dare laugh, Massimo Bianchi. Don't you dare!"

"But you are so very beautiful when you are angry," he said, saying the first thing that came to mind. "How else am I to respond but with joy and jubilation?"

Once more the men within earshot cheered and laughed, while Kendra threw her hands in the air in obvious disgust, grabbed her bags from the ground and walked away.

But it was too late.

Massimo had seen the devilish twinkle in her eyes, and knew he was already forgiven, for everything.

CHAPTER SIX

KENDRA TRIED TO stay furious at Massimo. Oh, she did her very best. Ignoring him while they gave their reports to the *polizia*. Giving him frosty yes-or-no answers when he asked her questions. Going off—pointedly alone—while she tried to figure out where on earth she was going to go, since her place of residence had been declared unsafe. Even glaring at him while he, so infuriatingly calm, suggested that she come back with him to his grandmother's *agriturismo*.

"She has space, so it won't be a problem. Then you don't have to worry about where you're going to stay until tomorrow."

She really wanted to tell him to go to hell, but somehow all she could remember was the sight of him climbing over the rubble, going to get her belongings, and most of her anger drained away. Then she recalled his saying she was beautiful, and the rest melted into nothing.

With a sigh of resignation, she agreed.

But when they were finally getting into his car where he'd left it by the clinic, she knew she couldn't just let it go.

"What you did earlier was incredibly stupid, Massimo. You could have been killed." Slamming her door for emphasis, she turned sideways in her seat, so she was looking at him, as she buckled her seat belt. "Did you hear the inspector say he was surprised the floor of that room hadn't come down when the other building hit Mrs. Ricci's house?"

He sent her a sideways glance, and his lips twitched. Kendra wasn't sure whether he was annoyed or holding back a smile.

"You were planning to go in there."

Kendra growled, which earned her a lifted eyebrow. "It was my stuff. And I'm lighter than you are. There would have been much less danger." When he didn't reply, she added, "Besides, think about it logically. You're one of three doctors serving two communities. You're far more important than an itinerate nurse."

"I disagree. And I'm sure your family would too."

Would they?

She didn't say it, but the thought sat heavily in her mind. The only member of her family she was close to was Koko. Even her aunt Raylene, Koko's mother, hardly ever reached out, although Kendra had lived with her the longest of all her relatives.

It was mostly the result of the peripatetic life she'd chosen, and there was no use fussing about the fallout of it now, but the moment of sadness lingered and had to be forcefully ignored.

"Besides," Massimo continued. "It's already done. There's no need to analyze it to death at this point."

Biting back a sharp retort, Kendra decided to leave well enough alone. While the memory of the fear she'd felt at his chivalrous—no, stupid!—actions was one she knew would never fade, she was honest enough to know he was right. She had planned on going into the house herself, and she wouldn't have given a second thought to how that would make anyone else feel.

She was used to looking out for herself, and doing whatever needed to be done. She hadn't needed a knight in shining armor, but perhaps it was a tad ungrateful to kick up such a stink about, for once, having one.

As for what he'd said, about her being beautiful when she was angry—well, she wasn't touching that with a ten-foot pole.

It was all nonsense anyway, designed to stop her in her tracks and get him off the hook. While she rather hated the thought that he'd won *that* round, she had no choice but to just let it go.

As they were speaking, Massimo had been driving up into the hills above Minori, on a narrow road that first dipped into a valley and then rose again, so that the lights of the coast became distant and milky. Wishing it were daylight, so she could see the surroundings and appreciate the view, Kendra wondered just how far away his grandmother's house was. And she couldn't help hoping it had a good supply of hot water.

She stank, and was covered in dust.

Lovely way to be introduced to Massimo's family...

That thought drew her up, sharply.

It wasn't an introduction, per se. Not in the sense of there being anything between them, and her needing to make a good impression. If it could have been avoided, completely, she would have much rather do that, but it was necessity born of happenstance, and she refused to think of it in any other way.

Just to make sure he realized that too, she said, "Tomorrow I'll ask around for somewhere else to stay."

"Mmm-hmm." The alacrity of his response left no doubt that he was in full agreement. "I can make inquiries too. There are a couple of places I can think of that aren't too far from the clinic, and although the season is in full swing, they may be able to accommodate you."

"Good. Thank you."

But there was a little corner of her mind asking why it was he was so eager to get rid of her.

The car slowed, and then turned into a driveway so narrow Kendra wondered how it fit through the stone gates at all. The drive itself was short, with a dip into a swale and then back up to reveal a cobbled parking area and her first glimpse of the farmhouse.

The stone building had a square, solid look, not unlike the man beside her.

"Welcome to Agriturismo Villa Giovanna," Massimo said, and there was no mistaking the pride in his voice. "While it does not look like much now, in the dark, in the daylight it is very lovely."

"I'm sure it is." She refused to tell him that even in the gloom of night she thought it fascinating, and couldn't wait to see inside. "Is it named after your grandmother?"

"No. No. The name is much older than she is. This farm has been in my grandfather's family for many generations. There have been times when they thought they would lose it but, somehow, we never have. When my *nonno* died, my father and his siblings tried to get Nonna to sell, because they knew she wouldn't be able to manage the land on her own. But, instead, she built villas and a common room where she serves her guests breakfast. She also accommodates group tours, focusing on the food we produce, as well as leasing out some of the farmlands."

As he brought the car to a stop, Kendra replied, "And saved it once again. Are none of your father's brothers or sisters interested in farming?"

Massimo shook his head, and his lips twisted into a rueful smile. "None. And in a way, Nonna is to blame, since she insisted that all of them concentrate on their educations. She always says, though, that it's her duty to preserve Villa Giovanna and the farmland for the generations to come."

"She's hoping you, or one of your siblings or cousins, will want to take it over." Kendra could completely understand that impulse—the desire to preserve the past—although it wasn't always feasible. "Do you think one of you will?"

Massimo paused with his door partially open, and looked back at her with a smile.

"It will probably be me. This place captured my heart from I was a little boy, and I doubt it will ever let me go, fully."

Something inside her softened, and once more she thought of the Nova Scotia shore—and of her father—and she understood.

"Then you should hold on to it, just as it holds on to you."

For a moment they were connected more intimately than they had when they were naked, their bodies joined together in ecstasy, and Kendra couldn't break away from his far-too-tender gaze.

His lips opened, but what he was about to say never got uttered, as the light over the front door flashed on, and they both turned toward it.

"Massimo. Are you coming inside?"

The elderly lady standing there was nothing like Kendra expected. Considering Massimo's size and height, she'd thought perhaps his grandmother would be tall and stout. And, having heard they were a farming family, she'd assumed Mrs. Bianchi would have the careworn look she'd seen on many of the faces of the elderly women who came to the clinic. Instead, the woman peering out at them was none of those things.

Diminutive and effortlessly elegant in a flowing dress

and chic sweater, Massimo's grandmother was the antithesis of everything Kendra had imagined. And even though she hadn't even gotten out of the car yet, she already felt huge and lumpish in comparison.

Not to mention filthy.

Even from a distance she was sure the older woman smelled lovely. Wildflowers, perhaps. Or some insanely expensive perfume.

"Come on and meet Nonna."

Massimo was already swinging his feet out of the car, and Kendra followed suit, somewhat reluctantly.

No amount of reminding herself she didn't care what impression she made, wasn't a guest, or even Massimo's friend, really, could totally beat back the thought that she didn't belong here. Had no right even crossing that threshold.

Getting out of the car, she grabbed her bags from the back seat, and went to catch up with Massimo, who was waiting for her at the edge of the parking area. As they approached the door, Mrs. Bianchi stepped back into the hallway beyond, and Kendra could see the worry on her face.

"Filomena called to tell me about the building falling and that you were there." Uncaring of his filthy state, she reached out and pulled Massimo close for a hug. "Were you hurt?"

Kendra stood back and watched as Massimo subjected himself to being patted and examined like a little boy, and she couldn't stop the smile spreading across her face. It was, for want of a better word, precious.

"I'm fine, Nonna. Not hurt at all." As though needing to distract her, he continued, "This is Nurse Kendra Johnson, who was staying with Mrs. Ricci. That house was damaged too, so I suggested she come and stay here tonight."

Now Kendra found herself under scrutiny, but, surprisingly, it wasn't uncomfortable. Perhaps it was because

Massimo and his grandmother shared that particular way of looking at a person—searchingly, but not rudely—and now she was used to it.

When the older lady extended her hand, Kendra put down her bags and moved closer to shake it.

She'd been wrong, after all. Mrs. Bianchi didn't smell of flowers, or perfume. Instead there was the distinctive, mouthwatering scent of fresh-baked bread surrounding her, which was even better.

"Of course she can stay here. You poor girl. Is that all you were able to save from Maria's house? Will you be able to get the rest at another time?"

"No, Mrs. Bianchi. This is everything."

Well, everything except her second pair of scrubs and the two pairs of underwear that had been hanging on a drying rack next to her window, and now were buried in the rubble of Mrs. Ricci's house.

"Kendra is a seasoned adventurer, Nonna, and travels light."

"I see." She said it slowly, as though she *didn't* see, at all, but there was no judgment in her tone, just honest surprise. "Well, you are very welcome, Kendra. I hope you'll be comfortable."

"I'm sure I will."

"Is there space in one of the villas, Nonna?"

At Massimo's question, she turned what looked like a shocked face his way.

"Oh, no. She stays here, with us. I just need to make up the guest room bed."

Best to make it plain, from now, that she didn't consider herself a real guest in their home, and certainly didn't need coddling.

"If you tell me where to find the sheets, I can make the bed myself, Mrs. Bianchi. I don't want to put you out."

"Oh, but…"

"I'll take her up to the guest room, Nonna, and give her clean sheets and a blanket."

Kendra knew that no-nonsense tone quite well, and apparently so did his grandmother, as she made no further argument, just said, "Well, by the time you both get cleaned up, I'll have some supper ready for you."

A little movement at the end of the hallway caught Kendra's eye, just as Massimo asked, "Where is Pietro?"

The little boy who had been peering around the corner pulled back, as though not wanting to be seen. From clinic gossip, Kendra knew Ms. Bianchi had taken in a foster child, and she assumed the little blond boy she'd glimpsed was that child, rather than a relative.

"He's in the kitchen, doing some work I set for him, so he doesn't forget everything he learnt this year over the summer. I know he'd rather be playing, but he's being a good boy. You can introduce him to Kendra when you come back down to eat."

She saw the hesitation in the way Massimo took a step toward the staircase but his focus remained on the other end of the hallway. And then he sighed, and Kendra could swear his shoulders slumped a little.

"Yes. Of course."

He reached back, and before she realized what he was doing, had picked up her bags from the ground and was heading for the stairs.

As she hustled to catch up, she resisted the urge to grab her stuff from him, but when they got to the landing, she said, "I could have carried those."

"Of course you could," he replied in a tone so serene she wanted to smack him. "You carried them into the house all by yourself, didn't you? But Nonna would skin me alive if I had allowed it."

And there really wasn't anything much she could say to counter that.

The room Massimo showed her to was lovely. While downstairs the floors were of red, hexagonal tiles, upstairs had beautiful wooden floors and, in the guest room, colorful rugs beside the bed that matched the curtains. The furniture was obviously antique and, although rather plain, quite lovely. There was the scent of a lemony polish and a calm, soothing atmosphere to the room—in fact to all she'd seen of the house so far—and Kendra started to relax.

"I hope you don't mind sharing a bathroom with me?"

Of course, he meant it innocently enough, but her mind immediately made the leap to both of them, naked, in the shower, together. Even as exhausted as she was, that image made her entire body heat, and had tension coiling her muscles into knots.

It took swallowing, hard, and a forceful effort to keep her voice level, so as to reply, "Of course not. Will you shower first, or shall I?"

She turned toward him as she spoke, and the expression she saw on his face made her internal temperature spike into the stratosphere. Somehow, she knew without a doubt he'd had the same fantastical thought as she had, and the same instinctive reaction to it. An invitation to share the shower rose to her lips, and had to be forcefully subdued.

He cleared his throat, and spun on his heel to head for the door.

"Ladies first. I'll go and find the sheets and towels for you."

As he closed the door behind him, Kendra let out a muffled groan, and only just stopped herself from flopping her dirty self down onto the clean white bedspread.

It was going to be a long, long night.

CHAPTER SEVEN

MASSIMO CAME DOWNSTAIRS the following morning, and found only his grandmother in the kitchen, which surprised him. He'd knocked on Kendra's door when passing, to tell her he would be leaving for the clinic in half an hour, and got no response.

"Where is Kendra?" he asked, as he went to pour himself a café latte.

"She left already," Nonna replied, taking a basket of oranges and apples to the table, in a less-than-subtle hint for him to eat something healthy, rather than just one of her freshly baked pastries. "She came down about an hour ago and asked if there were any buses coming by. I offered her some breakfast, but she said because of the incident last night she needed to see to some errands in town before work, and went to catch the bus."

Massimo only just bit back the curse that rose to his lips, but stifled it with a sip of his coffee.

"She could have just waited for me," he grumbled.

Nonna chuckled, but it was a rueful sound. "She's very independent, your Nurse Kendra. Besides, she'd not have been able to get anything done before work if she'd waited for you."

Again Massimo had to stop himself from saying what came first to his lips—that she wasn't *his* Kendra. But if he'd said it aloud, Nonna would read all kinds of things into his words.

That he didn't doubt.

The night before he'd seen her try to draw the younger woman out, with surprisingly little effect. With the candor he'd seen Kendra display in the clinic when questioned by other women, he'd thought she'd be more forthcoming. But although she'd been scrupulously polite, Nonna hadn't gotten much out of her.

Then Massimo had caught Nonna watching both him and Kendra at different times in the evening, as though trying to gauge their relationship. It had made him self-conscious, but Kendra either didn't notice or didn't care.

He'd tried to be as casual as possible but, as sometimes happened, the harder he tried, the more his brain kept turning to naughty, inappropriate thoughts. Like how earlier he'd instantly gotten hard at the thought of her in the shower, and how his damned penis was once again stirring just from that imagined picture.

Or fantasizing about her sneaking into his room later, and climbing into his bed with him. He would never be so bold as to do any such thing himself, but Kendra... Oh, Kendra was bold enough, sassy enough, secure enough to come to his room if she wanted to.

And he wanted her to.

As if all that wasn't enough, Pietro had been completely silent after mumbling a hello when prompted. No matter what was being said, he sat there, just watching each of them in turn, not joining in the conversation.

Not that the little boy was ever voluble. On the whole he was a quiet child, with an air of attentive caution about him. Nonna believed that once he felt secure in the house—with them—he would come out of his shell, but it had been months and Massimo had seen no sign of it happening.

It made him sad, and made him also wonder if the attention he was giving Pietro was sufficient.

If he were enough of a person, of a man, to be a good role model and mentor.

He would have liked to know how to draw the little boy out, encourage him to talk more, but as a man who only spoke when necessary himself, he didn't know how. Besides, perhaps that was just Pietro's nature and trying to draw him out more would only make him unhappy. How did one determine something like that, when they had no experience with raising children?

And it was no use looking at his own strained relationship with his father for inspiration. Papa never truly seemed to understand Massimo, or was interested in figuring him out. Instead, he'd poked fun at the son who only reluctantly participated in sports. The one who preferred to have his nose in a book than go out like his brothers did, and retreated into the background whenever possible to avoid the drama his siblings seemed to thrive on.

That had led to a certain amount of ridicule as Massimo was growing up, and even when he became a doctor, he was left with the feeling nothing he did would ever be good enough.

The only thing he knew was that wasn't how parenting should be done, but it didn't help him figure out the best way forward. As a result, Massimo found himself double- and triple-guessing his words and actions when interacting with the little boy.

"Where is Pietro?"

"He should be down soon." She glanced at her watch. "He's probably engrossed in one of his little projects, and losing track of time." Pietro liked to tinker with anything mechanical or electronic he could get his hands on. "I'll call him if it gets too late. But, before I do, I want to talk to you."

Not knowing what to expect, Massimo watched as his grandmother picked up her cup from the counter and came to sit across from him at the table.

"Okay. Is there something you need me to do?"

Nonna shook her head, and then shrugged. "Well, yes, although not in the way I think you mean. We are all set for our next guests, and you've done a wonderful job in helping me get ready, but…"

Her voice faded, and she took a sip of coffee before looking back up. By the time she did, Massimo was on pins and needles. He hated when she lost her habitual forthrightness, since it usually meant she was about to say something he didn't want to hear.

So he kept silent, watching her, until she shrugged again and said, "I think we should offer to have Nurse Kendra come and stay here."

"No." His refusal was instinctive, and foolish. Nonna's eyes narrowed in speculation, and he hurried to continue. "I don't think it would be a good idea. We are too far out of town, and she probably would prefer to be closer to the clinic."

"She's already discovered that there's a bus just down the hill," Nonna pointed out. "And you can drive her back and forth when your schedules coincide."

"Nonna, Kendra is a free spirit. I don't think she'd want to be stuck up here with us." He felt sad as he said it, and even a little silly. The villa was only a fairly short drive up from the village, and a twenty-minute walk downhill would take you right to the outskirts of Minori.

"No one is stuck here, Massimo, except perhaps you." He stared at her, annoyed and, although he hated to admit it, rather hurt too. "She can come and go as she pleases, just as you can, and if she spends time enjoying herself rather than locked away in the house, I say good for her. Perhaps she can set a good example for you, and you'll get out more yourself."

He wanted to argue, to say he was completely happy with his life, *grazie mille*, but the words stuck in his throat. Nonna wasn't saying anything he hadn't heard before, or knew to be untrue. He had turned into a hermit over the last few years, yet hadn't wanted to change that status.

The risk could be too great. The outcome too painful.

"I don't care what Kendra does."

He knew he sounded less like a grown man and more like a recalcitrant child, and when his grandmother snorted, he realized she'd heard it too.

"Then you should have no objection to her staying here."

Oh, he had all kinds of objections.

Like the fact he'd hardly slept a wink the night before, thinking about her just there, on the other side of his bedroom wall.

And the fact that being around her made him a little *pazzo*. Tempted to lose all caution and do things he'd never considered before. Like go into half-destroyed buildings, so she wouldn't have to, or try to entice her back into his bed, even if that bed was located in his *nonna*'s home.

"Massimo. The money she will pay in rent will go a long way to help me. You know this."

One last attempt to try to make her see reason.

"The villas are almost fully booked all the way to winter. You have at least five groups coming to do cooking tours, and the restaurants are open, so the farm produce is selling again, and you won't have to give much of it away like you did the last couple of years. Isn't that enough?"

Nonna shook her head. "Every bit helps, after what we went through. We should do this."

Desperate now, he again said, "Kendra may not want to stay here."

Pushing back her chair, Nonna stood up and gave him a long, hard look.

"At least ask her, Massimo. For me."

Then she went out into the hallway to call Pietro down for breakfast, leaving Massimo staring balefully into his coffee.

Cavolo!

By the time the clinic doors opened to the patients, Kendra had achieved a lot more than she'd expected to.

Found her way down from Villa Giovanna to Minori, without having to wait for Massimo.

Got breakfast of a café latte and pastry from the harborside café that opened before dawn to serve the fishermen and other early risers.

Then, taking her breakfast to go, she'd sat in front of the laundromat, knowing it wouldn't open for at least another hour and a half, but willing to wait. After all, her one surviving pair of scrubs was filthy, and she had to get them washed. Usually she'd do her washing herself, but today she was willing to pay extra for the proprietor's wife to do it for her, so she could get to work on time. Hopefully she could borrow something to wear, other than her less-than-professional white knit pants and band T-shirt.

She'd thought about asking Massimo or his grandmother for use of their washing machine the night before, but decided against it. Sitting around the kitchen table with Massimo, his *nonna* and Pietro had felt uncomfortable, but not in a way she would ever have expected.

There was that extreme awareness she always had around Massimo—that physical yearning she was able to subdue while at work—but which now, after all they'd gone through, was changed and heightened. She knew he'd endangered himself to help her and, in his own macho way, keep her safe. It both angered her and, somehow, lowered her resistance toward him.

Last night she was forced to acknowledge he had become even more of a threat to her peace than before, and that was saying a lot.

As if dealing with that weren't enough, there was Nonna, who turned out not to be the elegant doyen Kendra had assumed her to be on sight, but a far more dangerous beast: the mothering type.

There was absolutely no doubt in Kendra's mind that if she allowed that woman a toehold into her life, there would be all kinds of smothering and taking care of going on.

And that was the last thing she needed—or wanted—right now. Probably ever.

Yeah, definitely ever.

Then there was Pietro.

Seven or eight years old she judged, from his size and the fact that his adult upper front teeth were already in, but with the watchful light blue gaze of an old, old man. The type of man who's been through hell and is waiting for the other shoe to drop.

A gaze she knew all too well, from looking into the mirror as a child.

He tugged on her heartstrings—hard. She wanted to know what he was afraid of, here in this beautiful farmhouse, with people who obviously cared about him. Both Massimo and his grandmother made every effort to draw the little boy out, but he wouldn't budge from that cautious, disbelieving stance.

But it was clear he'd been with them for a while. There was a certain routine in how the three of them moved together.

When she'd come down from having her shower, Mrs.

Bianchi had said, "There you are, right on time. Pietro just finished setting the table. Massimo never takes long in the shower, so I'll start dishing out."

And Pietro had picked up a platter from the sideboard, and taken it to the stove for Mrs. Bianchi, with the easy manner of habit. Just like when Massimo came into the room and saw dinner already on the table, he'd gone to open a bottle of wine, and poured glasses for the adults. Then, in one of the sweetest gestures ever, he'd taken a bottle out of the refrigerator and poured some of its contents into another wineglass, which he set at Pietro's place setting.

There was such a homey atmosphere in that house, she almost couldn't stand it, and it made her even more curious about what had put that fear in Pietro's eyes.

She'd gotten out of there as quickly as possible that morning, just grateful that she'd been too exhausted to stay awake all night, thinking about Massimo being just a few steps away. But she had to admit that when she'd woken up and opened the curtains, she'd wanted, oh, so badly, to go down into the terraced garden and explore its beauty.

The view had made her breath hitch, and was another reason not to linger at Villa Giovanna.

Now, sitting outside the laundromat, surfing the web, looking for a shop close by that sold medical scrubs, she felt a strange mixture of sadness and relief at her swift escape.

"Buon giorno." Kendra looked up from her phone to see a man who looked vaguely familiar smiling at her. "You're the nurse who tried to punch Dottore Massimo yesterday. Such a strong blow! It's is very good he stepped away."

When he laughed, she couldn't help laughing with him. After he'd rehashed the entire building collapse, complete with wild hand motions and sound effects, he got around to asking her why she was there. On hearing she was waiting for the laundromat to open, he called the proprietor, who turned out to be his cousin. The next thing Kendra knew, the owner's wife came down and let her in, then promptly went back upstairs to finish feeding her family, leaving Kendra alone in the store.

Surprisingly, it was easy to find a place in Salerno that sold scrubs, and she placed an order for two new pairs, having learned the hard way that having an extra was wise.

You never knew when the house you were staying in might disintegrate, taking a pair of scrubs and a couple of pairs of panties with it.

So, by nine, she'd gotten to work under her own steam, had a full belly, clean scrubs and more on the way, and had told her coworkers the entire story about the night before.

What she didn't have was a new place to stay.

She'd started texting all her new friends in Minori the evening before, and although she'd had a number of people offer temporary accommodation, that wasn't what she was looking for. She really needed somewhere she could settle into for the next few months, until she moved on again. There was nothing worse than wasting valuable time constantly having to find and move to a new spot, when she could be exploring her surroundings.

But the tourist season was already in full swing, and the boardinghouses were full of seasonal workers. Plus, none of the *pensiones* were interested in negotiating a long-term lease, since short-term rentals and high turnover brought in a lot more revenue.

Having been in the storeroom when Massimo arrived, at least she didn't have to deal with seeing him immediately, and she wasn't scheduled to work with him either, which was a relief. She was sure he'd be annoyed that she'd left without waiting for him, or allowing his *nonna* to mollycoddle her with breakfast and more nosy questions. So, it was something of a surprise when he sent for her just as the clinic was closing for lunch, asking that she come to his office.

Already on high alert, she plastered a smile on her face before opening the door, although she didn't really feel particularly friendly. Or, to be more precise, felt perhaps too friendly toward him, as in wanting to grab him, kiss him, entice him into every naughty act they could manage.

"You wanted to see me?" she asked, standing in the open doorway, one foot in the office, the other still in the passageway.

Massimo looked up from the file he was making notes in, his expression so grim her heart faltered for a second.

"Come in, please. And close the door."

For a moment she considered refusing, but eventually did as bid. But she didn't walk any closer, staying just inside the door. He didn't ask her to sit down but, instead, rose and walked around to sit on the front edge of the desk. When he didn't immediately speak, but just sat staring at her with those unfathomable midnight eyes, her pulse rate went into overdrive. So she reacted the way she always did when feeling put on the spot.

She laughed.

His eyes flared with dark fire, and then narrowed, as she asked, "Am I in trouble or something? Maybe Nonna is upset because I ran out without breakfast?"

If the way his lips tightened meant anything, that had struck a nerve, but she ignored a pang of guilt, and kept smiling.

"She understood," he said in a low growl of a voice. "But that isn't what I want to talk to you about. *She* asked me to suggest that you rent a room from her at the villa."

The emphasis made it clear this was strictly his *nonna*'s

idea, and he wasn't as enthusiastic, which made it him and her alike. Yet there was a contrary part of her that wanted to feign enthusiasm, just to tweak his tail. Subduing it—and another bubble of amusement—took more effort than she expected.

"That's very nice of her, but I have some feelers out and expect I'll be able to find something soon."

He nodded and looked insultingly pleased with her refusal. Then he shook his head and frowned, as if reprimanding himself in some way.

"Nonna's business, like all tourist endeavors here, took a hard hit over the last couple of years. She's still worried that even though things have improved, she won't be able to catch back up financially. Having the extra money from you renting a room would make her feel a bit more secure, so if you don't find anywhere else to go, please consider her offer."

Now, that was understandable, and made it more difficult to refuse. Yet, could she really risk being not only in such constant contact with Massimo, but also immersed in the warm atmosphere of that lovely house? Everything inside shouted that doing so wouldn't be wise, but all she could do was hope she'd find somewhere else while still knowing better than to completely reject the opportunity.

She nodded, saying, "Sure. I'll keep it in mind."

And, by the end of the day, when no one else had come through, she had to acknowledge that Agriturismo Villa Giovanna may be her only option. But if she was going to stay there, she'd be doing it on her own terms, and no one else's.

CHAPTER EIGHT

MASSIMO WAS BOTH relieved and annoyed when he found out Kendra had asked to be able to leave the clinic early to run an errand. Since he hadn't finished examining Mrs. Lionetti the evening before, he'd arranged with Tino to go back and complete the elderly lady's checkup, but this time he had to take Fatima.

"Madonna!" she said, when she saw the still-impressive pile of rubble. "It's a wonder the injured man survived."

Massimo grunted in agreement, and once more his brain conjured the image of the rocks shifting, Kendra not moving out of the way. Sweat broke out along his brow and spine just remembering it.

Mrs. Lionetti was still so full of excitement about the building collapse, she omitted her usual acerbic comments, and the visit was quickly concluded. Massimo had drawn some blood, and told Tino he wanted her to go to the hospital in Salerno for additional tests.

"The memory problems you've described are concerning, and I want to try to discover what's causing them, before they get any worse."

Parting from Fatima not long after, Massimo made his way to his vehicle, which he'd left at the clinic. The streets were full of people, milling about, laughing and talking.

A few locals called out to him as he passed, but he simply waved and continued on.

He'd visited the area every summer since he was a boy, even younger than Pietro was now, and had lived here for almost seven years, but there were only a handful of people he'd call friends. He knew he had the reputation of being shy or retiring, but wasn't sure that was accurate. While at medical school in Roma, he'd developed a circle of acquaintances and had an active social life. That time of his life, he'd enjoyed the companionship, even though the living in the city wasn't to his liking. It had seemed appropriate to enjoy the bright lights and sometimes free and easy ways of youth.

That had continued for a while after he moved to Minori. Then, he had been far more outgoing, dining out some evenings, getting together with friends for various activities. It was during that time he'd met Therese, who had been hired as marketing manager at one of the nearby five-star hotels. She'd seemed everything he could wish for—smart, beautiful, charming—and he'd fallen hard from the moment he saw her sultry smile.

That had lasted just under three years. Despite her well-paying job, Therese had wanted to move on. Not out of ambition, but out of boredom with the Amalfi Coast and, he suspected, with him. Their final days together had been fraught with her biting indictments of his character and life, as though ridiculing him would somehow make her case stronger.

Now, when he considered his own shortcomings, instead of his father's jeers, which had haunted his younger self, now it was her voice he heard in his head.

Under those circumstances, was it any wonder that he preferred a quiet life, without fuss or dramatics?

At least that is what he told himself. Although loneliness niggled as he passed a trattoria, crowded with laughing, chatting patrons, and couldn't help looking to see if Kendra was in there.

But his grandmother had been right. His solitary life was a choice, and one he refused to regret. He was too old to change, and too cautious to risk his heart again, so the way things were was for the best.

Driving home, he found himself remembering the night before, when he'd had Kendra to keep him company. Even though much of the conversation was her berating him for going into Mrs. Ricci's house to get her belongings, tonight he found the drive too quiet, even with the radio going.

"Nonna, I'm home," he called out, as he walked in through the door.

"There you are," she said, stepping into the corridor and beaming at him. "I wasn't sure how late you'd be, but now that you're here, we'll eat. Kendra said not to wait for her, and so we won't."

He froze in the act of putting down his medical bag, and stared.

"Kendra?"

"Yes," his grandmother replied, stepping back into the kitchen, her voice fading. "She called to say she might be late, and I told her not to worry. We'll leave the door unlocked for her, and she can just lock it behind her when she comes in."

He was thankful Nonna wasn't looking at him, since he had no idea what the expression on his face was. Composing himself, he went into the kitchen, trying to be nonchalant.

"When did you speak to her?"

"She called this afternoon, about four. Thanked me very much for the offer, and said she would take me up on it.

We negotiated a price, and that's when she said she'd be in late."

Massimo stood in the doorway, unsure of whether what he was feeling was annoyance or excitement or both. Whatever it was, he was absolutely sure he didn't like it.

He'd been so sure she wouldn't accept Nonna's invitation, he'd never really considered the impact it would have if she did.

"Did you tell her the bus doesn't run along this route after a certain time?"

Nonna gave a shrug, and tasted the sauce she was stirring, before replying, "I mentioned it, but I am not worried. Your Kendra seems very capable and sensible. I'm sure she already knew that."

But now his mind was already gnawing at the idea of her walking up the steep hill by herself in the dark, although it wasn't really dark yet. Or perhaps accepting a drive from someone who might be unsavory. Or...

"Massimo, stop worrying." Nonna sounded as though she were trying not to laugh. "As our boarder, Kendra can come and go as she pleases, and I will not have you glaring at her as you are now just because she chooses to live her own life."

"I am not glaring," he said, automatically, which made his grandmother chuckle.

"Pietro, is Zio Massimo glaring, or no?"

For the first time in days, he saw Pietro's lips twitch into a little smile. "He is glaring, Nonna Bianchi."

"See? It's a wonder you haven't turned the milk sour with that face."

Massimo forced himself to relax, and smile. "But the milk can't see my face, Nonna, since it is in the refrigerator."

And he was so very happy to hear Pietro laugh.

It worried him, how solemn and silent the little boy was. Not that there was anything wrong with being quiet, as he himself knew all too well. But the feeling that Pietro perhaps wasn't happy here with them gnawed at him all the time. Wanting what was best for a child, and not knowing what that was, was heartbreaking.

"Let me go and wash up for dinner," he said, taking one last fond look at that small smile still on Pietro's face. "And then you both can tell me all about your day."

They had just sat down to eat when Massimo heard the unmistakable sound of a scooter coming up the hill. When it turned into the driveway, he exchanged a startled glance with his grandmother, and excused himself to go to the front door. Occasionally, although infrequently, they had guests turn up looking for accommodation without calling ahead.

But before he could get to the door, it opened and Kendra walked in, knapsack on her back, carrying her duffel and a couple of shopping bags.

She paused when she saw him, and for a long moment neither of them moved, or spoke. Massimo was aware of his heart thundering, and his muscles tightening, as though preparing for combat, but he tried not to let any of his inner turmoil show.

"I hope you weren't waiting for me to come in," she said, lips in a slight smile that didn't fool him for a moment.

She too looked as though ready for war.

"Of course not," he said, although it had been his intention to do just that. "When I heard the scooter, I didn't know it was you. I thought perhaps it was some tourists looking for lodging."

"Good," she said succinctly, closing and locking the door behind her. Then she started for the staircase. "I don't plan on being a disruption to your family routine, and I certainly don't need babysitting, so it's best to start as we mean to go on."

"Certamente." He was sure she was going to make him crazy over the next months but he'd be damned before he let her know that. "Did you rent the scooter?"

"No. Once I realized it made sense to take your grandmother up on her offer, I went to Salerno and bought it, secondhand. I don't want to have to depend on the bus—or you—to get around."

That shouldn't hurt, but it did.

"Ah, Kendra," his grandmother called from the kitchen. "Did you eat?"

"Yes, I did, thank you, Mrs. Bianchi." She was partway up the stairs, but paused politely.

"Good. Make yourself at home. Later, if you like, I will show you where to find everything."

"Thank you," she said again. "I'd appreciate that."

Then she was gone, and Massimo stood there, staring up after her until he heard her door close with a decisive snap.

Kendra closed her bedroom door, and let out a long breath.

This was such a bad idea, yet she'd had to admit to herself she didn't have a lot of choice when it came to somewhere to stay. None of the other avenues had panned out, and the people she'd spoke to didn't seem terribly optimistic about her chances of finding a new place to rent.

Sighing, she put her bags on the bench near the cupboard and, as though drawn by a magnet, moved to the window to look out at the view. Villa Giovanna was set into the side of the hill, the windows at the back overlooking the terraces below and then out to the distant sea. Beyond a hill she could see a bit of Minori, but the town didn't hold her attention. Instead, she found herself looking down into the gardens and groves below, lushly green and bright with flowers.

There was something about the landscape that called to her, but she refused to answer.

Just like she refused to do more than acknowledge the draw of Massimo Bianchi.

And his family too.

What she really needed to do was set very specific boundaries while she was here.

There would be no coddling. No happy roommates. No becoming part of the family.

To make it work she'd get up early and leave quietly, without stopping for even a cup of coffee—although Mrs. Bianchi had made it clear breakfast and dinner were included in her rent.

Come home late, after they'd already eaten, and go up to her room to watch movies and shows on her tablet.

Take off on the weekends to explore the surrounding area.

Those boundaries were more for her than for the Bianchis.

The atmosphere in the house attracted her deep down, and she knew better than to give in to the lure of "belonging."

That never lasted.

"Belonging" always turned into heartbreak when she once more became an outsider.

She'd long since given up believing she truly could fit in anywhere. Since she was ten, every time she thought she'd found a safe haven and people who wanted her forever, she'd been wrong. And now she was old enough, and wise enough, to know you only got hurt if you allowed others to get too close.

So she kept her distance.

And that's what she needed to do here, especially from Massimo.

He was even more attractive than the atmosphere at Agriturismo Villa Giovanna, especially the longer she worked with him.

A man that big, that solemn, shouldn't be so good with people of every age and condition, and yet he was. On the outside he gave the impression of standoffishness, but she'd seen him charm the crankiest *nonna* or gently calm the most frightened child with ease. With the men he was like a son, or brother, while he treated the younger women with genuine respect.

The first time she heard him sing a silly song to distract a scared baby, something inside her melted, and refused to solidify afterward. Massimo, in all his incarnations, threatened to derail her carefully constructed detachment.

She was honest enough to admit she still wanted him. That she couldn't help remembering just how wonderful he'd made her feel, and acknowledged it was torture to know he was right next door and she couldn't touch him. What she knew, however, was that the only way to survive the situation unscathed was to stay away from him as much as possible. Which was extremely difficult since now they both worked and lived in the same places.

And she needed to stay out of his family life too.

Even now, as she got ready to have her shower, she yearned to go downstairs and join them, be welcomed to take part in their evening ritual.

It was a yearning she'd given in to at every place she'd moved to after her father died, and his family started passing her around from one house to another. At each new relative's home, she'd try to integrate, to find a way to fit in, so she'd be one of the family, but it didn't really work, and soon she'd be passed on again.

Now, all these years later, she better understood that none of them had had the financial ability to raise her alone, and that they'd tried to do the best they could. Yet, the fact that not one of them thought to keep her made her sure there'd been something fundamentally wrong with her. If not, why didn't even one of her aunts or uncles try to find a way for her to stay with them?

No. Keeping a firm, polite distance while at Agriturismo Villa Giovanna was the best thing to do.

Her peace of mind, and her heart, demanded it.

CHAPTER NINE

SHE TRIED HER very best to follow her plan, but it fell apart far quicker than she'd expected.

A week in, to be precise.

That morning, when she opened her door to leave for work, she found a café latte and a pastry on a tray in the passageway. She stared at it for a long moment, considering whether to just ignore it, but she could never be so very rude. Not to someone who'd only ever tried to be nice.

Taking the tray, she went downstairs to thank Mrs. Bianchi, who was bustling about making breakfast for her guests, only to have her shrug in a way Kendra was beginning to realize was habitual.

"Pietro asked if he could take it up for you, and I told him yes. He's a sweet, kind boy and I think he was worried that you were going to work without any breakfast." She smiled, looking out the window to where the little boy sat on a bench, eating an apple, an open book on his lap. "I always tell him he must have something to eat in the morning, since it is oh, so hard to think straight on an empty stomach."

Kendra found herself melting, and tried to pull herself together. It was this kind of nonsense she had to guard against, but how do you harden your heart toward a lovely little boy like that?

"He's always thinking of others." Mrs. Bianchi sighed, still absently drying the plate in her hand, although she must've been in danger of wiping the pattern off. "I think it is because there were so many of them in the orphanage that the older children got used to taking care of the younger."

Oh, Kendra could understand that only too well. Hadn't she always bent over backward to try to help out so as to prove her worth?

It was heartbreaking to see it playing out in another young life.

And now her curiosity was aroused. How had Pietro come to be here? What were Mrs. Bianchi's plans for the youngster, going forward?

Even acknowledging it was none of her business, Kendra couldn't stop herself from asking, "How did you find Pietro?"

Finally putting down the plate, the older lady turned to Kendra. "My daughter-in-law Sophia, Massimo's mother, works for the child welfare agency in Napoli. I was visiting one day, and she asked me if I'd like to go to the orphanage with her, as they were doing a volunteer workday there—cooking a special meal for the children, playing games with them, that sort of thing. Of course, I said yes, and while I was there, I saw Pietro, and knew I had to bring him home with me."

"Just like that?" Kendra asked, unable to mask the skepticism in her voice.

"*Sì,*" she replied, with a firm nod. "It was like when I saw my darling husband, all those years ago. Love at first sight. Only this time, it was with a little boy who had no one, and needed to belong somewhere."

Kendra nodded, still unconvinced, but unwilling to say so.

Fingering the cross that hung from a chain around her neck, Mrs. Bianchi continued, "He was left in a *culla per la vita*, a baby hatch, in Napoli when he was just days old. They never found his mother, and he was sent to the orphanage." She placed a gentle hand on Kendra's arm, and said, "Sometimes, you just know something is right, and meant to be, and I knew that as soon as I saw him. I am too old to adopt him, but Massimo and I have decided that Pietro will always have a home here, with us, no matter what may happen."

Swallowing hard, Kendra didn't reply, ridiculously touched and unwilling to show it. Finally, when she was sure her voice would sound normal, she smiled and said, "Let me go and thank Pietro for my breakfast."

Then, taking her coffee with her, she slipped out through the glass doors into the cool of the morning, stopping to take a few steadying breaths before walking over to sit beside Pietro. He looked up, his too-old blue eyes surveying her for a moment before returning to his book.

"Good morning. I wanted to thank you for the coffee and pastry," she said. "It was very nice of you to bring them up for me."

"You're welcome," he said, his gaze steadfast on the page in front of him.

"What are you reading?"

Keeping his place with one finger, he flipped the book closed to show her the cover. "It's about two boys who run away to have an adventure."

"Is it any good?" she asked, amused at his succinct description.

He shrugged, the gesture so much like Mrs. Bianchi's signature shoulder movement it made Kendra smile.

"It's not bad, but I think they are really quite silly. When they left home, they took nothing useful or handy, just some bread and water."

"Well, at least they have some food. And everyone needs water to survive, don't they?"

Earnest blue eyes looked back up at her, as Pietro nodded. "*Sì*. But why do they have no compass, or even a map? And look at their shoes." He pointed to the cover, his finger touching the sneakers the boys were wearing. Old-school sneakers, with canvas tops and rubber toes, like the ones basketball players used to wear. "They are supposed to be going through rough terrain. Their feet should be hurting, all the time, and yet they never are."

So much logic from such a little chap. It made Kendra want to laugh, but she squelched the urge, knowing he would probably misunderstand. Instead, she nodded in agreement.

"You're right. They were being silly or, at the very least, not thinking things through properly before they started."

"Exactly." He nodded approvingly, his lips twitching up just slightly at the corners. "They didn't plan at all well, but I'll keep reading to see how it all turns out."

"I understand," she replied, keeping her face solemn. "I don't like not finishing a book I start either."

They exchanged a glance of sheer and complete understanding, and once more Kendra's heart melted. He really was the sweetest little fellow.

But there was still the matter she came out here to discuss with him. "While I appreciate the coffee this morning, Pietro, you don't need to bring me breakfast every day."

The smile faded and his eyes grew shuttered as he nodded silently, and she felt the connection they'd developed start to disintegrate.

"Why don't I come down and have breakfast before I leave, instead?"

His gaze flew back to her face, and he looked at her carefully, as if judging and weighing her words. Then he seemed to relax, and he nodded.

"That would be good. Nonna Bianchi wouldn't worry so much, then." She tried not to react to his words, but must have shown something, because he rushed on. "She worries about everyone. Zio Massimo, her family in Napoli, the guests who visit, even me."

Oh, Lord, this little man was dead set on breaking her heart completely, wasn't he? And what on earth was she supposed to say to that, when she completely understood exactly how he felt? Once you became used to being an afterthought, or a burden others had to bear, it was so difficult to break free from those thoughts.

But his situation was very different from the one she went through, and she wished there was some way to be reassuring, without making him feel she was just spouting platitudes.

"Pietro..." Her voice broke slightly, and she had to stop, swallow, clear her throat before she could continue. "Pietro, everyone deserves to be worried over. Besides, Nonna Bianchi doesn't just worry for no reason. She worries because she cares. Because she loves. And love isn't like a cake, that once you've cut it and eaten it, it's gone. Love lasts forever, no matter what."

Once more that probing blue gaze turned her way, and his eyebrows rose slightly.

"But how can she love so much?"

She said the first thing that came to mind. "I think we all can, if we allow ourselves to, and if we get enough practice, and Nonna Bianchi has had a lot of time to get it right."

He considered that for a long moment, and she could

almost see those logical gears in his mind turning over. Then he nodded.

"*Sì*, she is very old, and must have had a lot of people to practice on."

Kendra couldn't help the little chuckle that broke from her throat. "That's true, but maybe you shouldn't mention her age to her. Ladies don't like being called ancient."

To her surprise, Pietro giggled, and she couldn't help laughing with him, mostly from relief from having navigated a sticky conversation without getting all tangled up.

"Come on," she said, getting to her feet. "I need to get to work."

"Okay." Pietro carefully marked his place in his book, and got up too. As they walked back toward the house, he said, "I thought of something else those boys should have taken with them, on their adventure. A pocketknife."

"That's a good one," she said, as he opened the kitchen door for her, and stood back a little for her to precede him into the room. What a gentleman. "How about matches? In case they need to light a fire, and cook?"

"Ah! *Sì!* That is also a good one." He was beaming, as though she were the smartest person he'd ever met. "What else?"

She stepped through the door, and there was Massimo, sitting at the table, watching them. There was no way to gauge what his expression meant, but it sent alternating waves of hot and cold through her body.

"Cheese," she said, not knowing where that came from, but when Pietro laughed, she added, "I love cheese, and would *never* go on an adventure without some."

Which, thankfully, made Pietro laugh even harder, and allowed her to break free from focusing on Zio Massimo's face.

There'd been enough of having her heartstrings tugged on for the day, thank you very much.

The clinic was busy with waves of tourist patients, but although Massimo was kept hopping all morning, whenever he had a free moment his mind immediately turned to Kendra.

And Pietro.

How had she so easily broken through the little boy's normal reticence and got him to laugh like that?

Not that Pietro never smiled or laughed, but usually it took a great deal of effort to make it happen. Effort Massimo tried to put in, but that was not always successful either.

And the smile on her face had a different tone to it as well. As though all of her usual smiles and laughter were a facade, and this moment of enjoyment—of connection—was the real one.

Did that include the smiles and laughter she'd shared with him in bed?

He tried to think back to that night, which seemed horribly long ago, but the memory was clouded by a fog of lust and passion, and couldn't be trusted.

"Dr. Bianchi? We have a Japanese tourist being brought in following a fall at Villa Romana. The ambulance personnel report that he was traveling alone, and speaks no Italian and little English."

Before he could respond, he heard that familiar voice from behind him say, "I speak some Japanese. Perhaps I can translate."

Of course she would be the one to assist, at the time when he really least wanted to be around her, but Massimo bit back a sigh and nodded.

"Thank you."

He tried not to sound as grudgeful as he felt, but knew he hadn't been successful when she chuckled, which just brought on that crazy spike of need that drove through him any time he heard her do so.

She was driving him quietly insane. Just knowing she was in the house at night kept him awake and awash with desire. He was becoming so irritable, Nonna was avoiding speaking to him as much as possible. Strangely, though, his grandmother hadn't asked him what was wrong. Normally she'd have been probing at him like a dentist at a sore tooth, trying to find the root of the problem.

It was going to be an excruciating few months until she left.

But the thought of her leaving, and things going back to normal, just made him more edgy.

The Japanese patient was brought in with a laceration on his arm and a bump on the back of his head. According the Kendra, he was apologizing and saying he didn't need to be in the hospital, and although he couldn't understand what she was saying in reply, Massimo had no doubt she was being reassuring.

That was something he'd noticed about her—that there was a deep well of understanding and empathy beneath her jocularity and seemingly easygoing nature. Patients and coworkers alike gravitated to her and seemed to feel completely comfortable in her presence.

"He says he was walking backward, looking up, and didn't pay attention to where he was going. He thinks he slipped on a stone, and he put out his hand to try to grab onto anything to stop from falling, but cut his arm instead as he fell."

"Hematoma above the lower left parietal bone, but no signs of concussion. Ask if he's feeling nauseous or sleepy."

As Kendra asked the patient what he wanted to know, Massimo examined the laceration on Mr. Tanaka's arm.

"He admits to a headache, but none of the other symptoms. How is his arm?"

"Not too severe a cut, but it will need stitches. How long will he be in the area? He'll have to get the stitches removed in about ten days."

After some conversation, she said, "He'll be back home by then, and he promises he'll go to his doctor in Nagasaki and get them removed."

"Good." Massimo gave the other man a smile, but found Mr. Tanaka's gaze was trained on Kendra's face, and his expression made Massimo clench his teeth. "I'll clean and suture his arm…"

"Oh?" Kendra raised an eyebrow. "I can do that. You have other patients waiting."

"I like to take care of these things myself, for the tourists, when I can." True but, in this case, he had a definite ulterior motive—removing Kendra from the equation. "And that will free you up to take vitals on the next patient."

"But you won't be able to speak to Mr. Tanaka if you need to."

"I think we've covered everything necessary. If you tell him what's going to happen, you can give him the instructions about his wound before he leaves."

He thought he sounded reasonable, but Kendra gave him a long look and he thought she was going to laugh, but she held it back.

"Sure," she said, the corners of her lips twitching.

She spoke to Mr. Tanaka, and the disappointment on the other man's face was obvious. When his patient finally looked at Massimo, he knew his smile wasn't as kind as it could be.

But he didn't care.

CHAPTER TEN

THE PROBLEM WITH making concessions is that once you started, it was difficult not to keep giving ground. Which is how Kendra came to be having dinner with the Bianchi family one Thursday night, about two weeks after she'd first moved in.

It was impossible to say no to Pietro when he invited her, especially when he added, "It would make Nonna Bianchi happy, I think."

"Will it make you happy?" she asked, wanting him to know that, to her, his happiness was just as important.

And when he nodded, a tiny, hopeful smile tipping the edges of his mouth, she had to agree, even knowing being around Massimo was becoming achingly difficult.

While there was no escaping her physical reactions to him, it was his other attributes that had captured and held her attention.

The gentleness. His ability to make anyone he was speaking to feel as though he was completely focused on them. The way he treated his grandmother and Pietro.

Then there was the sight of him, one morning, just as the sun was rising, down among the lemon trees, carefully tending the plants and picking fruit for his grandmother.

Something about his demeanor, his calm surety as he moved from plant to plant, the motion of his hands—almost caressing—made her heart race, and a warm space open in her chest.

The more she got to know him, the more beautiful she found him, and she knew, deep inside, he presented a fundamental danger to her.

Exactly what that danger was, she wasn't sure. But it existed, and she didn't know how to handle it, or what to do.

And if she wasn't already aware of how strong the attraction was growing, it became completely clear on her last sightseeing trip, the weekend before. Although she'd made a point of coming down and having coffee in the kitchen before going to work each morning, she'd also made sure to make herself scarce most of the rest of the time. The first weekend after moving into Villa Giovanna, she'd taken a friend's suggestion and gone to explore Vietri sul Mare and the neighboring Cetara.

Neither of those small villages got the massive influx of tourists some of the other Amalfi Coast towns did, and the quiet, more laid-back atmosphere should have been calming. Yet, while she'd tried to enjoy the beauty surrounding her, investigating the myriad pottery stores in Vietri and enjoying the wonderful cuisine, the entire trip had felt surprisingly flat. It was as though something vital had been missing.

Again and again she'd found her mind turning to Massimo, wondering what he was doing, until she'd gotten completely annoyed with herself. She'd been tempted to cut her visit short, but forced herself to stay until Sunday, as planned.

So, when Pietro had invited her to join them for dinner, she'd really wanted to refuse. Nevertheless, having given her word, she presented herself at the dinner table, a little self-consciously but with her chin up, unwilling to let any of them see how unsure she was.

Mrs. Bianchi and Pietro greeted her with broad smiles, while Massimo gave her a comprehensive once-over that made her glad she'd changed into a knit sundress for the occasion. She'd also let her hair down, catching it back with a brightly colored band and letting it wave down her back.

"How lovely you look," Mrs. Bianchi said. "I don't know how you manage to be so chic while living out of a suitcase all the time."

It shouldn't be gratifying, but Kendra couldn't help the little glow of pride the older lady's words gave her.

"I long ago discovered the joys of knit clothing," she replied, with a grin. "And I tend to follow the sun, so I don't need heavy winter clothes. That makes packing light a lot easier too."

"I think your ingenuity and adventurous spirit is wonderful. I'm afraid I couldn't do what you do." Mrs. Bianchi looked around the cheerful kitchen, and shook her head. "I went from my parents' home to my husband's, and just…never left."

While her tone was rueful, there was no hint of sadness, and Kendra found herself wanting to say that she didn't blame her in the slightest. That life at Villa Giovanna seemed idyllic, so it was completely understandable. But, just then, Kendra's gaze got tangled up with Massimo's and, as her heart went into overdrive, she bit back the words.

The seemed too intimate, suddenly.

Too revealing.

But she realized halfway through the meal that all her reticence and hesitations had disappeared, as the conversation ebbed and flowed from topic to topic, drawing her in. The dynamic within the family was easy to become a part of, keeping her engaged and making her comfortable.

"Where are you off to this weekend?" Mrs. Bianchi asked, as Kendra helped her clear the table, and Massimo went to the fridge for the limoncello.

"Someone suggested I go to Capri, but the week has been so busy, I haven't made any real plans. I do have tomorrow off as well, though, so I might just do a day trip. I doubt Fridays are as busy as the weekend would be there."

"Oh, Capri is beautiful." Mrs. Bianchi gave a decisive nod. "You really should go. Massimo, do you know if Sergio is going to be at his villa this weekend?"

Who on earth was Sergio?

"I think he's still in Venice, on that project," Massimo said. "He's not due back for another couple of weeks."

"Well, then, you should call him and ask if you can stay at his villa and take Kendra to Capri. I know you're off tomorrow too, so you could make a long weekend of it."

"Oh, that's not—"

"I don't think—"

Both she and Massimo spoke at the same time, and stopped at the same time, which made Mrs. Bianchi look from one of them to the other. Yet, after that, she changed the subject, as though nothing untoward at all had happened.

Risking a glance at Massimo, she found him looking at her from under his lashes, and there was no mistaking his expression.

Desire.

Heat encompassed her entire body and Kendra tore her gaze away, but she knew without a doubt, should they go to Capri—or anywhere else—together, what would happen.

The lust swirling between them was unmistakable, and undeniable, no matter how hard she tried to ignore it or will it away.

Thankfully, just then, Pietro suddenly said, "Zio Massimo, why do you have a car, while Signorina Kendra has a scooter?"

Massimo's eyebrows rose, but he replied in his usual calm way, "I drive a car because I sometimes need to go longer distances, like when I visit Napoli. Besides, I have to carry my medical bag with me wherever I go."

Pietro seemed to consider that answer for a moment, and then said, "But Signorina Kendra carried all her clothes and everything here on her scooter, so there must be room. And I think her scooter is much nicer than your car. Wouldn't you prefer to ride a scooter?"

Relieved at the change of subject, and thoroughly tickled, Kendra bit her lip to hold back her laughter at the thought of Massimo giving up his comfortable luxury car for a small motorbike. But it became harder to contain her mirth when she glanced at Massimo's expression. He was trying so hard to remain serious in the face of the little boy's questions, but there was a decidedly amused twinkle in his eyes.

"I used to ride a scooter when I was young, at university in Roma, and it was a great deal of fun then."

Once more the little boy gave his reply some thought, then asked, "Was that so very long ago that you wouldn't like it anymore?"

Kendra choked on the chuckle that rose into her throat. Was the little devil calling Massimo old, without actually saying it?

For his part, Massimo stared blandly at Pietro for a long beat, and then said, "After I've finished my *digestivo*, with Signorina Kendra's permission, I'll show you that I am indeed still quite capable of riding a scooter."

She couldn't hold back her laughter anymore, even when Massimo sent her a glance best described as smoldering— which sent a thrill of need through her body.

"Oh," she gasped, hoping everyone blamed her breathlessness on her amusement, rather than deep desire. "Of course you may. I look forward to seeing that."

"You will most certainly see it," he replied, giving her a look from beneath his long lashes. "For you will be on the back of the scooter with me."

"Will I, now?" She tried to keep her voice amused and level, but her heart was suddenly pounding, and she knew she'd failed.

"Indeed," he replied, his voice deep and slow, which ridiculously increased the heat rushing through her veins. "I insist on it."

Mrs. Bianchi clicked her tongue and said, "When I was young, a boy asking me to ride on the back of his scooter was something my parents wouldn't approve of. In fact, the only person whose scooter I rode on, I ended up marrying."

"Luckily for us all, times have changed, Nonna."

It shouldn't annoy her to hear him say that. After all, she agreed with him. Yet, she had to squash a spurt of irritation.

"Not always for the better," the elderly lady answered. "Not always for the better."

"Perhaps you're right, Nonna." Massimo was looking down at his limoncello, those thick fingers twisting the glass back and forth, his eyes hidden so she couldn't read their expression. "There are definitely times when some of those silent but easily understood signals would be useful to have."

Was it her imagination, or was there a deeper meaning to his words? And was that cryptic message meant for her?

Just then his lashes rose, and he met her gaze with one that momentarily flashed with unmistakable fire. Heat that transferred itself right into her body and ricocheted—like a lightning strike—through her blood.

Which of them looked away first, she didn't know, but if she'd held his gaze a moment more, it would be impossible not to reveal the desire heightening her senses and making her thighs tremble.

She laughed—more to relieve the nervous energy sparking beneath her skin than anything else—and from the corner of her eye she saw Massimo tip the last of his *digestivo* into his mouth.

"Come, then," he said, getting to his feet. "Let us take a ride, Signorina Kendra."

And, for her, there really was no mistaking his meaning now.

"With pleasure," she replied, without thinking it through, which made her chuckle again.

Perhaps Kendra thought they'd just go to the end of the driveway and back to the house, but Massimo had other plans. It was time to get the situation between them straight, before he did something embarrassing, like try to kiss the amusement off her lips.

Under Pietro's watchful eyes, and Nonna's somewhat worried gaze, he got the scooter off the stand, and straddled it. After he'd started it, he looked back at Kendra, who was still chuckling, the sound going straight through his soul and sending his libido into overdrive.

She needed no prompting, but came and got onto the seat behind him and, snuggling herself to his back, put her arms around his waist. For them both to fit, he had to sit far forward, with his long legs bent slightly out, and he knew she couldn't be terribly comfortable, but she didn't complain.

And he realized, now, why his grandmother hadn't been allowed to ride on the back of men's scooters when she was young. There was something incredibly sensual about knowing he was cradled between Kendra's bare, spread thighs, and the way her arms gripped his waist. Not to mention the sensation of her lush breasts pressing against his back.

As he opened the throttle, the thought came to him that if she moved her hand down, just a little, she'd be able to grasp his erection. His instinctive reaction to that image made the scooter wobble.

Which made Kendra laugh even harder.

Which made him even harder.

In the distance he heard Pietro shout something, but couldn't make out the words. Then they were out the gate, and he was steering the vehicle up the hill, away from Minori. The family land extended for several acres on both sides of the road, and he had a special place in mind to take Kendra. It was one of his favorite spots on the property, and one few people knew even existed, and so would be deserted.

The road switched back, and he took the tight corner as fast as he dared. He was rewarded for his bravado when Kendra let out a *whoop* of enjoyment. Here, now, the land leveled off a little, and what looked like an untamed woodland lay to their right. He slowed and, once he was sure no traffic was coming, swerved onto the track into the trees. Slowing even more, they bumped along for a few yards, then he brought the scooter to a halt, and turned it off.

Putting his feet down to steady the bike, he waited for Kendra to alight, but she stayed where she was, arms tight around him, those delicious breasts firm against his back.

"What is this place?" she asked, her breath warm against his neck.

"It is part of the upper acreage of the farm," he replied, doing his best to keep his voice even, although his heart was pounding. "While it's cultivated farther along, we keep this part mostly wild, except for one place, which I'd like to show you."

Was it his imagination, or did her arms tighten slightly, before she let go and got off the scooter?

"Lead on," she said, as he put the scooter on the stand.

Getting off, he held out his hand, his breath catching in his chest until she took it, twining her fingers through his. The stand of trees wasn't very big, and he knew this land better than almost anyone alive, so it took only a minute or so to guide her to the spot.

"Oh!" The wonder in her voice, as she stared out at the field of wildflowers, made his heart sing. "Massimo, how beautiful. How did this come to be here?"

"My grandfather made this clearing in the trees and sowed seeds of native flowering plants to make sure his neighbor's bees would never lack for nectar and pollen. It's beautiful in spring, but this is the perfect time to see it, although different plants bloom all the way through to autumn."

She was still holding his hand, and her fingers tightened around his, but she didn't say anything.

Although he'd always loved this place, her stunned, silent appreciation caused him to look at the field in a new way. As though seeing it for the first time, instead of the thousandth.

The scent of the flowers rose in the warm air, and the low buzz of the last bees of the evening could be heard on the breeze. But it was the waves of colored petals that gave the field its beauty and majesty. Sometimes it was easy to take such sights for granted, or to focus on the ephemeral nature of the blooms, rather than living in the now. With intention, and the knowledge that life was too short not to grasp opportunities with both hands when they were presented.

"I want you." He said it as he felt it, with conviction, and no restraint. "And I wanted you to know it."

Once more she squeezed his fingers, but then she withdrew her hand from his. Still staring out at the flowers, she took an audible breath, and he couldn't help noticing that she didn't laugh.

He filed that away for later consideration.

"I want you too," she finally said, in a tone that conveyed nothing but the factual nature of her feelings. "But I respect your grandmother far too much to conduct any kind of ongoing affair under her roof."

"Understandable." And, in his mind, commendable.

"And," she continued, before he could say anything more, "you need to know there can be no emotional involvement. I'll be gone in a matter of months, and I don't like drama."

"Also understandable, and I don't like dramatics either."

As for a lack of emotional involvement, he would try his hardest not to get in any way attached. In this they were also in accord.

She'd been looking out over the field as she spoke, but now turned to search his face with an intent gaze.

"There also can't be any kind of weirdness at work. If we can't maintain our professional relationship at the clinic, then it would be best we don't get further involved."

He shrugged. "We slept together before you came to the clinic, and I think you'd agree we've been able to work together completely harmoniously, and without difficulties."

Kendra's eyebrows rose, as though she was about to argue the point, but then she just shook her head and said, "If you can figure out a way for us to be together that doesn't include your grandmother being aware of it, I'd be interested."

Her tone would suggest she were talking about a job, or

some other mundane matter, rather than the heart-stopping opportunity he felt it to be. And he was tempted to match her sangfroid, but something within rebelled against pretending a disinterest he truly didn't feel.

So, instead of replying, he stepped close, and pulled her into his arms.

"Let's make sure this is something we want to pursue," he said, dipping his lips close to hers, gratified to realize her breathing was rushed, relieved when she didn't hesitate to wrap her arms around his neck.

When she pulled his head down the final inch so their lips met, and immediately deepened the kiss into the realm of carnal and arousing, Massimo thought the top of his head would explode.

Finally, knowing that if they didn't stop, he would ease her down into the flowers and take the encounter to the next level, he reluctantly drew away. But they stayed locked together for another few long beats, as he drowned in the depth of her aroused, heavy-lidded gaze.

"Was there ever a doubt we'd want to pursue it?" she asked, the question obviously a rhetorical one.

Then, when she followed it up with a delicious round of laughter, it took all of his control to let her go.

CHAPTER ELEVEN

HE SUGGESTED THEY take advantage of his grandmother's suggestion and go to Capri the following day.

"My cousin Sergio is an actor and owns a villa on the island," he said, as he casually withdrew a small knife from his pocket. Opening it, he began to pick a handful of flowers. "If he's in agreement, we can stay there. If it isn't available, I can find us another place."

With an electric current still humming through her veins from their kisses, Kendra eagerly agreed. It had taken all of her willpower to let him go, instead of dragging him down into the flowers and having her way with him.

Bees, bugs and potential thorns be damned.

"Oh," she said, surprised and dangerously touched when he presented her with the flowers. "I'll try not to crush them on the ride down."

His lips quirked into a sly smile, as they made their way back to where the motorbike was parked. "And I'll try to be a bit more sedate with how I operate the scooter. There was something about having you behind me that made me rash."

As it turned out, they didn't have to do anything in furtherance of their planned excursion, having an unwitting coconspirator in their proposed affair. By the time they got back to Villa Giovanna, Massimo's grandmother had already contacted Sergio and arranged their accommodation.

"He said you should text him if you need the housekeeper to be on duty while you're there. Otherwise, he'll arrange for her to meet you in the morning and hand over the keys."

"I think we can manage on our own for such a short time," Massimo replied in a bland tone that sent little shivers over Kendra's skin, raising goose bumps in their wake.

She definitely wanted to have him alone in that villa, to do all manner of naughty things with and to him. Having someone else in the house didn't fit in with her plans at all.

Now that she'd made the decision to sleep with him again, she was all in. She'd never been a halfway type of person, and this situation called for a full-on assault. After all, hadn't she spent the last weeks desperately keeping her lust for him in check? Having given and received the green light to get back into bed together, she wanted everything she could get from him, and she had to lock her trembling knees as she considered what the next day might bring.

Thankfully, just then Pietro came barreling through the door into the kitchen.

"Zio, *signorina*, you are back. You were gone so long, I thought you had gone on an adventure far away."

Kendra couldn't help the little bubble of mirth that flew from her lips. "Zio Massimo took me to the flower field up the hill." Showing him the flowers she still had in her hand, she continued. "It is too late in the evening for adventures, especially if they involve pirates. I'm not fond of pirates."

"Zio Massimo would protect you." Pietro mimed pulling a sword and danced about, as though in the midst of an intense fight. "No pirate could harm you if he's there."

His fancy footwork had him bouncing into Mrs. Bianchi, who put out a hand to steady herself against the counter and said, "Careful there, Pietro."

Although she didn't sound cross at all, the little boy froze, his eyes widening in apparent fear, and Kendra felt her heart contract in sympathy. Before she could say anything, though, Massimo intervened.

"I think a proper sword fight should be conducted outside, don't you?" When Pietro didn't move, Massimo crossed the kitchen toward him, saying, "Come, young squire. Let us take up arms and practice to defeat our common foe."

Mrs. Bianchi ran a gentle hand over the little boy's hair, and said softly, "It is all right, Pietro. Go with Zio Massimo and play in the garden."

Obediently Pietro took Massimo's outstretched hand, and they went out together. As they walked away, Kendra could see the stiffness in both their gaits and hear the rise and fall of Massimo's deep voice, but not the words. Drawn to the pair, she moved closer to the door, and found herself standing beside Mrs. Bianchi, who'd done the same.

As man and boy moved across the grass toward the small shed at the edge of the garden, the older woman sighed.

"I worry about Pietro. Sometimes I think he's settled in completely, and is happy, and then…"

Kendra understood, and patted the other woman's shoulder.

"It will take time for him to fully feel secure."

She was speaking from experience.

It was only too easy to remember the feeling of waiting, wondering when, exactly, she'd be rejected again, and have to leave wherever she was. The sensation of walking on eggshells, afraid that if she did anything wrong, no matter how small, she'd be punished and sent away. Never wanting to make a mistake. Always trying her hardest to be good.

Perfect.

And yet, knowing that eventually she'd be shuffled off, proving once more that she was somehow unlovable, and easy to get rid of.

She didn't say any of that, though, and as Mrs. Bianchi had grown silent too, she simply watched Massimo march back out of the shed, Pietro like a little shadow behind him.

"Oh, dear," Nonna said, amusement now tingeing her voice. "The canes I use to tie up my plants are now to be swords. I wonder if they'll survive."

Kendra chuckled, tickled, and moved to see Massimo earnestly instructing Pietro on the classic dueling stance, and best way to hold the "sword."

"It's doubtful," she replied, as Pietro launched a somewhat timid attack on Massimo. "I hope you have more on hand."

"I do," she replied, giving the scene outside one more look before turning away. "Let me get you a vase for your flowers."

Kendra stayed put, her gaze fixed on the pair outside, watching as, little by little, they both relaxed, their earnest expressions morphing slowly into frank enjoyment as they play-fought.

So engrossed was she that she didn't even hear Mrs. Bianchi come back and stand beside her again.

"Isn't it strange how difficult it is to build confidence in oneself?" the older lady asked, in a musing tone. "Some people seem to do it effortlessly, while others need constant reassurance to develop it."

Kendra nodded in agreement. "And there are times I wish I could wave a magic wand and give it away to those who need and deserve it most."

A warm hand touched her arm, giving it a squeeze. "I do too, and have for a long time." The last part seemed incongruous to their conversation, but before Kendra could reply, Mrs. Bianchi added, "Here. Give me your flowers, and go out to join them. I'm sure you could teach them a thing or two."

Wanting to go was instinctual, but so was her hesitation. Mrs. Bianchi took the flowers from her unresisting fingers and gave her a little push between the shoulder blades.

"Go."

So she went, and her heart did a silly flip when both Massimo and Pietro saw her and grinned in welcome.

Massimo did his best to get Pietro involved in their game, and thought he was doing a fairly good job, until Kendra came out to join in and he saw the little boy light up.

Not that he minded. It was truly heartwarming to see Pietro come to life in that way, but it did make him wonder why Kendra was so easily able to connect with the child, while Massimo had to work so hard at it.

After Nonna called Pietro in to take his bath, and dusk was setting in, Massimo stopped Kendra from going into the house with a touch on her arm.

"Thank you for being so good to Pietro. He lets go and is just a child with you, while sometimes..."

He couldn't find the words to express what he was trying to say, but even in the gloom he saw the understanding in Kendra's eyes.

"It's probably because he knows I'm just a visitor, and have no bearing on whether he stays here or not."

Her words drove through him, freezing his blood for a moment.

"We treat him like family. Why would he think we were going to send him away?"

She hesitated, then gestured for him to follow her to the nearby bench. Once they sat down, she turned so she could look at him, and said, "Pietro has never *had* a family. How would he know what it feels like to be treated as a part of one?"

He could find no good answer, and while he sought one, Kendra sighed and rubbed at her cheek.

"It's not the same, but because of my own upbringing, I can understand why he acts the way he does."

There was no mistaking the reluctance in her voice, as though she'd have preferred not to talk about it, but felt compelled to do so anyway. No doubt for Pietro's sake.

And although there was no emotion in her voice when she next spoke, he realized that was just a smokescreen to hide her real pain.

"I was raised by my father, who'd been at university when I was born. And since he wasn't able to continue his studies with a newborn to look after, he went back to his mother's house in Nova Scotia. Then, like his father before him, he went back to fishing to earn a living."

She paused, turning her face to gaze into the evening gloom, instead of at him, and Massimo found himself holding his breath.

"He died in an accident when I was ten."

Again, a total lack of emotion, but the enormity of what she was saying vibrated in the air between them.

"I'm sorry," he said softly, receiving a chopping motion of her hand in response.

"It was a long time ago, and not the point I'm trying to make. After Dad died, my grandmother did her best to take care of me, but she couldn't manage on her own. All of my father's siblings lived in Ontario—a different province— and decided they'd each take turns looking after me. So, they passed me from place to place until I was old enough to take care of myself.

"All I wanted was the security of a family, like I'd had with Daddy and Grammy, and each time I had to move on, I'd get more withdrawn—more fearful. I'd be on tenterhooks, worried that if I caused even the slightest trouble, I'd have to leave."

She took a deep breath, and faced him once more.

"What I'm trying to tell you is that until Pietro *knows* he is a part of a family—not is *treated* as though he is—there will always be the fear in the back of his mind he'll be rejected. Even if he was adopted there may be times he'll still be unsure, trying not to do anything to make that happen. It will take a long time for him to believe it's forever, and not instinctively assume he's disposable."

He knew she was only telling him these things to try to help him understand what Pietro was going through, but Massimo had so many questions he wanted to ask. About what happened between her parents, her experiences after her father died, and if those experiences were the reason she lived the way she did. Never settling anywhere. Always on the move.

Yet, he knew she wouldn't appreciate his prying, so he said, "What do you suggest I do, then? Nonna has been deemed too old to formally adopt him."

"Why don't you do it, then?"

He should have seen that coming, but her question struck him hard in the chest, and he found himself shaking his head instinctively.

"I can't. The law won't allow it, since I'm unmarried."

Her gaze was searching, and he wondered if she somehow could see through his words to the heart of the matter.

Even if he could, he doubted he would be the type of father Pietro needed, and was unwilling to risk the little boy's happiness and future by being unable to parent him properly. Just as Pietro didn't know what it felt like to be a part of a family, Massimo didn't know what being an involved, encouraging father looked like either, and he lacked the confidence to try.

Kendra's eyes narrowed, and the corners of her lips turned down.

"That's a rather archaic law, I think, and a shame in this situation. So, what exactly do you plan to do? Suppose something happens to your *nonna*? Will they come and take him away?"

"My mother assures me she will help me retain foster parent status if Nonna is unable to take care of him."

"But what if your mother is no longer in a position to do so?" Her tone had gone from curious to concerned. "Massimo, you should find out if there is some way to be appointed co-fosterer with your grandmother, just to make sure."

His heart was now pounding, and a trickle of sweat crawled down his spine.

"Kendra…" He sought the right words, fumbling under the intensity of her scrutiny. "I don't know how to be a father figure to him—how to make sure I'm giving him all he needs."

Her gaze was intent, as though she sought the source of his misgivings. And when, without warning, she grasped his wrist, her fingers were surprisingly cold against his skin.

"No one does, really, when they become a first-time parent. Whatever your hesitations, get over them, for Pietro's sake. You care about him. I can see it, and I know it's not just that he lives here, or that your *nonna* loves him. You have the wherewithal to give him what he needs— a stable, forever home. Don't deny him—and yourself—

the opportunity to have a happy life together, because you won't make the right decision."

Then she let him go, and stood up to look down at him, her eyes darker than usual, all of her habitual laughter notably gone from both expression and voice.

"It's scary for you, but think how much scarier it is for Pietro. Being shown this lovely life, with people he's growing to love and depend on, but knowing it can all be taken away in a moment." She shook her head, a wry twist to her lips. "Believe me, I'm not judging you or trying to tell you what to do, but I'm asking you to just think about what I've said, okay?"

How he wished he could be honest with her—tell her that while he wanted, with all his heart, to see Pietro grow up in a loving, protective family, he didn't know how to go about making that happen.

Sometimes he thought that, through example, his own father had shown him what not to do, but then he remembered how his brothers had seemingly thrived under their papa's parenting style. Was the fact that he and his father had such a strained relationship not so much a deficiency in Papa, but one in Massimo instead?

Trying to work it all out and determine how to do the right thing for Pietro left Massimo in a mental and emotional tangle he didn't know how to sort through.

Besides, since his prospects of marrying were nonexistent, there was no chance of adopting Pietro either, or giving him the nuclear family, including a mother, he deserved.

Yet, there was no way to say any of this, and while it was tempting to dismiss her words out of hand, he also knew she was only trying to help.

And hearing her story made his heart ache for her, but she wouldn't appreciate his sympathy, or curiosity.

So, instead, he said, "I will give it serious thought, and speak to my mama too, to hear what she suggests."

Kendra's smile lit up her entire face, and his heart once more raced, but for a far more carnal reason.

"Good," she said, and then reached out to twine a curl of his hair around her finger, just for a moment, the movement catching him by surprise. "I'm glad."

Then she walked toward the house, leaving him on the bench with his muddled thoughts.

CHAPTER TWELVE

KENDRA WAS REMINDED once more of the fact that when Massimo had come to a decision, there was no hesitancy in putting a plan into motion. Before the end of Thursday evening he had the trip arranged, and suggested they awaken early and take the bus to Sorrento to catch one of the first ferries across the Gulf of Naples.

"During the high season, nonresident cars aren't allowed on the island," he'd explained. "So it doesn't make sense to drive. I hope that'll be okay with you?"

Kendra was used to not only traveling light but also roughing it, so she'd laughed and said, "Sounds positively luxurious in comparison to some of the trips I've been on."

"I'd like to hear more about your travels." He said it casually, but there was an undertone in his voice she didn't understand. "I've hardly been anywhere outside of Europe."

"The kind of life I live isn't for everyone," she replied, trying to figure out where the conversation was going. "Most people need roots to feel grounded."

Massimo's gaze was searching, and he seemed set to say something more on the subject, but didn't.

Then, the next morning, as they walked down the driveway to get the bus, he said, "I hope I don't have to say this, but I will anyway, so there can be no misunderstanding between us. As desperately as I want to get you back into my bed, I truly do plan to show you the best of Capri. I don't want you to think…"

She held up her hand to stop him.

"I won't lie and say the thought of us spending the weekend in bed didn't cross my mind, but while I think I'd like that very much, I've also learned you're a man of your word. So, since you said you'd show me the sights, I figured you'd do just that."

That gained her one of his sideways glances, but no answer. Sometimes his reticence, which seemed habitual, was both mysterious and frustrating.

She'd been rather hoping he'd change his mind about their itinerary once she said she was okay with not seeing even one of Capri's many sites. The way she was feeling, she'd be quite happy to see only the inside of his cousin's villa, as long as it meant she'd get some relief from the constant thrum of desire she felt around Massimo.

Even so, she also had to acknowledge how dangerous it was to give in to her longing for him. If she'd had any doubts about that, they had been laid to rest the night before, as they spoke about Pietro, and she'd opened up to him about her past.

She'd seen his curiosity, and the genuine sympathy in his eyes, and had been glad he'd refrained from asking any questions.

One of the few times his reserve worked in her favor.

It had been far too easy to tell him the parts she'd confided, considering she never, ever spoke about what had happened after her father died. And it had been oh so tempting to tell him the rest. To finally have someone outside of Koko she could talk to about everything.

Someone she knew would be understanding.

But she was used to holding her emotions close to her

chest, and that type of intimacy wasn't something she could risk.

Physical closeness? Sure.

But opening up emotionally, explaining all the experiences that made her who she was?

No.

And the reality was that the sex she was looking forward to would only last so long. If they were together alone in the villa the entire weekend, she had no doubt the temptation to get to know him better on a personal level, and have him know her, might be overwhelming.

All she needed to remember was that the enjoyment she'd get from sleeping with him would have a time limit, and she always moved on with a clean conscience and no drama.

He'd promised their relationship would fit within those parameters, and there was no way she'd be the one to move the goalpost.

The sun wasn't quite up over the hills when they went down the steps from Piazza Tasso to Marina Piccola in Sorrento, but light already suffused the air, giving the dockside and sea a golden aura. As Massimo bought their tickets, she took a moment to appreciate the sight of him from the back.

Broad shoulders showcased by a lightweight cotton shirt, which also clung enticingly to his strong upper arms.

Lovely butt encased in a buff-colored pair of linen shorts that came with the added bonus of showing off his beautifully muscled calves.

His effortless style was, Kendra thought, a subtle but unmistakable turn-on.

When he turned and caught her staring, she grinned, and Massimo's smile in return did crazy things to her libido, and sent her heart rate soaring. It took more determination to look away than she wanted to admit to.

Most of the people waiting to board seemed local, with only a few backpacked tourists among them.

"Like many places here along the coast, Capri has an influx of seasonal workers at this time of the year," Massimo explained, when Kendra commented as much. "But some find it cheaper to stay on the mainland, and commute by ferry there each day."

"Sure beats the average traffic-clogged drive to work most commuters face," she said, watching with interest as the ferry crew readied the craft. Portside bustle was as familiar to her as the inside of a hospital. "At the very least the views are far better, and the passengers can enjoy them."

Massimo nodded his agreement, but although his lips quirked slightly upward, he didn't smile. There was something different about his demeanor this morning—a tension she wasn't used to seeing—and she couldn't help a little shiver of anticipation. Was he, like her, on tenterhooks knowing they would, finally, be back in each other's arms by the end of the day?

It seemed telling that he hadn't touched her, even casually, that entire morning. Not even once.

No hand-holding or guiding touch on her shoulder to usher her into the bus. He'd even sat ever so slightly apart from her on the bus bench and offered no assistance on the stairs down to the dock.

None of these were, on the surface, important, except that she'd noticed in the past those actions were customary. Not just with her, but with everyone.

He was, despite his quiet nature, quite tactile. He would do the hand-on-the-shoulder thing with other staff members when he held the door open for them, as well as taking the *nonne* by the arm to walk them out. Ruffling children's hair, holding Pietro's hand, kissing his *nonna* on both cheeks when he came home, or before he left. All these things seemed to come easily and habitually to him, so his clear reluctance to touch her piqued her curiosity.

They'd taken up a position a little away from the people crowded together waiting for the stevedores to finish loading goods onto the ferry. As soon as the last of the cargo was in place, the gangway was opened and the crowd surged forward, but Massimo didn't move.

Instead, he hung back, waiting for the bulk of the people to board before he waved a hand toward the ferry and said, "Let's go."

"Okay," she replied, but before she stepped forward, she gave in to the irresistible urge that had been building inside to remind him what was to come.

Perhaps even to see, for herself, whether he was as on edge as she was at the thought of them being intimate again.

And definitely to show him that she remembered, with startling clarity, all his erogenous zones, and how to turn him on, sexually.

Using the tips of her fingers, she tickled along his spine, allowing her nails to lightly scrape, knowing he'd feel it clearly through the cotton of his shirt.

And she was rewarded by seeing him shiver.

"Okay," she said again, her voice husky with the longing flowing like a burning river through her veins.

Then she forced her trembling legs to move, before she could forget herself and kiss him senseless, the way she wanted to.

Kendra was playing with fire, and Massimo had no doubt that she was doing it on purpose.

With that one almost innocuous touch, she'd brought it all flooding back.

Memories of her limbs intertwined with his, her gasps and laughter filling his ears. Her surrender to his every caress, and demands that he surrender to hers. Touches and stimulation the likes of which he'd never experienced before, and found mind-blowingly intense.

Her cries of release when she finally, finally gave in to her orgasms.

Recalling those moments, knowing they were about to relive them sometime in the very near future, kept him rooted in place, watching her walk toward the gangway.

Oh, she had no idea what kind of beast she'd awoken when she scratched down his spine.

Watching the enticing sway of her bottom beneath the light pink knit dress she was wearing was enough to make his mouth water.

As he finally got his feet to move, Massimo followed her toward the ferry, and came to a rather frightening realization.

That beast had not really been slumbering at all. It had been lying still, held in control by his will—and hers. But its eyes had been on Kendra the entire time. It had been quivering, waiting for the moment to pounce, wishing and hoping it would get the chance to once more try to devour her with passion.

Getting to know her better hadn't decreased Massimo's desire for her. On the contrary, she'd grown in attractiveness the more he learned. The more he saw of her nature.

The kindness and courtesy toward Nonna and Pietro. Her easy way with patients and coworkers alike. Her adventurous spirit, so in contrast to his own more sedate and carefully planned actions and life.

He didn't want to like her more, or desire her more

than he already did. Down that road lay nothing but disappointment and pain. There was no way to avoid the
knowledge that not only would she be moving on, as she
always did, but also that he—so staid and boring—would
never be enough for her. The practical side of his nature
demanded he accept that and not become attached, but if
he had his way, Kendra Johnson would never forget him,
as long as she lived.

And he had the kernel of a plan for making that happen.

He was behind her as she got onboard and immediately
made her way to the upper deck, then to the prow of the
boat. Silently they stood side by side, her gazing out to
sea, while Massimo found himself considering her profile.
As the ferry got underway, Kendra lifted her face and he
saw her nostrils flare slightly on a deep inward breath, the
edges of her lips lifting into a smile.

Was that appreciation for the scene before them, with
Capri a rough gem in the distance, and the morning light
touching the waves, or pleasure for the power she had
over him?

Perhaps she'd forgotten that while she'd been learning
his body, he'd been learning hers, and remembered every
moment of their time together, which was indelibly etched
into his mind?

They were surrounded by people and, he reminded himself, were supposed to be just casual friends, so there was
no good opportunity to pay her back—right now.

Instead, he took great pleasure in anticipating his ret-
ribution and casually said, "I thought we'd go first to the
villa to drop off our things, and then go for a boat tour
around the island. It'll be a nice time to visit the Grotta
Verde. Then we can decide what you want to see next."

She gave him a sideways look, and a little chuckle,

which drove straight through his belly and lit a fire on its way through.

"Sounds great."

Having gotten Sergio's housekeeper's number, Massimo texted her to tell her when they'd be in, and got a reply saying she'd meet them when they docked to hand over the key. This pleased him so much, he found himself grinning.

"What are you smiling about?"

He turned to find Kendra giving him a speculative look, but couldn't erase the smile from his face.

His plan was falling very nicely into place.

"It's a beautiful morning," he said. "And I'm going on an adventure with a beautiful woman. Why wouldn't I be smiling?"

That earned him a snort, and a shake of her head.

"Will there be pirates?" she asked, those bewitching eyes with their slumberous lids gleaming with her amusement. "Or just booty?"

The last part was said in English, and luckily his knowledge of North American popular culture was wide enough for him to understand the double entendre.

If only she knew!

He nodded, holding her gaze and moving a little closer, so that her warmth permeated into the skin of his arm. "Booty, and plundering too," he replied, also in English, and he was enchanted to see color tinge her cheeks.

He'd never seen her blush before.

Shaking her head again, and releasing a breathy laugh, she turned back to watch as Capri grew closer, rising from the sea like a craggy, pastel-bedecked paradise.

Mrs. Casella, Sergio's housekeeper, greeted them with smiles on the dock.

"I've promised to take care of my grandchildren in Anacapri today, so this was the best way to get the key to you," she explained. "And Signor Sergio said I should remind you that the scooters and boat are all at your disposal, should you need them."

They all queued to take the funicular together, but Massimo was glad that Kendra took the lead in carrying the conversation with Mrs. Casella. His mind continued to be preoccupied with thoughts of what was to come.

"The villa is only about a fifteen-minute walk from the Piazzetta," she explained when Kendra asked. "And at this time of the morning it is pleasant indeed. Later it may get quite hot, so my advice is to sightsee now, and then find a nice, shady spot to while away the lunch hours."

"That sounds like a good plan," Kendra told the older lady, as the funicular was coming to a halt.

They said their goodbyes at the Piazzetta, and Massimo took Kendra's hand, as he led her through the main square to a small café. There they had a light breakfast, before once more setting off toward the villa. But he didn't rush, allowing her to browse and look around as they ambled along. It was still too early for many of the shops to be open, but she seemed to enjoy the window-shopping anyway.

As they got closer to Sergio's villa, Massimo saw the way Kendra was looking around, taking in any of the increasingly sumptuous homes visible.

"What did you say your cousin does for a living?" she asked.

"He's an actor, and his husband is a screen and stage writer. They've done very nicely for themselves."

"I'll say," she muttered, just as they approached the gate to Sergio's property, set into a high stone wall that had bougainvillea cascading over it at several points.

While the garden at the back of the house was nice, it was somewhat unassuming, and the house itself was situated in such a manner that the full scope of it was hidden. Massimo led Kendra up the modest staircase, and paused at the top to unlock the door. Once it was open, he stood back for her to precede him into the hall.

She stepped through, then came to a complete stop.

"Crikey," she said, her voice hardly over a whisper, as she took in the opulence of the entryway, with its triple-height ceiling, intricate moldings and massive crystal chandelier. "This is your cousin's house?"

"One of three," he said, easing her farther inside with a hand on the small of her back, and shutting the door behind them. "He and his husband, Robin—who is Scottish—have another in London, and an apartment in New York. Robin does quite a bit of work on Broadway."

Setting down the leather satchel with his clothes on the floor, he eased Kendra's ubiquitous knapsack off her back and placed it next to his bag. Then, taking her hand, he led her through and down the hall to the main sitting room. When he opened the door there, she once more stopped, gaping at the elegant, yet comfortable space.

Sergio was a man who loved both luxury and coziness, and although the preponderance of colorful silk and Persian carpets weren't to Massimo's taste, even he had to admit the effect was striking.

Kendra's gaze traversed the entire room, and her lips were slightly parted, as though in shock. But it was when she saw the view beyond the floor-to-ceiling glass doors that she finally moved, as though drawn to the vista, walking slowly that way.

He strode past her, opening the accordion doors so she could step out onto the wide stone terrace and look around. Even though this was a place for lazy days taking the sun and evenings sipping cocktails, with its overstuffed chairs, marble statues and verdant plants, it wouldn't be out of place in an architectural magazine. Then she was on the move again, her gaze now out at the sea where the Faraglioni jutted arrogantly from the Mediterranean, and she seemed to relax. When she got to the stone parapet surrounding the terrace, her eyes shifted to the formal gardens below, and he heard her draw a deep breath.

"This place is stunning," she said. "So beautiful and overawing. I feel underdressed, as though I should be wearing a lovely evening gown and diamond tiara."

He hadn't expected such an opening, and yet couldn't resist taking it. Moving behind her, he wrapped one arm around her waist, and twitched her long plait over her shoulder with the other.

"I disagree," he replied, his voice rough with the desire he no longer felt constrained to hide. "I think you are completely overdressed."

CHAPTER THIRTEEN

SHE MELTED. BURNED. All thoughts of not belonging in a place this magnificent fading to nothingness when Massimo wrapped her in his arms from behind.

And if she thought she was the only one who remembered all those erogenous zones they'd discovered that night in Positano, she was very much mistaken.

Massimo's lips were on her nape, causing her head to fall forward, giving him free rein. Then he lightly scraped his teeth across her skin as his mouth slid to the side of her neck, and caused a wave of erotic pleasure to flow like hot wax through her veins.

Her breath rushed, as his hands found their way beneath her dress, caressing up along her thighs.

"I've dreamed of this," he said into her ear, making her shiver with need. "Every night since Positano."

Kendra wanted to tell him she had too, but the intimate admission stuck in her throat.

He didn't seem to need a reply. Indeed, he was too busy driving her crazy, as he sought another of the spots he'd learned turned her on.

For his fingers were tracing around her hip bones, trailing fire in their wake. And his lips now were on the tender skin where neck and shoulder joined.

Her knees wobbled, and she raised her arms to twine

around his neck, then gasped as he turned his mouth into the crook of her elbow, tongue swiping against the sensitive flesh.

Oh, yes, his memory was truly excellent, she thought hazily.

She widened her stance, both for balance and in the hopes of enticing him to touch her in the place that truly ached for those thick, skillful fingers, but he ignored her silent plea.

"I want to strip you down right here, in the sunlight, and make love to you all day." His voice was a growl, and Kendra opened her mouth to agree—gleefully—to that idea, but he continued, "But, instead, I think we should find out just how much you truly love anticipation."

His words drove through her, weakening her legs even more.

"What do you mean?" It took so much effort to speak through a throat tight with desire, and there was no disguising the tremble in her voice.

"We will have a morning of sightseeing and foreplay— a boat ride, visiting the Grotta Azzurra, or swim in the Grotta Verde, finding a place to have lunch, whatever you like. We will kiss, and touch, and quietly revel in the anticipation of what will happen when we return here, later, and take pleasure in each other. If you let me, I will take you to the brink and then leave you there, until you tell me it's time for our play to end."

She realized what he meant then, and the sound that came from her lips was unlike any she'd ever heard herself make before.

Primal.

Needy.

Just like the emotions churning in her mind—the passion burning in her belly.

Those big hands slid around to her butt, fingers tracing lines back and forth across the sensitized skin at the very top of her thighs.

How crazy to be so very cranked up with those simple caresses of legs and neck and shoulders. They hadn't kissed. Nor had he touched her anywhere most people would consider intimate. Yet, she was already a trembling, yearning mess.

The thought floated into her mind that it was because he *knew*.

Knew what paying attention to those places would do.

And he understood just how much the thought of waiting, anticipating, would turn her on.

Understood, and became complicit in helping her seek—find—that ultimate pleasure.

"But what about you?" she found voice enough to ask, rubbing back against his erection to let him know exactly what she meant.

His chuckle was raw, and his voice little more than a hoarse growl as he replied, "I have been in an almost constant state of need ever since I heard your laughter in the clinic that first day. Another few hours won't cause me to expire."

Turning in his arms, she searched his expression, seeing both the want in his eyes, and the honesty.

Then, as though drawn by a magnetic pull she couldn't resist, her gaze dropped to his mouth.

How had she ever thought his lips too thin? The sensuality of their curves, the visceral recall of how their slick mobility had pleasured her, made another, hotter wave inundate her body.

"Kiss me," she demanded, pressing as close as possible and wrapping her arms around his waist.

He wasted no time acceding, and when their lips met Kendra felt herself surrender in a way she never had before.

Completely. Still caught up in the wonder of a man who seemed to unequivocally accept her just as she was, and didn't hesitate to offer her more than she'd ever dreamed.

"Mmm…" he moaned softly, lifting his lips from hers after a few exhilarating minutes. When he rested his forehead on hers, she sighed, resisting the urge to tug his mouth back to hers. "If we don't stop, my plan will go awry."

"I wouldn't mind," she retorted, waiting to see whether he'd take her up on the invitation, but he shook his head, before straightening.

"Oh, no you don't." His tone was firm, and he shook his head once, for emphasis. "This weekend will be memorable, and I, for one, am looking forward to our day, just as planned. Aren't you?"

There was a definite question in his eyes, despite the obvious desire, and Kendra shivered under that gleaming midnight gaze.

"I am," she admitted, the honest reply drawn from her by his focused attention, and the way his hands cupped her bottom, rhythmically squeezing.

"Then it is decided," Massimo said, in a tone that brooked no argument. "Let me call the marina and have them ready the boat."

Before she could respond, he gave her buttocks one more hard, thrilling squeeze, and then stepped back. Reluctant to let him go, she took her own sweet time, trailing her nails across from the center of his back to his rib cage, and couldn't help laughing when he growled, as though in warning.

Then he turned and disappeared into the villa, leaving her to sag, almost boneless, against the stones behind her.

Her mind was whirring, while her body hummed with a type of frightening electricity.

How had he reduced her to this state with a few kisses and caresses, and even fewer words?

More importantly, what was this strange sensation burning inside, at the realization that he not only understood her sexual proclivity, but accepted it, wholeheartedly? Had even come up with a plan to push the boundaries into fantasy territory.

He was offering her an experience she hadn't even known she wanted, but now craved with the type of hunger she'd never known before.

Would he touch her, intimately, here, before they left? And when—how, where—would he touch her again, while they were sightseeing?

What an incredibly naughty, arousing, crazy idea, and she had to acknowledge that she was definitely all in on it.

Just the thought of what was to come made her groan, and had another tremor rushing through her body. Her nipples were beaded tight beneath her bra, she knew she was already wet, and wondered if her panties were as soaked as she thought they were.

How was she going to last the morning at this rate?

Had she ever felt this unrestrained before?

She didn't think so.

All her adult life she'd been guarded, in control. What was it about this man, at this time, that broke through those barriers so easily?

That thought took her aback, just a little. Was she conceding too much to Massimo? Giving him too much access into her head?

Shouldn't she at least try to claw back some of her autonomy, before she lost herself completely in the experience?

But when it occurred to her what she wanted to do

next, it wasn't driven by those fears, but by a totally different thought.

Moving over to one of the plush loungers scattered around the terrace, she sat on the edge, letting the distant murmur of Massimo's deep voice wash over her. He was doing something for her that she'd never expected. Offering her an experience in pleasure beyond any she'd been gifted before.

She wanted it to be as good for him as it would be for her, and delayed gratification was her kink, not his.

His voice came closer, and she heard him bidding whoever was on the other end of the line goodbye, just as he stepped back onto the terrace.

"The manager of the marina where Sergio's boat is docked says it will be ready for us within the hour," he said.

"Oh, good. Then we have time."

Perhaps it was the timbre of her voice, or the expression on her face, that had him stopping in his tracks, his searching gaze bringing heat to her face—and other places too.

"Time for what?"

She beckoned him closer with a crooked finger. "Come here, and I'll show you."

For an instant she thought he'd refuse, and even when he approached it was slowly, almost hesitantly.

When he was within arm's length, she smiled up at him, as she reached for his belt.

"Wait." Those lovely large hands reached down to hold hers.

"Why?"

"You don't have to—"

Kendra laughed, and shook her head. "Of course I don't *have* to, but I *want* to."

And when she wriggled out of his grasp and set about

undoing his fly, then the buttons of his shirt, he didn't put up any further argument, only exhaled with a hiss as he stepped out of his shorts. Reaching down, he put one hand on her shoulder, while the other reached for her plait and wrapped it around his fingers.

She didn't hold back, and didn't let him either. Taking her time, savoring the taste, and scent, and texture of him, she took him to the edge, and held him there for a long moment. Growling her name, Massimo tugged on her hair. She set him free, so as to look up at him and laugh with pleasure. His face was tight, lips drawn back, two slashes of red staining his cheeks, his breathing ragged.

"You need to stop, now."

"No." She licked her lips, hoping he could see just how much she was aroused by what they were doing. "You need to let go, and give me what I want."

Still he hesitated and, held by her hair, unable to move toward him, Kendra stayed motionless. Looking up at him, she silently willed him to take a chance, to break out of whatever bounds were keeping him from accepting what she was offering.

If he couldn't trust her with his body—with his pleasure—could she trust him with hers the way she wanted to?

Something flashed in his eyes, and if she didn't know better, she'd have thought it was fear, but before she could properly analyze it, he gave in, and loosened his grip.

And she had only a moment to let out one huff of laughter before she took him back between her lips, and not long after, to ecstasy.

His legs were trembling, and he braced himself on her shoulders. As his breathing grew slower, his fingers loosened, and Kendra laughed softly.

"I enjoyed that," she said, just in case he didn't realize. "Can we do it again later?"

A strained chuckle was the reply, and Massimo slowly straightened.

What a gorgeous sight he was, naked except for his unbuttoned shirt, which, hanging open, only accentuated his thick, muscular trunk. Reaching up, she ran her hand over his chest, grazing one nipple, before following the line of hair that arrowed down to his navel.

He held her hand, and shook his head.

"My turn."

Heat spiked from her chest down into her belly, and her internal muscles gave a sweet little spasm.

"I'm not sure that would be wise," she warned huskily, although just then the thought of abandoning his luscious plan didn't seem such a bad thing. "I'm pretty much on the edge of coming right now."

He smiled, and the feral edge to it caused another ripple of arousal deep in her abdomen.

"I'll be careful. It is far too early in the day for your first orgasm."

Caught in his gaze, her body vibrating and hot, surrounded by the lush plants and growing warmth of the beautiful setting, something broke free inside. Something that had everything and nothing to do with lust. Everything and nothing to do with physical need. A sensation—an emotion—that bade her to give in.

Urged her to trust.

To push aside the sudden spurt of apprehension and open herself to the moment—to Massimo—without reservation.

But, as though mirroring Massimo's reluctance of before, she hesitated.

It felt familiar—the fear. The sensation of a turning

point, or the solid ground she'd built for herself shifting, ever so slightly, beneath her feet.

Yet, she'd never shied away from any challenge, and this was, indisputably, an adventure for the ages.

So she laughed, although it burned her throat slightly on the way out, and put her hands behind her, so she half reclined on the lounger.

"Do your worse. Or your best," she said, in English, too fuzzy-brained to find the right words in Italian. Taunting him a little and using bravado to keep from showing him her uncertainty.

"Always my best," he replied before, with a move almost too graceful for a man of his size, he sank to his knees, and pulled her closer with a tug. After he pulled down her panties and nudged her legs apart, he paused, looking down. She felt his gaze on her flesh like a touch, and trembled in reaction. "Only the best, for you."

Then he slid his hands under her bum, and lifted her while he dipped his head, and Kendra was completely, inexplicably, lost.

CHAPTER FOURTEEN

As HE STEERED the motorboat out of the marina, Massimo was feeling extremely pleased with himself, if still a little shaken. The encounter at the villa between Kendra and him had been erotic beyond belief, and the almost drunken look on her face before they left had made his ego inflate to ridiculous proportions.

No woman had ever made him feel the way she did.

Bold.

In charge.

But also vulnerable, knowing he was with a woman who possessed a self-assurance he could only ever wish for. Yet, with her it was easy to assume an air of confidence, and to allow himself to simply act rather than analyze every move he made, in case it was wrong.

With her he was comfortable in his own skin.

Perhaps too comfortable and confident.

After their tryst, she'd gone to change into her swim-suit and come back out wearing a pair of shorts. Massimo had shaken his head.

"Go and change back into your sundress," he'd said, surprising them both by the demand in his voice. "I want to be able to touch you whenever I want today."

Color flooded her cheeks and her lips had parted in silent shock. Then, without a word, she'd turned around and gone to do what he bade.

He'd never in his life been so commanding to a woman, and of all the women he'd been with, Kendra was the last one he'd have thought would comply without question.

Or without telling him to go to hell.

They were out on the open water now, but he kept the vessel at idle speed, taking the opportunity to look over his shoulder at Kendra, wondering if she were upset. Once she'd secured the line the dockhand had tossed to her, she'd settled into one of the seats behind him, rather than sit in the chair beside his.

She was half-sprawled on the bench seat, her head back, exposing the lovely long line of her throat. Her sunglasses were perched on the top of her head, and her eyes were closed.

"Are you sleeping back there?" he called, over the sound of the motor.

She half opened her eyes and smiled at him.

"No, just appreciating the moment, and wondering if this deprivation thing is really right for me. I'm so revved up I could explode just from the vibrations of the engine."

He loved when she spoke like that, so frankly sexual and open about her feelings, although it made him a little crazy too.

"Don't talk like that when I'm supposed to be concentrating on what I'm doing," he warned. "Or I'll have to come over there and make sure that when that explosion happens, I'm the one who causes it."

She pulled her glasses down and put them on with a chuckle, which just made his reawakening lust spike a bit higher.

"Oh, believe me, I'm holding out for that too."

"Come and sit next to me." He patted the seat beside the

pilot's chair. "I want everyone we pass to see the beautiful woman with me."

Another deep, husky laugh was the only answer he got, but she got up and moved to sit beside him, and Massimo felt his shoulders relax.

"This really is a lovely boat. The teak is amazing."

He grinned. "Lucky for me, our grandfather made sure all of his grandchildren learned three things. How to swim, how to know when a lemon was ready to be picked and how to operate a boat safely. Otherwise Sergio would never offer to allow me to take his baby out of the marina."

"I don't blame him. She's a thing of beauty." She stretched, and then, in a purely unselfconscious way, ran her hands over her belly and hummed. "What a glorious day."

He wanted to ask her if it was the weather making her say so, or if he had some hand in helping her feel that way, but the words stuck in his chest.

Then she looked over at him, and smiled in such a way he wished he could see her eyes instead of just his own reflection in her sunglasses. But even thus hindered, his body tightened, and he found himself smiling back.

He opened up the throttle a bit more, and started west along the coast, pointing out landmarks to her as they went.

"Would you like to go inside the Grotta Azzurra?" he asked, as they meandered along the northern coast. "It's not far from here. We can anchor and hire one of the rowers to take us in."

"I would. It's one of the things I was told I really should do while here."

Of course, Massimo had been in the sea cave many times before—had even gone back in the evening, after the tourists were gone, and swam in it—but now he was looking forward to showing it to Kendra. In a strange way, he felt as though she understood his love of the Amalfi Coast and all its beauty, even though it would never be as appealing to her as it was to him.

She'd seen so many places, and lived such an adventurous life, there was nothing here to hold her interest for long.

The thought made him angry and even more determined that once she moved on, she would never forget him. Steering the boat farther out to sea for about a mile, he set the engine to idle. While there were a few boats in the distance, they were, for all intents and purposes, alone, and he turned to face her, resting his hand on her knee.

Kendra was watching him, and she licked her lips, then visibly swallowed.

He didn't speak, not trusting himself to say the correct thing just then. Instead, he reached out and took off her glasses, tossing them onto the dashboard. Spinning her chair toward him, he stepped forward, and kissed her—hard.

There was no hesitation in the way she kissed him back. Tangling her tongue with his, then sucking on his lower lip, the motion bringing back vivid memories of the way she'd taken him into her mouth earlier.

Reaching up beneath her skirt, he found the edge of her swimsuit, and ran his finger lightly along the elastic circling her leg. There was a spot, just about there…

"Mmm," she moaned into his mouth, her back arching so her breasts rubbed his chest.

He drew back, bending to nip at her neck.

"I want to touch you." He said it into her ear, knowing it wasn't as sensitive as his were, yet that nevertheless she never failed to react when he spoke right into one, and was rewarded when she shivered.

"Do anything you want," she said, spreading her thighs, her head dropping back against the seat. "I give you permission."

"Anything?"

Her eyes were dark, yet sparked hot, her drooping lids giving her an even more sultry expression than usual.

"Anything."

He pulled her to her feet, and, bunching the hem in either hand, tugged her dress off over her head. She was wearing a two-piece suit, and he was ridiculously excited to note the top had a zipper down the front.

He made good use of it, baring her full breasts with their dark nipples now tightly furled.

Cupping them, he rubbed his thumbs over those enticing peaks, circling and then pinching them between his fingers. Entranced by the goose bumps that fanned out across her chest, he bent, and licked at her flesh. Starting at one peak, he drew patterns on her skin with his tongue until she laughed that breathy, sexy laugh, and her thighs tightened around his.

Without breaking contact between his mouth and her breast, he reached between them and cupped between her thighs, hearing her muffled cry of pleasure.

He didn't dare go beneath the cloth, knowing he wouldn't stop until she came. This game they were playing was much harder than he could have ever expected. It was only by putting her wants and needs ahead of his own selfish desires that he could restrain himself.

He wanted to sink his fingers into the velvet-wet heat he knew awaited inside her. Use lips and tongue on her clitoris until she cried for completion. Sheath himself inside her, and drive home until they both exploded and stars danced behind his eyes.

Unable to resist, he told her all those things, his hand

motionless on her mound, the other tugging at a nipple. Kendra groaned his name, her hips pumping against his palm, her fingers tangled into his hair, holding his head against her neck.

Realizing how frantic her movements were becoming, he drew his hand away, and reached up to free himself from her grasping fingers.

"There," he said, pulling her top back into place, but not before one last kiss on a nipple. "That's enough for now, I think."

He tried to sound factual, even casual, but it was impossible with his heart trip-hammering and his lungs barely able to pull in enough air.

When she huffed out a breathy passion-struck sound of amusement, it almost made him forget his promise, and he had to force himself to turn back to the controls, while Kendra fixed her top.

Kendra pulled the two sides of her bikini top together and tried to insert the end of the zipper into the tab. It was extremely difficult when her fingers were trembling, clumsy with arousal.

Her entire body felt sensitized, almost painful, and yet she didn't have a moment's regret for the pact they'd made.

She'd never felt more alive.

Massimo was turning the boat back toward land, going slowly, probably waiting for her to complete her chore, and it gave her the opportunity to examine his profile at her leisure.

There again was that slash of color on his cheek, the firming of his jaw speaking to his own unsatisfied need. He glanced at her and caught her staring, just as she got the zipper going.

"That was a close one," she told him frankly. "I almost lost it."

His nostrils flared slightly as he took a deep breath. "I realized."

"It was your fault, you know." He glanced at her out of the corner of his eye, his brow raised, as though in question. "I was fine until you started telling me all the things you want to do to me."

"Should I not do that?"

There was no amusement in the question, and she realized he was serious.

"Actually, I loved it." A chuckle broke free, borne on the sharpness of her need, and genuine amusement. "A little too much."

"Perhaps it makes you feel as I do when you laugh while we are intimate."

Genuinely surprised, she asked, "What?"

Massimo shrugged, the corners of his lips lifting. "Your laughter makes me hard, and when we are making love, it makes me lose all control if I am not careful."

"I'll have to remember that," she said, amused and in a weird way pleased.

"Actually, it makes me hard all the time, for it reminds me of the time we were in bed. When I would caress you and, finding a place you particularly liked, you'd laugh."

Why did that touch her, make a little glow start in her chest and spread slowly out from there?

Perhaps because in the past she'd been told her laughter was too loud, too robust, unladylike, and should be better controlled. Knowing it had that kind of effect on Massimo was revelatory.

But that was a fact she would keep to herself. She was even unable to tease him about it, knowing she couldn't pull that off without revealing at least some of what she was feeling.

Afraid he'd see the sheen of tears in her eyes, she quickly bent to pick up her dress and tug it on. Then, as added security, she grabbed her glasses and stuck them on her face, suddenly needing the separation they gave her from his all-too-knowing gaze.

"Next stop, Grotta Azzurra," he said, blithely unaware of how he'd rocked her to the core, and left her far more than just physically shaken.

"Carry on," she replied, pleased when her voice came out almost normal.

Hopefully he'd put the little tremor in it down to the desire still shimmering under her skin, where it mixed with that warm, tender sensation he'd stirred up.

Damn him!

The Blue Grotto lived up to its hype, a fact that totally blew Kendra's mind. There were so many tourist destinations that failed to be as beautiful as they were advertised to be, but there was no denying the sea cave was completely mesmerizing.

First was the unconventional way they had to enter— lying down in a small rowboat, as the oarsman pulled them in with hand-over-hand tugs on a rope through the low, narrow mouth of the cave. And then, inside...

Kendra gasped at the almost unbelievable blue of the water, which was, the oarsman told her, caused by light coming in through an underwater aperture. It was almost like being in a sea of blue fluorescent animals, made even more sublime by the flashing reflections on the walls.

Without conscious thought, she reached for Massimo's hand, and he twined his fingers with hers. The sensation felt so shockingly right, so intimate, she almost pulled away, but couldn't bring herself to do it.

It was an all-too-brief stop, and after a few minutes they were rowing back toward the entrance, their oarsman no doubt eager to collect another fare from the excursion boat anchored outside. But when one of the other oarsmen started to sing, Massimo asked him to wait, just for a minute, so they could listen, and for the second time in the day Kendra found herself close to tears.

The sheer beauty of the cave, and the singing, and having her hand held so very tenderly was almost too much to bear.

Thankfully, she was able to pull herself together by the time they got back out into the sunlight, and busying herself with pulling the anchor also gave her a little more breathing room.

Farther along, Massimo pointed out the site of a Roman ruin, then a series of forts along the western coast. Although he seemed little different from how he was the rest of the day, Kendra felt a strange atmosphere building between them, making her edgy.

It was, she reasoned, the sexual tension he'd so carefully cultivated, yet even to herself that didn't ring quite true.

Oh, there was no doubt she was still on a sexual high, irrespective of those moments in Grotta Azzurra that had shaken her so emotionally. But, even so, what had started out as an escapade—an arousing lark—had somehow started to morph into something different, and she wasn't sure what that something was.

Realizing she'd been mooning over his profile once again, she tore her gaze away and lifted her face to the sun. The sea breeze washed over her skin, and she inhaled deeply. It should have brought her peace, the way the ocean always did, but today that calm eluded her.

"I thought we could stop for lunch at a beachside restaurant near the Faraglioni." Massimo's voice pulled her out of her reverie, and her gaze was drawn back to him. Unable to resist, she reached out to brush the hair back from his forehead, and was rewarded with a smile. "But if you're not yet hungry, we could stop for a swim at the Grotta Verde first."

What she really wanted was to drag him back to his cousin's villa and have her wicked way with him, in the hopes that once that was over this sense of being on a tilt-a-whirl would go away. Telling him that, though, would be far too revealing, so she smiled instead.

"I'd like a swim, I think. It's getting quite hot now, even with the sea breeze."

He nodded, and sent her a sideways glance that raised the simmering desire beneath her skin at least ten degrees.

"There will be others in the grotto, but even so I will touch you again. I can't keep my hands off you for much longer."

And the huff of delight that broke from her throat had little to do with amusement, and a lot to do with need.

CHAPTER FIFTEEN

Massimo was true to his word, although he was extremely discreet in how he caressed her while they frolicked in the emerald waters of Grotta Verde. Now that he knew she also liked when he told her all the things he longed to do to her, he used his voice as well as his touch to turn her on.

And the list of sensual, sexual actions he came up with surprised even himself. He'd always thought of himself as conventional—even dull—in his needs, but the beast Kendra unleashed in him was anything but staid.

He wanted her in every way he could think of. Nothing off-limits, unless she was unwilling, and she didn't seem averse to anything he suggested, which made him even wilder with desire.

Keeping their association on a strictly carnal level wasn't easy, however. His curiosity kept growing apace with his passion. Yet, as he discovered, getting her to talk more about herself, especially her earlier life, wasn't easy.

After they'd swum back to the boat, and he was drying off, he saw her once more turn her face up to the sun, and inhale, taking in the briny air, a smile lighting her face.

Something about her posture resonated with him, and Massimo found himself saying, "You really love the sea, don't you? I remember the first time I saw you, looking out over the bay at Spiaggia Tordigliano. I thought you looked as though you wanted to scoop the water up in your arms and hug it."

Her smile widened, and she sent him a sideways glance. "It sounds poetic when you say it that way, but yes, that's exactly how I feel whenever I see the sea. I inherited the love of it from my father."

Without thought, he asked, "And what did you inherit from your mother?"

All signs of pleasure dropped away from her face, and her lips twisted for a moment as she shrugged.

"I have no idea. I've never met her, and never will."

His heart stuttered, and he said the first thing that came to mind. "Is she deceased?"

Another shrug, but while now she tried to smile, he saw through it. That was the way she looked when she was in retreat, but didn't want anyone to know.

"I don't know that either." There was a moment of hesitation, and he thought that would be the end of the conversation, but then she sighed. "She was a foreign grad student at the university Dad attended. They had an affair and when she got pregnant he offered to marry her, but she wasn't interested. According to my aunt, she told him her family would never accept him because he was Black, and wouldn't accept me either. So she hid the pregnancy from her family, had me and then took off back to Argentina."

Dumbfounded, he shook his head. "Astounding. She has no idea of the joy she's missed, by not knowing you."

Kendra glanced at him out of the corner of her eye, then turned away, so he couldn't see her face.

"It's no big deal. I learned to accept it a long time ago."

But he believed that statement just as much as he'd believed that distancing smile she'd given him just moments before.

Then, before he could persist with the conversation, she

said, "Now I'm definitely hungry. It's been a long time since breakfast."

Without further comment, he started the motor, and they continued along the south coast. Restless now, not with unsated desire but with anger at her mother's defection, he opened up the throttle, putting the powerful boat through its paces. As they cut through the waves, he glanced over at Kendra and her smile of pleasure eased some of the pain around his heart.

No matter how difficult his home life had ever been, at least his parents were always around. Despite his father making his disappointment with Massimo clear, and both parents so focused on each other it sometimes felt their children were an afterthought, at least he'd had his grandparents' support. He may have felt lost in the shuffle, something of an outsider because of his retiring nature, but there had never been a time when Massimo had felt truly alone.

How had Kendra managed, growing up without her mother, losing her father when she was ten?

And what impact had her mother's defection had on her development?

It all just made him want to know more.

Reminding himself that she would be gone from his life within a short time reined in his curiosity. Seeing her retreat from the conversation warned him that she wouldn't appreciate his prying any further.

But hearing her talk about the exciting aspects of her life would help him to remember the vast difference between them, and squelch any inclination he may have to get closer to her, emotionally.

They anchored near the seaside restaurant he'd chosen, and a dory came to ferry them ashore. Once they were seated at a table overlooking the famous rocks and had ordered, he leaned back in his chair, and said, "I've been curious about how you ended up in the army."

She smiled, and seemed to relax. He hadn't noticed how tense she'd been since their earlier conversation until her shoulders dropped at his question.

"It was a matter of finding a way to do what I wanted to, which was travel," she replied. "That's the simplified version of the story, anyway."

"What's the complicated version?"

He held his breath, wondering if Kendra would retreat again, but saw no change in her demeanor, and breathed out as she put down the glass she'd been sipping from and replied.

"Well, when I was about fourteen, I went to live with my aunt in an area adjacent to a pretty notorious neighborhood in Toronto. I started hanging out with a group of friends she didn't approve of but, having hit the rebellious stage, I kept seeing them anyway. Then, one of the group got arrested for shoplifting, and my aunt decided I needed something else to do after school, and enrolled me in a program at the community center."

Her smile widened, as though the memory was a good, rather than bad, one.

"One of the ways they tried to help the kids in the program—many of whom came from really disadvantaged circumstances—was to find mentors, and I was paired with a doctor whose family had moved to Canada from the Caribbean." She shook her head, her gaze growing distant, as though remembering it all. "Dr. Amie really turned my life around. She's a real Renaissance woman, you know? She was interested in everything, from music to nature, other cultures too, and, of course, the sciences. She'd take me to museums and concerts, even to the ballet and opera, but also got me into reading, and art appreciation—everything. Through her I started to realize there was a great big world out there, waiting to be explored."

"She sounds wonderful," he said, as Kendra paused to take another sip of her wine. "I'm surprised she didn't encourage you to become a doctor."

Kendra laughed. "I think she secretly wanted me to become one, especially when I told her that was what my father had wanted to do too, but she wasn't into pushing anything on me. What she did was broaden my horizons, then got me thinking about what I wanted, and how I could get there. The future really wasn't something I thought too much about at that point, you know? But she encouraged me to keep my grades up, explaining that was the way to keep my options open and then, finally, one day she sat me down and asked what I wanted to do when I left school."

"And you told her you wanted to travel the world."

She nodded, her eyelids lowering for a moment, so he couldn't see the expression in her eyes.

"And she asked what I planned to do to make that happen." Kendra chuckled, and tucked a stray strand of hair that had escaped her plait behind her ear. "Needless to say, I hadn't given that a lot of thought, and shrugged the question off. But the next time we were together, she forced me to think it through. Would I want to go to college, and get a degree that would enable me to travel? Could I become a travel writer, or agent? How else could I finance this peripatetic life I wanted? After going over all the options, I figured it would be best to join the military, and train to be a nurse. Then I wouldn't have student loans to pay off, and I'd also get to travel while in the military too."

For an instant his mind flashed on an image of his own carefree time at school—difficult, because he'd chosen medicine, but not because he'd had to work his way through, or think about tuition.

His respect for Kendra, for the way she'd risen above her childhood and made her dreams come true, on her own terms, rose to new heights.

"So volunteering for the army was a means to an end, as was nursing?"

"I guess so." She chuckled, the sweet, warm sound wrapping around him. "Although I chose the career carefully, not just at random. Dr. Amie made sure of that. For a while it was a toss-up between nursing and culinary school, but after doing a volunteer stint at a hospital, I was hooked."

Surprised, he cocked an eyebrow at her. "You like to cook?"

"Love it. I started fooling around in the kitchen, making meals for my cousins and myself when we got home from school, and it grew from there." A thoughtful, almost sad look crossed her face. "It's the one thing I really miss when I'm on the road." Then her expression lightened. "But whenever I go back to Canada, my cousin Koko makes sure I cook for her. She says she doesn't have many good, home-cooked meals while I'm away, but makes sure she doesn't let her mother hear her say it."

And as they laughed together, Massimo was left once more considering just how much he admired her, and wondering why it all made him want her even more.

What was it about Massimo that made him so easy to speak to—to bare parts of herself she rarely, if ever, shared with anyone?

Settling into the small dinghy that would row them back to the boat, Kendra avoided looking at Massimo, feeling raw. Exposed.

Instead she looked up at the majestic rock formations jutting from the sea and then, as though unable to help it, at the outline of the villa's roof, visible from this position. Massimo had pointed it out to her earlier, and she'd shivered, imagining getting back there—finally experiencing the release she'd been craving all day.

Now, staring up at the house, she knew she was ready. More than ready, although that knowledge came with another spurt of fear.

It was supposed to be a no-strings-attached situation, and it was usually the men she slept with who tried to change the script. Now it was she who was battling against a connection she'd felt from the first moment she saw him, months ago at the beach.

She didn't believe in instant attraction, really. Or even less love at first sight. But there was no escaping the fact that the draw she felt toward Massimo—both physically and emotionally—was stronger than she knew how to handle.

Already she had to admit to herself that sleeping with him again was probably the worst idea she'd had in a long time, from a peace-of-mind standpoint, but it was too late to back out now. Not that he would try to force her. In fact, she knew without a doubt, if she told him she'd changed her mind, he would immediately accept her decision.

No. The real problem was that she wanted him, and all that he had to offer, too much to resist.

She'd take this weekend, and all he had to give here on Capri, then figure it out afterward. Make the hard decisions.

But as she looked up at the rocky coastline, and breathed in the salty air, she finally admitted she'd be leaving a piece of herself here when she left. And, for the first time in a long, long time, the thought of moving on brought no joy.

Back onboard, Massimo started the engine while she weighed anchor and, once they were underway and she'd neatly stowed the line, she moved aft to where he sat at the controls. Sliding in behind him, she leaned her chin on his shoulder, and turned her head so her lips almost touched his ear.

"I'm ready," she whispered, and felt him shudder. "No more stops. No more waiting. Let's go back to the villa."

He didn't reply, just opened the throttle, and the boat jumped up on a plane as it carved through the water. Grabbing the back of his chair to keep her balance, Kendra laughed, and ran the tip of her tongue along the edge of Massimo's ear, earning a growl that was clearly audible above the engine noise.

Then she realized that instead of following the coastline as it curved north, he was heading out into open water, and her heart began to hammer. Far out from land, he put the boat in Neutral, and turned to her.

All around them lay the glorious blue of the ocean, Capri just a gray-and-green lump in the distance. Here there was just the low hum of the idling engine and the cries of gulls feeding a little way off.

Massimo's eyelids drooped, and his lips tightened for a moment before he spoke.

"You're ready for our game to end?"

"Yes." She nodded in emphasis.

"I'm not sure I am," he replied, still seated, making no effort to move, or to take her into his arms. "At least, not in the way I envisioned."

It never occurred to her that he might be having second thoughts too, and her heart plummeted at his words.

She lifted her chin, determined to maintain her poise. Not let him see her fear and disappointment.

"You've changed you mind about us sleeping together?"

As hard as she'd tried to keep her voice steady, it still came out weaker than she'd have liked, but when Massimo shook his head, the rush of relief she felt turned her knees to jelly.

"Not at all. I feel as though if I don't make love to you, I will… I don't know what I'll do, but it wouldn't be good."

Tilting her head to the side, she asked, "Then why are we here, instead of racing back to the marina?"

He didn't answer her question, but gestured with his chin to the bench seat.

"Go. Sit."

Oh, why did she turn to mush when he became demanding? She wasn't sure there was another man alive who could boss her around this way and get away with it, much less have her almost mindlessly comply.

But it was Massimo, and so she turned obediently and took a seat.

By the time he got up and came to stand in front of her, she was trembling all over, and her toes were curled against the deck. When he sank to his knees, another of those crazy, untamed sounds broke from her throat.

Massimo's hands were on her outer thighs, and he looked up at her.

"I don't know what it is you do to me, Kendra." His voice was low, rough, and the sound of it seemed to vibrate into her skin. "I know myself to be a staid man—you might even say dull—but around you I become…" He hesitated, seemingly searching for the right word. "Wild. Like an animal. Operating on instinct and primal needs alone."

Surprised, she huffed. "The man who whispered into my ear all those incredibly sexy ideas about what we can do in bed is anything but staid. Or dull."

He shrugged. "You prove my point. I have been called *tedious. Too careful. Boring.* And before meeting you I would have agreed. Now, I hardly know myself."

She sat up straight, then leaned forward to lift that wayward lock of hair that always flopped onto his forehead.

"The people who called you those things clearly didn't know you well. The man who went into that damaged house was almost ridiculously bold and daring. And the way you ride a scooter and drive a boat tells me there is a daredevil just under your quiet surface, waiting to bust out." Then she leaned closer yet. "And the man who has given me a day that can only be described as fantastical, who's kept me so aroused there were times I could hardly function normally, is anything but tedious."

Reaching up, he pulled off her sunglasses and tossed them aside, searching her gaze, as if trying to see if she meant what she'd said.

"You've brought that out in me," he replied, and his hands slid up under her dress. When his fingers slipped into the waistband of her bikini bottoms, she instinctively lifted her hips.

"Maybe," she said, forcing the words out through her suddenly dry throat. "But I didn't create that in you, and couldn't bring it out if it wasn't already there."

He grunted in reply, apparently too busy pulling her bottoms off to say anything more.

"What are you planning?" she asked, not liking the suspense and wondering what his change of tactics actually entailed.

He looked up, holding her gaze, and in the bright sunlight, out here on the water, golden lights seemed to gleam in the depths of his eyes.

"I want to make you crazy," he said, as though that would be something new. As though he hadn't been doing just that all day. "And then I want to watch you lose control. Then, when we get back to the villa, I want to do it all over again. And again. And again."

As he spoke, he parted her thighs, and slid his hands up until they rested on that sensitive area just below her hip bone.

Kendra gasped, pulling a short hot breath into her lungs, and spread her legs even wider, urging him on.

Massimo slowly parted her labia with his thumbs, and Kendra arched, feeling the slick slide of his flesh against hers.

Then the sweet, erotic torture began, lasting until she was begging, *begging* him for surcease, and her laughter and cries of release joined the raucous shrieks of the gulls.

CHAPTER SIXTEEN

KENDRA WATCHED CAPRI dwindling into the distance behind the ferry with almost heart-wrenching regret.

The three days in Capri with Massimo had flown by, filled with laughter, fun and mind-blowing lovemaking. Massimo had taken her to heights of pleasure unlike anything she'd experienced before. The knowledge he'd gleaned about her body, his way of taking what she'd always considered a silly predilection and elevating it—and her—to a whole new level of eroticism had turned her inside out.

It should be enough.

Physically she was sated, but mentally, emotionally, she craved more.

More closeness, like the evenings, after dinner, when they'd shared a lounge chair out on the terrace at the villa, sipping wine and talking. Leaning back against Massimo's broad chest, having his arm around her waist, feeling him drop kisses onto her temple, had brought Kendra an indescribable sense of peace.

She'd wanted to stay there forever, never having to move out of that warm embrace. Wanted to tell him everything there was to know about her, learn everything about him, so that the bond she already felt could grow into something strong, and true.

Every time she looked at him, even in the most banal of situations, her heart skipped a beat, and a strange, non-sexual warmth threw her mind into disarray.

It was, in a word, *inexplicable*.

Sex she was used to, and was quite happy to indulge in. Even a loose type of friendship was typical of her encounters with men, but that was where she usually drew the line.

Yearning for emotional closeness and support, longing for a relationship built on more than lust, was verboten.

There was no place for any of it in her life.

Or is there?

The whispered thought wafted through her brain and refused to go away, even when she pushed against its allure.

Massimo Bianchi was a man who had a solid place in the world, she reminded herself, while she was, in her own word, a vagabond. Settling down in one place wasn't in the cards for her—a fact she'd accepted long ago. Only by moving, by exploring, could she feel complete.

She'd tried staying in one place after she'd left the armed forces, but the restlessness wouldn't leave her, until her apartment—her life—became stifling. She truly believed she was born to rove, to seek in far-flung and distant places so as to find the meaning of her existence.

Even if Massimo were interested in trying to build something with her, could she take the chance that she wouldn't be able to deliver what he needed, long term?

Especially when she factored Pietro, and even Mrs. Bianchi too, into the equation, the risk didn't seem worth it. The little boy needed a solid, loving, stable home, and Kendra knew she wasn't capable of delivering one.

Or if she attempted to, it might not last.

How could she risk making the attempt, letting all the residents of Agriturismo Villa Giovanna get used to having her around, only to realize it had been a mistake to stay? Her heart ached at the thought of how Pietro would probably feel—abandoned, unlovable—and how the experience may set him back.

It wasn't a chance she wanted to take.

Some people just weren't meant to remain forever in one place, and she was one of that wandering tribe. Why hurt others when it was completely avoidable?

"Everything okay?"

Caught up in her less-than-happy thoughts, Kendra started, not realizing Massimo had returned from the commissary and was standing beside her.

Pushing her sunglasses more firmly up on her nose, she sent him a smile, even though it took a huge effort.

"Of course," she replied, accepting the bottle of water he held out for her, and opening it. "Just woolgathering."

She'd said the last bit in English, unable to think of the Italian equivalent, and Massimo turned to lean on the railing so he was looking directly at her. Something about his expression, the way he seemed to focus in on her face so intently, set alarm bells ringing in her head.

"I've noticed," he said slowly, "you usually only use English when you're upset. Your Italian is really exemplary otherwise."

She forced a laugh. "I'm not upset. How could I be, after the hedonistic weekend we just had?"

Massimo didn't reply and, as she took a sip of water, Kendra mentally patted herself on the back, glad to have reminded them both what the weekend had truly been about.

Sex.

Incredible, heart-stopping, almost-break-the-bed, blow-off-the-top-of-her-head sex, but just sex, nonetheless.

Even if she'd just finished berating herself for thinking otherwise.

Massimo took a long drink from his bottle, his gaze still trained on her face. After he'd swallowed, he said, "I would like to have such a weekend with you again. Or even just a night, here or there, if that is all we can arrange."

Kendra's heart stuttered, and she bit the inside of her cheek, so as not to agree immediately. Wouldn't it be better to start letting things cool down from now, rather than continue on what had become, for her, an increasingly slippery slope?

"I'm not sure how that would work out," she finally replied. "I don't want your grandmother to get the wrong idea, which she will, if we keep running off together."

He snorted. "Nonna may be old-fashioned, but she's well aware of the way modern relationships work. She's not the type to assume that if we are sleeping together, it means anything more than that."

Another revelation, as Kendra—who never gave a fig what anyone thought of her—realized that in Mrs. Bianchi's case, she actually did care. Losing the older lady's esteem and friendship was not something she wanted to do.

"Maybe so, but why take the chance of giving her the wrong impression? Like most grandmothers, I'm sure she wants to see you settle down. It would be worse for you in the long term if she even has the thought that it might be a possibility, and then I leave."

"Perhaps you're right," he said, but there was a note in his voice she didn't know how to interpret. "Have you decided where you're going next—when you leave Minori?"

She was the one who'd brought up leaving, so why did her hackles rise because he'd mentioned it too, as though already eager to see the back of her?

Even knowing she was being silly, her voice was cool

when she replied, "Not yet. I have out a few feelers in other parts of Europe, but I'm actually considering going back to Canada for a while. It's been a few years since I saw my family, and I know I can pick up work there, easily."

"You had said you wanted to see more of Italy. I thought perhaps you'd travel here for a while before you left."

How on earth did he remember that?

"It depends on how quickly I need to find a new position." Now she was just making stuff up, on the fly. She always had a nice contingency fund in place, just so as *not* to have to rush from job to job. "I've also been thinking of going to Spain, although nurses aren't on the shortage occupation list, so I'd have to find something else to do. I hold a teaching certificate, so that might be an option."

The last bit was totally off the cuff, since she hadn't looked at the Spanish government website in a few years.

"Well, you have a little time to make a decision. Just under two months, right?"

He'd been keeping track of the time she had left too, then. Was he counting the days they had left together, or how quickly it was he'd be rid of her?

"Seven weeks. Which isn't very much when you think about all that goes into moving around like I do. Hell, when I first thought of coming here, and applied through the program, it took me a year to put it all together, not counting the eighteen months I was stuck in Dubai. I'm glad you reminded me that I need to make some solid plans. If I don't start now, leaving might turn out to be more expensive than I want."

But, as she changed the subject, she suspected that no matter what plans she made, the cost of leaving Minori was already more than she wanted to pay.

Not in cash, but in emotional currency.

* * *

As the ferry drew closer to Positano, Massimo led Kendra toward the front of the ferry, then excused himself, telling her he would return momentarily. Walking to the other side of the boat, he leaned on the railing, needing a few minutes to compose himself, away from her and the pull she so effortlessly exerted on his senses.

He knew she'd be leaving, Massimo reminded himself. This was not something new, or unexpected.

So why did it hurt so much to hear her speak of it in such a cool manner?

The weekend with her had left him raw. Needy.

It had opened his eyes to parts of his own character he wasn't sure he'd even known existed, and cracked open the shell he'd so carefully built around his heart.

Even when he'd kept reminding himself that none of this would last, that she'd soon be gone, that it was supposed to be only sex, Kendra was undermining the very foundations of his life.

Of whom he thought he was, and what he'd always thought he'd wanted.

He didn't want to let her go, even though he fully knew he had no say in the matter.

There was also the frightening thought that it would be easy, should she crook her little finger, to leave what he'd built and follow her wherever she wanted to go.

Of course, it would be anything but easy, and not even possible.

Not just was Minori his home, but he had a responsibility to Nonna, and to Pietro, that tied him to that home even more securely than his deep and abiding love for the Amalfi Coast.

There would be no running off into the sunset. No casting all to the wind in the name of love, even if Kendra had been even the slightest bit interested in him doing so.

Which she was making very clear she was not.

This too was not news, although for the last three days he'd willfully pushed that knowing aside, pretending that somehow, someway, there was a chance for them.

Or, more precisely, a chance that she would fall for him, the way he'd fallen for her, and choose a life together over one of excitement and adventure.

He suppressed a harsh snort at that thought.

For a few moments he'd believed her when she told him he was neither staid nor boring. He'd wanted to believe it. Needed to, as a sop to his ego, and a reason to step out of his comfort zone and give her all she wanted, sexually. Now, looking back on the weekend just ending, he hardly recognized the man he'd been, or pretended to be, when with her. That man had been far bolder and more demanding than Massimo of old had ever been. It had been an illusion—created more for himself, he thought, than for Kendra's benefit. A fantasy of the man he'd always wanted to be.

No, that man had lived a brief existence, and it was time to admit there was no use for him in real life.

Yet, as the ferry drew closer to the dock and Massimo made his way back to his bewitching companion, he had to admit the weekend had fundamentally changed him in other ways.

He'd told himself, over and over, that Therese had been the one. That love at first sight dictated it was so, because hadn't he fallen for her immediately? Now he realized Nonna had been right. He'd been infatuated by a beautiful face and willowy figure and, having placed her on the pedestal of first love, only love, when she'd tumbled off that lofty perch, he'd been convinced his heart was shattered.

Convinced it was impossible to love again.

How terribly, horribly wrong he'd been.

Drawing near to where he'd left Kendra, he saw her in profile, noted the tightness of her lips, the way her fingers grasped the rail, as though to anchor herself, and he paused.

She'd all but told him outright that she was through with him as a lover. When he'd suggested they continue the affair, she'd balked, and he hadn't wanted to listen.

Hadn't wanted to read between the lines and hear what she was saying.

If for no other reason than the love he had for her, he needed to accept that decision. He never wanted to make her uncomfortable, and he certainly didn't want her pity. For eventually she'd realize his feelings, and that would, if nothing else, make things awkward.

Best now to lock away those feelings and try, as best he could, to go back to being the colleague she'd once slept with, and now held at arm's length.

Taking a deep breath, retreating behind the wall she'd all but destroyed, he moved forward, just as the ferry eased into the dock.

He was tempted to touch her arm, but knew that was an impulse born of the very need he had to suppress, so instead he cleared his throat to get her attention.

"I think you're right," he said, as she glanced around at him. "It's best we leave this weekend behind, and go back to the way things were before."

She nodded slowly. "If things were different, we could keep seeing each other, but they're not. So, yes, let's not complicate things any more than we already have."

"Concordato," he agreed, although the word felt like acid in his mouth. "No more complications."

It looked as though she might say something more but instead just nodded again, and turned away to look out at the dock, leaving him to wonder how long it took a shattered heart to mend. If it ever did.

CHAPTER SEVENTEEN

KENDRA HAD ONCE heard someone say that when you're young the days are short, and the years long, but when you're old the days are long and the years short. But it was only now, as her time on the Amalfi Coast was coming to a close, that she truly understood the sentiment. Although, of course, for her it wasn't years that flew by, but weeks.

The days were torturously long, spent as they were almost constantly in Massimo's presence. Even when she couldn't see or hear him, as long as she knew he was around her system stayed on high alert.

It was worse at the villa, even though she'd gone back to her old plan of being there as little as possible. At night, knowing he was just steps away stole whatever scrap of peace she may have otherwise achieved.

Having promised Pietro she would, she still had her breakfast in the kitchen, but nothing would convince her to come in early enough in the evenings to eat dinner with the family. Mornings were hard enough.

Having to put on a smiling face so none of them would realize she was slowly dying inside.

Being treated with cool courtesy by the man who'd once made her feel like the most beautiful woman on earth, who'd made her scream with pleasure and beg for more, was too painful.

Thankfully, she was a master at concealing her agony behind smiles and laughter, although the effort it took to produce either was exhausting.

Whenever anyone at the clinic or in the village asked where she was going when she left Minori, she told them back to Canada, although she hadn't told anyone there that she was coming. The truth was, she didn't know what she was going to do, or where she was going to go, and had no interest in making firm plans.

"You still haven't said where you'll be going next," Koko said, three weeks before Kendra's contract with the clinic would be up. "Usually by now you'd have some kind of plan."

Glad that her cousin couldn't see her face, Kendra chuckled.

"I have some feelers out, and am still doing some research. Besides, I didn't get to see much of the rest of Italy before starting the job, so I'll probably do that before I move on."

Her cousin had accepted her explanation, but Kendra knew the real reason why she hadn't made plans. There was a tiny, stupid part of her heart still whispering that she should consider staying here, on the Amalfi Coast. That perhaps if she did, somewhere down the road she and Massimo could find a way to work things out.

Definitely a stupid idea.

It wasn't Massimo who was the problem, but her. Even if he wanted her—which didn't seem to be the case—she didn't trust herself to be able to give him what he deserved.

Someone who would stay by his side, and never leave.

A woman he'd want to spend the rest of his life with, instead of one who always seemed to eventually disappoint those she loved, and became disposable.

As that thought flowed through her head, Kendra realized her greatest fear had been realized.

She was in love with Massimo. Deeply, honestly. Truly.

What else could this sensation be? This need to make sure he was happy—that whatever she did was in his best interests, rather than her own. The constant conflict of wanting to be near him, yet having to keep away, so that what happened between them wouldn't end up being a source of pain for him.

Thankfully the revelation came while she lay, sleepless, in her bed, staring out the window at the moon, which seemed almost close enough to touch. The bright orb wavered, filtered through the tears filling her eyes, but Kendra refused to let them fall. Instead, she blinked them away and clenched her fingers into fists.

This was the life she'd chosen. One that made sense in the context of whom and what she was.

There was no use pretending she could be anything else—anyone else—and that was all there was to it. Wasn't she used to heartbreak? To having to walk away? No matter how she ached at the thought of leaving Massimo—leaving this idyllic life he and his little family lived—doing so was for the best.

For all of them.

Although the flow of tourists had abated, the clinic was still busy, mostly with locals, and Kendra was glad of the workload, even though it often meant working alongside Massimo. Pretending everything was fine and dandy, when just being near him gave her pain a keener edge since she'd admitted to herself the depths of her feelings.

"You're still here, young lady?" Mrs. De Luca asked, as Kendra met her in reception to take her back to the examination room. "I thought you were only in Minori for the summer."

"I leave in a few weeks, but the other, full-time nurses are taking their holidays now, so I'm filling in until they get back."

"Well, I was talking to some of my friends and we all agree you're the best of the summer nurses we've had over the last few years. Even Amelia Lionetti sings your praises, after you took the time to explain to her about how to manage that sleep disorder she has."

Thankfully, Massimo had been able to determine that Mrs. Lionetti had non-24-hour sleep-wake disorder, rather than Alzheimer's or one of the other possible diagnoses. Getting the elderly lady to understand what that was, and what they would be able to do to help, hadn't been easy, but Kendra had patiently explained until it sunk in.

Hearing she now had the approval of the village *nonne* was gratifying, to be sure, but it did nothing to heal the broken place inside. The void created by love, and the fear it created.

Just as she got Mrs. De Luca into the examination room, Kendra heard the sound of breaking glass coming from reception, raised voices and then a truncated scream.

"Stay here," she told the elderly lady, before running back down the corridor.

The scene that met her eyes had her freezing for a moment, and her perception slowed, so that it felt as though it took minutes, rather than seconds, to survey the room.

One panel of the front door broken.

A woman curled on her side on the floor, unmoving and bleeding, in the shards.

The reception staff and waiting patients frozen in place.

A man she didn't recognize, holding what looked like a metal pipe in one hand and a knife in the other, standing beside the fallen woman.

"I told you not to come here," he said. "I told you to keep

quiet." It seemed as though he was talking to the woman on the floor next to him, but his eyes kept darting from side to side, keeping tabs on everyone in the room. "Get up. Get up, damn you."

Strange how the mind works, Kendra thought, still in slow-motion mode, because it was only then she realized the man was speaking in English.

When the woman on the floor didn't move, he shouted again, "Get up!"

He was escalating, the situation becoming more dangerous by the second.

Holding up her hands, Kendra stepped forward.

"Sir," she said, keeping her voice level and firm. "Sir, I need you to calm down. Let me—"

"Shut up! Step back!"

"It's okay," she said, not stopping, but pacing slowly closer. "It's all right. I'm just going to help you get your friend up, so you can leave."

"No!" That flat gaze, wavering back and forth, then settling on Kendra again. "She's fine. We don't need your help."

Then he glanced down at the woman, and Kendra took what might be her only opportunity.

A side kick catching him just above the diaphragm, hopefully sending it into spasm, was meant to put him down, but didn't. Instead, he staggered backward, hitting the unbroken side of the door, bouncing off and straight at her, teeth bared, knife held high.

He didn't expect her to go low, but that's what she did. Grabbing his leg, using upward momentum to flip him up and over, hearing the clatter as the pipe and the man hit the floor. Spinning around, heart pounding, getting into a fighting stance, watching as he got up again, still holding the knife. Knowing he was about to charge her again. Ready for it.

There was a movement, just a flash in her peripheral vision, and she somehow knew who it was, and what he was going to do. Watched in horror as Massimo rushed forward, flinging one strong arm around the drug-crazed man's neck, putting him in a choke hold.

The knife flashed at least once before Kendra could get to them, and she didn't even care that she'd probably broken the man's wrist when she disarmed him.

But it took the combined strength of both her and Dr. Mancini to get Massimo to let go of the now-unconscious man.

Then it was all a blur. Shouts and motion, a sick sensation when she saw the blood on Massimo's shirt.

"Are you hurt?" she asked him, trying to find the source, checking chest and rib cage, stomach, then grabbing his arm, seeing the gash in his sleeve. In the flesh exposed beneath.

Cursing, holding back the tears, wanting to scream at him, stanching the blood with her hand, since she had nothing else available.

And through it all Massimo didn't move. Didn't say a word. But his chest was heaving, and when she looked up to tell him to come with her so she could examine the gash, he was staring down at her, and the look in his eyes sent a chill down her spine.

Unmistakable fury.

She knew what it was, because she felt the same way.

"You can scream at me later," she said, keeping her teeth clamped together so as not to let loose at him. "But right now, I want you in exam room two so I can examine your wound."

His eyes narrowed, and a muscle ticked in his jaw, then he gave one stiff nod.

"I'm taking Dr. Bianchi to dress his wound," Kendra said to the room at large, not caring if anyone heard or not.

All she cared about was making sure Massimo was all right.

Massimo couldn't speak. Didn't dare say one word, as Kendra unbuttoned his cuff and turned back his sleeve.

He didn't even feel any pain from the slice on his arm. He was still caught in the nightmare of seeing Kendra fighting with a knife-wielding madman. Still filled with the type of rage he hadn't even known himself to be capable of.

She'd told him he could scream at her later, and he hoped she was ready for that, because, oh, yes, it was coming.

In the meantime, it was all he could do to maintain some semblance of sanity.

It had been hard enough over the past weeks to do so, when all he was wrestling with was loving a woman who would soon disappear from his life. This incident—near tragedy—threatened to push him over the mental equivalent of one of the famous cliffs along the Amalfi Coast.

"I knew what I was doing, Massimo." He heard the steel in her voice. Turned his head away, unable to even look at her just then. "I had it under control."

Luckily for her, the door opened just then, and Fredo Mancini came in.

"The police are here, and they'll need to take your statements," he said, coming over to take a look at the wound on Massimo's arm, palpating around it. "Clean slice. Not too deep. Have it cleaned up and some stitches and you'll be fine."

"Can you ask one of the other nurses to take care of it, please, Dr. Mancini?"

Now he couldn't help whipping his head around to look at her, took in her stoic expression, the lines bracketing her mouth and wrinkling the skin between her brows.

"I'll do it myself," Fredo said.

And then Kendra was gone.

"Her hands were shaking." Fredo had his back turned, getting the supplies he needed. "And I'm not surprised." He shook his head, as he pulled on a pair of gloves. "Mine would be too, if I'd just fought a madman like that. I didn't see it, but I heard she was magnificent."

But thankfully, when Massimo made no reply, Fredo lapsed into silence.

They had to close the clinic, of course. Alessio Pisano, who'd been out at the time of the incident, came rushing back to oversee the cleanup and boarding over of the broken door, and sent everyone home.

By the time he'd gotten his stitches, Kendra had already left, taken off by the police to give her statement.

The shock was wearing off, but not the rage. He knew he needed to contain it, but it kept bubbling up, needing release.

Knowing how the village grapevine worked, he made sure to call his grandmother to let her know he was all right, only to find that Kendra had done that for him.

"Oh, Massimo. What a terrible thing. Kendra said you'd been hurt but the wound wasn't serious, and I'm glad she did. I've had so many calls, and the story gets worse each time I hear it. Is it true Kendra fought him off? She didn't mention that when she called. Was she hurt?"

Reassuring Nonna took some doing, and he was exhausted by the attempt.

Exhausted but still furious.

He needed to find Kendra.

For some reason now his mind insisted on playing tricks on him, telling him she wasn't all right. That the scene he remembered in his head, as frightening as it was, wasn't the way it actually happened.

That it was worse, and Kendra had been hurt.

Perhaps even killed.

He called, but got no answer from her cell phone, so he hung up and sent a text.

Where are you?

Then, when there was no response, another.

I need to know you're okay.

Finally...

I'm fine. Just needed to clear my head.

Where?

Another seemingly interminable wait, and then:

On the beach.

Of course. If he'd been thinking straight, he would have known she'd head for the water. A place that brought her peace, and reminded her of her father.

He hoped she'd found some of that peace there. For him, for the first time in his life, the familiar surroundings of his beloved home brought no comfort at all.

With rapid strides, he traversed the streets from the clinic down to the shore, stopping on the boardwalk to search the shoreline, eventually spotting her sitting on the sand near the water. Legs crossed in front of her, head tilted back, her face to the afternoon sun, which dipped toward the horizon a little sooner every day, she should have looked relaxed. But he knew her now. Intimately. Had studied her, even when his brain told him to stop looking, and everything about the line of her back, and the set of her shoulders, screamed tension.

Just like that, as though a switch had been thrown inside, his terrible rage drained away. Oh, he was still angry, but the urge to shout, to lose all control, had waned. Enough that he felt confident to toe off his shoes and, holding them in his hand, walk down to sit beside her.

When he looked over at her, he saw the tear tracks on her cheek, and his heart contracted. Reaching out, he touched her damp skin.

"You scared me," she said, before he could find words. "I was afraid you'd die, and…"

She turned her face away, so that all he saw was the curve of her cheek, the long line of her throat. He waited, wanting to hear what she would say, but she didn't finish her sentence.

He leaned closer, wanting to touch her—*needing* it—but holding himself in check, even when he saw another tear trickle down her cheek.

Then it came to him that although they were to part, although he was not, and never would be, enough for her, if he'd learned one thing today it was that tomorrow was not a given. They would go their separate ways, but, at least on his part, it would be in honesty.

"I was afraid for you too, Kendra. Desperately so. I thought *you* would die and I would have missed my chance to tell you that I love you."

She froze, her face still turned away from him, and another tear trailed down her face.

Wanting to comfort her, not knowing how best to, Massimo touched her shoulder.

"I didn't say that to hurt you, Kendra. Nor do I expect you to say it back to me. I just want you to know."

Then, before he could do or say something he'd regret, he got up and walked away.

CHAPTER EIGHTEEN

KENDRA LET MASSIMO GO.

Not because she didn't want to call him back, or tell him she loved him too, but because the fear was unrelenting.

She knew not admitting she felt the same way would hurt him, and that was the last thing she wanted to do. But hurting him by staying silent was a far smaller pain in the long run than making promises she couldn't keep.

For all intents and purposes, she was better off alone. Living a solitary life meant she didn't risk complications or cause damage to anyone else. Since she was eighteen, she'd only ever had to think about herself. What did she know about being a part of a couple? A part of a family?

Nothing.

Not anything of substance, anyway. Not enough to be sure she could make it work. That she wouldn't screw it all up.

Using the heel of her palm, she swiped at her tears, heartsick.

No. It was better for everyone if she stuck with the plan and left. Kept traveling. Fulfilling that childhood dream, born in the library stacks, museums and concert venues of Toronto. That plan she envisioned all those years ago had given life meaning, even if her life probably was—in other people's eyes—a truncated one.

One without ties to bind or choke and, perforce, without the elusive emotion that seemed to cause nothing but pain to anyone who felt it.

Hadn't it caused the end of her father's dream to be a doctor?

Devastated both hers and Grammy's lives, when Dad died?

Looking back on the plethora of broken homes and dashed dreams she'd seen in her lifetime, she shook her head.

All caused because someone, at some point, fell in love.

Which was all well and good, except love rarely seemed to bring true happiness.

The people she would hurt when it turned out love wasn't enough—when they realized *she* wasn't enough—didn't deserve that pain.

No. No, no, no.

She had to leave before Pietro got attached. Before she succumbed to Nonna's mothering. Before Massimo discovered that she wasn't deserving of the emotional investment he would make.

Because she knew, deep down, that a man as steadfast and true as he would give her his all, in every way. And the fear of what that would do to him if she stayed, and tried, and failed, was too much to bear.

Love, in her mind, meant making the best decisions for those you cared about. Hard choices, but the right ones in the end.

A crisp evening breeze blew off the sea, churning high, gray clouds across the darkening sky, and Kendra lifted her damp cheeks into it, inhaling the scent of the ocean. Where in the past her thoughts would turn to her father, now she knew whenever she was by the water, she'd think of Massimo. Think of the love she came so close to having, and had to walk away from.

It was time to move on, before she caused any more harm to the most wonderful man she'd ever met.

"What are you looking for, when you travel?"

It was as though Massimo still sat beside her, asking the question once more, as he had in Positano the first night they'd officially met.

Once upon a time that had been an easy question to answer.

Adventure.

Freedom.

Meaning.

Now, none of those words had any resonance. None sparked pleasure. There was a hollow ring to them, as though the drum skin of her life, once so taut and melodic, had been punctured.

Perhaps beyond repair.

Sighing, feeling tears stinging behind her eyes again, she glanced at her watch and was surprised to see how late it had become. Only a pink haze still lay on the horizon, the sun having gone down while she was so lost in thought its setting had gone noticed.

Getting to her feet, she picked up her shoes and knapsack from where she'd left them, and started back toward the clinic to get to her scooter. But, on arrival she realized it was gone, most likely stolen.

"Oh, great."

She was too tired to even curse, knowing it was best to save that energy for the hike to the police station.

"Signorina Kendra."

The voice came from the small café across the street, and she turned to see the proprietor walking quickly toward her, waving both hands over his head.

"Good evening," she said, as he reached her. "Did you by any chance see who took my scooter? It was right here."

"Dr. Massimo paid one of the young men to ride it up to the villa, *signorina*, and asked me to watch for when you came back. After what happened today, he thought perhaps you might prefer to be driven, rather than ride. I have called for a taxi for you already."

"Oh…"

"It is the dinner hour, *signorina*, so I must go back. *Buono notte*."

As he trotted back across the street, the taxi he'd summoned arrived, and Kendra sank into the back seat with a grateful sigh.

How considerate of Massimo to think of her, even in the midst of his own turmoil and upheaval. He'd been angry—*furious*—with her after the incident earlier. She'd seen it in his eyes, and had prepared herself as well as she could to face it. After all, at the time she'd been furious too.

And more frightened than she'd ever been before. Not for herself, but for him. Seeing the blood on his shirt, knowing that knife wounds inflicted when adrenaline was high sometimes didn't even hurt, and the patient could be slowly bleeding out inside, almost took her to her knees.

A world without Massimo in it was unthinkable.

Just imagining it made her stomach twist and had sweat breaking out on her brow, as the flash of the knife slicing down played behind her eyelids like a sick horror movie scene.

Thankfully, the man driving the taxi didn't seem inclined to speak, and it was a quiet ride to the villa.

If she'd had to talk about what had happened earlier again, she might burst into tears, and she'd already cried more today than she had since the day her grandmother died. Which was the last and one of a very few times she'd cried as an adult.

Somewhere around the age of twelve, she'd already learned crying didn't help. It was when she'd been moved again, going to her uncle, leaving behind the cousins she'd grown to love, the dog one of the neighbors had gifted her, and the aunt who'd taught her to cook. She'd cried and pleaded to be allowed to stay, but her aunt had just shaken her head.

"Nothing can be done about it, Kendra. It's time to go, and no amount of crying can change that."

No amount of crying can change that.

Harsh words to a little girl, but all too true.

The taxi approached the driveway, and Kendra's heart stuttered at the sight of Massimo's car parked a bit haphazardly in its usual spot.

Where else would he be but at home, you idiot?

Opening the door, she tried to pay, but the taxi driver lifted his hand.

"Dr. Bianchi paid me already, *signorina.*"

Even that he'd taken care of. Much of her childhood, and all of her adult life, she'd done everything for herself. No wonder that, on a day as fraught as this one had been, an act of kindness—of care—made her once more well up.

She got out and watched the taxi drive away, taking a few minutes to compose herself before heading toward the house. When she opened the door, there was a screech from the kitchen that froze her blood, and then the sound of a chair falling over. Dropping her bag and starting down the hallway at a run, she saw Pietro round the corner from the kitchen, going as fast as his feet could carry him toward her, his arms outstretched.

Without hesitation, she scooped him up, her heart

jackhammering, as she wondered what she'd see in the kitchen…

"Zia Kendra, you're all right!" Pietro was crying into her neck, clinging to her so hard it hurt. "Zio said you were, but I was worried anyway."

"He wouldn't go up to have his bath until he'd seen you for himself." Mrs. Bianchi stood in the doorway to the kitchen, and the anxiety on her face was unmistakable. "We heard what happened, and were both concerned about you."

Wrapping him tighter in her arms, Kendra rocked back and forth, rubbing Pietro's back, in tears again herself. "I'm fine, my sweet boy. I'm fine. Don't cry."

"Let me take him." Mrs. Bianchi came forward, but Kendra shook her head.

"No. No, I've got him. We're all right, aren't we, sweetheart?"

Mrs. Bianchi reached out and touched Kendra's cheek gently, and then nodded toward the kitchen.

"Come through and sit, then. He might not be huge, but Pietro is getting quite big, aren't you, darling?"

The little boy's sobs had abated somewhat, but he was shivering, and Kendra went to the chair in the corner of the kitchen and grabbed the blanket draped over the back. Then she sat down and wrapped it around the thin, trembling shoulders.

Even thus occupied, she looked around, but there was no sign of Massimo.

She wanted to ask where he was, but hesitated. Then she took a deep breath, knowing she had to face him sometime.

"Massimo?"

"He's in the garden. He said he needed some air."

"He looked sad," Pietro whispered into Kendra's neck. "I think his arm was hurting. Will you look after him, Zia?"

Such a simple question. Childlike and innocent.

But for Kendra there were so many layers to it, she didn't know how to answer.

Then something snapped inside her heart, broke apart to release a wave of such sweet pain she bit her lip so as not to make a sound.

It was then, with Pietro's slight weight in her lap, his arms still holding her so tight, and Mrs. Bianchi's worried, motherly gaze on her face, that everything fell into place.

And it all suddenly made sense.

So, she gave Pietro another gentle squeeze, and replied, "I will, Pietro. I will."

It was almost completely dark in the garden, the clouds overhead blocking the moon, the breeze fresh on his face.

Rain was coming. He could smell it on the wind, feel the moisture in the air. It was one of the things his *nonno* had taught him as a little boy. How to read the signs so as to be prepared for whatever came, whether on the land or sea.

Nonno understood weather patterns, and how all of nature interconnected perfectly.

"Except man," Nonno had said with a shake of his head. "Man thinks himself above it all, when we're little better than organized dust and water."

From Nonna he'd learned more about people—how empathy differed from sympathy, and why both were important in life. When to hold his ground, and when to let go.

They'd both emphasized honesty, integrity and taking care of those around him. They'd guided him through the harsh maze his younger life had been, giving him guidance, acceptance and the love he'd lacked at home. Massimo credited them both with his life path and whatever happiness he'd been able to grasp.

Now, as he sat in the garden one of his ancestors had

planted, he wished Nonno was here. Just to talk to. To give him some of that down-to-earth advice.

Massimo shifted, letting his gaze lift to the sky, accepting the pain. Settling into it, knowing it would be with him for a long time.

Probably forever.

He didn't know what he'd expected, when he'd admitted his feelings to Kendra. It wasn't as though he'd thought he had a chance. Yet, although he'd steeled himself for rejection—whether hard or gentle—somehow her silence had hurt even more.

For her, usually so forthright and sure, to not respond at all had been more heartbreaking than he could ever have expected.

A shaft of light flashed for an instance on the grass, then was gone, but he didn't turn around. Nonna, he thought, coming to check on him, to try to coax him inside. Although she wasn't born into a farming family, like her husband, she'd learned the signs and would know it would soon rain. She'd be angry if he stayed out in the damp.

"You once asked me what I was looking for, when I traveled."

His heart leaped, but he didn't turn at the sound of Kendra's voice. He was still too raw, and he didn't want her to know. His response came automatically, as though from someplace deep he had little control over.

"You said adventure, freedom and a wider worldview than the one you grew up with."

"You remember."

She sounded surprised, and that made a harsh chuckle break from his throat. He remembered everything. Too much.

"Yes."

"Well, I want you to forget I said it." She sounded closer,

and he was sure he hadn't imagined a soft brush against his shoulder. "I realized today that was bull."

He shook his head, not understanding where the conversation was going. If she was now ready to let him down, he wished she would get it over with.

"Don't you want to hear the real answer?"

He shrugged. "Certainly. If you want to tell me."

"I've been looking for a home. For somewhere to belong. For someone to love me—just the way I am—and take all the love I have to give."

Soft arms around his neck, her familiar, beloved scent filling his head. A kiss on the top of his head, followed by her twirling a lock of his hair around her finger.

He didn't dare move, or speak.

Or hope.

Yet his heart was pounding, and he had to clench his fingers into fists to stop himself from reaching for her hands.

"I think, if you really love me—not just because we're crazy good together in bed, but all of me—the way I love you, I could find those things here."

That caveat, her lack of surety about his feelings, finally galvanized him. Reaching behind to swing her around, he pulled her into his lap and kissed her until he was sure the moon had fallen from the sky just to shine on them.

When he finally broke the kiss, it was so he could trail his lips to her ear, and say, "The first moment I saw you, at Spiaggia Tordigliano, I fell for you, but refused to admit it. And every time since then I have fallen a little more, until now I can't imagine life without you."

"Massimo." She made his name sound like a song. One only she knew how to sing in the perfect key. "I fought my feelings as hard as I could, afraid, because I'm not sure I know how to be what you want. What you need. I've never been in love before. Didn't really believe in it, until I met you. Suppose I get it wrong, or mess it up?"

He cupped her face, and kissed her gently, wishing now that it weren't so very dark, so he could see her eyes.

"You are perfect in every way, Kendra, and I love you for all you are. Your adventurous spirit, your independence, your laughter and tears. I love you even when you shout at me, or try to punch me because I have given you a fright."

Then he knew he had to admit his own fears. Give her a chance to change her mind.

"But it is I who know I might not be what you need. I can't promise to run off with you to exotic places, should you desire to do so, for my life is here and I am committed to helping so many people."

She laid a finger against his lips.

"My vagabond days are over. All I want is to build a life here with you, if you will have me."

"If I will have you?" He squeezed her against his heart, and heard her sigh. "Now that you have pledged yourself to me, my home will be with you, always."

"Always," she repeated, wrapping her arms around his neck and whispering in his car, "I like the sound of that."

EPILOGUE

SUMMER HAD COME again to the Amalfi Coast, and the wild-flowers in the upper woods were a riot of color, their perfume filling the air.

"Make sure you pick many pink ones for Nonna." Now twelve, Pietro had appointed himself the arbiter of taste, style and comfort at Agriturismo Villa Giovanna. "They are her favorite."

Massimo and Kendra exchanged a look, and when Massimo whispered to her, "You would never believe I've known her more than three times longer than him," Kendra had to laugh.

As the sound echoed into the woods, Massimo's eyes grew hooded, and Kendra shivered, knowing exactly what was on his mind.

Even after four years, he still had the ability to turn her on with a look, and remind her that when it came to love, her laughter was, for him, a constant aphrodisiac.

Moving to where they'd left the wagon they would use to transport the flowers back to the house, Kendra surveyed the bounty destined to grace the villas for their guests to enjoy. Pinks and purples and blues still predominated, with the hot-weather flowers making a slow start this year, because the area had stayed unseasonably cool after Easter.

As they were placing the last of the blooms into the cart, a voice called, "Oo-ee," from the road, and Pietro immediately looked at Massimo.

"That is Tonio," he said. "I told him I would be here this morning."

"Oh?" Massimo raised his brows, and Pietro squirmed slightly.

"Yes. Yesterday he showed me a stream on his father's land and invited me to come and fish in it." His brow creased in that cute, old-mannish way he had. "Although I don't think there is anything to catch. It is a very *small* stream."

"Did you tell Nonna you would be going?"

"I did, and she told me to ask your permission, but I forgot. May I go, anyway?"

Kendra was inclined to say yes, but then she was usually inclined to say yes to Pietro, who was still as sweet, as kind, as he'd ever been. Instead, though, she let Massimo take the lead.

Massimo, the wretch, let the little boy squirm a little, before saying, "I will allow it, but next time you ask in advance, before your friends arrive to whisk you away."

"Yes, Papa." He sounded contrite but couldn't stop himself from doing a little jig. "I will."

"Off you go then."

"Thank you, Papa. Thank you, Mama."

And then, running to hug and kiss them both, he took off at a gallop, his long thin legs flying along, so that he disappeared into the trees in the trice.

"Ah," Massimo said. "That is what summer is about, isn't it?" Wrapping his arms around her waist, he pulled Kendra close, and bent to nip at the base of her throat. "Running wild with friends, fishing in fishless streams, getting filthy."

"Nonna won't be pleased when he tracks mud into her kitchen later," she replied, dancing her fingers down his spine, and smiling when he shuddered.

"Mrs. Bianchi, if you do such things, I will be forced to take my revenge, here and now."

She laughed, looking around, tempted. Then common sense took over.

"Not with a small battalion of preteens running amok around here, our son among them."

It still gave her a thrill to say "our son" that way. They'd had to wait until they were married for three years before they could legally adopt Pietro, but the wait had given them all time to create a new normal.

Pietro had sobbed when she and Massimo had asked if he was willing for them to adopt him formally, and Kendra had cried right along with him when he vehemently said yes. Massimo had been equally moved, and the sight of the tears he couldn't contain had made Kendra feel as though her heart would burst with love.

Nonna had suggested she move into one of the villas, to let the newlyweds and Pietro have the farmhouse to themselves, but none of them would entertain that idea. With a marked lack of reluctance, Nonna had stayed right where she was, and life settled into a beautiful rhythm.

Kendra was the on-call locum nurse for the clinic, working the summer months and stepping in if any of the other nurses went on holidays or took sick leave. For the rest of the year, she kept busy helping around the villa and farm, learning new recipes and cooking techniques from Nonna, and being Pietro's Mama.

And Massimo's wife—a role she'd found, despite her initial fears, suited her down to the ground.

They were still discussing when and how to expand their family, but neither of them felt the need to rush. Making sure Pietro felt secure had been their main concern. Now that he was, they were talking about trying for a baby, but also considering adopting again.

Kendra had never been happier, and she told Massimo so every chance she got.

"So, if I can't have my way with you against one of these wonderfully handy trees, may I do so later, at a time and a place of your convenience?"

Kendra laughed, and saw his eyes grow even darker, the sight giving her anticipatory goose bumps. He really did know how to turn her on, and keep her simmering.

"I would be very upset if you didn't," she replied demurely. "Very upset indeed."

"Let us go home, then," he said, reaching for the cart's handle.

Overcome with sweet emotion, she touched his arm, and when he turned his midnight gaze her way, she said, "When I'm with you, I am already home."

And immediately found herself exactly where she was happiest. In his arms, held tight against his heart.

"As it is for me," he whispered into her ear, causing a shiver of delight to trickle along her spine. "And will be forever."

* * * * *

COMING SOON!

We really hope you enjoyed reading this book.
If you're looking for more romance, be sure to
head to the shops when new books are
available on

Thursday 18th August

To see which titles are coming soon, please visit

millsandboon.co.uk/nextmonth

MILLS & BOON®

Coming next month

HER SECRET RIO BABY
Luana DaRosa

The door opened, interrupting their conversation, and Dr Salvador strode back into the room. The fierce protectiveness in Diego's eyes vanished, leaving his face unreadable.

Eliana's eyes were drawn to the emergency doctor, who stepped closer. She was wearing an expression of medical professionalism on her face that quickened her pulse. She knew that look. She had given it to patients herself.

She whipped her head around, looking at Diego, and whatever he saw written in her face was enough to make him get off his chair and step closer to her side. A similar look of protectiveness to the one he'd had a few moments ago was etched into his features.

'Would you mind giving us some privacy?' Sophia asked him, and a tremble shook Eliana's body.

The nausea came rushing back, her head suddenly felt light, and Eliana reacted before she could think, her hand reaching for Diego's and crushing it in a vice-like grip.

'It's okay if he stays,' she said, in a voice that sounded so unlike her own.

Something deep within her told her she needed him to stay. Whether it was premonition or just a primal fear gripping at her heart, she didn't know.

Diego stopped, giving her a questioning look, but he stayed, and his hand did not fight her touch.

'Well, it looks like it's not a stomach bug, but morning sickness. Or, in your case, late-afternoon sickness.' She paused for a moment, before confirming the absurd thought that was rattling around in Eliana's head. 'You're pregnant.'

Eliana opened her mouth to speak, but no words crossed the threshold of her lips. Pregnant? How was she pregnant? Her head snapped around to Diego, and whatever expression she was wearing on her face seemed to convey to him all the words she didn't want to say in front of the doctor.

The baby was his. They were pregnant.

His hand slipped from her grasp as he took a step back. The shock she felt at the revelation was written on his face.

'How long?' she asked, even though she knew it didn't matter.

Eliana had only slept with one person in the last six months, and that was the man standing here in the room with her.

Continue reading
HER SECRET RIO BABY
Luana DaRosa

Available next month
www.millsandboon.co.uk

MILLS & BOON

THE HEART OF ROMANCE

A ROMANCE FOR EVERY READER

MODERN

Prepare to be swept off your feet by sophisticated, sexy and seductive heroes, in some of the world's most glamourous and romantic locations, where power and passion collide.

HISTORICAL

Escape with historical heroes from time gone by. Whether your passion is for wicked Regency Rakes, muscled Vikings or rugged Highlanders, awaken the romance of the past.

MEDICAL

Set your pulse racing with dedicated, delectable doctors in the high-pressure world of medicine, where emotions run high and passion, comfort and love are the best medicine.

True Love

Celebrate true love with tender stories of heartfelt romance, from the rush of falling in love to the joy a new baby can bring, and a focus on the emotional heart of a relationship.

Desire

Indulge in secrets and scandal, intense drama and plenty of sizzling hot action with powerful and passionate heroes who have it all: wealth, status, good looks…everything but the right woman.

HEROES

Experience all the excitement of a gripping thriller, with an intense romance at its heart. Resourceful, true-to-life women and strong, fearless men face danger and desire - a killer combination!

To see which titles are coming soon, please visit

millsandboon.co.uk/nextmonth

JOIN US ON SOCIAL MEDIA!

Stay up to date with our latest releases, author news and
gossip, special offers and discounts, and all the
behind-the-scenes action from Mills & Boon...

 @millsandboon

 @millsandboonuk

 facebook.com/millsandboon

 @millsandboonuk

It might just be true love...